Furiously Inappropriate Magic

Book VII of the Magic of Magic Series

Clayton Taylor Wood

Books by Clayton Taylor Wood:

The Runic Series
Runic Awakening
Runic Revelation
Runic Vengeance
Runic Revolt
Runic War

The Fate of Legends Series
Hunter of Legends
Seeker of Legends
Destroyer of Legends
Avenger of Legends

Magic of Havenwood Series
The Magic Collector
The Lost Gemini
The Magic Redeemer

The Magic of Magic Series
Inappropriate Magic
Ridiculously Inappropriate Magic
Ludicrously Inappropriate Magic
Absurdly Inappropriate Magic
Insanely Inappropriate Magic
Chaotically Inappropriate Magic
Furiously Inappropriate Magic
Epically Inappropriate Magic

The Masks of Eternity Series
Elazar the Magician

Special thanks to Howie and Nancy, who have a kind of inappropriate magic all their own. And to the hidden magic within each of us, waiting patiently to be found.

DISCLAIMER:

This book contains (furiously) inappropriate depictions of (furiously) inappropriate people doing (furiously) inappropriate things. Including, but certainly not limited to, inappropriate language and very thinly veiled connotations of the naughty variety.

And of course, (furiously) inappropriate magic.

Table of Contents

Furiously Inappropriate Magic

Prologue

When destiny knocked on Fury Little's door, her sort-of-aunt Nettie decided she'd better answer it for the girl.

Nettie happened to be visiting Chauncy and Valtora's quaint little home in Southwick at the time, during a much-needed break from her duties at the Order of Mundus. A little vacation she'd taken to the Little household without her husband Harry, which was a shame. Still, he was busy on some sort of mission, and besides, absence made the heart grow fonder, or so they said. And while for most marriages that would most certainly be true, for Nettie and Harry, spending time apart was a painful thing to do.

In any case, she found herself at the kitchen stove at the time of destiny's arrival, cooking up a nice little dinner for her sort-of-niece. For Fury happened to be the only one home, seeing as how Valtora and Chauncy had decided to take advantage of Nettie's presence by enjoying an impromptu date night.

"Almost done sweety," Nettie declared, stirring the stir-fry she'd made. Fury, already seated at the table and awaiting the meal eagerly, beamed at her with her customary good cheer.

"Yay!" she exclaimed, clapping her hands. Nettie glanced at her, unable to help but smile. For Fury was a simply lovely child, a joy to be around always. About as deep as a dried-up puddle, but hey, no one was perfect.

"Here ya go," Nettie declared, grabbing a plate and serving Fury. She set the plate down before the girl, who hopped up and down in her chair with excitement.

She really was quite lovely, in more ways than one. For she'd inherited her mother's looks, the poor girl, and puberty had been particularly generous. Fury had beautiful brown hair, a similar shade as her father's, but wavy like her mother's. Or rather, like Zella Trek's hair, whom Valtora had stolen, by virtue of stealing her body. Fury's hair flowed all the way down to her lower back, and had not a single split-end. Her eyes were big and beautiful, and were the strangest shade of purple Nettie had ever seen, and her

1

lips were full. Much like the rest of her, whom nature had seen fit to fill to overflowing in all the right parts, while sparing the rest.

She really was utterly lovely, her outside perfectly matching her lovely soul.

Nettie sighed, serving herself then, wondering exactly at what point the poor girl would have that lovely soul crushed by the dark forces waiting outside this safe little home. For a fragile, sheltered, innocent girl like her would invariably have her heart broken and her dreams crushed, by the various evils that existed beyond the bubble Chauncy and Valtora had built for their precious daughter. Lovely souls and bodies were too often doomed to be preyed upon by unscrupulous others, after all.

But as fate would have it, Nettie didn't have to wait long for her answer. For that was precisely the point that destiny knocked upon Fury's door.

"What in the...?" Nettie blurted out, slapping more stir-fry on her plate. She set it aside, then waddled up to the front door, wondering who the hell it could be. Chauncy and Valtora had left only a half-hour ago after all, and their date nights usually went far into the morning. Entailing what exactly, Nettie had no interest in ever knowing, knowing Valtora.

Again came the knock, even before Nettie could reach the door, which implied an annoying amount of impatience. And as Nettie knew too well, when one person lost their patience, everyone else around them tended to.

"All right all right," she yelled. "Hold yer damn horses."

She reached the door, turning the knob, and flung it open irritably. Then she froze, her eyes widening.

"You!" she blurted out, staring in disbelief.

For there, standing on the front porch, was an exceedingly elderly man, even by Nettie's standards. He was tall and thin, his back stooped with age, and clad in a brilliant blue cloak and pointed hat. And in his right hand was a big ol', perfectly twisty staff, topped with a big ol' blue crystal. He eyes her with equally blue eyes, stroking his long, thinning white beard.

"Hello Nettie," he greeted.

"Imperius!" she replied. "What the hell're you doin' here?"

"The same thing I always do," he replied evenly. "Delivering a Chosen One their destiny."

"No one's home," she replied. Which was a lie, but close enough to the truth to pass for it. "Date night."

"I didn't come for Chauncy or Valtora," Imperius replied. "And I already know that Chaos is otherwise occupied."

Which was true, Nettie knew. For Chaos, having recently turned nineteen, had flown the nest last week, so to speak, traveling to Grissam to be with Destiny. Supposedly to continue his training as a warrior-wizard, although Nettie suspected that Destiny was providing a more well-rounded education for the boy, being rather pleasantly well-rounded herself.

"So who the hell'd you come for?" Nettie pressed. And then immediately narrowed her eyes. "No," she blurted out.

"Yes," Imperius replied.

"No," she repeated. Imperius arched a bushy white eyebrow.

"Yes."

"You don't understand," Nettie protested. "She's...not Chosen One material."

"That is not for you or I to say," Imperius chided gently.

"Then go away," Nettie replied.

"Now now Nettie," he began.

"You want her, you gotta wait for her parents," Nettie interrupted. "I can't be makin' decisions for her without their consent." Which was a really *really* good way to weasel herself out of any responsibility for this unfortunate event.

Imperius eyed her in a scolding sort of way, but to her surprise, he inclined his head.

"Very well," he decided. "I will return in one day."

And with that, there was a *poof*, and he vanished in a burst of blue sparkles.

Nettie stared at where he'd been, watching as the sparkles touched the ground and vanished. Then she sighed, turning around and letting the door close behind her. She cleared her throat, then waddled back into the kitchen, doing her best to look nonplussed.

"Mmm!" Fury exclaimed, still eating her meal. "So *yummy* Nettie!"

"Glad you like it hon," Nettie replied, grabbing her plate and sitting down to eat. The stir-fry was just okay, hardly worthy of Fury's exclamations. A bit dry and poorly seasoned. But Fury seemed to enjoy it just the same. As evidenced by the fact that she danced in her seat as she ate, humming to herself merrily.

Poor idiot, Nettie thought, forcing herself to finish her meal. Her guts squirmed, whether because of the food or due to unease, she wasn't sure. But she knew damn well that when Chauncy and

3

Valtora returned from their little escapade, she'd have to inform them of Imperius's pending re-visit.

And she was *not* looking forward to that, no siree. Not one bit.

Chapter 1

The bowels of Hell were hardly a place the uninitiated would care to visit, all hot and stinking of sulfur and filled with demons and such. But of course, much of the unpleasantness of Hell was merely good marketing, in that it made good people avoid going there at all costs. This had the rather pleasant effect of only attracting rather naughty people to come instead. And as Chauncy and Valtora would certainly attest to, naughty people could be so much *fucking* fun. In the case of this particular date night, quite literally so.

"Oh *yeah* baby," Chauncy exclaimed, lying on his back on the warm stone of a rocky pillar some five hundred feet above a lake of pure magma. Gasping for air and sweating, for perfectly pleasant reasons. "God I missed this."

"Yeah, we don't say that name here," Valtora chided, lying on her back at his side. She was quite spectacularly nude, and he was also nude, though rather disappointingly so, at least in his view. Yet somehow he happened to be just what she liked. Or rather, one type that she liked. For as their various trysts in Hell over the years had shown, Valtora enjoyed many types of man. And woman, too.

And while this had of course once filled Chauncy with all sorts of feelings, including inadequacy, insecurity, rage, shame, and despair, now it was just another way to enjoy a date. In this case, with the Incubi and Succubi, Valtora's and Chauncy's favorite people, respectively. Well, other than each other, of course. And their children. Except for Epic, that was. Who as you'll recall, dear reader, had vanished during Chaos's adventure six years ago…and had never been seen or heard from again. Along with Zora, who Chauncy missed far more than his strange son, though he would never admit it to anyone.

"Sorry," Chauncy replied. Then he sighed. "Ready to go back?"

"I mean I *guess*," Valtora stated. "Honestly, I could go one more round."

"I don't have it in me," he stated apologetically.

"Fine," she grumbled, clearly realizing that if he didn't have it in him, she wouldn't have it in her, so to speak. "Oh *Zo-Monsterz!*"

Almost immediately, Chauncy felt a weight on his pelvis, and saw a large cat laying across it. A cat three times as big as a regular housecat, with golden-brown fur speckled with black, and big, purple-pink eyes that gazed at him. Sexily, as always.

"Reowr," she meowed. Whilst purring.

"Oh," he blurted out. "Hey Zo."

"Can you pwetty pweez bwing us home?" Valtora asked, using universal crazy cat-lady intonation. In response, ZoMonsterz's eyes began to glow with an unholy orange-yellow light...and in a flash, they found themselves back home. On the living room floor, which was awkward, because Nettie and Fury were on the couch. And because Chauncy and Valtora were still quite naked.

"Gah!" Chauncy blurted out, rushing to cover his dangly bits. Which were already covered by a Hellcat who'd been doing a more than adequate job, considering the rather unimpressive proportions involved. His sudden movement startled poor ZoMonsterz, who leapt off him rather violently.

Unfortunately, that meant she accidentally scratched him with her extremely long, ridiculously sharp hind claws. In a particularly personal place.

Deeply scratched. Like, all the way through.

Chauncy *shrieked.*

Blood shot all the way up to the ceiling, and Chauncy shrieked again, covering his groin with his hands. He felt a part of him roll off onto the floor with the motion, which firmly confirmed his greatest fears.

"FUCK!" he cried.

"Daddy?" Fury blurted out, wide-eyed.

"For the love of...!" Nettie shouted, leaping from the couch. "What in hell?"

"Rooter!" Chauncy screeched, trying in vain to stem the bloody jets painting the ceiling.

"Come on girlie," Nettie said, yanking Fury off the couch and pulling her up the stairs. A moment later, Nettie came back down with Rooter, the small rocky golem with a plant atop his head. A plant that was significantly bigger than it'd been a decade or two ago. Rooter walked up to Chauncy, doing his healing thing, and to Chauncy's immediate relief, he was whole again.

"Now get some damn clothes on!" Nettie barked, leaving the room again and going upstairs. Chauncy heard a door slam, and Nettie didn't come down again.

"Oh thank goodness," Chauncy blurted out, and to his shame he burst into tears. "Thank you thank you thank you."

"What is...oh," Valtora said, picking something up off the floor. It was, Chauncy realized a part of him he'd lost, but had regrown thanks to Rooter. "It's so small," she noted. Which was distressingly true. But on the receiving end of this statement was none other than Tip, the demonic mod for his rod.

"I'm...dying..." Tip gasped, his eyes glowing less brightly than before. "Save...me!"

"Rrhhhg," Chauncy heaved, putting a hand over his mouth. And then he promptly passed out.

* * *

The next morning, Chauncy woke up in his hot-pink four post bed with Valtora at his side, and immediately looked under the covers to sneak a peek at what'd been so recently clawed. For he'd suffered a nightmare about the event, which had ended with him parting ways with Tip yet again. To his relief, he was still quite whole...and to his further relief, Tip had been reattached to him. The little demon was still sleeping, but had only recently settled down from an apparent nightmare, jerking his head from side to side and moaning from time to time. Luckily, at a non-considerable length, the demon had settled down.

After a shuddering sigh, Chauncy slipped out of bed, making sure not to wake Valtora. For while she was normally an early riser, she'd had a long night, and it was best to let sleeping mommies lie.

Down the stairs he went, dodging an errant sock placed by ZoMonsterz for the purposes of accidently killing him, and then made his way into the kitchen, finding Nettie already there. She was wearing a bathrobe and making breakfast, and to Chauncy's relief, Fury was nowhere to be found. After what'd happened last night, he had absolutely no desire to see her, or to explain exactly what'd happened.

"Heya Chauncy," Nettie greeted, her expression carefully neutral. Which could only mean terrible things. "Have a seat," she added. "We need to talk."

7

Chauncy felt the blood drain from his face, and sat down at the kitchen table, feeling numb. For if there were any four words more terrifying to a man than those – in that specific order – he didn't know of them.

"I'm sorry," he blurted out. "I was stupid." He paused. "It's my fault," he added. Standard lines in response to the four deadly words, as any adult man should have learned.

"Shut up and listen," she grumbled, having a seat opposite him. "Before ya ask, this ain't got nothin' to do with whatever dumb shit you two did last night."

Chauncy paused, then relaxed. A bit.

"Oh," he mumbled.

"Fury got a...visitor yesterday," she told him, giving him a rather significant look.

"Oh, I know," Chauncy replied, feeling quite relieved. "She's been getting her periods for years now."

"Not *that* visitor, ya dipshit!" Nettie shot back. "Imperius Fanning."

The blood left Chauncy's face a second time, this time vowing not to return.

"What?" he blurted out. "Why?"

"Why else?"

"But...she's...ah...Fury," he protested. Which was, to anyone who knew her, all that needed to be said. "What does destiny want with *her*?"

"Hell if I know, kid," Nettie admitted. "But I suppose she'll find out soon enough." She sighed. "Imperius is coming back today, so he can deliver her destiny."

"But...no!" Chauncy protested.

"That's what I said," Nettie replied. "But Imperius wouldn't have it."

Just then, Chauncy heard footsteps coming down the stairs. Light footsteps, dainty even. Which meant that they most certainly weren't Fury's. Sure enough, Valtora came 'round the corner, walking into the kitchen, also with a bathrobe on. Hot pink, naturally.

"Hey," she greeted with a yawn.

"Imperius is coming for Fury!" Chauncy blurted out, unable to contain himself. Valtora blinked, then frowned, then gave an incredulous look.

"For Fury?" she said. "Oh *hell* no."

"That's what I said!" Chauncy replied.

"Me too," Nettie piped in.

"Does he even *know* Fury?" Valtora protested, putting her hands on her hips. "Uh uh. Nope. No way."

"Right?" Chauncy replied, feeling rather vindicated. For like everyone else in the house, he couldn't help but feel guilty for the negative thoughts he had about his daughter. Particularly in light of all the wonderful positive thoughts that she inspired. But in many ways she was like a child, to the point where he'd decided to hide the various realities of life from her. He'd even managed to get Valtora to do so as well, which was a fricking miracle.

"Well Imperius is coming for her today, so..." Nettie warned, giving Valtora a significant look. Valtora crossed her arms over her chest.

"Let him," she replied. "I *dare* him..."

Knock knock.

"...to," she finished. "Fuck," she added.

"I'll get it," Chauncy replied automatically. And then stayed right where he was, in classic Chauncy fashion.

"*I'll* get it," Valtora countered, and promptly turned to stomp toward the door. But at the same time, there came another stomping. A stomping from upstairs. Going downstairs, right toward the door. At alarming speed.

"I got it!" they heard Fury cry. Valtora cursed, breaking out into a sprint.

"No!" Chauncy blurted out. But by then it was too late. For Fury beat Valtora to the punch, so to speak, reaching the door and flinging it open with her usual gusto.

And there, standing on the doorstep, was none other than Imperius Fanning himself.

"Ah," he stated. "You must be Fury. It appears I've come right on time."

* * *

"Imperius!" Chauncy blurted out, trying to push past Fury to get between them. But Imperius shoved him back with the butt of his staff, shaking his head at Chauncy in warning.

"I came for Fury, not for you," he stated coolly. "Please let me have a word with her."

"Um..." Chauncy stated, wringing his hands.

9

"Alone," Imperius added, giving him a warning glare. And, being a coward at heart, he backed down. For, no matter how many times he'd worn the mantle of a hero, he still felt most comfortable after taking it off.

Valtora took Chauncy's place, peeking over Fury's shoulder.

"Hey Impy!" she greeted. "Hi!"

"Hello Valtora," Imperius replied.

"Fury's gotta go now, bye!" Valtora informed him, pulling Fury bodily back from the door.

"Oh," Fury exclaimed, quite confused as to what was going on.

"Enough!" Imperius snapped. And so suddenly booming and powerful was his voice that everyone froze in place. The legendary wizard glared at everyone. Except Fury, of course. "What will happen will happen, regardless of your attempts to avoid it," he warned. "But as your superior in the Order of Mundus, you test my patience at your own peril."

A chill ran down Chauncy's spine, and he cowered under Imperius's imperious gaze. Even Valtora remained speechless. Almost certainly not because she was cowed, but because she knew where this was going. Imperius was right, and they'd all witnessed the inevitability of his destiny-deliverances.

This was going to happen whether they liked it or not, and resisting would only make it worse. A phrase reminiscent of one that Chauncy had heard from his roommate while in prison in Tabula to the south, which had provided the incentive he'd needed to escape.

"Step back and close the door, and leave me with Fury," Imperius commanded. "Please."

Everyone reluctantly obeyed, and Valtora closed the door on Fury and Imperius, looking quite defeated. She turned to Chauncy, giving him an embrace, and Nettie watched on, her eyes moist.

"Sorry kid," she told Chauncy.

"Yeah," he replied. "Me too."

For whatever was in store for Fury, he knew that, in the end, there would be no way to protect her childlike innocence from the evils of the world. Not anymore.

Chapter 2

Fury stared at the wizard before her, standing on *her* porch, at *her* house, no less. And who'd wanted to speak with *her*.

It was impossible. Unbelievable. A dream that had, at long last, come true. After all, throughout her entire life, every other member of her family had been asked to answer destiny's call. Well, except for poor Epic, who'd vanished long ago. But still, she'd spent her whole gosh-darn life just *waiting* for Imperius Fanning to say it was *her* turn.

And here she was, and here *he* was, and it was actually, honest-to-gosh happening.

"Wow," she breathed, taking this feeling in. A feeling of utter awe and delight. It was a marvelous sensation, and she hardly wanted to rush it, so she soaked in it instead, enjoying it for as long as it allowed her to. She found herself clutching the necklace she'd worn since she was a baby, the magical artifact Fang hanging from it. A gift from Daddy, the best-est man in the whole wide world.

"Fury Little," Imperius began, his voice delightfully deep and booming. So much so that Fury clasped her hands together in delight. "Our world is in grave danger," he warned, his tone darkening wonderfully. "An ancient evil has risen in the Dark Forest, southwest of Tabula. Even now, its armies are spreading across Grissam like a great plague. Without your help, they will destroy everything you know and love!"

"Really?" Fury gasped, covering her mouth with her hands.

"Really," Imperius confirmed.

"I wanna help!" she decided instantly, putting her hands on her hips all determined-like. Heck, she even scowled fiercely, even though she wasn't *really* mad. It was more of a determined ferocity, an internal vow to not allow anything to stop her in her quest. For if people were in trouble, why, then by golly it was her responsibility to do something to help them.

"Then journey past the Kingdom of Pravus, and seek the fabled land of Ferra Lin," he replied. "There, you will find what you need to face the evil that threatens these lands."

"Okay!" she replied instantly. Then she paused. "Ooo, can I start now?"

Imperius paused, eyeing her critically.

"Yes," he answered.

"Yay!" she exclaimed, then rushed forward and gave him a big ol' hug. He tensed up, as people sometimes did, but then relaxed and hugged her back, which *all* guys did in the end. Because guys were just the nicest, sweetest people, honestly. Unlike girls, who for some reason tended to be standoffish and irritated with her.

Her delight adequately expressed, Fury stepped back, beaming at Imperius. Then she waved goodbye.

"Goodbye!" she exclaimed, and then burst forward, running past Imperius and down the stairs of the front porch, making her way across the walkway toward the sidewalk.

"Wait!" Imperius shouted. Fury froze, then turned around.

"Oops...did I do something wrong?"

"Ah...it's just, it might be better for you to have your parents and Nettie help you prepare for your trip, is all," Imperius stated, giving her a funny look. A look she got often, from most people after a while, so she didn't really pay it much mind.

"Okay," she agreed. And walked right back to the front door, shoving it open eagerly. Her parents stumbled backward from the door, Nettie close behind. "I'm gonna save the *world!*" Fury exclaimed, thrusting her arms in the air.

And that, dear reader, is the very beginning of this particular tale, one that is sure to bring you down a very different road than you've traveled before. But never fear, for in the end, inappropriate magic is bound to appear, and old friends are sure to pop up. But buyer beware, for there's no telling just how dark this tale may get, or how surprised you may be at the end. Read on, dear reader, and trust that at the very least, you'll be inappropriately entertained along the way.

Chapter 3

Having been bestowed a grand destiny by none other than the great Imperius Fanning, Fury Little set off immediately to prepare for the epic journey to come. And of course, her wonderful family set out immediately to help her in this preparation, so eager were they for her to finally have her adventure.

Daddy went to the store to get her a pack, while Mommy and Nettie went to one of Addie's grocery stores to get provisions. Fury took the opportunity to pack some clothes, which was a particularly hard job, considering just how many outfits she had. Each outfit was spectacularly colorful, of course, though heavily leaning on the pinks, purples, and turquoise. And she had colorful socks that had to be precisely matched to fit each outfit, and even underwear, though no one would see it. Because *she* would know, and it would bother her incessantly if she didn't match.

This done, she considered her accessories, including the most important of all: the hair ties. For these too had to match her outfits, and she needed plenty of options for her daily change in hairstyle. In lieu of packing said hair ties in a bag, however, she deemed it more efficient to carry them on her person. The smallest on her fingers, the rest on her forearms and wrists. In colorful patterns, naturally.

Then came the earrings, rings, necklaces, gold and silver braces for her wrists, toe rings, chokers, decorative fingerless gloves, and cute hats. Because when it came to going on a wonderful adventure, she wanted to look her very best. Not for the purpose of impressing, for this didn't even occur to her. Rather, she found that the more her outside represented who she was inside, the better – and more authentic – she felt.

This monumental task complete, Fury went downstairs with her stuff in tow, finding that her parents and Nettie had returned from their respective shopping trips. They seemed a bit quiet, and exchanged glances, and were even a bit teary-eyed.

"Aww," she cooed, giving Daddy an impromptu hug in the kitchen as he laid out a hot-pink backpack with purple highlights, and a glittering rainbow-colored unicorn embroidered on it. Which was just *exactly* what she would've picked. "Tank yew Big Daddy Nyum-Nyums." Which was her nickname for her sweet, dear father.

"Anything for you," he replied, his lower lip trembling a bit. He cleared his throat, glancing at Mommy, who was busy shoving the non-perishable provisions she'd bought into Fury's awesome new backpack. Fury added the stuff she'd packed, which turned out to be far too much stuff for the pack. So she was forced to take out her less-favorite outfits. A minor disappointment, quickly forgotten. Because she was going on a frickin' journey, and in the end, that's what really mattered.

"There," Mommy said when the pack was...packed. "What else?"

"Gonna need some way to defend herself, ain't she?" Nettie asked.

"Right," Dad replied. "I've got some weapons and stuff at the shop she could use."

"Yay!" Fury exclaimed, for she'd never been allowed to use any of Daddy's creations. Not in the weapons aisle, anyway.

"You thinking what I'm thinking?" Mommy asked.

"Rod of Fire," Chauncy replied.

"Yes," Mommy agreed.

"Rod of Fire!" Fury exclaimed, thrusting her fists in the air. For it was her favorite weapon in the shop by far, at least in theory. A red metal rod topped with a pretty red gemstone that absorbed and released heat, it was just the kind of weapon she'd imagined wielding as a wizard...and an upgrade from the Rod of Burning, which Daddy had made before Chaos had been born. Everyone else in her family – except poor Epic, wherever he was – was a wizard, and gosh darn it, she wanted to be one too.

Off to the shop Daddy went, returning a short time later with the Rod of Fire in hand. He presented to her in grave Daddy fashion, which was just simply exactly the way she'd imagined this moment would go.

"Be careful with it," he advised, more tears coming to his eyes. She adopted a similarly grave expression.

"I will," she replied, taking it into her hands. "Thank you Big Daddy Nyum-Nyums."

14

Daddy grimaced, and Nettie gave him a look, then rolled her eyes.

"Yeah," he mumbled. "Um, so what else?" he asked. Not Fury, of course, but Mommy.

"Um..." Mommy began, rubbing her chin with her glittering diamond hand.

"Hmm," Daddy mumbled, rubbing his chin as well.

"Guess that's it," Mommy said at last. Daddy frowned.

"No," he countered.

"Yes," Mommy replied.

"I feel like we're missing something," he pressed.

"Like what?"

He paused, then snapped his fingers.

"Transportation!" he answered. Mommy's eyes lit up.

"Ooo, I'll grab Peter!" she exclaimed.

"Peter!" Fury gasped. For she absolutely loved the pretty unicorn. And he matched so many of her outfits, which was just *perfect*.

Mommy went to the foyer and opened the front door...and then gasped. For Imperius Fanning himself was standing at the doorstep, awesome magical staff in hand.

"No," he declared.

"Huh?" Mommy replied, taken aback. As evidenced by the fact that she took a step back.

"She goes on foot," Imperius clarified. "No Peter. No carriage."

"But..." Mommy began.

"No," Imperius insisted.

"She has soft feet," Daddy argued.

"And a soft head," Nettie grumbled.

"They'll toughen up with time," Imperius replied. He gave Nettie a disapproving look. "As will the rest of her."

Daddy and Mommy glanced back at Fury, looking torn.

"Really?" Daddy said in a high-pitched sort of way.

"Really," Imperius confirmed. He patted his gut then. "Has my gut ever been wrong?" he inquired with a truly epic arching of one bushy white eyebrow. Why, it gave Fury chills to witness it.

Both of her parents hesitated.

"No," they replied in unison. Reluctantly.

"Then trust it this time," Imperius insisted. "Come Fury," he added, gesturing for her to do just that. She rushed up to him,

15

clasping her hands to her bosom in excitement. He stared at her. "Your pack," he reminded her.

"Ooo, right!" she replied, rushing to retrieve it. This done, she returned to his side excitedly. Mommy and Daddy rubbed their faces, then gave each other a hug, which was cute. "Aww," Fury cooed. "Triple-hug?"

"Sure," Daddy replied.

She joined in on the lovin', and at length they separated, and Fury turned to Imperius, adopting a serious expression. A fierce countenance that screamed "I'm ready, come get me." Or rather, "I guess I'll come get you, destiny. Let's do this."

"Let's do this," she stated, never one to hold a thought back.

"So you shall," Imperius replied. "Go south through the Gate to the Kingdom of Pravus, then head east until you reach the ocean," he instructed. "Follow the shore and it will bring you to tall cliffs," he advised. "When you reach the tallest cliff, search the area for the fabled land of Ferra Lin. There, you will find the means to fulfill your destiny."

"Which is?" she asked.

"To travel southwest of Grissam to the Dark Wood," he answered. "And destroy the source of evil within."

"Okay!" Fury agreed. "You can count on me!"

"One more thing," Imperius stated. "To help you in your journey, first follow the road through Pravus to a stone bridge, and seek the help of Rocky."

"Shmookie tookums?" Mommy asked.

"The same," Imperius confirmed. "But he is only to accompany you to the Gate to Grissam," he added. Then he turned to Daddy and Mommy. "You are not to intervene in any way," he warned, his tone quite grave. "Nor are you to follow or watch her journey. To do so would end in utter disaster. Are we understood, Chauncy Little?"

"Who, me?" Daddy replied. Innocently. Imperius just stared at him in a stern, wizardly sort of way. Which was just so cool to watch. Daddy's shoulders slumped. "Fine," he grumbled.

"Promise me, Chauncy," Imperius pressed. Chauncy hesitated, wringing his hands.

"Can't I just go and save the world?" he asked. "Isn't that...more practical?" he added, glancing at Fury.

"Remember the stakes," Imperius replied. "If you die, the universe dies with you. You must stay here, safe and sound, for all our sakes."

Daddy grimaced.

"But it's not like you have a whole lot of guards or anything protecting me here," he argued.

"My gut protects you," Imperius replied, patting his belly. "It tells me to keep you here, so that's what you'll do. Now promise me you'll stay out of Fury's quest."

Daddy hesitated, then sighed.

"I...promise," he replied. Imperius turned his gaze to Mommy and Nettie.

"I promise," both grumbled.

"Very well," Imperius declared, smoothing out his cloak with one hand. "Go now, Fury, and fulfill your destiny!"

"Okay!" Fury replied instantly. Imperius paused, glancing at Daddy and Mommy, then returning his gaze to her.

"Tell me where you're going," he prompted.

"Through the Gate, follow the road to the stone bridge, find Rocky, head east to the ocean, follow the shore north to the tallest cliff, get to the highest spot on the cliff and find the fabled land of Ferra Lin, then go to southwest Grissam to defeat the great evil in the Dark Forest," she recited. For when it came to her memory, she was much like her Mommy. In fact, some of her fondest memories were of snuggling with Mommy on the couch, memorizing the dictionary and thesaurus together.

"Right," Imperius replied, giving her a relieved smile. And with that, the great wizard vanished in a poof of pretty blue sparkles.

"Ooo," she breathed, watching as they fell to the ground and disappeared. Then she turned to her parents. "Hugs before bye-byes?"

"Of course," Daddy replied.

She hugged Daddy and Mommy and Nettie, then waved goodbye, leaving and closing the door behind her, backpack on her back and Daddy's rod in her hands. And with that, her fated journey began!

Chapter 4

The sun shone from the east as Fury made her way past A Little Magic, continuing down the main street toward the Gate ahead. Its ginormous silver doors gleamed brilliantly in the sunlight, like two gigantic pieces of jewelry. While their function was to bar the way into the magical Kingdom of Pravus, it was also to convey the beauty and majesty of way lay beyond. For if the kingdom had managed to create such a beautiful work of art of what otherwise could've been purely functional, then they clearly had their heads – and their hearts – in the right place. It hinted at what other magnificent and magical things might exist beyond…and enticed anyone who saw them to find out. Or if not that, then at least to dream.

This is how Fury felt about the Gate, and how she'd felt about them since she was thirteen.

She strode right up to the Gate, finding a gruff and tough looking guard guarding the twin silver doors. But when he spotted her coming, she gave him a smile, and he couldn't help but smile back.

"Hi!" she greeted, giving him a little wave.

"Hey," he replied, studying her outfit. Which was cute, if she did say so herself. A pink crop-top with a V-neck, and purple tights with pink shoes and purple socks, it was classic Fury. A fashion the man clearly appreciated. And kept appreciating, which was awfully flattering.

"Going through," she stated.

"Uh huh," the man mumbled.

She skipped up to the doors, touching one of them, and waiting for the *thunk* that was to follow. But there was no *thunk* at all, to her surprise.

"Am I doing it wrong?" she asked no one in particular.

"Huh?" the guard asked, continuing to appreciate.

"Oh, it's just that it's supposed to unlock," she explained. "I'm a wizard," she added. He blinked.

"A wizard?"

"Yep!" she confirmed. "My Daddy's Chauncy Little."

The guard frowned.

"Wait, you're one of the Littles?" he asked.

"Yep!"

"Huh," the guard replied. "Met your brother Chaos," he told her. "Back when he was going on his adventure." He paused. "Gate's not opening?"

"No," Fury replied, furrowing her brow in consternation. "Strange, right?" She furrowed her brow harder, trying to figure it out. But before she could come up with a reason why, there was a *thunk*...and the silver doors began to swing open. Fury stepped back, as did the guard, and watched as the magical Kingdom of Pravus was revealed...and what's more, a man standing on the other side of the Gate. He was at least eighty, and would've been seven feet tall or so had his back not been quite bent with age. And he had short red hair with patches of white, with silver glasses and bright blue eyes. His outfit was quite unique, in that he wore a chestnut brown shirt and suspenders, with matching pants and shoes, topped with a vest composed of a lattice of stones, pieces of metal, and even some wood chips of various hues.

"Harry!" Fury exclaimed in delight, rushing forward and leaping into the man's arms. She found him as hard as ever, not so much as budging with the impact of her love. She gave him a big ol' squeeze, followed by a smooch on the cheek, then disengaged, beaming up at him.

"Heya Fury," Harry greeted in his warbly voice. "How'n the hell are ya?"

"Great!" she replied immediately.

"Ya sure are," he said with a grin.

"Imperius came and I'm on my way to my destiny," she explained.

"Makes sense," Harry replied. "Where's Nettie?"

"With Mommy and Daddy," she answered. Then she pouted. "You're visiting?"

"Sure am," he confirmed, adjusting his glasses. Which was hopeless, because like his back, they were chronically crooked.

"Aww, I'm gonna miss it," she said with a pout, and a stomp of her foot.

"Tell ya what," he replied. "I'll visit again when ya come back."

Her countenance immediately brightened.

"Yay!" she exclaimed, giving him another hug. "Thanks Harry!"

"See ya," he replied. "And have fun."

"Will do," she replied.

With that, Harry left, and Fury watched him go with a wistful smile. Then she turned back to the open Gate, taking a deep breath in. She gazed upward at the gleaming doors, struck by a sudden feeling of awe. That she was *here*, right *now*, doing what she'd so often dreamed of doing.

This was the moment she'd imagined for so long, and it was happening. And by golly she was going to enjoy every second of it.

She realized then that the guard was still staring at her, and it occurred to her that she might be overstaying her welcome.

"Sorry," she apologized. "Just enjoying it."

"Don't be," he replied, seeming happy to enjoy the moment himself.

"Bye!" she said, giving him a wave. And he waved back, naturally. Then she turned forward, and took her first step into the magical Kingdom of Pravus. For while she'd been there once before, it'd been as an infant, and thus she hadn't taken any steps on the land's magical ground. Her feet tingled as she strode past the threshold of the Gate, her heart filled with giddy glee. For each step she took from here on out was one step closer to her destiny!

* * *

The road leading into Pravus was not so different than any other road, being made of packed dirt. In fact, it was, at least from an engineering point of view, far inferior to the immaculate stone roads of Southwick. But from a different viewpoint, the road was extraordinary indeed, not in the details of its construction, but in its function. For it was Fury's guide into a legendary land, one filled with magic and wonder. The fact that it was merely stomped-on dirt was a bonus, for it represented an ancient way of travel, before humanity had overly exerted its compulsive control over nature, forcing everything to live in a simplified, boxy, boring human world.

Fury skipped along said road, feeling mighty fine indeed, her brown waving hair swinging side-to-side as she went. Then she stopped, for it occurred to her that her backpack should be jingling with every step. She took it off, removing some bling. Two necklaces, to be exact; she looped them 'round the straps at the bottom, then gave the pack a shake. They jingle-jangled just as she'd hoped…and thus she continued her skip-stepping journey in a more musical way.

She found herself humming as she went, leaving the Gate gradually behind. With the sun warming her skin and a breeze in her hair, it really was just the perfect day.

"Thank you, day!" she exclaimed, for when one carried gratitude in one's heart, it was important to express it. And as with fashion, Fury's preference was to express the inside on the outside. It didn't matter that the day didn't reply, for expressing joy was as much for her as for others. Acting out of joy only magnified it, whereas to magnify negative emotions required holding them inside to let them grow. But both types of emotion rippled outward, affecting everyone connected to her, and expressing joy created joy in others, who would express it, and so on and so forth. In short, being happy made others happy, which made her happier still.

Onward she went, until she grew tired of skipping, and she settled into a pleasantly paced walk instead. Just taking in the sights and sounds, the scents of flowers and grass and dirt, enjoying the whole shebang.

Time passed, the sun slowly making its way on its usual celestial path, until it was high overhead. The day, already warm, grew even more so, until it was rather hot. So Fury stopped again, grabbing a flask of water and drinking until she was sated. Then she poured the water over her body to cool off a bit. Which wet her clothes, but she hardly minded, for wetness, dirt, and grime didn't bother her in the slightest.

This resulted in her using up most of the flask's water, and she squeezed the bottom, where Daddy had put a Wetstone inside. This filled the flask back up, and she put it back in her pack, slinging the pack back onto her back. Then onward she went, enjoying the cool of the breeze on the wetness.

A few minutes later, she spotted a sign ahead. One that read: "Village of Erp, population sixty-eight." At only a bit past noon, which should strike you as a bit odd, dear reader. For as you may or may not recall, Chaos had only reached said village after a full day and a half of travel. Also recall, however, the meandering, non-linear manner in which he'd made the trip, which had more than tripled the distance he'd had to walk.

21

In any case, Fury found herself skipping again, and skipped right into the village, which consisted of three buildings: a general store, an inn, and a bar. There was a man standing outside said bar, a brawny balding man wearing brown coveralls – russet brown in contrast to Harry's chestnut – and chewing on a length of straw.

"Hey," he greeted, eyeing her as she skipped. Particularly her still-wet clothes. She imagined he was puzzling over the mystery of why they were wet, considering it hadn't rained and there were no bodies of water nearby. "Hey," he repeated, continuing to eye her. "What's your name pretty girl?"

"Fury," she answered. "Fury Little," she added, for completeness's sake. She kept skipping along, and he stepped away from the doorway, walking toward her.

"Whatcha doin' visiting Erp?" he inquired.

"Just passing through," she replied. "I'm on a Quest," she added, including the capital 'Q'" for the important noun, though she knew it wasn't grammatically correct.

"A quest huh?" he asked, continuing to stroll toward her. "Why the big rush?" he asked, moving to step in front of her. She stopped her skipping. "Come to the bar and stay awhile," he prompted, giving her a smile that included quite a few less teeth than she was accustomed to seeing. "My treat."

"Oh, I'm too young to drink," she countered cheerily. "Bye!"

She went to step around him, but he grabbed her wrist, stopping her.

"Come on," he pleaded. "I insist."

"No thank you," she replied. "But thanks for the offer…you're very kind."

"I sure am," he replied. "Gentle too," he added, though his grip on her wrist implied otherwise. "And firm," he added, which she supposed was true, though his physique was decidedly not. Though she couldn't help noticing he was starting to bulge a bit, beneath his bulging gut. To her confusion, he pulled her hand toward said southernly bulge, and she resisted with rapidly increasing alarm.

Just then, the door to the bar burst open, and a middle-aged woman barged out. She was remarkably similar in shape to the man, and clearly not one bit pleased.

"What 'n the damn hell *fuck* do you think yer doing, Earl?" she barked, stomping up to him. He let go of Fury's wrist instantly, whirling around to face her.

"Just welcomin' this fine young woman to our town, Heggie," he explained. Heggie eyed Fury, then the bulge Fury had inspired, regarded the man rather furiously. And promptly slapped him upside the head.

"Woman?" she blurted out. "She's a damn *girl*, Earl!"

"I was just..." Earl began, but was slapped again. This time across the aforementioned bulge, with a meaty *thwack* that made him squeak.

"Get your fat ass back in the damn bar, Earl!" she snapped.

"But..."

"Now!" she barked. And pointed to the bar, in case he'd forgotten where it was. Earl took once last lingering glance at Fury, then strode dejectedly back to the bar, standing at the door and chewing his straw once again, his eyes – and groin – downcast.

Heggie turned to eye Fury then, looking her up and down, then shaking her head.

"Get the hell outta here if you know what's good fer ya," she grumbled. And then stomped back to the bar.

"Bye!" Fury said, waving at them both, then began skipping through the town again. And so small was the village of Erp that she was soon leaving it far behind. She thought it a bit rude for Erp to grab her wrist, and to try to force her to touch his manly bits. But on the other hand, he'd called her a woman, which was nice. It was clear he'd liked her, even if he hadn't had the best of manners, but then again manners could be taught.

Onward she went, a-skipping at times, walking at others, and taking the occasional break for water and getting watered on. And while with the Wetstone water was essentially infinite, food was not, so she made sure not to eat yet. Not until she was good and famished. Besides, there was a certain pleasure in looking forward to things, and as such, her increasing hunger merely conjured visions of sating it...visions that were pleasant indeed.

At length the sun had swung all the way to the horizon, its rays painting a gorgeous scene on the clouds. Including the gorgeous-est of pinks and purples, nearly matching her outfit, which was a nice touch. The going got a bit more challenging, considering the increasing darkness, and Fury realized she'd soon have to make camp. So she did, stopping and taking off her backpack and putting down her Rod of Fire. Then she sat by the road to rummage through her pack. She took out her sleeping bag, and then munched on some nuts. Cashews, which were her favorite, though she was a fan of salty nuts in general.

She sighed a content sigh then, rather proud of her day's effort. Gazing up at the sky, she enjoyed the steadily cooling air, and the sounds of crickets and other insects having their chirpy-chirp conversations. At length, she yawned, then stretched, and decided to unzip her sleeping bag in preparation for snuggling inside.

And that was when she spotted something in the distance, near the road ahead: two glowing silver-blue eyes.

Fury frowned, standing up. The eyes were at least a hundred and twenty feet away, and cast a faint silver-blue light on the area ahead of them. And in fact, she spotted two more sets of glowing eyes on either side of the first, these closer to the ground.

"Hello?" she called out.

There was no reply. But the three sets of glowing eyes continued to stare unblinkingly at her...and what's more, they appeared to be getting closer.

"Hi?" she ask-greeted. And for the second time that day, she felt a bit uneasy. A feeling which made her doubly uneasy, because it was a feeling she almost never felt. But still, there was no answer...and the silver-blue glowing eyes continued to approach. It wasn't long before they were close enough for her to make out their forms:

It was a man, still mostly shrouded in darkness, with a wolf walking at either side.

"I'm Fury," she greeted, taking a step back involuntarily. "Hi," she added, offering a nervous little wave.

But to her consternation, the figure didn't wave back. And he kept striding toward her, picking up his pace. Until he suddenly broke out into a sprint, charging right at her...and his wolves did the same.

"Oh!" she blurted out, taking another step back, then another. The man was closing the distance with frightening rapidity, the wolves breaking ahead of him. Only thirty feet away now.

Twenty. *Ten.*

"Wait!" she cried, holding out a hand for them to stop.

And then the first of the wolves leapt at her, slamming into her chest and throwing her to the ground!

Fury struck her back on the grass with a *whump*, her head bouncing off the hard ground. Stars exploded in her vision, and she gasped, feeling a heavy weight atop her. The wolf's silver-blue eyes locked on hers, and it pinned her down with its big front paws.

The other wolf stopped at her left side, and then she heard footsteps approaching to her right. It was the man, she realized; he strode up to her, stopping at her right side. He was tall and slender, wearing ragged, torn clothes that smelled absolutely rotten. And his flesh was awfully pale, and what's more, there were deep gashes in his chest and arms. And to Fury's horror, the left side of his face was just...gone. No flesh, just pearly-white bone.

He knelt before her, his eyes locked on hers. And try as she might, as terrified as she was, she froze, unable to look away.

"You..." the man growled, his breath hissing through the missing left side of his lips.

Fury just stared at him, unable to move.

The wolf atop her bared its long, awful fangs, and she realized with fresh horror that it too was missing hunks of its fur and flesh. All the way down to the ribs on its right side, in fact. Its cold drool dripping onto her neck, making her flinch.

"Ka-La-Meh-La...calls," the man gasped, silver-blue light seeming to swirl like mist inside his eyes. He grabbed her Fang necklace in one hand, staring at it with those terrible eyes. Then he raised his right arm up, and to Fury's terror, a gleaming silver dagger was clutched blade-down in his hand. She cried out, watching as he brought it high above her chest, its wicked edge gleaming in the moonlight.

Then she screamed...right as he brought the dagger plunging down toward her heart!

Chapter 5

Despite it being a particularly fine – and unseasonably warm – autumn day, King Pravus the Eighth was having a particularly *un*-fine day. Mostly because he'd been forced to cut his morning workout short to attend to his obligations instead. But to be fair, the magical kingdom that bore his name wasn't faring any better. For while autumn had only just arrived, news had reached his kingdom only a day ago. Dire news that, despite the weather, had chilled him to the bone.

He found himself standing quite peevishly before the Southern Wall, the section of the two-hundred-foot-tall stone wall surrounding his kingdom bordering Grissam, staring at the nearly two-hundred-foot-tall golden doors of the Gate there. Closed, as they should be, for only a wizard could open them, other than himself of course. Which was quite vexing, because apparently something had come through them. Without consent, which was rude. And also illegal. As such, he'd brought a ridiculously large contingent of soldiers with him. Not for protection, for with the magic of his monarchal uniform, he hardly needed it. No, when governments put gobs and gobs of soldiers on display, it was always for show. A sort of geopolitical theater that told any would-be enemies to knock it off already, because just *look* at how many friends I have.

"Desmond!" he barked.

"Yes sire?" Desmond droned. The old man was standing beside him after all, looking for all the world like a mostly melted candle. Well, not so old anymore, considering he'd earned another quaff of a potion of youth. One that'd transformed Desmond into a fifty-year-old man. Ish. But somehow his body seemed as decrepit as ever, as bodies tended to be when not tended to for an appreciable length of time.

"You told me the Gate had been opened," he accused, glaring down at the man.

"Indeed sire."

"It's closed," he stated, gesturing at the doors.

"An open and shut case then," Desmond replied evenly. Pravus rolled his royal eyes.

"So where's the threat to my kingdom?" Pravus pressed. Which was a two-part question. The first assumed that a wizard had opened the Gate, allowing a threat to pass through. The second posited that the wizard was the true threat, because if they'd done it before, they could do it again. Desmond paused, clearly aware that an old game was being played. One where he would have to come up with the right answer to both questions, lest he earn Pravus's disrespect.

"Undetermined," he replied at last. "The Grande Wizard of the Court should have his report shortly."

There was a sudden *poof* of black, choking smoke, and Pravus turned a haughty glare at it. Sure enough, the smoke cleared to reveal none other than Skylar, Pravus's demonic wizard. One with deep red skin and spikey black hair streaked with white. As well as a similarly striped black goatee, large horns that curved backward from his head, and eyes that glowed with an unholy orange light. His robe of flames burned, but did not burn him; still, Pravus could feel the heat on his face. Which did nothing to ward off the chill of foreboding in the air, of course.

"Unhappy anniversary," Skylar greeted. Then he paused. "My liege," he added reluctantly, bowing oh-so-slightly. Pravus grimaced.

"Indeed," he muttered.

It was the sixth anniversary of the Dark Rising, the now-legendary night when the dead had risen in Grissam. As the story went, zombies had been seen coming out of the Dark Forest…a forest southwest of Tabula, the capitol city of Grissam. Which was the city he and Templeton had visited six years ago, before almost single-handedly saving the cursed city of Old Langsroth. In any case, soldiers had been sent into the Dark Forest to kill the zombies, but no matter how large a force Grissam sent, no one returned.

Then had come the Dark Rising, when the dead had risen from their graves in the nearby towns and cities, massacring the people there. And every citizen who'd died had added one more undead soldier to that dark army…until all but one of southwest Grissam's towns and cities had been wiped out.

27

Now, six years later, the only southwestern city left standing was Belfast. A city that served as the only land passage north to Tabula...and beyond Tabula, this very Gate. As such, Belfast constituted Grissam's best chance at preventing the hordes of undead from reaching the Gate, considering that while Tabula was a mesa, and thus quite defendable, it was easily avoided by going around it. The wide-open plains around Tabula would serve as an essentially undefendable passage north, toward the magical kingdom of Pravus. Small, tight passages were far easier to defend...and to open up only to those whose passage in and out was preferred.

"I discussed the matter of the Gate's opening with the Order of Mundus," Skylar revealed.

"And?" Pravus snipped.

"None of their wizards opened it yesterday," the demon revealed. "Nor do they have knowledge of who did."

"I can guess," Pravus muttered.

"As can I," Skylar replied. "But a guess is not necessarily the truth."

Pravus rolled his eyes. For they both knew damn well – or rather, guessed damn well – that only one wizard could have done it. The same wizard that he was quite sure was behind the Dark Rising.

The one and only Zarzibar.

A good guess, considering the zombies in Old Langsroth and in the Dark Wood shared the same glowing, blood-red eyes. And because Zarzibar was the only lich or necromancer or whatever known to currently reside on the continent, at least according to the Order of Mundus.

"Pardon Grande Wizard," Desmond interjected. "You said that none of the Order's wizards opened it yesterday."

"Correct," Skylar confirmed.

"Did they open it any other day?" Desmond pressed. Which was a damn good question.

"Not within the last year," Skylar answered. "Destiny was the last to open it."

Pravus blinked.

"Destiny, the paladin of Vita," Skylar clarified.

"Ah," Pravus replied. "Well, we must assume the worst..." he began.

"Always, sire," Desmond interjected.

"…that Zarzibar has opened the Gate to allow undead to enter my kingdom," Pravus continued, ignoring the dour man. "Or even worse, that *he* has entered the kingdom, and plans to raise an army of undead to attack our lands."

"Agreed," Skylar replied. "Our scrying magic should have let us see who was opening it, but somehow the enemy blocked it."

"Evidence of insidious intent," Pravus deduced.

"Perhaps," Skylar stated. "The only other wizard who could possibly frustrate the Order's scrying magic is Chaos Little."

"Who is in Borrin," Pravus replied, suddenly done with the process of deduction. "So what is our plan?" he inquired, eyeing the Grande Wizard of the Court. For as the pre-eminent wizard in the kingdom, he was the best suited to answer this question.

"We should continuously surveil this Gate, to ensure that no further intrusions occur," Skylar answered. "Or that if they do, we are immediately aware of it."

"And I suggest flying scouts to surveil the countryside," Desmond advised. "Perhaps dragons, or wyrms," he added. Wyrms were, of course, smaller cousins of the dragons. Like small dogs and small-minded men, they were loud and vicious and profoundly insecure.

"Very well," Pravus replied. "Make it so."

With that, Skylar vanished in a puff of smoke, accompanied as usual by the stink of sulfur. Pravus held his breath until the smoke mostly dissipated, then turned to Desmond.

"I'm done," he declared. "Back to Cumulus."

"Yes sire," Desmond droned.

And with that, Pravus turned away from the Gate, striding back toward his trusty fire dragon. A truly massive dragon that'd been waiting behind him all this time. Much to the consternation of his soldiers, who still didn't feel comfortable around a giant lizard that could roast them all if it chose to. Which was ironic, because the fire dragon had served them all quite loyally for nearly two decades, helping to save the kingdom – and the world – on many an occasion. Had the creature been human, the soldiers would have lauded it and declared it a great hero, worthy of near-worship. But as it was another species, it was treated with mistrust. Such was the curse of human nature, and the nature of many other species. In that any considerable difference between groups was seen as a reason to erect psychic walls, in hopes to keep the "other" out.

"Desmond," he stated as he strode.

"Yes sire?" Desmond inquired, from a considerable distance behind Pravus, on account of his profoundly underdeveloped physique.

"Set up a meeting with Lord Lucus when I get back," Pravus ordered.

"Yes sire."

Pravus mounted the fire dragon whilst Desmond took a wingéd horse, and soon Pravus found himself flying high over his lands. His eyes were drawn far south of the Gate, to the southwest, in fact. Somewhere out there, the enemy was gathering. Growing stronger with each passing day.

He sighed, feeling the weight of the last six years pressing down not on his shoulders, but his very soul. For, ever since learning of the rising threat of undead hordes, he'd spent almost every waking minute trapped in his role as king. With each passing year, he'd felt more and more alone, such that even his sweet cousin Templeton's company was no longer sufficient to fill the void within him.

Focus, he told himself. *The world is counting on you.*

But after six years since the Dark Rising, and despite Pravus's aid to Grissam, no headway had been made against the undead. And while Pravus had defeated the Fallen Sky that'd cursed Old Langsroth, Zarzibar, the evil lich that'd created it still lived. Or rather, un-lived. Or existed, or whatever.

Pravus turned away from Grissam, focusing on his kingdom to the north. A pristine landscape, untouched by undead hands. But even as he left Grissam behind, he couldn't help but feel a chill run down his spine.

Zarzibar's army was growing. And if someone didn't do something soon, it would spread across the world like a great plague, and destroy everything Pravus knew and loved.

Chapter 6

Fury screamed as her undead attacker plunged his dagger downward at her heart, turning her head away at the last second. A horrible pain shot through her chest…

…and then there was a loud *whump*, and the man was catapulted right over her, taking the wolf atop her with him.

Fury gasped, looking down at her chest, and to her relief, it was intact. No dagger handle sticking out, quivering with each beat of her heart. Her pain had been purely anticipatory. She heard the thump, thump of incredibly heavy footsteps stomping past her from behind, and the remaining wolf leapt at whoever was behind her.

There was a loud yelp, and Fury saw the wolf shoot upward and away from her, well over thirty feet from the ground. It reached the peak of its flight, then fell, landing some two hundred feet away.

Fury stared at the sight, hardly believing her eyes. And also terribly confused. Then she heard a loud grunt from behind.

She scrambled to her feet, then whirled around, expecting to see something equally awful and ready to kill her. But to her surprise, the creature that stood before her was neither awful nor undead. Rather, it was a creature at least twenty feet tall, with a blocky head, shoulders as big as boulders, and skin that looked to be half made of stone. He stared down at her, his hands curled into fists, and grunted again.

Fury's eyes widened, and she gasped, covering her mouth with her hand. For though she'd never seen him before, at least to her recollection, she'd heard stories of a creature matching his description.

"Rocky?" she blurted out. He frowned, or at least she thought he did. His expressions were a bit stiff, after all. "I'm Fury," she greeted. "Imperius Fanning told me to find you!"

Still the dwarf-giant looked unconvinced.

"My Mommy calls you shmookie tookums," she offered. "My parents are Valtora and Chauncy Little."

With that, Rocky's eyes widened – or at least as much as they could – and he broke out into a stiff smile.

"Freeeend!" he declared, relaxing his fists. And with the act of uncurling his fingers, he transformed them back into hands. He knelt before her, opening his arms wide.

"Ooo, hugs!" Fury exclaimed. "Yes please!" And she promptly hugged his leg. Which was quite hard, being half made of stone. "Thanks for saving me, by the way," she added, recalling her recent brush with death. She shuddered at said memory, for she'd never once been treated so disrespectfully. Other than by Earl, in a far less deadly way.

Rocky put his hands on her back with surprising gentleness, then stood.

"Wuuut Impeee saaay?" he inquired.

"He wanted me to meet you here and have you come with me east to the ocean," she explained. "Then north to the tallest cliff. I'm supposed to find the fabled land of Ferra Lin there, so I can complete my destiny."

"Oooo," Rocky replied, seeming quite impressed with this.

"Wanna come?" she asked, biting her lower lip and giving him googly-eyes.

"Shuuur," he replied.

"Yay!" she exclaimed, coming in for another hug. One that Rocky was happy to receive. That done, they set off, Rocky walking at Fury's side. "Where's your bridge?" she asked.

"Neeeer," he answered, pointing down the road. "Waaant carreeee?"

"Ooo," Fury replied. "Sure!"

He got on all fours, lowering himself down so she could climb up. Then she sat on his back, and he continued eastward, traveling far faster than she ever could on all fours. Yet somehow he managed to keep his back mostly level, so that it merely swayed nicely. An exceedingly pleasant ride, she had to admit. So she did.

"This is a *super* pleasant ride," she told Rocky. Who made a happy noise in reply. He picked up speed a bit, the sun fully set now. But while before she'd been quite sleepy, her brush with death had given her a substantial second wind.

She spotted a pair of glowing silver-blue eyes ahead, and realized it was the wolf that Rocky had thrown into the air. It was lying on its side, its legs shattered, sharp bone-ends sticking out grotesquely. And quite strangely, there was a silver-blue glowing mist swirling out of said wounds, identical in hue to its eyes.

Rocky veered toward it, which made Fury rather nervous. But then he trampled it, flattening its head with one massive hand. An act of violence that made Fury flinch, but tempered by the realization that the wolf wasn't really alive.

It wasn't long before Fury spotted something ahead: a wide river with a cute stone bridge arching over it.

"Is that your bridge?" she asked.

"Yaaaa," Rocky answered. "Huuurd yewww yell," he added.

"And you came to rescue me," she deduced. "Awww!" she exclaimed, throwing herself belly-first on his back and giving it a hug. "Thanks shmookie tookums!"

"Welcuuum."

She sat up, putting on a determined face, and even put her hands on her hips.

"Imperius told me to head east to the ocean after going over your bridge," she declared. "Let's go!"

"Okkeeee," he agreed.

They went over the bridge, and turned right, leaving the road behind, forging their own path eastward as Imperius had prescribed. It wasn't long before Fury's adrenaline faded, however, and she found her eyelids growing heavy once again. At length, she could barely hold them open any longer, and decided it was time to make camp. Rocky brought them to the top of a small, grassy hill, then lowered himself to the ground so she could get off safely. With sunset far behind them, the stars twinkled merrily in the heavens, the quarter-moon seeming to smile down on them as they built a fire. Which was easy with the Rod of Fire. They simply gathered some brush and chunks of long-dead wood, then tapped it with the rod's crystal top. Boom, campfire. Just. Like. That.

"Sleepy time," Fury announced, unfolding her sleeping bag and snuggling inside. "Mmm," she murmured, feeling all comfy-cozy. "So *nice*."

"Niiice," Rocky agreed, lying opposite her, with the campfire in between. "Niiite," he added.

"Nighty night," she murmured back. And then closed her eyes and went to sleep. Or at least she tried to, without success. For she found herself simply too darn excited to surrender to sleep's embrace. She turned to glance at Rocky. "Can you tell me a bedtime stowwy pweese?" she asked, even giving a little lower-lip pout along with some doe-eyes.

"Stohhhry?" Rocky asked.

"Mmhm."

Rocky gave her a doubtful look.

"Pretty *please*?" she pressed, offering maximal doe-eyes and pouty-lip. Rocky grunted, then reluctantly complied. For it was soon apparent that he was not much of a storyteller, being minimally capable of speech. So what came out of his stiff lips was largely unintelligible. And what's more, his pacing was terrible and he definitely could've made use of a thesaurus, as he tended to use the same words again and again. But still, in the end, it wasn't so much the substance of the story but the fact that he was telling it that worked on Fury's brain, and as luck would have it, she missed the tale's end. For before the gentle dwarf rock giant could conclude his tale, he found her fast asleep.

* * *

The following morning, Fury woke to find the sun playing peek-a-boo at the horizon. She smiled at it, crawling out of her sleeping bag and stretching her arms over her head. Rocky was already awake, and smiled stiffly at her as she stretched. Then she yawned, and then farted. Quite loudly.

"Oopsie," she blurted out, giving Rocky an apologetic look. But he honestly didn't seem to mind. And to her relief, there'd been nothing liquid or solid that'd escaped during her impromptu gaseous release.

"Go?" the dwarf giant asked.

"Sure," she replied. "I'll eat on the way." Then she paused. "Actually, I'll, um, be back, kay?"

And with that, she ran away from Rocky as quickly as she could, aiming for a large group of bushes in the distance, for she had urgent business to attend to. After finishing said business, she returned feeling much relieved.

"Okay," she declared. "Onward, Rocky!"

She climbed on Rocky's large, flat back, and he made his way east, using the sun as a celestial compass. Fury took the opportunity to change into a new outfit, not at all concerned that Rocky might see her nude. She'd inherited her mother's unconcern with being naked, because in the end, everyone was, at least under their clothes. Not to mention that she'd also inherited her mother's figure, which gave a truly massive boost of confidence by itself.

Fury changed into a dark blue and turquoise ensemble, seeing as she was hoping to match the ocean when they got there. Which, after another few hours – at high noon, in fact – they did. The relatively flat grassland gave way to a wide, sandy beach, one that stretched to the north and south as far as her eyes could see.

And since she'd never seen the beach or the ocean – except for in paintings, and in illustrations in Daddy's magic books at the shop – Fury found herself gazing at the splendid sight in the spirit of wonder.

"*Wow*," she breathed. "Isn't it beautiful, Rocky?"

"Yaaah," he replied.

"I wanna go in!" she exclaimed, leaping off his back and charging through the sand. Which was wonderfully squishy and soft underfoot, she found. A fact that made it fun to try to run on. Eventually she reached the water, which was doing the strangest thing: rising up in a long line parallel to the shore, then falling over itself in a churning, hissing mess that slid gently toward her feet, then backed away. Over and over and over again.

Fury watched this exotic play of water, wondering at how it all worked. Why rise? Why hiss? But she didn't really care if she never found out. For the experience of experiencing it was more than good enough.

She stepped into the water then, feeling it lap at her shoes. Which got instantly soaked, but she didn't mind. The water was surprisingly cold, in a refreshing sort of way. She bent down to cup her hands and get some of it, then brought it to her lips and drank.

"Ooo, salty!" she exclaimed, rather liking this surprise. For she loved salty things quite a lot. But after a few gulps, she found it a bit too salty to have a whole lot of.

After splish-splashing around for a while, Fury went back to Rocky, mounting him again.

"Let's follow the shore north to the tallest cliff!" she exclaimed, pointing the way rather unnecessarily. And with that, they were off again.

* * *

As it turned out, Rocky and Fury didn't make it to the cliffs overlooking the ocean that day, and ended up setting up camp that night, a hundred feet or so from the beach. The vegetation here was more limited, making it take a bit longer to gather materials for a fire, but Fury certainly didn't mind the task. After all, searching for dead, dried vegetation under a brilliant star-filled sky, with a moon smiling down on her and casting its silver light on the crashing waves nearby...well, it was as magical as any spell a wizard might perform. And to be able to share it with Rocky was extra special indeed.

"There!" she said as she placed the last of the dried brush. She grabbed her Rod of Fire then, scowling as she imagined a powerful wizard might. "Alight, mine campfire!" she exclaimed in an epic-sounding voice, as if she were Imperius Fanning himself. So the brush did, and soon they were relaxing before a merrily crackling fire. "This is nice," she mused, smiling from ear to ear, sitting beside Rocky. She leaned over to rest her head on his rocky thigh, and he grunted approvingly.

"Niiizzzze," he agreed in his rumbly sort of way.

Fury gazed at the flames, her mind wandering pleasantly.

"I wonder what my magic will be?" she...well, wondered. Rocky shrugged. "Whatever it is, it's gonna be *so* awesome," she declared. Which of course was undeniably true. For even having magic was, well, magical to her. So any magic would do.

They sat next to each other, enjoying each other's presence. Until at last Fury's eyelids grew heavy, and started to close. The next thing she knew, Rocky was carrying her to her sleeping bag, and tucking her gently in.

"My sweet, gentle giant," she murmured gratefully. "I love you."

And with that proclamation, Fury went fast asleep. And dreamed dreams of a fabled land of Ferra Lin, where she would discover her magic at last.

Chapter 7

It took the better part of a week for Chaos Little to travel from Southwick to Belfast, a journey that triggered fond memories of his quest some six years ago. In stark contrast to his first foray out of Borrin, he'd prepared extensively for his travels, purchasing a horse and having a backpack and saddlebags filled with all the essentials he might need. Not the least of which was his trusty Omen-63 Tactical Shovel, a tool and a weapon enhanced with magic by his father Chauncy. Magic that allowed the shovel to absorb rock and dirt, then throw it outward at enemies. Magic that'd proved useful indeed, especially during his quest to defeat Old Langsroth.

In any case, the trip through the Gate from Southwick to the kingdom of Pravus – then to the golden Gate leading to Grissam – had been far less eventful this time around. Then again, he was a far different person than he'd been six years ago. Ever since his quest to Old Langsroth, he'd followed Destiny's advice, developing daily rituals to develop himself. He'd trained in the use of his shovel as a deadly weapon on a near-daily basis, and gained skill after skill. Cooking, cleaning, sewing, fighting, carpentry, plumbing…just about everything he could learn. And in doing so – in spending each day with intention, rather than drifting passively through – Chaos had become a useful man indeed. Which was a far cry from the useless boy he'd been.

Destiny had visited him in Southwick a few times a year since their time together in Old Langsroth, spending most of the rest of her time on the front lines of the war against the undead hordes of the Dark Rising. She'd stationed herself in the critical city of Belfast…and had sent a carrier pigeon to him a few weeks ago, dropping off a letter instructing him to come to visit *her* this time instead of the other way around. Which he found himself more than happy to do, considering they hadn't seen each other for nearly a year. An amount of time that was particularly difficult for him, all things considered. And by all things, we of course mean one thing in particular.

Something that, sitting atop his sleeping bag by the campfire he'd made expertly less than an hour ago, a half-day's travel away from Belfast, he found himself focusing rather hard on.

"Hnngg!" he grunt-moaned, working feverishly to provide himself with a poor facsimile of what he so desperately missed. Sweat dribbled down his forehead, stinging his eyes. "Rrrgnnnooohhgawd!" he blurted out, rounding the corner to what would surely signal the end of his day. He closed his eyes, picturing things that will go unmentioned, dear reader. But suffice it to say, it was a carefully curated narrative he'd developed over the years, which he unfortunately found necessary to bring things to a head. For he'd let the ol' evil build up for a bit too long, and he was determined to get it out.

Then, with a sort of hunched over, violent vigor, gasping for air, then holding his breath, Chaos finally came to the conclusion he'd been hoping for.

"F...unghh...DestINY!" he cried, toes curling in the throes of it now. And in the interest of avoiding being *too* graphic, that's all I'll say about that. For it would be far better not to have a visual of what had just occurred...as the two tan-armored Belfastian soldiers patrolling the area on horseback would surely attest to.

"What the...!" one of them blurted out, witnessing evil's release.

"Oh," the other man exclaimed, turning his head away far too late.

"Gah!" Chaos blurted out, scrambling to his feet. While still being in the process of evil's release. The campfire sizzled rhythmically, and everyone just sort of stayed where they were, frozen in place. Until the sizzling rhythm finally stopped. Eventually.

Chaos cleared his throat then, facing the two men awkwardly. While hoping quite fervently that they would kill him.

"You done?" one of the soldiers asked, still looking away.

"Um...yep," Chaos replied, still wanting to die. The soldier turned around with great hesitation, then relaxed. A bit.

"Who're you?" he demanded.

"Uh, Chaos," Chaos replied. And then immediately regretted it. The guard's eyebrows went up.

"Oh, you're Destiny's boyfriend," he stated. Chaos grimaced.

"Um..."

"Chaos Little, yeah!" the other soldier stated. "The wizard who helped her beat Old Langsroth!"

"Not the only thing he's beat," the first soldier joked.

"Ha!" the second soldier replied, pointing a finger at the first soldier. "Good one!"

Chaos glanced at the campfire, seized by the sudden urge to throw himself into it. A painful death to be sure, but on the other hand, quite definitive.

"Gets lonely on the road, eh?" the first soldier mused.

"Sure does," the other agreed. "Why, I remember one time when…"

"No," the first soldier blurted out, cutting the man off. "Just…no."

The two just sat on their saddles, eyeing Chaos, who cleared his throat.

"Uh, gonna uh, go to sleep now," he informed them.

"Tuckered out eh?" the second soldier replied.

"Feeling beat I bet," the first piped in.

"Ha!" the second soldier replied, pointing at his fellow again. "Anywho, we'll let ya go now," he added. "See you in Belfast."

Chaos's face paled.

"You're…going back?"

"Oh ya," the second soldier confirmed, to Chaos's dismay. "This is as far as we scout. Night!"

"Sweet dreams," the first soldier stated. "Don't worry, we'll be sure to let Destiny know you're coming."

"Ha!" the second soldier exclaimed, pointing yet again.

And then the two men turned their horses around and left. Chaos watched them go, then sat down by his sleeping bag, staring into the fire for a long, long while. At length, he stirred.

"Fuck!"

And with that, he got in his sleeping bag, closing his eyes. But despite feeling beat – and quite drained – it was a long, long time before he finally fell asleep.

Chapter 8

The following morning, Fury climbed out of her sleeping bag to greet the day, with a great big smile and a satisfying stretch. And her morning proclamation of gratitude, of course.

"Good morning, day!" she exclaimed. Then she gazed at the blue sky and its fluffy clouds, and the ocean and the sand and just…everything. "Thank you world, for letting me be," she added. For it was quite literally true. Without the ground both holding her up and pulling her down, and the air to let her breathe, the sun's warmth, and so many other lives living so that she could eat and such, she would never have been. Thus it was practically a miracle that she existed, and she simply refused to take that for granted.

"Huuuy," Rocky greeted, seated nearby.

"Morning tookums!" she replied, rushing up to him and giving him a big ol' hug. Or rather, a small hug, relatively speaking, but with a big ol' dose of love. "Wanna go?"

"Shuurr," he answered, getting on all fours. She mounted him eagerly, then rode him north, following the shoreline toward their mutual destination. One she had no idea how long it would take to reach. But with Rocky protecting her – especially from icky zombies – she had little fear of what might come. Instead, with his protection, she could face the future with happy anticipation instead of anxiety and dread.

Off they went, galloping just to the left of the beach, the going easier on the short, tough grass there compared to the sand.

After a good three hours, Fury was surprised to see an upsloping of the land ahead. Pleasantly surprised, in fact. For this upsloping created a steadily taller cliffside that dropped down to the ocean.

"We're getting closer!" she exclaimed, clapping her hands, then clutching them to her chest. Which had been technically true since the start of her journey, of course. But they were getting *closer* closer now, which was extra exciting. Sure enough, just as Imperius had predicted, the slope kept rising, until they reached the tippitytop of the cliffs, as evidenced by the fact that everywhere she could see was at a lower elevation. Coming to the edge of the cliff, Rocky and Fury saw that the ocean was a good thousand feet below. A formidable distance indeed.

"Wow," she breathed, taking in the remarkable scenery. Seagulls glided far below, the waves crashing against the side of the cliff in vigorous sprays of hissing foam.

"Waaaaw," Rocky agreed, similarly transfixed.

At length, Fury had her fill of the sights, and turned away from the cliffside to get down to business. Which she made clear by putting her hands on her hips, whilst scowling good-naturedly.

"All right," she declared. "Time to find the fabled land of Ferra Lin!"

"Waaare?" Rocky asked.

"Imperius said to search the area when we reach the highest cliff," she recalled, eyeing the terrain. It was quite rocky, with no plant life whatsoever, and splatted with a fair amount of white seagull poop. It also stretched forward and to either side for a considerable distance – at least two miles, if not more – and as such, it was a terribly large area to search. Although now that she thought about it, Ferra Lin – being fabled – should've been easy to see in a relatively flat, barren area. "Huh," she mumbled, rubbing her chin thoughtfully.

"Spleeet uuup?" Rocky suggested.

"I guess," she replied. Then she remembered the zombie attack she'd nearly been killed by. "But we need to stay within line-of-sight," she added. Rocky gave her a blank look. "We need to be able to see each other wherever we go," she clarified.

"Okeee," he agreed.

"Can you carry my backpack for me?" she asked. For on the uneven, rocky terrain, she was worried it would increase the risk of losing her balance and falling.

"Okeee," he agreed, taking the backpack from her.

With that, they split up, Fury heading right while Rocky went left. She stepped carefully over the uneven, rocky ground, not wanting to roll an ankle. Consequently, it took her quite some time to get to where she wanted to go. At first she found herself impatient, but not liking this way of being one bit, she decided to change her perspective. She was on an adventure, searching a great, tall cliff for a legendary place. One that would finally show her what her wizardly magic was.

41

In this frame of mind, she turned her frown into a much more comfortable smile, the giddy rush of high adventure filling her with newfound vigor.

"I should search the area up and down methodically," she told herself. Which was almost certainly true. But she didn't particularly feel like doing so, because it would transform this adventure into a simple back-and-forth scanning task. So she decided against it, wandering here and there, going wherever she felt like in the moment, or wherever happened to catch her eye.

In the throes of this wandering wanderlust, Fury found herself heading toward a slight depression in the terrain, flanked by two large boulders that'd attracted her attention. As she drew closer, she realized that they weren't boulders per se, but rather *extremely* weathered sculptures. Of what appeared to be twin fangs rising into the air, curving inward as they went. But time had managed to wear them down, rounding their tips and breaking off stone hunks here and there. She stepped up to one of them, peering at its surface, and found hints of intricate symbols that'd been carved into it.

"Huh," she murmured, running her fingers over said symbols. They were so faded they were hard to read, and she knew darn well she wouldn't have been able to read them anyway. Still, they were marvelous things, hinting at an ancient civilization with a language all their own, and a grand history spanning generations that had been all but lost to time.

Why, to even imagine such a grand sweep of time, of a culture, art, and countless stories of lives lived here...it was simply *wonderful* to consider.

Fury found herself smiling as she ran her fingers down the symbols again, and imagining what they'd looked like when they'd first been carved. Then she turned to look at the other stone fang to her right, and strode toward it to study it.

Which would've been nice, and super interesting. But as it turned out, fate had something else in mind for poor Fury. For as she stepped toward the other fang, the rocky ground caved in under her weight.

She didn't even have time to scream.

Darkness enveloped her as she plunged downward, her gut lurching as she entered into free fall. Faster and faster she fell, her heart leaping into her throat.

Then there was a sudden *froosh!*

42

Shockingly warm water engulfed her, and she plunged downward into it, the impact knocking the breath from her lungs. She froze, then scrambled blindly upward through the water, using a breaststroke. A shockingly powerful current pulled her forward, and she burst through the surface, taking a gasping breath in...

...and then felt herself go off the edge of something, and fall again.

This time, Fury did scream, her voice echoing back to her hollowly. And after a few terrifying seconds, she plunged into water again.

The current was even more powerful now, and yanked her forward at frightening speed. She swam to the surface, taking another gasping breath in, doggy-paddling to stay at the surface. She was still surrounded by utter darkness, unable to see a thing no matter where she looked. The only sound was the roar of what she could only assume was the waterfall behind her, the one she'd fallen off.

Minutes passed, and Fury noticed that the current was slowing down. At length it slowed so much that she couldn't tell if she was still moving forward or not.

It occurred to her then that she'd fallen who-knew-how far, and was now deep underground. And further, that Rocky had no idea where she was, on account of her not having cried out when she'd fallen. Even if he tried to go after her, he'd just end up trapped here as well. For she knew that it was entirely possible – even likely – that she was now in a subterranean river of sorts, and that there might be no way for her to get out.

The thought inspired a fresh wave of terror, that she might end up treading water in this utter blackness for the rest of her life. A short life, where she eventually tired, and could tread water no more. Then she'd slip under the surface, holding her breath for as long as she could...before giving in at last to the desperate desire for life-giving air, and drowning to death.

No!

Panic rose within her, threatening to carry her psyche away much like the water's current had. A feeling even more alarming because frankly, she'd never felt it before.

Her whole life, she'd felt perfectly safe and secure. But now, for the first time, darkness threatened her...both inside and out.

Trust Imperius, she told herself, remembering the great wizard's words. After all, he wouldn't have sent her here just to die. Would he?

A fresh spike of fear shot through her guts, panic rising within her far more powerfully than before. Her breath started coming in rapid gasps, as if there wasn't enough air in the cavern.

You're going to die.

Her heart pounded in her chest, a scream threatening to burst from her lips. She held it back, but the harder she resisted it, the greater her terror grew.

Then she did scream, a bloodcurdling *shriek* that echoed through the inky-black cavern. And screamed. And *screamed.*

She screamed until her voice became raspy and hoarse, until she could scream no more. Instead, she fell into a fit of coughing, then crying...and crying out for help. But no help came...and none ever would.

Fury was trapped, floating in an underground sea. She was going to die...and there wasn't a damn thing she could do about it.

Chapter 9

How long Fury floated in a sea of darkness, she had no way of knowing. For time lost its meaning when the senses were deprived, and when there was nothing to do but tread water. After what seemed like an eternity, her terror had passed, replaced by a numb exhaustion. One so powerful that Fury didn't even have the energy to fear her own mortality.

So she floated onward, treading water, her limbs feeling like leaden weights.

And such was the curious property of being put in an unsolvable situation that Fury found herself just wanting it to be over. For this awfulness to end, even if it meant letting go of her life and letting herself slip below the surface, never to re-emerge again. She found it strange that a person who loved life as much as she did – and had wanted so much to continue living before coming here – could, in the space of a few hours at most, so fervently wish to die.

So she floated, feeling the weakening current continue to carry her along, until she was so exhausted that she could barely keep her head above water.

She felt herself sinking below the surface, and clawed her way back up, gasping for air. A fresh bolt of fear gave her limbs newfound strength, and she doggy-paddled more vigorously now. But fear faded, and she began to sink again, her head inevitably plunging below the surface. This time, she started to take a breath in underwater, and stopped just in the nick of time. Still, an immediate surge of warm fluid filled her mouth. She scrambled to the surface, swallowing some of the fluid, then spit the rest out, gasping for air again. The fluid, to her surprise and dismay, was thick and salty, and slightly metallic tasting. Far different from the nice ocean water she'd enjoyed before.

She spat repeatedly, struggling to keep her head above water...or whatever this liquid was.

But no matter how hard she struggled, her resolve weakened along with her limbs, and soon it was all she could do to allow herself to sink underwater for a bit, then swim upward for quick little breaths of air.

You're dying, she realized. But this time, the thought didn't bring with it a fresh wave of fear. Rather, it came with a peaceful acceptance, that this was the way things had turned out. She'd done her best to go on, and the world had decided that she wouldn't. And that was that, the end of her story. A life truly enjoyed, but shorter than she'd wanted it to be.

It's okay, she told herself. *You can let go.*

She felt a sudden sadness, and knew that she was mourning the loss of the life she'd had. And that, too, was okay. A part of letting go.

Fury closed her eyes, feeling the warm fluid around her, and how she rose in the water when she took a breath in, then sank with every breath out. She opened her eyes, taking one final breath in.

Goodbye, she thought, holding the breath in.

Then she let it out, sinking below the surface again.

But before she'd finished doing so, she thought she'd spotted something to her right. She forced herself to resurface, wiping wetness from her eyes. And to her surprise, there *was* something to her right. A faint crimson glow, so faint that she wondered if she was just imagining it. But no matter how many times she closed, then reopened her eyes, it was there.

A fresh burst of hope re-energized her, infusing her limbs with newfound strength, and she breast-stroked toward the light. As she grew slowly closer, she saw that the glow was coming from a triangular hole in what appeared to be a stone wall...a hole that led to a tunnel with a floor only a foot above the surface of the water.

Fury swam toward it eagerly, her acceptance of death vanishing instantly. But even as she did so, the weak current carrying her threatened to pull her leftward of the hole, forcing her to swim against the current as well. Which, despite her surge of vigor, soon proved increasingly difficult.

Come on!

She pushed herself, forcing her limbs to obey her commands. Visions of Daddy and Mommy came to her, and Chaos and Nettie and Harry. Even Rocky. All weeping because she'd died. Because she hadn't tried hard enough. She had to go on, for their sakes if not for her own. Or at the very least, she had to *try*.

You can do it!

Fury struggled mightily against the current, making her way with agonizing slowness toward the hole in the wall. Until it became the only purpose of her existence, to reach it at last. And at long last, despite everything, she *did* reach it, grabbing on to the stone ledge a foot above the surface and clinging on.

Yes!

She tried to pull herself up onto the ledge, but her arms were far too weak. So she just clung to the ledge, gathering her strength. When she tried a second time, she managed to pull herself up enough to get her upper body onto the ledge, with her legs still dangling down. A minute later, she tried again, crawling onto the cool stone floor bathed in that faint crimson light. Until at last she was on firm ground again, safe…at least for the moment.

Then Fury turned to lie on her back, staring up at the peak of the triangle-shaped tunnel she'd found herself in. Elation filled her to bursting, and she cried out in glee. After which she promptly burst out into tears.

A long while later, after her tears had ceased to flow, Fury's eyes drifted closed, and she fell into a merciful sleep.

* * *

Fury's eyes opened.

She found herself lying on the same cool stone floor as before, the peaked ceiling above bathed in dim crimson light. She groaned, rolling onto her side, then her belly, her whole body stiff and sore. Such that pushing herself to her hands and knees proved painful and difficult, her limbs wobbling with the effort.

But she was alive, which was all that mattered.

She rested in this position for a bit, then got to her feet. Her shoulders were awfully sore from swimming, as was her chest and middle back. She stretched, then turned to look out at the water she'd nearly drowned in. The crimson light barely illuminated the first few feet of water, which looked red and opaque in its glow. She swallowed past a lump in her throat, remembering how hopeless she'd been. How willing she'd been to die.

Then she turned away from the river and that darkest of moments in her life, choosing to gaze down the tunnel into her future instead.

The tunnel went forward a few yards, then made a sharp, 90-degree turn to the left. She stepped forward, then frowned; her clothes felt awfully sticky and stiff, which was strange, and were of course pure red in the crimson light. Which was coming from somewhere beyond the turn in the tunnel, she realized. She kept walking, making the turn...and saw a long hallway beyond, bathed in that same red light. But this hallway was a bit wider, perhaps eight feet, and had four statues standing on stone pedestals by either wall, facing each other...and a fifth statue facing an empty pedestal.

Statues with eyes that glowed with a dull red light...and were clearly the source of the light that'd led her here.

Fury continued forward, stopping before the first of the statues on her left. It was of a man hold twin scimitars, curved swords that were really swords and not stone. In fact, his amor was real armor as well...only his body was made of a strange, dark red stone. His red eyes glowed with that eerie light, one that was both oddly compelling yet unnerving at the same time. In addition, she noted that the backs of his hands had large circles in the middle, that glowed with the same red light.

"Huh," she murmured, studying the statue for a bit longer. Then she turned to the one to her right, seeing that it was much the same, though a shorter man with long hair, and wearing rotted scale armor instead. He carried daggers in his hands, and the backs of his hands had those same glowing circles on them. The sight of his daggers made her realize she'd lost her own weapon, the Rod of Fire.

Well shoot, she thought, feeling a bit sad. For it'd been a present from her loving dad.

At length, Fury continued down the long hall, which eventually turned left again. This led her down an even wider hallway, and a set of stairs leading up a good dozen feet. She went up them, seeing more statues on either side...and an opening in the tunnel beyond them. She strode down this hallway to the opening, finding a bridge continuing onward across the dark water of the river below. She'd circled back to the river, she'd realized, and was now crossing it. Beyond, she could see a brighter red glow, for the bridge led to another tunnel carved into the stone of the subterranean chamber.

Fury paused, then made her way toward it, since there was nowhere else for her to go. Over the bridge and down the tunnel, which led to another set of stairs, these going down…a considerable distance more than they'd gone up in the stairwell before.

At length she reached the bottom, seeing the tunnel extend another thirty feet or so before making a 45-degree turn to the right. A much brighter crimson light was coming from somewhere beyond this turn, as if beckoning her to continue.

With little choice but to do so, Fury did.

Making the turn, she found that the tunnel opened up into a large chamber beyond. One arranged in a hexagon, with a ceiling well over thirty feet high. The chamber itself had to be at least fifty feet in diameter, with more of the warrior-statues lining the walls nearest her. But at the far end of the chamber, she saw the source of the bright red light. Which was something that quite literally took her breath away.

It was a huge statue of a three-headed dragon, wrought of that same dark red stone, with one head following the rear wall left, and one right. Aqueduct-like structures came through the upper part of either sidewall, angling down toward these side-heads, going right into their wide-open mouths. Aqueducts within which crimson fluid flowed at a considerable rate. It had to be water from the river she'd been in earlier, seeing as how the stairs had brought her below the water level, so to speak.

And the middle head, well, its great big neck came from all the way up at the ceiling, arcing down to rest its head on the floor in the center of the chamber. Its mouth was also open wide, baring upper fangs; but surprisingly, its lower fangs were missing, their twin sockets glowing with a red light. Each head's eyes were also glowing, far more brightly than the statues she'd seen earlier had.

Fury stared at the rather unexpected sight, feeling a sense of awe.

"Wow," she breathed, devouring this scene. For while creepy, it was aesthetically quite pleasing. With a mother whose magic was bedazzling, Fury was well versed in aesthetic theory. Which was how she knew that this chamber had been designed impeccably.

She stepped into the chamber, studying it more closely.

She found that her initial impression had not been quite correct. For while the aqueduct did carry water into the leftmost head's mouth, the right one actually carried that water away. Which meant that the water was flowing up the slope of the rightmost aqueduct, strangely. In addition, there was something she hadn't noticed at first against the rightmost wall: a cylindrical vertical shaft a good three feet in diameter, which opened up in an arched doorway leading inside. And inside of it, a continuous waterfall of...water, that went who-knows-where.

"Huh," she murmured.

Fury turned to look at the central head's eyes then, somehow drawn to its brightly glowing red eyes. Eyes that were level with hers, so large was the dragon. She stared into them, feeling a strange sensation...a kind of pressure pulling at her face and chest. As if her blood was rushing to her skin there, pulling her forward.

A voice boomed in her head, deep and powerful. Not heard in words, but in thoughts understood instantly.

Remove the shackle that binds you.

Fury blinked, the presence within her mind sudden and terrifying. Goosebumps rose on her flesh, a chill running through her. She tried to take a step back...but found that she could not.

Then she felt something warm on her chest, and looked down, seeing her necklace there. It was Fang, the necklace with the large fang at the end, a gift from her father. Something she'd worn pretty much her entire life, and had refused to ever take off. But as she stared at it, it grew hotter and hotter...until it was burning her flesh.

"Gah!" she blurted out, tearing the necklace off and throwing it to the side. It fell to the floor with a clatter, glowing a faint red.

Come closer, the deep voice boomed, reverberating through her brain. And with that command, she felt the pulling sensation become more powerful...followed by an urge to obey. But a part of her resisted, struggling against that urge. Her heart pounded in her chest, faster and faster, sweat beading up and dripping down her skin. It stung her eyes, and she wiped them with the back of her hand.

Soon her heart was beating so loudly in her ears that the sound seemed to fill the large chamber. And with each beat of her heart, the dragon's eyes seemed to pulse...and the water flowing in and out of the left and right heads seemed to flow in a more pulsatile way as well.

Touch me, the voice urged, the crimson light within the empty sockets of his lower fangs pulsing as well.

Fury stared at those twin sockets, the pulsing light hypnotic, timed perfectly with her heartbeat. As if the light somehow *was* her...or that she was the light.

TOUCH ME.

The command *boomed* in her mind, and Fury stepped forward involuntarily, reaching the dragon's open maw at last. Her heart beat ever faster, hammering in her chest now, the light from the empty sockets before her matching pace.

Fury felt a *pulling* sensation in her hands, and extended them palm-down toward those glowing sockets, drawn to them somehow. She rested her palms on them, and gasped. For the stone there was warm, and seemed to vibrate with power.

The light from those sockets shone even brighter at her touch, so bright that she could see their light penetrating her hands, the bones and veins visible as dark shadows encased in her flesh.

You are worthy.

Without warning, dark red fangs shot out of the sockets, bursting upward so rapidly that they pierced right through Fury's palms, exiting out of the backs of her hands. Long, curved fangs coated in her blood.

The pain was instantaneous...and agonizing.

Fury *screamed*.

She yanked her hands backward, but they were stuck in place, and the attempt only sent a fresh wave of pain through them. She screamed again, falling to her knees, her arms above her head. The pain intensified, as if the fangs were getting hotter and hotter, searing her flesh.

And then there was blood.

It poured out of her palms, gushing down the dragon's fangs and into its mouth, forming a rapidly deepening pool within. And as it did so, that pool began to swirl within the dragon's mouth, starting to glow with the same light as its eyes. Fury shrieked in terror as her blood poured out of her, pint after pint spilling into the dragon's maw.

She felt suddenly lightheaded, her vision starting to blacken...and then the fangs retracted almost instantaneously, pulling out of her hands and vanishing into the glowing sockets they'd come from.

Fury shrieked, yanking her hands away from the dragon's mouth, staring at them in horror. For in the center of each palm was a hole she could see all the way through. Panic gripped her, threatening to carry her into sheer madness.

Place them in the blood, the deep voice in her head ordered.

"No," she mewled, shaking her head. She sobbed, tears streaming down her cheeks. "Please no more, please!"

DO IT.

The voice compelled her, and despite every inch of her being screaming at her not to, she stood, eyeing the glowing red blood resting in the bottom of the dragon's mouth. She lowered her hands, plunging them into that pool of blood…

…and watched as the blood flowed *into* the holes in her hands…and into *her*.

She gasped, feeling a sudden ecstasy in her hands. It mingled with the pain, agony and ecstasy combining in a freakish union. Yet still the pleasure grew, until it was many times more powerful than any she'd ever felt. The pain grew with it, matching its intensity, until each became so powerful that they threatened to overwhelm her.

To *obliterate* her.

Fury cried out, but this time it was not a scream, but a desperate need to be released of this impossible duality of extremes. It was a moan of pleasure and pain, so great that she couldn't hold it in anymore.

And with that cry, the blood finished flowing back into her at last…and she was released from this impossibly sweet torture.

She collapsed, her hands slipping from the dragon's mouth, as she fell onto her side on the floor. She curled in the fetal position, her hands clutched to her bosom, her eyes closed.

At length, Fury stirred, the pain and pleasure gone. Utterly gone, as if they'd never been. But they lived on in her memory, as they would until the end of her life. And she knew in that moment that no experience would ever match it. Ever *could* match it.

Rise, the voice in her head commanded.

Fury stirred, opening her eyes. She got onto her knees, then stood, her legs no longer wobbly. There was no soreness, no fatigue. She felt absolutely fine.

Looking down at her hands, she saw red circles the size of large coins seemingly tattooed on the fronts and backs. Her flesh had healed somehow, the holes closed with that crimson flesh…a color that, to her surprise, didn't rub off.

We are bound, my Proeliator, the voice boomed. And while she'd never heard the word before, she knew it was an ancient term for warrior.

"B…bound?" she asked.

But instead of an answer, the flow of liquid in the aqueducts slowed, then stopped…and then flowed in reverse. Including the waterfall going down the cylindrical shaft at the wall to her right. The fluid shot violently upward now, to who knew where.

Return to your world, my Proeliator.

Fury hesitated, staring at the glowing eyes of the middle dragon head. But unlike before, no force drew her toward it, nor away. She was in control again. She was herself. Even her heart had slowed back down to a relatively normal rate.

She glanced back down at her hands, turning them over. The red circles were still there, but again, there was no pain. Then she gave the dragon once last glance, before striding toward the arched doorway leading to the red fluid gushing upward.

RISE.

The voice boomed in her mind, and she obeyed, stepping through the doorway and into that violent geyser. It shot her upward at terrifying speed, roaring around her, and within its dark, watery fury she could not see or breathe.

Then she saw a sudden burst of bright blue light from above, and felt her ascent slowing. She shot out of the ground, flying a few feet into the air, then landing on a flat, rocky surface. The impact knocked the wind out of her, but didn't injure her, to her relief.

She scrambled to her feet, then looked around, seeing rather familiar rocky terrain all around her, the beautiful blue sky high above. And, only a few dozen yards away, she saw none other than Rocky running toward her, calling out her name.

Chapter 10

Upon returning to his castle in Cumulus, King Pravus met Lord Lucus in the man's office. Which was unnecessarily large, but not even close to as large as Pravus's. For no man in the kingdom could have anything larger or more ostentatious than the king, by royal decree. It was human nature to assume that bigger was better, after all, and thus no one could be bigger or better than royalty. He found Lucus seated in his chair at his desk, leaning back and twirling one tip of his truly magnificent handlebar mustache, an evil gleam in his eyes.

"What do you need, my liege?" he inquired in his silky, slimy voice, arching an eyebrow. Evilly.

"Your...unique perspective," Pravus replied. For it was well known that Lord Lucus was perhaps the evilest lord in the kingdom. But fate had seen fit to balance this out with profound laziness. As such, he'd fallen comfortably into the usual administrative role, content to steal the fruits of his men's labor whilst making their lives rather miserable, in the manner of the typical middle-manager.

"Mmm-go on," Lucus prompted, twirling a bit more vigorously.

"Regarding the situation in Grissam," Pravus began. "You're familiar with the latest developments?" Which was, of course, that there had been *no* developments. No progression. Just a stalemate at the fortress city of Belfast, which was losing men week after week. Pravus had sent repeated rounds of reinforcements over the years, understanding that to lose Belfast would be disastrous. But he was running out of extra soldiers to give...and every soldier lost to the undead horde was a soldier the undead gained.

"Naturally," Lord Lucus purred.

"I fear our current strategy is doomed to fail," Pravus confessed.

"It is," Lucus agreed. "Classic, really." Pravus arched an eyebrow.

"How so?"

"The old 'wear and tear,'" Lucus mused, his eyes twinkling with mischief.

"Pardon?"

"A strategy best used again a larger enemy force," Lucus explained, twirling his tip even more aggressively. "Apply constant moderate pressure for an extended period of time, causing repeated injuries and damage to infrastructure."

"And?"

"And eventually the cost of repairs and medical treatment – and the loss of morale – will be too great to maintain," Lucus explained.

"But the enemy will suffer as well," Pravus pointed out.

"Not the undead," Lucus argued. "They don't have morale. Many injuries don't bother them. And everyone they kill adds to their army."

"Indeed," Pravus agreed with a grimace.

"Not to mention that undead don't require food or water," Lucus continued with inappropriate cheer. "Logistics win wars...and the logistics of maintaining an undead army are just so *easy*."

"Yes, well," Pravus grumbled. "We require a novel strategy, which is why I'm here."

"Marvelous," Lucus replied, stopping his twiddling to steeple his fingertips. Also evilly.

"What do you suggest?"

"Undead are like infections," Lucus stated. "They spread from host to host unless all hosts are destroyed."

"Go on."

"Quarantine the undead, destroy them...and you'll still lose," Lucus continued. "For the source will still remain."

Pravus eyed him shrewdly.

"You're referring to whatever is creating the undead," he deduced. Lucus smiled wickedly.

"Indeed," he confirmed. Pravus considered this.

"So we continue to supply troops to Belfast, but have a separate force go into the Dark Forest to find the source," he concluded.

"And while the bulk of the undead forces are preoccupied with Belfast, your forces in the Dark Forest will hopefully encounter far less resistance," Lucus stated.

"Hopefully?"

"The fog of war hangs heavy over the Dark Forest," Lucus replied. "We know nothing of what lurks inside."

"We need reconnaissance," Pravus realized. "But no one who's gone in has ever come out." Which was why they'd stopped trying to penetrate the cursed place.

"Then find someone who will," Lucus shot back.

"Such as...?" Pravus asked.

"A wizard," Lucus answered.

"Wizards require Imperius Fanning's blessing to go on quests," Pravus argued. He found it strange that Imperius hadn't prompted a Chosen One to defeat the Dark Forest already, but he was not about to question the Arch Wizard of the Order of Mundus's magical gut.

"True, but we could find a way to...compel them," Lucus pointed out. "Let them dip their little fingers in our honeypot, so to speak."

Pravus considered this, rubbing his chiseled chin thoughtfully. It was a sound plan, and the one thing they hadn't tried yet. The Chosen Ones had always risen to save the day in the past, when evil threatened the land. Indeed, he himself had risen to destroy Old Langsroth six years ago. Along with sweet Templeton, who'd never failed to help Pravus with a rising of a far different kind. One that also resulted in a purging of evil, which perpetually built up in his mind.

"What about a hero?" Pravus compromised, feeling a stirring from deep within his soul.

"Definitely a wizard," Lord Lucus replied. Rudely.

"In any case, thank you," Pravus stated. "I believe you've been most helpful."

Lucus made a face as if slapped.

"I mean *clever*," Pravus corrected. Lucus's expression relaxed.

"Indeed," he purred, a-twiddling his fingertips.

And with that, their meeting met its end, and King Pravus left Lucus's office to find his favorite cousin in the whole world: sweet, dearest Templeton!

Which would've been nice, if his plan hadn't been so rudely interrupted by a sudden burst of blue sparkles in the hallway ahead of Pravus, followed by the appearance of none other than the great wizard Imperius Fanning.

"Oh," Pravus blurted out, stopping before the old wizard. Who eyed Pravus with a look that Pravus wasn't at all comfortable with. Mostly because it was a sort of disappointed glare. Or perhaps Imperius was just terribly old, and thus terrible to look at. "What?" Pravus snapped.

"Your destiny was to venture forth into Old Langsroth," Imperius declared in his typical dramatic tone. "To the catacombs beneath the great city."

Pravus frowned.

"Pardon?"

Imperius continued to glare at him, crossing his feeble arms over his underdeveloped chest. Which prompted Pravus to place his own, far more massive arms in a similar position.

"I already did all that," he stated imperiously. And accurately, at least from his point of view. "I defeated that villain in Old Langsroth myself." By cutting him in twain, most heroically.

"To the catacombs beneath the great city!" Imperius snapped.

"What?"

"You were supposed to go to the catacombs beneath Old Langsroth!" Imperius clarified. "I specifically told you that only there would you uncover the means to defeat what may be the greatest villain of your generation...and save the world from utter devastation!"

Pravus paused.

"You did say that," he conceded, a bit abashedly. But not too abashedly, for it would undermine his authority to do so.

"I did," Imperius agreed. "And yet here we are."

"So...you're saying I need to go back to Old Langsroth, to the catacombs beneath the city, and uncover the means to defeat the greatest villain of my generation," Pravus stated.

"Yes!" Imperius snapped. Pravus paused. Awkwardly.

"I see," he stated at last. He paused again. "May I use the dragon this time?"

"You may," Imperius proclaimed.

"And my magic uniform and sword?" Pravus pressed, daring to hope. For his uniform made him nigh invincible, whilst his magic sword made everything killable.

"You may not."

"Marvelous," Pravus grumbled.

"One more thing," Imperius declared. "You may bring your cousin with you, until you see the submerged stone. But at the entrance to the catacombs, you must part with him and go it alone."

And with that, Imperius vanished in a burst of blue sparks, in precisely the manner he'd come. Pravus stood there, watching as the sparkles fell to the floor, passing through it. Then he sighed.

"Right," he grumbled.

He strode down the hallway, still determined to fetch Templeton. But not, as he'd thought, to go to the Dark Forest to fight the undead. Rather, it was to go to Old Langsroth for some unfinished business instead.

Chapter 11

"Fuuur-eeee!" Rocky called out as he approached, slowing down, then stopping before her. His eyes widened in horror, and he put a big rocky hand to his mouth. "Ohhh nooo!"

"What?" Fury asked. "What's wrong?"

Rocky just stared at her. Then pointed at her, while still covering his mouth with his other hand.

Fury blinked, then looked down at herself...and realized that she was covered in blood. Like, *covered* in it. Her clothes were saturated with blood, as was her hair. Blood spattered the ground around her, and was dripping from her. It occurred to her then that the "water" she'd seen in the strange, underground place she'd been might not have been water after all. Which explained why it'd been so salty and metallic-tasting, and sticky and gross and stuff.

"Ugh," she blurted out, trying to wipe the stuff from her chest. But of course it was a pointless exercise. "Gross!"

"Neeeed Rooooter!" Rocky urged, looking absolutely aghast.

"Oh no no," Fury blurted out. "It's not *my* blood."

Rocky blinked.

"I'm not hurt," she insisted, flashing him what was almost certainly an unconvincing smile. "It's...ah...a long story, but I'm okay."

Rocky paused, then lowered his hands to his sides.

"Wuuut...happpen?"

"I uh, fell through the ground, 'cause it collapsed under me," she explained. "Then I landed in a big river of uh, blood, and it carried me um, back, eventually." Which was awfully vague, and more than a bit deceptive, which was why Fury was sucking so badly at trying to get away with it. She'd only ever told the truth for most of her life, having no need to lie. Because most of her life – up until now – she hadn't had anything to hide. But now something terrible had happened to her, except for the ecstasy part. Which had also been terrible at the same time, but...not.

"Ohhh," Rocky replied, seeming to accept this quasi-lie. "Keeep suuurch?" he asked.

"Um...yeah," she answered. "But I wanna clean up first."

There were two ways to do this: with her Wetstone-enhanced drinking flask, or by taking a dip in the ocean. The ocean was much farther away, so Fury took the least laborious route, pouring the Wetstone's seemingly endless supply of water over herself. It took far longer than she'd expected to get fully clean, for as it turned out, blood tended to stick to things. In the end, her clothes were permanently dyed red, but her hair and skin were clean.

Luckily, she'd given her backpack to Rocky before falling into the river of blood, so she had plenty of clothes to change into.

She stripped off her bloody-ish clothes, again not at all worried about Rocky or anyone else seeing her naked. Then she chose an outfit of purest white – white sleeveless shirt, white shorts, white socks – to cleanse herself aesthetically of the bloody ordeal she'd endured. This done, she mounted Rocky's back, riding him across the hilly terrain. And for the rest of the day, they searched for the land of Ferra Lin...without any success whatsoever.

As the sun set over the horizon, Fury and Rocky were forced to abandon their search. For without a light source, they wouldn't be able to see very far past their noses. With this in mind, they made camp, this time without a fire. For Fury's Rod of Fire was gone, lost to the river of blood far below them, in the subterranean realm she'd so recently explored.

Still, if it hadn't been for the red circles tattooed on the fronts and backs of her hands, Fury would have started to doubt that she'd ever had that strange adventure at all. Indeed, lying in her sleeping bag, all comfy-cozy, with Rocky at her side, it seemed impossible that she'd nearly died earlier that day. Or that dragon-statue fangs had been shoved straight through her hands. Or that she'd been named Pro-something-or-other of whatever voice had boomed in her head. The only other evidence of her terrifying trip was the absence of her necklace Fang. Having lost it saddened her terribly, for it was something precious from her past.

Fury closed her eyes, snuggling in her sleeping bag, feeling herself slowly falling asleep. But as she did so, she had visions of twin dragon eyes staring into hers, and of her own glowing blood flowing into holes in her hands.

Rest my Proeliator, that strange voice seemed to tell her, even as her visions faded, slowly replaced by the oblivion of deep sleep. *You're going to need it.*

* * *

The next morning, Fury woke just as the run rose over the horizon, and she leapt to her feet as if a spring were under her, as she usually did.

"Hello day!" she exclaimed, smiling at the sunrise. Then she frowned, rubbing her chin, considering what outfit she'd spend the day in. Rummaging through her pack, she selected a gold dress, gold bangles, and golden hair ties. In honor of the golden sun, of course.

This done, she packed up her pack, mounting Rocky and continuing their search for Ferra Lin. But despite spending most of the morning searching for the fabled land, once again, they found nothing.

"Well darn," she swore, putting her hands on her hips. And to her surprise, she felt a rather unfamiliar sensation. A sort of uncomfortable-ness in her chest, along with an urge to stomp her foot. Which she didn't do, because she was sitting on Rocky. But she had the urge, which was odd. "Where the heck is it?" she demanded, the feeling only growing stronger.

"Meee not noooo," Rocky admitted.

The uncomfortable feeling only grew, to the point where Fury was starting to get alarmed. So she closed her eyes, taking deep breaths in, whilst reaching to touch Fang. Which, she realized with fresh dismay, was no longer hanging around her neck, since she'd lost it in…well, wherever she'd been.

"Well *crap*," she blurted out, opening her eyes and pouting. And then she covered her mouth with her hand. "Omygosh!" she gasped.

"Wuuut?" Rocky inquired.

"My potty mouth!" she exclaimed, quite aghast. For while she'd said "crap" before – and lots of crap worse than that – she'd never said it when upset.

"Eeeet ookaaay," Rocky reassured her. But she wasn't reassured at all.

"Well, I guess we'll have to look again," she decided.

"Ohhh nooo," Rocky complained. For it was clear he was getting rather sick of it.

"One more hour," she pleaded. "Pretty *please* shmookie tookumses?"

Rocky sighed.

"Okee," he agreed. Reluctantly.

And so they set off, doing a rather rapid scan of the terrain. But once again, their efforts were in vain. A fact that made Fury feel that awful feeling again.

"Gosh *darn* it," she swore, gritting her teeth. "Sorry!" she blurted out, covering her mouth with her hand again. She sighed then, feeling suddenly hopeless. For despite her best efforts – and Rocky's – she'd failed in her mission. Something that she'd never heard of happening, not once. Well, except for that time Greg, Nettie and Harry's first apprentice wizard, had died after dodging into Magmara's lava blast. But no one in *her* family had failed a quest.

If she was the first, why, her parents would be so disappointed. And so would Imperius Fanning.

She sighed dejectedly, feeling even worse now.

I'm a failure, she thought. And for the first time since she could remember, it was a thought she felt compelled to keep to herself. She hardly wanted to burden Rocky with her bad thoughts, after all, and bring him down with her. *Keep it to yourself*, she told herself. And so she did.

But in doing so, she felt the awful truth stay in the pit of her stomach, seeming to weigh her down. She *was* a failure, unlike the rest of her family. And suddenly, the thought of returning home to them and admitting this was too much for her to bear.

"Well, maybe *this* is the land of Ferra Lin," she proposed, which she knew was a lie. "Maybe we found it, and now we have to keep going."

Rocky made a dubious-sounding sound.

"Well we've looked everywhere," she argued, feeling peeved. So much so that she slid off Rocky's back, putting her hands on her hips and giving him a bit of stink-eye. "Where else could it be?"

He stood up from all fours, frowning and rubbing his blocky chin. Then he shrugged. Fury sighed, kicking a pebble. It clattered across the ground, coming to a stop in a depression. Which was exactly where Fury's mind went.

"Well now what?" she complained.

"Go hooome?"

"But…"

"Chaaauncy help," Rocky reasoned. Which was perfectly reasonable; Daddy would be happy to help her, as would Mommy. But then she remembered that Imperius had forbid her parents from helping her…and in fact had warned that them doing so would result in catastrophe.

"No," she stated. "I have to do this by myself. With you," she added hastily. She set her jaw firmly. "We tried to find Ferra Lin, but we didn't succeed. I guess we'll have to keep…"

There was a sudden burst of blue sparkles, and none other than Imperius Fanning appeared before her!

"Oh!" she blurted out, taking a step back. Imperius scowled at her. Or just looked at her while being very, very old. Frankly, it was hard to tell.

"You already found it!" he snapped. And promptly vanished in more sparkles. Which then vanished after touching the ground.

Fury stared at the spot where Imperius had just been, then glanced at Rocky.

"Did I just imagine that, or…?"

"Eeet happen," he assured her. Fury frowned, then her eyes widened.

"Wait, the underground blood river temple place!" she exclaimed, her spirit soaring. "That must've been it!"

"Oooooh," Rocky breathed.

"I mean *duh*," Fury said, slapping herself in the forehead. "God, I'm such a fucking idiot."

Rocky drew in a sharp breath, and so did Fury, covering her mouth with both hands this time.

"Oh *fuck*, I swore!" she…swore. And then swore again, because she'd sworn. Again. "Shit!" she added, to her chagrin. And then sank to a squatting position, feeling absolutely horrified. She said nothing at all then, terrified that another naughty word would escape her lips.

Rocky just stared at her, clearly stunned.

At length she stood, lowering her hands from her mouth, and gave Rocky a terribly apologetic look.

"I'm so sorry," she blurted out. "I…"

"Eeet okaaay."

"No," she insisted. "I shouldn't have said all that." But Rocky just shrugged. She took a deep breath in, then released it, struggling to feel some sort of control over herself. But after a lifetime of not *having* to control herself, she found herself not quite up to the task. Thus, the terror of another X-rated utterance stayed with her, and she decided that it was best if she said nothing at all. Other than what she said next.

"Let's go to Grissam," she prompted.

She mounted Rocky, and he made his way due southwest. Toward Grissam and the Dark Wood...the next leg of Fury's quest.

Chapter 12

The morning after his unfortunate camp-side meeting with the two mounted soldiers, Chaos set off on the last leg of his trip to Belfast. And while he'd spent most of his journey practically bursting with excitement to see Destiny again – especially after a year apart – now he found that excitement replaced by fear. For he knew beyond a shadow of a doubt that the soldiers would tell Destiny of their chance meeting with him. And in particular, how they'd, uh…come to find him.

Fuck, he swore to himself as he strode through the forest northeast of Belfast, up the gentle slope of a large hill. For, having trained in innumerable skills over the last year, he'd been hoping to impress her with how very *useful* he'd become. Destiny was, after all, an incredibly competent person herself, and had only become more so since he'd first met her when she'd been fourteen. *Shit*, he added, a visual of what'd happened the night before assaulting his mind's eye. Along with the sound of his campfire's repeated sizzling.

He rubbed his eyes as if to cleanse them of said visual, but it was no use. The mind never forgot, not until death or dementia. Which for him would take far too long to come.

Thus, it was in the spirit of repeatedly and metaphorically beating himself that Chaos reached the top of the large hill. Which, being quite a bit taller than the land around it – by definition – gave him a spectacular view of what lay beyond.

It was, he found, a steep drop-off to a valley far below…and beyond this, a vertical drop to a mile-wide canyon over a thousand feet deep that stretched as far to the left and right as he could see. The only way across was a narrow rocky land bridge that cut the canyon in two, supported by three massive rock pillars. In the center of this passage, the ground flared out to form a great big flat circle above the middle of the canyon, upon which a walled city had been built.

The great city of Belfast.

"Wow," he breathed, taking it all in. For it was as grand a sight as he'd seen, at least since saving Old Langsroth six years ago. Even from way up here, it was obvious that Belfast was a heavily fortified city, and that its primary purpose was to defend.

He gazed at the sight for a while, mostly because it was epic, but also because he was kind of dreading meeting Destiny, on account of the previous evening's invasion of his privacy. A fact that was profoundly irksome, because he'd been looking forward to being with Destiny for a year now, and to be frank, his public display of yesterday had tainted everything.

"Fuck," he swore under his breath, his guts squirming at the memory. Still, he steeled himself against the future, forcing himself to continue his journey toward Belfast. Which involved going leftward to follow the cliffside, toward a wide path that led down the face of the cliff...and all the way to the northern wall of the city. He made his way to the path, then followed it downward, his legs more than up to the task. For while he'd been a weak, rather pathetic kid when he'd first met Destiny six years ago, now he was anything but. Near-daily training had made his legs strong, and the rest of his body rather muscly if he did say so himself. Which he didn't, because it was far better to have others sing your praises than try to sing them yourself.

In any case, it wasn't too many hours later that Chaos found himself walking across the land bridge, nearing the entrance to Belfast. Which was blocked by a large portcullis at the sixty-foot-tall wall surrounding the city, and guarded by four soldiers in Belfastian tan-colored chainmail armor. A color that made them blend almost seamlessly with the tan rock of the surrounding landscape, and the tan walls of the city itself.

"Name!" one of the soldiers barked, in a warning sort of way.

"Chaos Little," Chaos answered.

"Oh!" the soldier replied. "We've been expecting you," he stated. Chaos grimaced.

"I bet," he mumbled under his breath. Still, he strode up to the portcullis, while the soldier called out to the soldiers inside the wall to open the portcullis.

"Enter," the soldier prompted after said portcullis lifted. "Destiny awaits."

"Har har," one of the other soldiers replied, rolling his eyes. Chaos inclined his head, stepping through the gateway into the city.

"Thanks for coming!" the soldier called out from behind, once the portcullis had lowered again. The other soldiers sniggered and chortled, and Chaos grit his teeth, his face burning. He strode across the wide city street beyond the gate, doing his best to keep his posture straight and his expression dignified. Though he strongly suspected that his best was not particularly good.

The city of Belfast was arranged much like Southwick, in that its squat, tan stone buildings were arranged in a grid. More in a militaristic sense, for the city had clearly been built for this primary purpose. Every building was extensively fortified, and ramparts and watchtowers on the wall surrounding the city hosted soldiers with bows and crossbows. Soldiers patrolled the streets, with the occasional armored carriage parked on the street. And while most of the soldiers had the tan armor of Belfast, some wore the black and gold of King Pravus's men.

Okay, Chaos thought as he walked down the street. *Now I just have to find Destiny.*

Her last letter had informed him that her residence was the tallest building in the center of the city, so he made his way in that general direction. It wasn't long before he found something that met that description: a huge belltower smack in the middle of the city. He made his way toward it, having to introduce himself to nearly every single soldier that passed. For they were all quite paranoid, it seemed. To his chagrin, every single one of them broke out into a knowing smile when he told them his name, and were all too happy to direct him toward Destiny's domain.

At length, he made it to the belltower, taking the stairs all the way up to the floor just below the bell itself. The stairs led to a wooden door that was old, but clearly recently cleaned and sanded, which all the evidence Chaos needed that his Destiny was here. He cleared his throat, then knocked on the door.

"Come in," a woman's voice called out from within.

Chaos opened the door, seeing a large room beyond, one with plain tan walls and a tan stone floor, with a narrow bed set against the wall to the right. And there, sitting at the edge of said bed, was a woman. A very *attractive* woman. One with big golden eyes and full lips, and full...other things. She was dressed in her usual golden shirt and pants, her silver flanged mace with golden runes propped up against the bed. But to Chaos's surprise, her long golden hair was nearly gone, a very short buzz-cut all that remained.

"Hey," he greeted, his tongue promptly tying itself into knots. He just stood there in the doorway, grinning at her stupidly.

"Hey yourself," Destiny replied, standing from her bed. She arched an eyebrow. "You can come in," she added.

"Oh," Chaos mumbled, stepping into the room.

"Close the door," she prompted.

"Oh," he repeated, turning around and doing just that. And then turned around again, just staring at her with a big ol' stupid smile on his face. She strode up to him and grabbed his head, pulling him in for a kiss. And in contrast to her personality, her kiss was wonderfully soft, making him melt into it.

"Mmm," he murmured, giving as good as he got. He wrapped his arms around her, pulling her into him. "God I missed you," he proclaimed when she pulled away to breathe.

"So I heard," she replied. He frowned, then blushed.

"Uh...?" was all he could stammer.

"Couldn't wait, could you?" she mused, shaking her head. His blush deepened, and he scratched the back of his head.

"Uh," he repeated, not knowing quite what else to say.

"At least you were moaning *my* name," she stated. He grimaced.

"I can explain," he began. And then expected her to interject. But she didn't, just standing there, putting a hand on her hip. He grimaced again. "I was uh, I missed you."

"We've established that."

"Aren't you going to tell me you missed me too?" he asked. She frowned.

"Why would I do that?"

"Ass," he grumbled.

"I missed you," she admitted, leaning in and kissing him again. She smiled then. "I couldn't wait either," she confessed.

"Oh yeah?" he replied, waggling his eyebrows. Which wasn't sexy at all, but clearly genetic, given how his father had a propensity to do the same.

"Luckily I have all these soldiers around to take care of me," she mused. He blinked, then drew back from her, terror gripping his guts.

"Wait, *what?*"

"Kidding," she replied, smirking at him. He glared at her.

"Not funny," he grumbled. He paused then. "You didn't, right?"

"Of course not," she replied. "I know how insecure you are."

"I'm not," he protested. Which was a lie.

"The only people who take care of me are you and me," she assured him. "No soldiers. Though believe me, it isn't for a lack of them trying," she added wryly. "Everyone's hard-up here. Prostitutes would make a killing, if there were any."

"No women?" he asked.

"Not enough," she replied. "Turns out women and kids don't want to live in a city under siege by zombies every night."

"Makes sense," Chaos replied. "Poor bastards," he added. "Gotta be hard for them."

"To be so hard all the time?" she asked.

"Yep."

"Don't feel too bad for them," she stated. "By this point, most of them have gotten desperate enough to take care of each other."

"Huh?"

"They're a close-knit group," she told him. "Always willing to lend a hand to their fellow man."

"Ah," Chaos replied, blushing again.

"Speaking of which, we need to end this dry spell," Destiny stated, shoving him toward the bed. "And there won't be any time for sex after sunset."

"Why not?" he asked. Dumbly.

"Duh."

"Right, zombie hordes," Chaos mumbled, feeling stupid. Which was something he'd been determined not to be in front of Destiny this time around. "I swear I'm not this dumb unless you're around," he added.

"Uh huh," she replied. Maddeningly. Still, she shoved him onto his back on the bed, then proceeded to initiate precisely what he'd been looking forward to for the last year. An act that will remain obscure, for the purposes of maintaining decorum. Suffice it to say that Destiny made it quite clear that Chaos's smarts had nothing to do with why she wanted him around. And when she was finished communicating this fact, he stopped giving a damn about how he appeared and focused on how good he felt.

"Wow*ee*," he breathed, gasping for air. She smirked at him, then sat up, lowering her head a bit. A golden glow appeared in her eyes, spreading across her body to her hands...and she placed said hands firmly on Chaos's personal space. Which, in addition to glowing with golden light, became firm once again. "Wha...?" he blurted out. "Let me guess...Vita's Boundless Vigor?"

69

"Yep," she replied.

"Didn't know it could do *that*," he stated, gesturing at the prayer's effect.

"Again and again for hours," she told him, breaking out into a smile. "We've got a year to make up for."

"I'm on it," he replied with a salute.

And, shortly thereafter, to his utter delight, he was.

Chapter 13

Two days after nearly drowning in a river of blood, then having her palms penetrated by a demonic-looking dragon statue, Fury finally made it to the area before the golden double-doors that served as the Gate into Grissam.

Which was, she found, absolutely *teeming* with soldiers. Soldiers on foot, on horseback, and even on horses with wings. All guarding the Gate, it seemed.

"Ooo!" Fury exclaimed, hopping up and down and pointing at the winged steeds. "Look Rocky!"

The soldiers spotted her and Rocky rather quickly, on account of Rocky being a dwarf giant. His presence inspired a fair amount of alarmed shouting and brandishing of weapons and such, so Rocky stopped a good hundred yards away from them, after Fury leapt off.

"Go," Rocky prompted, gesturing for her to continue onward.

"Aren't you coming?" she asked.

"No...supposed tewww," he reminded her. Which was true. Imperius had told her that Rocky could only accompany her to the Gate, but not beyond.

"Aww," she pouted. Then she teared up a bit. "My widdle shmookie tookums!" she exclaimed, rushing up to him and hugging his leg. He reached down, gently embracing her back. "I'm gonna miss you," she told him.

"Meee miss yewww," he replied, his eyes similarly moist. He stood then, gesturing for her to go.

"Thanks Rocky!" she said, waving goodbye. And then she turned away, walking toward the soldiers a hundred yards ahead. Who were still eyeing Rocky warily, and her far less so. As she approached the nearest ones – who held crossbows at the ready, while others brandished swords – she smiled at them and waved cheerfully. "Hello!" she greeted.

"Who are you?" a tall guard inquired.

"Fury," she answered, walking right up to him and stopping a few yards away. Much to the discomfort of the other men. "Fury Little," she added with a little hair-toss, just 'cause she was feeling a lil' bit sassy. The guard watched this display, then blinked, then frowned.

"Of the Little family?" he asked.

"Mhmm," she confirmed. "My Mommy's Valtora and my Daddy's Chauncy," she added.

The soldiers hesitated, then relaxed. A bit.

"I'm Lieutenant Askov," the tall guard greeted. "What brings you to the Gate?"

"Imperius Fanning came to my house and told me to go to the kingdom of Pravus and then meet my friend Rocky at a bridge, then go east to the ocean, then go north to the tallest cliff, then find the fabled land of Ferra Lin, *which I did*, and then go to southwest Grissam so I can save the world from the great evil in the Dark Forest," she answered. And then took a deep, gasping breath in. "So like, yeah," she concluded. "Here I am!"

Askov paused.

"What?" he asked.

Fury repeated said run-on sentence, more than happy to do so. Then she said it a third time. And as they liked to say – whoever "they" were – the third time's the charm. Which in this case, was correct.

"I see," Askov stated. "Well, we'll have to get permission from King Pravus. No one goes in or out without his approval."

"Oh, okay," she agreed instantly. And stood there, waiting. Askov gave her a funny look.

"It's going to be a while," he warned her.

"I'll wait," she replied.

"Like, days. Or weeks," Askov pressed. She gave him a look.

"What? No," she countered. "I need to save the world. Can you ask him now?"

Askov gave her another funny look.

"No," he replied.

"Why not?" Fury pressed, putting a hand on her hip. Again, she felt that uncomfortable feeling, one that made her want to glare at him and stomp her foot. Which she did, because self-control was a skill she'd never had the opportunity to practice.

"Because he's a king, and you're an adolescent girl, and that's just not how life works," the soldier answered.

"Imperius sent me," Fury insisted.

"Sorry kid," the man replied. "I have my orders, and I have to obey them. Nothing personal," he added.

Fury crossed her arms over her chest, shooting him a glare. And while it was an expression quite foreign to her – and thus felt uncomfortable to perform – it also felt oddly *good*.

She turned around then, spotting Rocky still standing about a hundred yards away. She cupped her hands to her mouth.

"Oh *Rocky!*" she called out. "I need help!"

"Now wait a minute," Askov began.

And then Rocky starting bounding toward them.

* * *

Lieutenant Askov watched in sphincter-spasming terror as the massive giant with rocky skin charged toward him and his men. He backpedaled quickly, drawing his sword. Which seemed not-at-all appropriate for the battle that was to come.

Fuck, he swore to himself. While maintaining the icy-cold demeanor of command. Also while metaphorically shitting his pants.

"Incoming!" he barked.

Fury turned to face him, looking rather pleased with herself. And behind her, the giant – named Rocky, apparently – was only a hundred feet away now.

"Ready arrows!" Askov commanded, taking a few more generous steps backward. But before Rocky reached them, the giant skid to a stop before the girl, gazing down at her. And while the girl was petite – no more than five foot one, probably – the giant was at least twenty feet tall, towering over her. And everyone else.

"Rocky, they won't let me through," Fury said with a pout, stomping her foot again. Which would've been annoying and immature to Askov, except the girl was awfully cute. And what was even more uncomfortable for him, *incredibly* hot. Like, a total ten out of ten. Maybe even an eleven. Which made it incredibly hard to be too hard on her. While also hard *not* to be incredibly hard around her.

"Ohhh-pun," Rocky ordered, turning a glare on Askov. While curling his big blocky hands into fists.

"I need permission from the king," Askov protested, taking another step back.

"Ohhh-pun," Rocky repeated, taking a step forward. Which was, to Askov's dismay, equivalent to a good four steps forward for a human.

An arrow *fwipped* through the air over Askov's head, slamming into Rocky's chest. And bouncing off with a *clang*, because of course it did.

"Hold your *fucking* fire!" Askov barked, taking another few steps back. Rocky just continued to glare down at him. "Sorry about that," he stammered. "Look, I'm under orders here," he insisted. "I…"

"OHHH-PUN!" Rocky roared, taking another step forward. The resulting foot stomp make the ground under Askov's feet tremble.

"Please," Fury added.

"Um…" Askov began, eyeing the giant, then his men. Then the giant again. "I'm sure King Pravus will understand," he told himself. "I mean, if Imperius sent you, and you're a Little, then…"

Rocky took another step forward.

"What the heck, let's do it," Askov replied. For while he'd braved many battles for his king, fighting dreadful enemies of all kinds, if he had to choose between his king's wrath and certain death, wrath seemed the lesser of the two evils. Risking his life for the safety of the kingdom was one thing, but risking it to prevent a Little from saving it was quite another. "Everyone, give way!" he barked.

His men were only too eager to do so, parting to give Fury and Rocky a wide path to the double-doors.

"Thanks!" Fury exclaimed, beaming a gorgeous, heart-melting smile his way. And wouldn't you know it, he smiled back, because *damn*.

Lieutenant Askov watched as Fury skipped in a carefree sort of way, all the way up to the double-doors. Then she put a hand on one of them, and there was a *thunk*…and the door swung open. Which proved that she was, in fact, a wizard. Fury turned to Askov, waving one more time.

"Bye bye!" she called out.

And then she turned and went through the doors, vanishing behind them.

The door closed, and to Askov's relief, the giant stomped away from them, leaving him and his men unmolested. Askov heard one of his men coming up to him from behind, and turned to see Yolev, his second-in-command.

"You're fucked," he told Askov.

"Yup," Askov replied. "But at least we're still alive." He sighed. "I'll take all the blame," he added with grim resolve. "You guys'll be okay."

"Thanks boss," Yolev replied.

They both turned to the Gate, staring at the double-doors.

"How old you think she was?" Yolev asked.

"Hell if I know," Askov replied. "Used to be able to tell, but I can't guess their ages anymore." He paused. "Maybe nineteen?"

"Pfft, looks the same age as my fifteen-year-old," Yolev replied. Askov grimaced.

"Either way, she's still just a kid," he grumbled.

"Try telling that to my daughter," Yolev shot back, shaking his head. "They think they're all grown up when they're still barely more than babies. Problem is, they look grown-up too. Especially that one," he added, gesturing at the Gate.

"That's what I worry about with my daughter," Askov replied. Then he sighed. "Go on then," he stated. "Go back to Cumulus and tell them what I did." He paused. "And be kind."

"You saved our lives," Yolev replied. "And if the girl's right, you might've just helped save our kingdom." He smiled. "I'll do everything I can to make sure King Pravus sees it that way."

Chapter 14

After being prompted rather peevishly by Imperius, King Pravus summoned Templeton to the castle for another adventure. And while he still felt a bit irritated that he'd failed to finish his first one in the proper fashion, the prospect of heading off on another quest – or rather, the second part of his previous quest – with his sweet cousin was tantalizing indeed. For he fondly recalled his memories of said quest, some which warmed his heart upon remembering, and others which he used for fondling.

"An adventure!" Templeton declared cheerfully from behind Pravus as they rode their old friend the fire dragon over the two-hundred-foot-tall wall surrounding Cumulus, the capitol of their kingdom. The dragon followed the course of the King's Passage, quickly leaving the great city behind. Why, Pravus could practically *feel* Templeton's eyes twinkling. "Brings back memories, doesn't it?"

"That it does," Pravus replied with a twinkle of his own. He'd even decided to wear his old purple-pink platemail armor from his time in Tabula six years ago, and his purple-pink greatsword. Armor that only he could wear, for its weight was too much for most anyone else to bear.

"I daresay it's been too long," Templeton stated. "A man's heart craves adventure, does it not, my king?"

"Please, call me cousin," Pravus replied. "Indeed it does," he agreed. "I'd say every two years or so would be perfect."

"And I would agree," Templeton concurred. "Enough time to recover between quests, and to build a good yearning without building resentments for being stymied!"

"Just so," Pravus replied, feeling a burst of joy. An emotion he'd felt less and less over the years. Ever since he'd heard of the Dark Rising, actually. Being one of the few leaders capable of helping to stop the northern march of a massive undead horde was a terrible responsibility...one that'd been terrible for his peace of mind. A seemingly unwinnable game was no fun at all to play, especially day after day. Now that the proverbial game involved a much smaller – and more approachable – problem, the possibility of winning it filled him with renewed vigor.

"I confess to some confusion regarding our mission," Templeton...well, confessed.

"In what regard?"

"Well, we've been tasked to go to the catacombs beneath Old Langsroth," Templeton replied. "But as I recall, everything below the ground floor is submerged."

"True," Pravus stated. For Old Langsroth had once been flooded with blood from the Fallen Sky, a cursed storm created by a necromancer long ago. With the death of the Fallen Sky, only water had remained, still flooding the city, albeit at a lower level. Still, water from the Great Flat had been backflowing into the city when they'd left six years ago, and it was only natural to assume that so great a volume of water hadn't simply evaporated since. Which made entering the catacombs problematic, seeing as how breathing water was generally considered bad for one's health. "I suspect part of our quest is to solve this problem when we get there."

"I suspect you're correct," Templeton agreed.

They rode the dragon in silence then, each enjoying the other's company without needing to fill the moment with pointless verbalizations. For such a thing was a nervous habit, hinting at a baseline insecurity. Instead, Pravus found himself enjoying the scenery, the wind howling in his ears, and the satisfying *whump*, *whump* of their dragon's wings as it flew.

It occurred to him then that they'd just passed the point on the road where they'd battled Gavin Archibald Merrick Senior, and the devastating power of the cube-shaped Order. Another adventure, one of many he'd been lucky enough to experience in his relatively short life.

"We've lived quite the lives, haven't we," Pravus mused. "Lives many men would envy."

"Maybe," Templeton replied, "...though I'd prefer they be inspired by our lives than envious of them."

Pravus nodded, having thought the same himself on many occasions. For in living one's life well, it made others give themselves permission to do so. It was far more often the case that people held themselves back from a good life rather than being held back by others…a fact that most would deny, though in the end it was tragically true.

"Perhaps our station gives us the confidence to take risks," he mused.

"And in taking risks, we reap the rewards," Templeton replied.

"As with the gym," Pravus noted. Not in the way of attempting to lift far more than one should, or in risking injury for the sake of bragging rights. Rather, it was in having the courage to push the slightest bit past the borders of one's competence, and in doing so, achieve a reward without undue risk. In just the same way, Imperius had surely sent Pravus back to Old Langsroth because he knew that Pravus was up to the task. A challenge to be sure – and one where death was a real threat – but not a task that was insurmountable.

He realized then that there was an art to matching a person with a quest. Too little risk, and the reward would be of little worth. Too great, and the chance of success would be so miniscule that few men would make the attempt.

"I wonder how this quest will test us," Templeton stated, clearly thinking along a similar vein. He really was a soulmate for Pravus, which was a damn shame. For Pravus knew in his heart that he could never have his cousin, not in the way he wanted. And this left a hole where his cousin could have been, had Templeton only been so inclined to fill it. A hole that was tearing Pravus apart inside.

He wondered just how much longer he could go on like this…and whether he would ever gather the courage to let his dream of a life with Templeton go, and finally fill the void within him…with someone who wanted to do so.

Chapter 15

Having passed through the Gate to the kingdom of Grissam, Fury found herself traveling alone once again...and immediately missing her cootsie wootsie big ol' dwarf giant friend. A fact that made her pout a bit as she followed the wide dirt road beyond the Gate, one that led her across grass-covered rolling terrain. Like waves of the ocean, its hills and valleys never got very tall or deep, content with pleasantly undulating. What trees there were had started losing their leaves, on account of it being autumn. The wind carried said dead leaves across the land, adding bits of color to everything.

Which was just so *pretty*, really. Why, it was enough to make Fury smile, and forget how much she missed her best-est friend Rocky.

"Doo-dee-doo," she sang as she skipped across the terrain, enjoying the sun warming her skin. She tilted her head from side-to-side as she went, making her hair flip from side-to-side on a whim. Because when people were happy, they did happy things, like sing and dance and smile. And since skipping was as close to dancing as a person could do while ambulating, she managed to do all three.

"La-dee-da," she continued, enjoying the jingling sound her backpack made with each skip. Then she spotted a butterfly flitting over a few flowers by the side of the road, and stopped with a gasp. "Flutter-by!" she exclaimed, for it was what she'd called butterflies as a child. She watched as it flitted, eventually flying away.

Then she continued skipping, coming up onto a small hill. It was only when she was at the top of it that she spotted something on the downslope of the hill: a horse-drawn carriage parked a few yards from the side of the road. It was quite cute, made of polished brown wood with streaks of lighter brown, and windows tinted purple, which was a nice touch. And its wheels were very big, nearly as tall as she was.

All-in-all, it was a beautiful carriage, so much so that Fury decided to skip her way down the road to get better look. Whilst singing her la-dee-da song. As she drew near, she spotted a few people outside of the carriage: four men and one girl. Two of the men were dressed in beautiful purple coats and pants, with nice purple hats; one of them was opening the carriage door rather hurriedly and searching for something inside, while the other one was lying on the grass near the carriage, staring up at the sky.

The other two men were dressed in rather shabby brown clothes, and looked rather greasy, as if they hadn't showered in a while. These men were guarding the carriage with swords drawn, keeping guard over the man searching the carriage.

The girl, in contrast, was about Fury's age, and stood near the man who was lying on the ground. She wore a beautiful purple and gold dress, one she'd apparently spilled a rather large amount of tomato juice on. And it was obvious she was quite distressed by this, as well she should be.

"Aaaaaiiiee!" she screamed, staring down at her tomato-juice-stained dress. Then she took a deep breath in, and screamed again.

"Hello!" Fury greeted as she drew close, giving them all a little wave. She beamed them a cheery smile, veering off the road toward them. The two men guarding the carriage were clearly alarmed at this development, turning to her and eyeing her warily.

"Who the hell are you?" one of them demanded, pointing his sword her way.

"Fury Little," she answered immediately, stopping a few yards from him. "That's a *gorgeous* carriage," she added.

"Yeah," the other guard replied, eyeing her up and down while licking his lips. "Sure is."

"Mmhmm," first guard replied, stealing a glance at her. "I like the trunk too," he added, his gaze lingering. Then he turned back to the screaming girl and searching man. "Hurry it up already!" he barked, almost certainly worried that the man searching the carriage was taking too long, and that this could compromise general safety.

"That's a beautiful dress too," Fury said, addressing the girl. "Don't worry, the stain should come out with some vinegar, ice, and detergent." After all, as a bit of a klutz – and a lover of fashion – she'd spilled almost every imaginable fluid on every imaginable kind of fabric, and as a result, knew just what to do.

The girl looked up from her dress, staring at Fury.

"Wh…what?" she blurted out.

"Soak the stain in vinegar, add detergent, then rub it in with ice," Fury instructed. "If there's still a stain, add more vinegar, then wash as usual."

The girl continued to stare at her.

"It'll be as good as new," Fury insisted with a smile.

"The *fuck* is wrong with you?" the girl nearly screamed. Fury blinked.

"Huh?"

"You think I give a *shit* about my *dress?*" she shrieked. Incredulously.

"Hurry it up asshole!" the first guard-person urged. Which was rather rude.

"That's rather rude," Fury stated. The man turned his sword on her again, pointing it right at her chest.

"Shut up!" he barked.

"I'm just trying to help," she protested.

"Go away!" the girl snapped. "Idiot!"

"Gee," was all Fury could think of to say. Because honestly, she'd never been spoken to this way. She crossed her arms over her chest. "I never," she added. Because as mentioned just before, she'd never had.

"On your knees!" the guard pointing his sword at her barked, jabbing it at her rather threateningly.

"Why?" Fury asked. The man blinked.

"Because I said so, idiot!" he explained. Which was not a great explanation at all, but was the standard reasoning given by those who relied on perceived authority to control others rather than reason.

"That's not nice," she scolded. "I think you should apologize."

"On your *knees* bitch!" the guard snapped, jabbing the point of his sword at her belly. The tip actually *hit* her, penetrating her cute green shirt and jabbing her tummy.

"Ow!" she blurted out, flinching backward. She looked down at her belly, relieved to see that the jab hadn't drawn blood. She glared at the guy. "What the *heck?*"

"I said on your knees girly girl," the man snarled. "I ain't gonna ask again."

"Don't hurt her too bad," the other greasy man said. "Not yet. I wanna have some fun with her before we go."

"Me too," the jerk who'd jabbed her said, his lips curling in a lopsided grin. "Why, she's prettier than all 'em jewels we gonna get."

"Mmhmm," the other grease-ball agreed. "Both these gals are."

Just then, the man who'd been searching the carriage pulled out of it, a sack of coins and jewels in his hands. He was sweating profusely, and looked awfully pale.

"H-here," he stammered. "Just t-t-take it."

"We w-w-will," the man guarding him mocked with a smirk. "Drop it on the ground, then walk away. Don't turn back, if you know what's good for ya."

"O-k-kay," the man stuttered. And did just that, sprinting away from the carriage just as quickly as he could. The girl in the purple dress turned to do the same.

"Stay!" the guard barked. The girl froze in place.

Fury eyed the two greasy men, who she was starting to think weren't guards at all. For it seemed that she'd just borne witness to something she'd only heard of in books and scary campfire stories:

A *robbery*.

"Gasp!" she gasped, covering her mouth with one hand. "You're *bad* men!"

"The dawn breaks!" the guard pointing his sword at her said.

"Dumb as rocks, ain'tcha," the other one mused. "Pretty though."

"Pretty perfect," the first man agreed. "Take off your shirt and show me how pretty you *really* are."

Fury blinked, her face screwing itself into a bewildered frown. "What?"

"Pull off that shirt and show me yer pretties, pretty," the man ordered.

"The *fuck* I will," Fury shot back. With a sudden vehemence that shocked her. "Oops," she blurted out, covering her mouth with one hand.

"Do it!" the man barked, jabbing at her shoulder this time. The tip hit her shoulder obliquely, cutting her sleeve and skin.

"Ow!" she blurted out, stumbling backward in surprise. This time, the blade had made a shallow gash in her flesh. A gash that drew blood. Her eyes widened at the sight, and she turned back to the man, suddenly filled with a strange emotion. An incredibly *powerful* emotion, one that came on so rapidly it was downright frightening. "Mother *fucker!*" she shouted.

The man lunged forward, kicking her right in the belly with his boot. The air blasted from her lungs, and Fury fell onto her back, pain spreading through her guts. So much so that she had the sudden urge to puke. Which, not being one to hold back urges, she did.

"Blarrghhh!" she barfed, turning her head to the side just in time. Nasty acidy stuff spilled onto the grass. "Urrghhmmff," she added, bringing up some more.

"That'll teach ya," her assailant stated with a greasy smirk. "Now get up on yer knees," he added. "I got somethin' to show ya."

Fury groaned, clutching at her achy abdomen. She rolled onto her belly, pushing herself up onto her hands and knees…but her left shoulder stung terribly with the movement, blood pouring out of the gash there. She got to her feet, glaring at the man who'd stabbed and kicked her.

"I said on your knees, bitch!" the man snapped. Fury grit her teeth, putting a hand to her bleeding shoulder.

"No!" she replied. Which was, admittedly, a waste of an opportunity for a bad-ass line.

"Fine," the man replied. "Guess we're gonna hafta do this the hard way."

"*Oh* yeah," the other man piped in. "We're *both* gonna be hard."

And so, dear reader, well, you know what happens next in situations like this. Suffice it to say that life is not at all fair, and that bad things do happen to good people. Innocence is something eventually lost by all of those who live long enough to have the veil of childhood lifted from their eyes, and to see the world for what it is, warts and all. A tragic state of affairs, I'm afraid, and poor little Fury Little could hardly be said to be the first kind-hearted soul to suffer at the hands of rapacious men. But men and women such as this do exist, and thus tales of their misdeeds must be told, if only to warn others that such things can, in fact, happen. For this is the very purpose of a cautionary tale.

That being said, as it turned out, things turned out quite a bit differently than the two robbers expected…and the cautionary tale was not for Fury, but for *them*.

Fury gripped her stinging shoulder, blood soaking her hand. She felt its warmth spread across her palm, then seem to spread to her whole hand, then her wrist and forearm.

Then it spread across her chest, to her other arm, and then across her whole body, like a wave of warmth. Warmth that grew hot, and then *burned*. Not painfully, but rather, pleasantly.

"Ohhhh," she moaned, her eyes rolling up in her head. "Ohhh-*fuuuuck!*"

"The hell?" the man threatening her blurted out, taking a step back. The girl in the purple dress took one look at Fury, then bolted.

"Her eyes!" the other man exclaimed. "Holy shit!"

The heat filled her, seeming to *pulse* within her. She closed her eyes, seeing the stone dragon before her, its glowing red eyes seeming to stare into her very soul.

Surrender to me, Proeliator, the dragon's voice boomed in her head, echoing through her consciousness. She gasped, feeling a sudden pressure in her palms. As if something was trying to shove out of each of them.

"Nnngghh," she moaned, pressure building in her palms.

SURRENDER!

Fury cried out, giving herself up to the presence within her, yielding to the unimaginable pressure of its will. And right as she did so, she felt a sudden, piercing pain in her palms, as if they'd been stabbed by the dragon's fangs again.

Fury *screamed*.

Her eyes snapped open, and she stared at her hands, seeing...*things* coming out of the red circles in her palms. Red circles that were glowing with an unholy crimson light. They were shafts made of what looked to be red stone dragon-fangs, each about two feet long. And as she watched, they finished coming out of her, her hands reflexively gripping them...

...and then blood poured out of each of the shafts, forming the shape of meat-cleaver blades.

The blood seemed to crystallize, hardening until it was shiny like obsidian. Until she was holding twin meat-cleavers. With edges as sharp as *fuck*.

"Holy...!" the robber standing before her exclaimed, backpedaling frantically. Fury lifted her gaze to him, gripping her meat-cleavers tightly.

"Come out," she told him, strolling toward him. "I want you *inside* of me."

The man blinked.

"What?" he blurted out. She scowled at him.

84

"I wasn't talking to *you*," she snapped. "I was talking to your *blood*."

"Oh," the man replied automatically. And then thought about it for a second. "Shit."

He turned to run, and Fury wound up with her right hand, chucking the meat cleaver at his back. It went a bit low, embedding itself right into his ass-crack with a meaty *thump*. Like, *deep* into his ass-crack.

He screamed, tumbling to the ground.

Fury strode toward him, then spotted the other robber grabbing the bag of jewels and coins.

"Sorry Filbin," he offered, and ran the frick away.

"Come back!" Fury called out after him. He ignored her, which was rude. So she flung her other meat cleaver at him. It whirled after him, but her aim was off; it fell to the ground, burying itself into the dirt.

She turned back to the creep with the cleaver in his ass-crack, who was trying in vain to scramble to his feet. Apparently having his butthole cleaved was making this difficult for him. Fury glared at him, storming up to him and reaching down to grab the bone-handle. But he crawled away.

"Stop *moving*," she snapped, reaching for it again. But he didn't, which was rude. She cursed, sprinting and leaping at him feet-first, driving her heels into the small of his back. Which made him scream, satisfyingly enough. "Ass," she grumbled, stepping off him, then grabbing the cleaver-handle. She yanked it out of said ass with some difficulty, which was also satisfying. For he screamed with every second of the attempt.

As she pulled the cleaver free at last, blood spurted from the gaping wound. Like, a *lot* of it. But as it did so, it did something quite strange. In that each bloody butt-spurt slowed in mid-air...and then flew toward the hollow bottoms of the handles of her cleavers, getting sucked right in.

Fury froze, staring at this odd development, utterly confused. So much so that she didn't even realize that the robber had managed to stand, and was hopping away on one leg...toward his horse, no less.

"Hey!" she shouted, rushing toward him and whipping her cleaver at him as hard as she could. But again, it was off-mark, missing him by a wide margin. She ran after him, but the bastard managed to reach his horse, climbing into the saddle and galloping away.

She cursed again, watching as he fled down the road. Then she stomped after her cleaver, retrieving it. Its handle was warm, and seemed to pulse in her palm; she realized that she still had to get the other one. Which she did with more cursing, hardly minding each naughty word issuing from her lips. For instead of feeling awful to utter, they felt awfully good.

At length she found her other cleaver, holding each in her hands. She was alone now, except for the guy lying on the ground and gazing up at the sky. Who wasn't blinking, she realized. And hadn't since she'd arrived.

"Oh," she mumbled. For he was clearly dead.

With no one left to piss her off, Fury's fury slowed subsided. Which was too bad, because she suddenly didn't want it to leave. As it did, however, something else strange happened: her crystallized red cleaver-blades melted before her eyes, sucking back into the handles. And then the handles moved of their own accords, sucking butt-first back through the glowing circles in her palms. As they did so, she felt a powerful pulsing from the handle of the cleaver that'd sucked up the robber's blood...and an identical pulsing sensation filling her palm and traveling up her arm. Her veins there bulged, as if ready to burst out of her skin...and her eyes rolled into the back of her head, an incredible sensation spreading up her arm and to her chest, then all the way through her body.

"Gnnnggghhh!" she moaned, shuddering in ecstasy.

But the sensation lasted a disappointingly short time, and soon it was gone. The handles vanished within her, the red circles on her hands ceasing to glow.

And with that, Fury's fury was gone.

* * *

The aftermath of Fury's impromptu battle was terribly confusing.

She stared at the bloody scene for a long, long time, then lowered herself on shaky legs to the ground, sitting on the grass. Just staring. At the carriage, at the dead man's body lying near it. Visions of what'd just happened came to her, and she recalled them over and over again, trying to make sense of what'd happened. But none of it made sense to her.

Why would those robbers have attacked the carriage? Why kill a man…just for some coins? Just for the ability to buy some stuff? For "stuff" was just that. It couldn't make anyone happy for long. Stuff was dead. It couldn't love. Even beautiful stuff was good because of the beauty, not the stuff. Beauty wasn't for *having*, it was for appreciating when it came.

But that was only part of what she didn't understand.

"Why'd I do that?" she asked no one in particular. For as much as she hated to admit it, she'd acted very *very* badly. She *cussed*. And what's worse, she'd *hurt* someone. Like, thrown a gosh-darn meat-cleaver at him. And made him bleed.

It didn't make any sense. Not one bit. For she'd never gone and done anything like that before. Not in her whole life.

"Why?" she pressed, shaking her head slowly. Tears dripped down her cheeks, and she wiped them away with the back of her hand. They were hardly the first tears she'd shed after the robbers had fled…and she knew they wouldn't be nearly her last.

But at length, she'd cried enough, and no amount of questioning or reliving the event had helped. So she stood on wobbly legs, giving the carriage one last look, burning it into her memory, before turning away from it and leaving it behind. She made her way numbly back to the road, then stood there for a while, turning forward, then back the way she'd come.

Suddenly, she wanted nothing more than to go back home. To rejoin Rocky and rest on his back while he brought her back to Southwick, where she'd be safe and secure and content for the rest of her life.

You have to save the world, she thought, recalling Imperius's declaration. That it was her destiny to save people from a great evil within the Dark Wood. A destiny she had absolutely no desire to fulfill, for she'd had her fill of violence.

But if she *didn't* forge onward, then innocent people might die…including her beloved Daddy and Mommy, and even Chaos and Uncle Willard and Auntie Gretchen. And lots more, considering that if she didn't succeed, the world itself would end.

Fury felt a heaviness come over her, a terrible weight that threatened to bring her to her knees. It was suddenly all *too much*.

It wasn't fair.

She sighed, then spotted the hole in the sleeve of her shirt where the robber's sword had jabbed her. To her surprise, the blood staining the fabric was gone. She lifted her sleeve, expecting to see a wound there. But instead, she saw a dark red line where she'd been stabbed…but the skin was otherwise intact. It wasn't a wound, but more like a crimson tattoo.

One that was exactly the same color as the circles on her hands.

She stared at it, sliding her finger over it again, without a hint of pain or soreness. Then she lowered her sleeve, gazing up the road back to the Gate…and Southwick. A path that promised the comfort of the familiar, and of being who she'd always been. Back in Southwick, Daddy and Mommy would ask nothing more of her than that. She wouldn't have to grow, or be uncomfortable, or feel that anything was *too much*.

But maybe – just maybe – it felt like too much because she'd never had to carry any weight at all.

Fury stared up the road, then turned to face the other way, at the unknown road beyond. Where it would take her, she had no idea. What she might do if she walked it, she couldn't know.

The only way to find out was to take it, for better or for worse.

She swallowed past a lump in her throat, looking down at her hands, then at the carriage. And then she forced herself to take one step forward down the road. A single step. But with that step came another, for the momentum of the first made the second easier than stopping. And the third and fourth steps were the same. With that momentum, the path she'd resisted became the path of least resistance.

And with that, Fury made her way toward her destiny, mystery that it was. But no sooner had she made this decision when she heard a voice call out from behind her.

"Hey!"

She stopped, whirling around…and saw the girl in the purple dress running down the road toward her. The girl slowed, then stopped a few yards away, eyeing Fury warily.

"Oh," Fury mumbled. "Hey."

"What the hell was all that?" the girl demanded, gesturing at the carriage.

"All what?" Fury asked.

The girl put a hand on her hip, glaring at her.

"The whole part where your eyes starting glowing red and your hair turned red and meat cleavers came out of your hands," she clarified. Which to be fair, was pretty much what Fury had been expecting. Fury hesitated, then shrugged helplessly.

"I don't know," she answered.

"You don't know?"

"I don't know," Fury confirmed.

"How can you not know?" the girl pressed incredulously.

"Um…because I don't?" Fury replied. "It's the first time that's ever happened to me."

The girl frowned, then lowered her hand from her hip.

"Oh," she replied. "I see." A pause. "Thanks for scaring those dickheads off," she offered. "I guess you saved my life."

"I did?"

"Sure," the girl replied. "They would've killed me to stop me from identifying them to the authorities."

"Oh."

"…or raped me," the girl continued. "Probably repeatedly. And *then* they would've killed me."

Fury gave the girl a blank look, for she'd never heard of "rape" before. But given the context and the way the girl had said it, Fury assumed it was something bad.

"It's true," the girl insisted, crossing her arms over her chest. "I'm pretty hot," she added. Which, Fury found, was quite true. She had long, straight black hair and rather tanned skin, with big brown eyes and full lips. And while she was shorter than Fury, she had long legs, and excellent aesthetic proportions. Proportions that Fury found herself appreciating. Not in a jealous way, for Fury had been bedazzled by her mother to be aesthetically pleasing herself, but in a "hubba hubba *wowee*" sort of way. Which was a bit startling, for Fury had never felt a "hubba hubba *wowee*" kind of feeling before, much to her mother's consternation.

"You totally are," Fury replied. A reply which the girl clearly enjoyed. "Um, so what's your name?"

"Bree," the girl replied. "Yours?"

"Fury," Fury answered. The girl frowned.

"Your parents named you Fury?"

"Uh huh," Fury replied.

Bree stared at her for a bit, looking her up and down, then looked down at herself. Namely her purple dress, which was still stained with what was definitely *not* tomato sauce.

"Ugh," she complained.

"I've got extra clothes in my pack," Fury offered. "You can borrow some."

"Thanks," Bree replied, and promptly pulled off her dress. Which revealed that she wasn't at all a fan of wearing anything else. A revelation that was a revelation for Fury, who stared, then turned away, blushing furiously. She cleared her throat, taking off her pack and handing it to Bree. Without looking again, naturally.

"Take whatever you want," Fury mumbled, staring at her feet.

"You can look you know," Bree told her. "I'm not shy or anything."

"Oh," Fury replied, continuing to not look. At length, Bree handed the pack back to her. She took it, stealing a glance at Bree, and to her relief the girl was dressed. In one of Fury's favorite outfits, no less: a pink and purple halter top with pink and purple shorts. "You might get cold," Fury warned.

"I run hot," Bree replied. And although Fury had never seen Bree run, she believed it. "Where are you headed?"

"To Belfast," Fury answered.

"Belfast?" Bree asked incredulously. "Why?"

"It's my destiny," Fury explained. Which apparently wasn't explanation enough. In the interests of maintaining *your* interest, dear reader, we'll simply say that Fury recapped Imperius's arrival and everything else that'd happened up until the present moment. You're welcome.

"Wow," Bree murmured, taking this all in. "So you're a wizard?"

"Um…" Fury replied. Then she shrugged. "I think so?"

"Totally explains the glowing eyes and shit," Bree stated. Then she frowned. "Why are your eyes purple?"

"I dunno," Fury replied with a shrug. "My Mommy's are too." Bree hesitated.

"Mind if I tag along?"

"It might be dangerous," Fury warned.

"With my looks, being alone is more dangerous," Bree replied, gesturing at herself. Which, while true, was a bit off-putting. Beautiful things were most beautiful when they simply *were*, after all, and didn't constantly reference the fact. As Fury's mom had often said, if you were full of yourself, you'd be less likely to be filled by anyone else. Whatever that meant.

"Okay," Fury replied reluctantly.

"Let's go," Bree prompted. And promptly started walking down the road. Fury rushed to catch up, slowing to a walk beside the girl. She stole a glance at Bree.

"So like, how old are you?" she asked.

"Sixteen," Bree answered.

"Really?" Fury asked. "You don't look it." She would've guessed eighteen at the least. Bree gave her a dark look.

"I get that a lot," she grumbled.

Fury paused.

"Aren't you going to ask how old *I* am?" she asked.

"Don't care," Bree replied. Fury blinked.

"Oh," she mumbled.

And with that, the two girls fell into a bit of an uneasy silence, their steps falling into a matching rhythm as they made their way down the road toward Fury's destiny...and toward whatever dangers awaited them next.

Chapter 16

After a thoroughly satisfying day and early evening, Chaos and Destiny took their rest on her narrow bed at last. But, bolstered as they were by Vita's Boundless Vigor, their rest was more because of a sated appetite for each other rather than for their bodies.

"Getting dark," Chaos noted, eyeing the narrow window opposite the bed. He sat up, watching as Destiny got dressed.

"Enough loving," she stated. "Time to fight."

"Oh boy," Chaos replied, getting dressed himself. He grabbed his shovel – his trusty ol' Omen-63 Tactical Shovel, that was – while Destiny grabbed her mace.

"It's going to be bad," she warned.

"As bad as Old Langsroth?" he asked.

"Yep," she replied.

"Well, I'm a lot older now," he pointed out.

"Maybe I'll have to save your ass less this time then," Destiny shot back with a smirk. He rolled his eyes.

"I've been looking forward to this," he admitted, taking a few practice swings with his shovel.

"You wouldn't look forward to it if you knew what was coming," she warned. "The enemy is getting stronger…and bolder."

"I'll be careful," he promised. "And besides, with you at my side, I have nothing to fear."

"*Less* to fear," she corrected. "All right. Time to go upstairs."

"Upstairs?" he asked. For he'd assumed they'd go *down*stairs.

"The belltower is our best vantage point to see the enemy coming," she explained. And with that, she led him out of her room, then up the stairs to the top of the belltower. As expected, there was a big bell there, one made of bronze. But there were no walls blocking the panoramic view. All of Belfast was visible from their vantage point, including the relatively narrow passage across the canyon to the south. This was lit by tall stone pillars set at regular intervals along the edges of the land bridge, each topped by a flaming brazier. Beyond this, Chaos spotted a vast, dark forest, one with mist hanging over it.

"That's the Dark Forest," Destiny stated.

"The source of the undead," he replied.

"So we assume," Destiny said. He eyed her sidelong.

"Have you gone there?"

"No," Destiny answered.

"Why not?" he pressed.

"Vita told me not to," she answered. "She said I would die."

"Oh," he replied. "Well, then I'm glad you haven't gone there," he quipped.

"Bet you are," Destiny replied with a smirk. "Now shut up and be a lookout."

"Yes ma'am," Chaos replied, and promptly did as she'd prescribed. He gazed out beyond the city, at the passage leading south to the Dark Forest. The passage over the canyon looked pale silver in the reflected moonlight, barely visible in the darkness of the night. "What am I looking for?" he asked.

"Movement," she answered.

"What are these zombies like?" he inquired.

"Same as the ones in Old Langsroth," she answered. "Weaker ones are slow, stronger ones are fast and strong."

"Any Zhimeras?" he pressed, referring to the powerful zombies with extra limbs and other body parts glommed together into one deadly beast.

"Yep."

"Wonderful," he quipped, with more confidence than he felt. He'd had nightmares of the awful creatures for the last six years, after all. While he was more than eager to face one and defeat it with his Omen-63, his inner child was still terrified of the prospect.

"Focus," Destiny chided, but not in an insulting sort of way. He did so, watching…and waiting.

Minutes passed, and then nearly an hour. Chaos resisted the urge to speak, knowing that now wasn't the time.

Then he spotted them: pale shapes coming out of the Dark Forest, making their way rather quickly toward the canyon pass. Still over a mile away, but coming.

"I see them," he announced.

"Ring the bell," she stated.

Chaos turned to the big bronze bell, and was about to ask how to ring it when he spotted a rope hanging down for that purpose.

He pulled on it, then let it go…and covered his ears before needing to be told to.

DONG!

Even with his ears covered, the sound was deafening. It rang across the city, echoing over and over again.

"Three times!" Destiny yelled. Chaos obliged.

DONG! DONG!

Then he stepped back from the bell, waiting for the bell's ringing to fade before uncovering his ears.

"Now we join the soldiers downstairs," Destiny informed him. "We'll hold the line at the southern gate. It's the only entrance into the city from the Dark Forest."

"I take it the entrance is blocked by a portcullis?" he asked as they made their way downstairs.

"Yes."

"Do we really need to fight then?" he asked. "I mean, how can the zombies threaten us if they can't get inside?"

"We've replaced the portcullis dozens of times," Destiny replied.

"Ah."

"We're down to half the forces we had at the beginning," she warned. "And that's with regular reinforcements from Tabula, the kingdom of Pravus, and Bevinshire."

"Bevinshire?"

"A country west of Grissam," she explained. "Point is, we're getting weaker and the enemy is getting stronger."

"Yeah, but *now* you have a wizard on your side," Chaos replied, puffing out his chest and thrusting his shoulders back with unsubtle machoism.

"Who?" Destiny inquired. He gave her a look.

"Me," he answered. "Ass."

"I love you," Destiny stated. "But your magic sucks unless it's a last resort."

"I love you too," he replied. "And *you* suck." Because she did, and quite well at that. But Destiny didn't take the bait, reaching the bottom of the belltower and continuing down the street. Soldiers were pouring out of the surrounding buildings, most of them making their way toward the southern wall of Belfast. The wall facing the oncoming zombie horde. Chaos felt a little thrill as he joined their march, Destiny at his side. He'd been dreaming of this moment for over a year, of being able to fight alongside his love again. This time not as a frightened, sheltered boy, but as a man.

As he watched, archers made their way up the stairs running up the side of the wall ahead to get to the ramparts above, while some of the infantry made their way through the still-open portcullis to the massive land bridge beyond. Chaos spotted row after row of large wooden barricades set along the land bridge, clearly positioned to slow down the zombie army's march. There were ten in total, he saw, each row extending all the way to the edges of the land bridge. Each was about eight feet tall, and had sharpened wooden stakes that projected outward, designed to impale any would-be attackers.

Just behind the nearest barricade, Chaos saw a large wooden structure standing. It consisted of two massive pillars and a cross beam. Attached to the middle of this crossbeam was a large, metal, log-shaped pendulum, one that had been primed for swinging, held up and to the right.

"Why are those soldiers leaving the protection of the wall?" Chaos asked.

"If they don't, the enemy will be able to bash down our portcullis without us being able to fight back," Destiny replied.

"What do you mean?" he pressed. "The archers can take out lots of zombies." Destiny gave him a look.

"Arrows don't stop zombies unless it's a head shot," she explained. "And even then, it has to take out enough of their brain. If other zombies pull out the arrow, or if it goes all the way through, the zombies will just slowly heal."

"Really?"

"Each zombie has glowing blood in it," Destiny explained.

"Just like the ones in Old Langsroth," Chaos realized.

"Right. Most have just a little, but it's enough to let them regenerate, at least eventually. And we've seen zombies giving blood to fallen comrades to heal them."

"Oh," Chaos replied. "I see why archers wouldn't be helpful." He paused. "But the infantry will have the same problem, won't they?"

"We aim to cut off heads, but limbs will help," Destiny replied. "That way, even if a zombie is revived, it won't be able to move well, or do much damage."

"Have you tried throwing them off the land bridge?" he asked. For the passage over the canyon was only about thirty feet wide or so.

"Every chance we can get," Destiny answered. "That's the best option, but our main goal is to bide our time."

"Until sunrise," Chaos guessed.

"Right," she replied. "Let's go up to the ramparts."

They followed the archers up the stairs to the ramparts atop the great wall surrounding Belfast, and Destiny went up to the edge, looking over the rampart wall, which was waist high. This gave Chaos an excellent view of the battlefield beyond...and the army of pale figures marching out of the Dark Forest, making their way slowly but surely toward the city.

"At this rate, they won't reach us before sunrise," Chaos joked, glancing at Destiny. She didn't reply, her expression grim as she watched the pale zombie horde. Chaos grimaced, turning back to watch as well...

...and then a large group of zombies burst out of the Dark Forest behind the first wave, surging forward at terrifying speed. They shoved their way through the zombies in front of them, cutting through them and charging across the land bridge toward the southern wall of Belfast.

"Oh crap," Chaos blurted out, taking an involuntary step back.

These faster zombies reached the first of the wooden barricades, about halfway across the land bridge. Some ran right into them, impaling themselves on the sharp ends of the logs the barricades had been made from. Others tried leaping *over* the barricades, landing atop them and impaling them like the others.

Chaos glanced at Destiny, whose expression hadn't changed. Nor had she made any attempt to move, or shout orders, or...anything. He was struck with the urge to ask why, but resisted it.

Trust her, he told himself. She'd been through hundreds of nightly battles, after all. Now was not the time to talk, but to watch...and learn.

The fast zombies continued to pile up in front of and on top of the barricades...which had the unfortunate effect of forming a ramp of zombies before them. A ramp that more fast zombies ran up...and then jumped, leaping over the first of the barricades and clearing them. Destiny turned to face the soldiers in the city behind the wall.

"First barricade breached!" she shouted. Which made sense, because most of the soldiers within the city couldn't see what was going on.

The fast zombies continued a good twenty feet to the next row of barricades, throwing themselves on it with abandon as they had with the first…and more followed, until a ramp of their bodies had accumulated to the point where the ones who followed managed to leap over it.

"Second barricade breached!" Destiny shouted.

This pattern repeated itself for the third row of barricades, then the fourth. At which point the enemy army ran out of fast zombies, and the slow zombies reached the first barricade at last. They climbed up the ramp of fast zombie bodies with considerable difficulty, then fell over the barricade to land beyond, picking themselves up and shambling onward to the second barricade. They did this until they reached the fourth barricade, which, due to the failure of the fast zombies to complete a ramp up it, the slow zombies were stymied by. So they simply ran into it, impaling themselves on the sharp wooden ends, then sort of writhing pathetically and probably graarrghing and such.

"Awfully inefficient," Chaos noted.

"They can afford to be," Destiny replied grimly.

He watched this display of zombie incompetence, of wave after wave of the things mindlessly throwing themselves at Belfast's defenses. As with traffic jams he'd seen in Southwick, it wasn't long before a considerable column of zombies had backed up behind their fallen comrades. In fact, so numerous were the zombies that soon even the slow zombies formed a gentle slope up the fifth barricade, halfway to the city. Such that even a slow zombie could step over it, tumbling to the land bridge beyond.

"Fifth barricade breached!" Destiny shouted. "Staves up!"

Some of the soldiers beyond the fifth barricade hoisted long bo-staves, rushing to the right of the zombies that'd made it beyond the barricade. When the zombies stood, the soldiers shoved them backward with the ends of their long staves…right off the left side of the land bridge. More zombies fell over the barricade, and the soldiers swept right then, doing the same thing.

"Smart," Chaos murmured, watching as zombie bodies fell a good thousand feet off the land bridge. "Taking them out of circulation."

The soldiers did this for a bit, then retreated, and were replaced by fresh soldiers who repeated the process. Again, a smart tactic, to ensure that soldiers never got too fatigued. It was quite clear to Chaos that the men had done this many times before, acting in perfect harmony with each other. It made sense; with battles every night, people had to either be cooperative and competent or die.

After six years of daily battle, the soldiers of Belfast were perhaps the most competent in the world.

"What about fire?" Chaos asked, eyeing the mass of zombies still pouring in from the south.

"Ran low on oil a long time ago," Destiny replied.

"Ah."

The staff-wielding soldiers did their thing for a few minutes longer, but it wasn't long before the zombies falling over the fifth barricade were too numerous to handle by poking. The soldiers switched it up, having two soldiers hold either end of a staff at hip height, then rush toward one edge of the land bridge, shoving multiple zombies off at a time. This was far more exhausting, requiring soldiers to switch up each time.

It worked – for a bit – but soon the soldiers guarding the sixth barricade were overwhelmed.

"Sixth back!" Destiny barked.

The soldiers threw their bo-staves over the sixth barricade, and their fellows behind the barricade went to either side of the wooden structure, taking two metal poles and setting them into holes at the sides of the barricades. The beleaguered soldiers swung on these like monkey bars in a kid's playground, getting behind the barricade. Then they pulled the metal poles free, presumably so that the zombies couldn't use them. Not that any slow zombie would be capable of such an acrobatic feat.

"Clever," Chaos stated. "How are we doing?" he asked Destiny.

"Better than last night," she answered.

"So…good?" he pressed.

"We either see the sun rise tomorrow or we don't," she replied.

Chaos nodded, watching as the slow zombies surged over the fifth barricade, piling up in front of the sixth. It was only a matter of time before their bodies made a slope up to the top of the barricade, and began tumbling over it.

"Sixth barricade breached!" Destiny shouted.

"What happens when they reach the portcullis?" Chaos asked.

"We stop them from breaching the portcullis and the wall," Destiny answered.

"And if they do breach the wall?" he pressed. She turned away from the scene ahead, her golden eyes boring into his.

"Then we fight until we die," she replied.

He swallowed, then turned to face the hordes of undead…and spotted something at the far end of the land bridge. Something far bigger than the zombies around it. It was a Zhimera, he realized. A zombie chimera with one human head and a body composed of numerous zombie body parts fused together. This one had a dozen segments connected end-to-end, each composed of three torsos fused to its central torso. And each side-torso had a many-joined human arm, three times as long as a normal one. It looked for all the world like a human centipede…and it moved with *terrifying* speed, climbing over the slow zombies and rushing over the land bridge toward Belfast.

"Oh shit," Chaos swore. "Look at that thing!"

"That's not what I'm worried about," Destiny replied. He frowned.

"Really?"

She shook her head, pointing off at the Dark Forest. Chaos followed her finger, spotting something emerging from the tree line.

Something *huge*.

Chapter 17

The land bridge leading from the Dark Forest to Belfast teemed with countless pale zombies, some walking while others fell to their bellies, crawling over each other in a writhing mass of bodies. All making their way inexorably toward the southern wall of Belfast...and thus, toward Chaos and Destiny.

The centipede-like Zhimera charged over this zombie army, crushing zombies under each of its long, many-segmented limbs. It moved with shocking speed...and considering that most of the barricades' pointy bits were covered by soft zombie bodies, the Zhimera had no trouble going right over them. It charged over the first four barricades, then leapt right over the fifth one, clearing it easily.

"Archers!" Destiny shouted.

The archers beside them on the wall lit a fuse on each arrow, then aimed...and shot the arrows at the centipede Zhimera, who crouched down in preparation for a leap over the sixth barricade. The arrows struck true, slamming into the Zhimera's body, the fuses sparkling. The Zhimera leapt into the air, sailing over the sixth barricade...

...just as the arrows *exploded*, blowing the Zhimera to pieces.

"Yeah!" Chaos exclaimed, pumping a fist in the air. While absolutely no one else cheered, embarrassingly enough. He lowered his fist, blushing a bit. "Go team," he added. Lamely.

"We used to do that," Destiny stated. "Now we don't celebrate until daylight."

"Right," Chaos mumbled. And no sooner did he state this reply when he was reminded why. For there, at the tree line, was the enormous creature they'd seen coming out of the forest: a hulking humanoid over twenty feet tall, with massive muscles rippling as it strode onto the land bridge. It was, Chaos realized, a dwarf giant like Rocky. But unlike Rocky, it didn't have rocky skin. And also unlike Rocky, it was clearly a zombie. One with eyes that glowed with a bright crimson light...which indicated that it was far more powerful than the typical undead. It carried a massive warhammer in one hand, one at least a dozen feet long.

It stomped slowly northward toward the southern gate of Belfast, shoving other zombies aside like rag dolls. Those that didn't get out of its way were crushed underfoot. Messily.

But even as the thing made its way toward them, the slow-zombie hordes cleared the seventh barricade.

"Seventh barricade breached!" Destiny shouted. "Staves up!"

The soldiers with the long metal staves did their thing, sweeping zombies off either side of the land bridge as best they could. But soon they were at risk of being overwhelmed, and Destiny ordered them to evacuate. Hundreds of zombies fell over the seventh barricade, then got up to shamble to the eighth. Which meant there were only three barricades between them and the front gate of the city...and they were less than an hour into the night.

"We're in trouble, aren't we," Chaos realized.

"Yep," Destiny replied. She turned to the archers. "Move right," she ordered. "When that thing gets close enough, shoot at its center of gravity. We need to try to blow it off the left ledge."

"Yes ma'am," the archers replied, moving to the rightmost section of the rampart.

"That thing looks awfully heavy," Chaos noted. "I'm not sure those arrows are powerful enough."

"They aren't," Destiny agreed. Unexpectedly. Chaos gave her a questioning look, but she ignored him, watching the zombie horde below. They piled up against the eighth barricade, forming a slope of bodies leading up and over it...and went over it.

"Eighth barricade breached!" she barked. "Staves up!" The soldiers behind the barricade rushed to comply. But even as they got busy shoving zombies into the canyon on either side, the dwarf giant zombie reached the first barricade. It swung its big-ass hammer in an uppercut motion, shattering the middle of the barricade and sending hunks of wood flying...and more than a few of its zombie-fellows as well. Then it stomped up to the second barricade, giving it similar treatment.

"Damn," Destiny swore, her mouth set in a grim line. "He's going to destroy all of them."

Chaos watched as the giant zombie did just that, realizing that it would take time to rebuild the barricades. If it took more than a day, it would mean that even if they survived the night, that tomorrow night they'd be relatively handicapped. Every day was a race against time, for the zombies came every single night. There was no rest for these men, and there hadn't been for six years. Perhaps some of them rested, fighting every other day, but even then, the psychic pressure of knowing that the battle raged on had to have an effect on one's peace of mind.

These men are the real heroes, he thought as he watched the soldiers ahead of the ninth barricade sweep zombies off the land bridge. Their sacrifice was far greater than his had been, six years ago. Two days in Old Langsroth – and a single heated battle – was nothing compared to what the soldiers of Belfast had been through.

He might be Chosen One, but he had a lot of work to do before he was a true hero.

I'm not worthy, he told himself. *Yet.*

And in that moment, he vowed that he would be. That he would one day be worthy of standing with these men. And with Destiny, who'd been right with them most of the time. He turned to gaze at her, the full weight of her sacrifice striking him. Those few times she'd taken a break from the fighting to visit, a few times a year at most. To be honest, he'd sometimes been irritated with how seldom she'd come to see him, and how exhausted she'd been when she'd arrived. How she'd wanted to do nothing but rest and have him hold her. Now he knew why…and why she'd seemed so distant sometimes when she'd visited. The faraway look in her eyes had not had anything to do with him, but with *this.* For while she was away, her comrades still had to fight.

Chaos swallowed past a lump in his throat.

"Thank you for coming to visit me all those times," he told her. She turned to glance at him, then smiled, holding out a hand. He took it, squeezing it. And while she said nothing more, that simple gesture said enough.

They both watched as the zombies continuing to pour over the eighth barricade, eventually overwhelming the soldiers there. The soldiers retreated in the usual way, zombies piling up behind the ninth barricade. Which meant there were only two barricades left before the zombies reached the portcullis. Behind the tenth and last barricade, soldiers with heavy shields and maces formed a wall before the portcullis, just behind the pendulum-structure Chaos had noted before.

"We're losing ground too quickly," Destiny muttered, shaking her head. "Ready the pendulum!" she shouted.

A soldier rushed up a ladder against the rightmost pillar holding up the pendulum, grabbing a lever that Chaos assumed would release it. But the soldier didn't pull it, of course, for the zombie hordes had yet to breach the ninth or tenth barricades. Ahead, the giant zombie shattered the third barricade, stomping up to the fourth. It was a juggernaut, slow but inevitable. It would reach them, and when it did, they were in deep, *deep* shit.

"Ninth barricade breached!" Destiny shouted as zombies poured over it. In the distance, the zombie giant smashed the fourth barricade with its massive hammer, sending wood and zombies flying. More zombies fell off the edges as the giant waded forward through the undead masses to the fifth barricade. Destiny turned to Chaos, letting go of his hand. "When the tenth barricade goes, we join the soldiers outside."

"Got it," Chaos replied. While feeling remarkably uneasy inside. For the prospect of leaving the protection of the wall to face literally thousands of zombies – and a zombie giant, no less – was hardly something to look forward to. This despite the fact that he'd spent the last few years dreaming of this day, when he'd finally get to test his mettle against the zombie hordes. As was often the case in life, what was desirable in fantasies was decidedly undesirable in reality. And so it was that years of yearning were instantly proven to be a total waste of time.

The zombie hordes pressed ever-forward, until they formed a slope up the tenth barricade. And beyond, the zombie giant smashed through the fifth barricade, its baleful red eyes locked on the southern wall of Belfast.

"Tenth barricade breached!" Destiny barked as zombies fell over it, landing beyond. They rose to their feet, shambling forward toward the wall of soldiers between them and the front gate. They reached the pendulum, mere feet from where the first line of guards held their shields firmly before them. "Pendulum, now!" Destiny shouted.

The pendulum released, the huge metal beam swinging downward in an arc to the left. It slammed into the front line of zombies, sending them flying off the edge of the land bridge. More zombies came forward to take their place, reaching the shields of the front line. The soldiers shoved them backward with those shields…and right into the pendulum's next swing.

"We're up," Destiny declared, turning and rushing down the stairs to the city street below. Chaos followed her to the portcullis, guarded by many Belfastian soldiers. "Open," she ordered.

"Yes ma'am," one replied.

They opened the portcullis, and Destiny strode through, Chaos following suit. The guards closed the portcullis behind them with a *clang*, leaving them standing behind the rows of soldiers ahead. Soldiers that were the only thing standing between them and the zombie army.

Destiny walked up to the rearmost soldiers, and they parted for her, as did the soldiers in the rows beyond. She walked right up to the first row, who thankfully *didn't* part for her, considering that would've let the zombies pour through. She lowered her head in prayer, her body beginning to glow with a golden light. Then she touched the guards in the first row, two at a time, blessing them with Vita's magic. When she'd finished blessing the first row, she blessed the second, then walked back to Chaos.

"What was that?" he asked.

"Vita's Boundless Vigor," she answered.

"Not regeneration?"

"If they fall, they won't heal fast enough before the zombies kill them," she reasoned. "Better they don't fall at all."

The pendulum swung with a *voomp-voomp*, smashing into zombies with each swing. Chaos was surprised to find that it wasn't swinging any less over time, despite the resistance the zombies provided. He spotted soldiers on either side of the pendulum, pulling ropes that apparently kept it going.

"Bringing the light," Destiny warned, closing her eyes to pray again. A warm golden light appeared high above her head, illuminating the land bridge ahead. The zombies nearest them grarrrghed, shielding their eyes from the light...and seemed to slow under its power. But it was nowhere near as powerful as the sun, which would have stopped the zombies altogether. Still, it was something.

Beyond, the zombie giant crashed through the eighth barricade, then stomped up to the ninth one, smashing it with another uppercut-swing of its big-ass hammer.

"Get ready," Destiny warned, grabbing her mace from its holster at her waist. Chaos readied his Omen-63, grimacing at his paltry weapon. What good could a shovel do against a zombie giant?

Whelp, you're about to find out, he muttered to himself, switching his grip on the shovel's shaft. His hands were slick with sweat, for obvious reasons.

The giant crashed through the ninth barricade, charging for the final one.

Voomp-voomp.

The pendulum sent more zombies a-flying, and the first row of shield-bearers stood firm, despite the sight of the dwarf giant zombie lifting its hammer to smash to tenth barricade.

BAM!

The barricade split under the weight of the hammer's massive head, and the giant shoved through, roaring at the top of its beastly lungs. Zombies poured through the gap around him, rushing in slow-motion toward the still-swinging pendulum. The giant strode toward the pendulum as well, even as it continued *voomp*ing side-to-side, sending zombies flying.

"Hold the line!" Destiny barked. Chaos grimaced, for he himself had taken an involuntary step backward. "Archers, get ready!" she commanded.

The giant stomped up to the pendulum, lifting its hammer and setting up for a big swing. Which it executed, bringing the hammer right onto the swinging pendulum in a horizontal smash. The blow slowed the pendulum...but tore the hammer from the giant's hands, sending it flying off the side of the land bridge and into the canyon far, far below.

A fact that made the giant *extremely* unhappy.

It roared again, the sound making the hair on the nape of Chaos's neck stand on-end. Then it charged forward toward the shield-bearers...

...and was struck full-on in the lower legs by the pendulum.

The giant flew to the left with the pendulum, nearly toppling off the side of the land bridge. But it grabbed on to the metal beam, swinging back...and its weight brought the pendulum to a halt. The crossbeam creaked...and then snapped with an eardrum-splitting *crack*. The metal beam and the giant fell to the ground, making the earth quake under Chaos's feet.

"Fall back!" Destiny shouted. "Through the portcullis, go, go!"

The rows of shield-bearers backpedaled, still facing the zombie hordes and the giant. The portcullis opened behind Chaos, and he backed into the city, the rearmost shield-bearers coming in after him. But to Chaos's dismay, Destiny stayed outside the city, facing the zombie army and the giant, who was rising to its feet.

"Destiny!" Chaos shouted.

* * *

"Stay put!" Destiny yelled at Chaos through the closed portcullis. She closed her eyes then, lowering her head in prayer...and a dome of pure golden light appeared around her, expanding outward in all directions rapidly. The dome struck the front lines of the zombie army, sending them flying backward violently. But the giant merely stumbled backward a bit, barely budging with the magical blow...and the zombies standing directly behind him were similarly unaffected.

Damn, she thought, watching as the giant recovered its balance. It glared at her with its baleful glowing eyes, clenching its huge hands into fists. But instead of taking a swing at her, it leaned over, grabbing the metal beam-pendulum and lifting it. It shifted its grip to hold it like a two-handed club, hoisting it over its head.

"Shit," Destiny swore. "Open the gate!"

She heard the portcullis opening behind her, and waited until the giant's wind-up was complete, its makeshift club held overhead like an axe ready for a downward chop.

"Arrows!" she barked, closing her eyes in prayer at the same time, sending a request of Vita.

A second dome of golden light shot outward at the giant, at the same time as explosive arrows slammed into its right side. The expanding dome struck the giant, making it stumble backward, the weight of the beam behind it knocking it off-balance...and the arrows exploded, shoving it to the left.

The giant toppled over like a felled tree, landing on its back on the land bridge with a *boom.*

Zombies flew from the impact, others crushed under the giant's weight. But instead of rushing through the open gate to safety, Destiny rushed at the giant, leaping onto its crotch and sprinting over its belly and chest toward its head. She reached it, swinging her mace downward in an overhead chop, striking the beast right between the goddamn eyes.

The mace smashed into the creature's forehead with a *crack*...but bounced off the thing's thick skull. She stumbled, then regained her balance, swinging again and again. But the giant's skull was terribly strong, and while her blows turned its flesh into mush, its bone held.

The giant roared, reaching to grab Destiny from behind, and she dodged out of the way, running back toward the portcullis. She ran through the open gate, skidding to a stop inside the city.

"Close!" she ordered. And so the portcullis did.

* * *

Chaos stood beside Destiny, peering out at the giant from beyond the portcullis, watching as it got to its feet. Its forehead was a mashed mess, but the wounds only appeared to have irritated it. It roared, then grabbed a handful of nearby zombies, throwing them. Not at the portcullis, but over the wall...and right into the city itself.

The zombies landed with meaty *thwacks*, then rose to their feet, graarrghing and shambling toward Chaos, Destiny, and the large number of Belfastian soldiers present.

Needless to say, said zombies were immediately dismembered.

More zombies flew over the wall, the giant taking handful after handful and chucking them into the city. Some landed on a few unlucky soldiers, smashing them into the street.

"Take cover!" Destiny ordered, rushing toward the stone overhang at the entrance of one building. The soldiers did just that, some rushing into nearby buildings, while others joined Destiny under the overhang. More zombies rained down on the streets, rising to their feet and charging at the soldiers in a slow-motion attack. And while separately the zombies were rather pathetic, and easy to dismember, in large numbers they were a force to be reckoned with.

"We need to take that giant out," one of the soldiers stated. "Or we're screwed," he added with depressing accuracy.

"Archers, aim for the wound on its head!" Destiny called out, even as more zombies rained down. A whole bunch of them came toward the overhang, and Chaos gripped his Omen-63, winding up to give it a good ol' swing. One that decapitated the nearest zombie, which was awfully satisfying. Especially considering how much he'd been practicing said swing over the last year or so.

Destiny fought as well, beating the zombies off with her mace, and the soldiers fought valiantly with their clubs and swords, making quick work of the nearest zombies. But no matter how many they beat off, more and more came, forcing them to keep up the fight. Chaos decapitated another zombie, then another, smashing a third across the temple with the back of his trusty shovel. It fell onto its back, and he thrust down at its neck, decapitating it as well...and burying his magical shovel a few inches into the street.

Oh, he thought as he pulled the shovel free. For he'd forgotten about its magical properties. His father's magic had made it so that the shovel absorbed and released stone and dirt.

"I have an idea," he called out. But he never got the chance to share it. For quite suddenly, a large metal beam smashed through the closed portcullis, taking out a section of the wall in the process. It retracted...and then smashed into the upper portion of the wall above the portcullis, taking down more of the wall.

"Fuck!" Destiny swore.

And fucked they most certainly were. For the giant had grabbed the pendulum-beam, and was making mincemeat of the southern wall of Belfast.

"We're dead," a soldier declared. Which was awfully unhelpful. And awful, because it was true. Destiny ignored the man, turning to fix Chaos with her golden-eyed gaze.

"We stop that thing or we die," she stated. Chaos nodded.

"I'm ready to fight," he declared valiantly. Though to be honest, he was honestly terrified.

"We don't need a fighter," she retorted. "We need a wizard."

Chaos hesitated, and she put a hand on his shoulder.

"This isn't about proving yourself," she told him. "This is about seeing the sun rise."

Chaos swallowed, then nodded.

"Alright," he replied, setting his Omen-63 aside. "One wizard coming up."

And with that, he strode up to the hole in the wall where the portcullis had been, dodging zombie-grabs as he went. The wall directly over the hole collapsed, revealing the giant standing before him. Chaos gazed up at the thing, then cracked his knuckles.

"Alright asshole," he declared. "Time for a surprise."

He reached out to the universe then, feeling a *shift* as its great order was disrupted.

And then the land bridge right before the wall of Belfast collapsed under the giant, sending it – and a whole frick-ton of zombies – to their dooms.

Chapter 18

After a day of travel on her own two feet, Fury's feet were quite sore. Unaccustomed as they were to extended use, the bottoms of her feet had earned some blisters. A fact she discovered after heading a ways off the side of the road with Bree to make camp that evening. They sat on the grass far enough away to avoid being seen by anyone using the road, wary of unsavory characters like the robbers they'd met earlier.

She thought about making a fire, but without the Rod of Fire, she didn't know how. And besides, a fire would only attract the interest of strangers…and at the moment, her relationship with strangers was decidedly poor. Except for Bree, of course.

Fury pulled her sleeping bag out of her pack, laying it on the ground. Then she paused, glancing at Bree.

"Um…I only have one," she stated apologetically.

"Is it big enough for both of us?" Bree asked.

"We could try," Fury ventured. And so they did, and while it was awfully tight, they both managed to snuggle into the sleeping bag. Which made it quite warm, thankfully. For the autumn nights were getting cooler, a hint of winter's future chill in the air.

Fury closed her eyes, enjoying Bree's warmth on her back. For she'd chosen to be the little spoon, so to speak. In fact, Bree's closeness made Fury feel some kind of way, which was both pleasant and at the same time strange. For it was similar to that "hubba hubba *wowee*" feeling she'd gotten earlier that day. Still, she found it hard to truly enjoy this novel sensation, for every *snap* of a tree branch or rustle of a yet-to-fall leave made her ears prick up, sending her heart a-pounding. As if enemies were everywhere, or that the robbers she'd attacked were coming back to get their revenge.

It was only the weighty pull of exhaustion that ended this special kind of torture, a weight that pulled on her eyelids first, forcing them closed. Then it pulled her down, down…to the depths of an uneasy sleep. One where dreams of a stone dragon

109

with glowing red eyes burned her with its unblinking gaze, consuming her until nothing was left.

* * *

The next morning, Fury woke with the sun as she always did.

It took her a moment to remember why there was a warm body all smooshed up against her back. After a rather lengthy period of enjoying this, she wiggled her way out of the sleeping bag, disturbing Bree, who was clearly still sleeping.

"The *fuck?*" Bree snapped. And then promptly fell back asleep.

Fury did a bit of a stretch, then smiled at the sun.

"Hello day!" she greeted, waving at it with a smile. For like the sun, she liked to shine her warmth on everything.

"Shut the fuck up!" Bree snapped, rolling angrily in the sleeping bag to face away from Fury.

"Oh," Fury mumbled, quite taken aback. She stared at the girl, then got changed quietly, choosing to walk a fair distance away from the girl before doing so. She searched through her pack, trying to find just the right outfit for the day, and decided on a hot-pink shirt and white skirt, with white and pink polka-dot socks. She began stripping off her clothes…and noticed the hole in the sleeve of her shirt.

The previous day's events came back to her in a horrid rush, making her heart sink.

"Crap," she blurted out. And then covered her mouth with one hand. "Darn," she corrected. She eyed the outfit she'd chosen, shoving it back in the pack. She chose a black shirt and shorts instead, changing quickly. And wore no bling, for bling was a celebration of the joy she felt inside, and right now she felt none at all.

She returned to their little camp, eyeing Bree nervously. Because she was ready to go, but the girl was still asleep. And terrifying.

So she waited. And waited. And *waited.*

At length Bree groaned, tossing and turning in the sleeping bag. And then opened her eyes, glaring at Fury. For like, no frickin' reason. Fury looked away, feeling awfully confused. She hadn't done anything wrong, had she? Why was Bree so gosh-darned *mad* at her?

Bree got out of the sleeping bag, folding it up and handing it to Fury.

"Here," she grumbled.

Fury put the sleeping bag back in the pack, then slung said pack over her shoulders to rest on her back. All while eyeing Bree dubiously.

"What?" Bree grumbled, clearly still irritated.

"Did I...do something wrong?" Fury asked. Bree blinked.

"What?"

"It's just...you seem really mad at me," Fury explained.

"Nah," Bree replied. "I'm just a total bitch when I wake up."

"Oh," Fury stated. She paused. "Why?"

"Why what?"

"Why are you uh, mad when you wake up?" Fury clarified. Bree shrugged.

"Hell if I know," she replied. "I get it from my mother."

"Huh," Fury murmured. For it was quite odd to her that this should be so. After all, she always awoke from a refreshing sleep feeling...well, refreshed. And therefore happy and just *marvelous*. She couldn't imagine waking up any other way, really.

"Can I have a snack?" Bree asked, eyeing Fury's pack.

"Sure."

Bree ate, but Fury did not, as she didn't feel particularly hungry. Then they walked back to the road, making their way toward Belfast. Or wherever the road was taking them, anyway.

"Where does this road take us?" Fury asked, figuring Bree would know.

"Tabula," Bree answered. "It's where my uncles were taking me."

"What for?"

Bree grimaced, lowering her gaze to her feet.

"Sorry," Fury offered. "You don't have to..."

"They were going to sell me," Bree interrupted. "So I could...work in Tabula."

Fury frowned.

"Sell you?" she asked. For the idea seemed ludicrous. "How can they sell you? You're a *person*," she added incredulously. Bree eyed her.

"You're really that naive?" she asked.

"Huh?"

111

"Never mind," Bree grumbled. "Anyway, now that they're dead, I'm free. And I sure as hell ain't going to Tabula."

Fury considered this as they walked.

"So…you're happy they're dead?" she asked.

"Hell yeah," Bree confirmed. "Assholes," she added, rather viciously.

Fury considered pressing this line of questioning, but decided against it. Thus they fell into a silence as they walked, which allowed Fury's mind to wander back to the events of yesterday. Images of the man she'd hurt came to her, and the pleasure she'd gotten – at least in the moment – at having hurt him. She'd never once enjoyed someone else's misfortune, not once in her whole life. But she hadn't just enjoyed it.

She'd *relished* it.

Her stomach growled as she went, but she paid it no mind. Despite the fact that she hadn't had dinner the night before, nor breakfast this morning, she had no desire to eat. Nor to walk for that matter, but she had a duty to fulfill, and there was nothing else she could really do. So onward she walked, following the road to her destiny.

An hour passed, and to her relief, she saw no more carriages on the road, nor any ne'er-do-wells. Just an endless landscape spread out before her and Bree, mostly meadows with forest in the distance. She found her gaze lingering on the flowers sprinkled over the meadow, and enjoyed their subtle perfume as she passed them by. Still, the contrast between the ugliness and violence of the robbers and this flower was jarring to her. That the world could harbor both was beyond her comprehension. For how could a world of flowers and sunlight and warmth – a world that supported her and all life in so many ways – allow for such awfulness?

It occurred to her then that perhaps the price for freedom was the ability to make bad choices. Which meant that that she either had to make good choices, or have good choices made for her. And perhaps that was what Imperius Fanning was doing, in ordering her to go on this quest. Which meant that he might be preventing her from making bad choices by doing so.

At length, the sun was directly overhead. Which meant it was noon, and therefore lunchtime. The ground had begun to slope upward toward a path that seemed to have been cut deep into a hill. Fury's stomach growled more insistently, and though stopping to eat seemed like far too much work, this time Fury obeyed her body's command.

"Do you want lunch?" she asked Bree right before reaching the hill-path.

"Sure."

They both stopped on the road, and Fury grabbed some jerky from her pack, giving Bree some, then taking some for herself. Luckily her parents had packed plenty of non-perishable foods. They continued their journey, chewing on the jerky as they walked. It wasn't long before the sheer walls of the hill were flanking them on either side, the area cast in shadow. They made it about a quarter mile before exiting the hill, the landscape opening up again around them. To Fury's surprise, there was a magnificent view ahead: for there, only a few miles away, was a grand city built atop a mesa perhaps a hundred feet tall. A city that matched the rusty red color of the mesa itself, as if each building had sprouted from the rock like a living thing.

"Wow," she breathed, stopping to take it all in. It was just as her brother Chaos had described it to her, after he'd returned from his own quest. "Tabula!"

"A city of criminals and drunks and rapists, yay," Bree muttered. Fury pointedly ignored her.

"Wanna check it out?" she asked. Bree stared at her as if she was stupid.

"What are you, stupid?" Bree blurted out, confirming this. Fury frowned.

"I don't know," she admitted. "I guess I *wouldn't* know," she added. She paused, mulling it over. "Maybe anyone a lot smarter than me would think I was, but people as smart as me or dumber wouldn't," she reasoned. "So maybe I'm just stupid compared to you."

Bree stared at her, then grimaced.

"Sorry," she mumbled. "I just...no, I don't want to go there."

"Okay," Fury stated. "We won't then."

Bree paused then, eyeing the city.

"What is it?" Fury asked.

"It's just...I know that the guys that were going to buy me will do it to some other girl," she answered.

"Buy them?"

"Right," Bree replied.

"Why would they buy a girl?" Fury pressed. Innocently. Bree gave her a look that showed she *definitely* thought Fury was stupid.

"Um, to whore them out as a prostitute?" she answered, as if it should be obvious. "Duh," she added, which meant it should've been. Fury just stared at her blankly, for she'd never heard of the term. "To force them to have sex with guys for money," Bree explained.

Fury continued to stare at her blankly.

"Sex?" she asked. "What's that?"

Bree opened her mouth, then closed it. Then stared at Fury for a bit longer.

"You don't know what sex is?" she asked incredulously.

"Nope," Fury replied.

"Um...it's when..." Bree began. Then she lowered her face to her hands, rubbing vigorously for a bit. After which she looked up at Fury again. "You *really* don't know?"

"Nope," Fury confirmed.

"It's like..." Bree began. And then proceeded to describe the act as best she could. A description we'll spare you from, dear reader, but one that, suffice it to say, Fury found quite perplexing.

"But...why?" she asked.

"Why what?"

"Why would people do that?" she clarified. Bree furrowed her brow.

"It feels good," she answered. "Haven't you ever...um, you know what? Never mind."

"So wait, your uncles were going to...?"

"Yep," Bree replied.

"But why?" Fury pressed incredulously.

"Because they're assholes," Bree explained. "*Were* assholes." She paused. "Say, what you did to them...could you do it to someone else?"

"Um...I have no idea, actually," Fury admitted. "I wouldn't want to though."

"Not even to help save someone?" Bree pressed. Fury hesitated.

"I mean...I don't know," she replied. "I don't want to hurt anyone."

"Yeah, well if you don't, they'll hurt someone else," Bree pointed out. "So if you *can* do something, you should."

Fury furrowed her brow.

114

"But…if everybody has to do everything they can for everyone else, then no one will have a chance to live for themselves," she protested. Bree frowned, giving her a funny look. "What?" Fury asked.

"Nothing," Bree replied. "That's just…pretty not dumb."

"Aww," Fury said, clutching her bosom and breaking out into a smile. "Thanks!"

"Anyway, maybe we don't have to do *everything* we can do, but we should still do something sometimes," Bree compromised. "If I had the power to find and stop those men, I'd do it."

"Well I don't know if I do," Fury stated. "I have no idea how I did all that, or if I could do it again."

"Well, one of the robbers stabbed you first," Bree reasoned. "Maybe getting hurt did it. Or getting angry *because* you were hurt."

"I mean maybe," Fury replied noncommittally.

"Well we need to figure it out," Bree stated. Fury frowned.

"Why?"

"Because we might get attacked again," Bree pointed out. Which was a really good point.

"Okay, but how're we going to find it out?" Fury pressed. Bree hesitated, then shrugged.

"No idea," she admitted. "And frankly, I don't want to be the one testing it in case you go all psycho on me."

"I agree," Fury replied, feeling relieved.

"But I still think you should do *something* to stop those guys in Tabula," Bree pressed.

"Me?"

"You're supposed to be a hero, right?" Bree asked. "Heroes save people."

Fury considered this, realizing Bree was right. She *was* supposed to be a hero. Or rather, she was supposed to become one. And that meant she had to do heroic things. Which meant she had to *try* to do heroic things…and preventing grown men from putting their pee-pees in underage girls certainly fit the bill. She took a deep breath in, then let it out.

"Alright," she agreed. "Let's go to Tabula."

Chapter 19

The trek to Tabula took over an hour, and in lieu of talking – something that Bree apparently didn't feel like doing – Fury's mind wandered. Unfortunately, it decided to focus on negative things. Which was unusual for Fury, but quite common for other people's minds to do. The prospect of meeting more bad people, and then actually maybe *hurting* those people, made her feel a bit anxious. A foreign feeling for Fury indeed.

But unlike most minds, Fury's had a hard time focusing on the negative for very long, and thus it wasn't long before Fury found herself focusing on the terrain between them and Tabula instead. It was quite beautiful, the red dirt and stone all around, with tufts of short grass and a few flowers growing here and there. Witnessing this natural beauty made her stride a bit lengthier, her shoulders not quite as slouched. While her mind still reeled with visions of the day before, the fact that beauty existed in such abundance tempered her anxiety a bit. In fact, as she gazed out over the landscape, peaceful and colorful as it was, massaged by a gentle breeze and warmed and fed by the sun, she realized that beauty was abundant in far greater proportion than ugliness. In her experience, people had been almost universally kind, except when hungry or tired or otherwise stressed. Or when waking up, in Bree's case, apparently.

It was one bad day she told herself, standing a bit straighter at the thought. *One bad moment in a* good *day*, she corrected, for it was true. Which made it rather silly to be such a fuddy-duddy, all things considered. She broke out into a smile, feeling the urge to skip. Not one to hold back her urges, breaking out into a skip was precisely what she did. With that motion came a change in emotion, for the two were inextricably linked. To be depressed was to be chained to the past, which slowed one down until it kept them in place. To be anxious was to be chained to the future, which forced one to move far too quickly, neglecting the present to get the future over with already. But to skip or stroll was to be

116

chained by nothing, and that allowed her spirit to be free in the moment…which in the end, was all there was.

"The hell are you doing?" Bree blurted out, staring at Fury incredulously.

"Skipping," Fury replied. Bree looked at her as if she'd gone mad. Or as if she was incredibly stupid. It was hard to tell.

"Why?"

"Because I feel like it," Fury replied. Which was as good an answer as any. She ignored Bree's grumpy looks, enjoying herself without a care. Still, the fact that Bree's attitude was rather ugly made that "hubba hubba *wowee*" feeling fade. Not entirely, of course, but considerably.

In her pleasant frame of mind – which owed itself mostly to the jerky in her tummy – Fury continued her journey with renewed vigor, happy to be happy again. And during the hour or so it took to reach the base of Tabula's mesa, whenever a bad thought or memory would come her way, she managed them by avoiding them. Which mostly involved gazing at the puffy clouds in the sky, or spotting a butterfly flitting over the occasional flower. All while Bree flashed her strange looks, strangely.

But as you know, dear reader, avoiding one's problems is the surest way to continue suffering from them. Which meant that Fury's strategy was doomed to fail, at least eventually. So when she reached the wide path sloping up the side of the mesa that led to Tabula, she found said strategy failing.

"Are you sure we should be doing this?" she asked Bree as they strode up to the guards guarding the start of the winding path upward.

"Relax," Bree replied. But as anyone with any sense would know, telling an anxious person to relax was utterly pointless, akin to telling a person who'd been lit on fire to stop burning. For an anxious person's mind was incapable of relaxing by its own power…and in any case, an inability to relax was what anxiety was all about.

One of the guards held up a hand to stop them. It was a big and tough looking man with gold and red chainmail armor, wearing a helmet with a symbol of a sword pointing blade-down.

"Morning ladies," he greeted. "Your names?"

"Bree and Fury," Bree answered.

"Reason for entry?" the guard pressed. Bree glanced at Fury.

"Um…business," Bree replied.

117

"What manner of business?"

"My uncles own a...personnel business," Bree explained. "Service industry."

"Which service industry?" the guard asked.

"Um...massage," Bree replied.

"Length of stay?"

"A few days," Bree answered.

"Very well," the guard decided. "You'll have to register at the Visitor's Center."

"M'kay," Bree sort-of-agreed. The guards parted, and Fury and Bree started up the winding path. This led to a red stone wall surrounding the city, with an arched gateway leading in. One guarded by guards identically to the previous ones. They went through the same question-and-answer session, followed by an order to visit the Visitor's Center. And with that, they gained entry into the capitol of Grissam.

Tabula was quite different than Southwick; whereas Southwick's streets were straight and laid out in a simple, flat grid, Tabula's narrow cobblestone streets were twisty-turny, and the city had many different vertical levels to it. It was a far more colorful city as well, in that the throngs of people clogging the city streets actually wore colorful clothes. Not the muted colors so popular in Southwick, where only children were allowed to enjoy bright colors, and it was considered an adult rite of passage to transition to a palette bordering on grayscale.

The cootsy-wootsy signs above each shop – or rather, 'shoppe' as they were called here – were also quite colorful, and whimsical to boot. Whimsy was Fury's favorite form of artistic expression, so it was natural that her eyes widened at the sight of them.

"W*owee*," she breathed, slowing to take it all in. Bree elbowed her in the ribs. "O*wee*," Fury yelped, rubbing said ribs gingerly.

"Come on," Bree grumbled. "Mission first, gawk second."

"So...where are we going, exactly?" Fury inquired.

"My uncles said they were going to meet my buyer at a bar," Bree answered. "It's called The Moist Cookie," she added. "Be on the lookout for it."

Fury nodded, and they went down a random street, following behind a throng of people going in the same direction. At length, Fury spotted a kindly-looking old man sitting on a bench beside the road.

"Excuse me," she said. "Can you help me find The Moist Cookie?"

His eyes lit up, his lips curling into a grin.

"Come a little closer and I will," he replied.

"Okay," Fury agreed, stepping toward him…only to be yanked back by Bree.

"Nope," the girl chided, pulling Fury past the old man. Who looked awfully disappointed that he hadn't gotten a chance to help.

"But…" Fury protested.

"Stop talking to people you idiot," Bree snapped. Fury grimaced, lowering her gaze. She found herself utterly confused, having no idea what she'd done wrong. But doing something wrong didn't mean that Bree could treat her wrongly.

"Be nice," Fury scolded. Gently.

"Sorry," Bree grumbled.

"Thanks!" Fury replied, feeling instantly much better. Such was the power of apology, after all; why it was magic as potent as any wizard's spell. Yet everyone could wield it, if they chose to. Which many did not, for as with any magic, apologies had their price: the risk of losing status, whatever that was worth. For those happy to be themselves, of course, status was of little concern. Which was why Fury was quick to apologize if she felt she'd done someone wrong.

They made their way down the street, looking at signs as they went. Eventually they found what they were looking for: a large tavern with an unmistakable sign, of a huge cookie hovering over a glass of milk, which the dripping cookie had clearly just been dunked in.

"Ooo!" Fury exclaimed, pointing excitedly. And hopping. Bree slapped her arm down, shooting her another glare.

"Can you try *not* to stand out for once?" she complained.

"Well," Fury began, but Bree grabbed her by the wrist, hauling her toward the entrance to The Moist Cookie. A big, burly, rather greasy man was guarding it, one wearing a brown shirt with the tavern's logo printed on it. He grinned from ear-to-ear when the two girls drew near.

"Hello ladies," he greeted, eyeing them both.

"You guys open?" Bree asked.

"The Moist Cookie is always open for business," the man replied. "You'll be glad you came!" Which, Fury noted, was what was written on the man's shirt. A catchy tagline, she had to admit. And she hoped it was true.

"Come on," Bree told Fury, pulling her close to her side. The man opened the door for them, and they stepped into the tavern. It was rather poorly lit, with lots of circular tables surrounded by chairs on one side, and then rows of chairs facing what appeared to be a dance floor. The bar was extensive, with tons of bottles of liquor and wine and such displayed behind it. Fury had never drank alcohol, and she'd never seen her parents drink it either. But she'd heard enough about spirits that she knew the basics. Which was basically to either never drink, or if you did, to do it at home with a bunch of trusted friends. And while there were quite a few people sitting at the bar, they weren't Fury's friends. *Yet.*

One of the men at the bar turned around in his barstool to eye Fury and Bree, a rather rotund man, yet with disproportionally short, skinny arms. He wore a black leather jacket and pants, and had short curly brown hair, and an amount of acne that could only be described as grossly unfair.

"Hey *girls*," he greeted, in a rather nasal voice, eyeing them hungrily. More hungrily than he'd eyed his plate of chicken wings a moment ago. He put his hands on his prominent belly. "What brings a couple cute lil' cookies like you to my bar?

"My uncle Rupert and uncle Hedric," Bree answered. The man's eyes lit up, and he rubbed his belly eagerly.

"Oh *yes*," he practically purred, lowering himself from his stool and waddling up to them. Whilst eyeing Fury preferentially. "You brought a friend," he noted.

"They thought you might like her," Bree explained. "For double the price."

"Done," the man replied instantly, switching to rubbing his hands instead of his belly. He made it to Fury, looking her up and down. "My *my*," he purred. "Oh but this is going to work out just *fine.*"

"You're the buyer?" Bree asked.

"No no," the man replied. "I'm Percy, the owner. I…facilitate the ah, transition to employment, so to speak. In return for carrying out…" he paused, his lips curling into a smile, "…a bit of 'new employee training.'"

"Hurgghh," Bree replied, covering her mouth. "Sorry, bad breakfast," she added hastily.

"It's the water," Percy replied sagely. "All out-of-towners have to get used to it."

"So where's my buyer?" Bree inquired, looking around the bar.

"I'll fetch 'em," Percy replied. Then he paused. "I must say, you're handling this awfully well."

"My uncles trained me," Bree explained.

"And where are they, exactly?"

"At the Visitor's Center," she replied. Cleverly. The man's eyes widened in alarm.

"You didn't...?"

"We didn't register," Bree assured him. Which seemed to reassure him quite a bit.

"Ah, good," he replied. "Stay here," he told them. "Herbert? Go get these ladies' buyer," he asked of one of a scrawny middle-aged man seated at the bar. Percy turned to his bouncer. "Do a sweep outside, will you?" he prompted. He gave Bree an apologetic smile. "Can't be too careful."

The bouncer left, and so did Herbert.

"Why don't you girls slip into something more comfortable?" Percy offered. He gestured at a door behind the bar. "There's a changing room down the hall and downstairs. Pick some good...ah, uniforms. Something *stimulating.*" He paused. "After you take a shower," he added a bit apologetically.

"Sure," Bree grumbled. She pulled Fury to the door, opening it and heading down a long hallway to another door at the end. This led down a stairwell to a long hallway with doors on either side. Bree opened the first one on the right; there was a bed there, and little else. The door on the left revealed the same. Eventually they made it to one of the last doors on the left, finding the bathroom with a shower. "Thank *god,*" Bree grumbled, starting to peel off her clothes. "I frickin' stink."

"Not me," Fury replied, eyeing Bree a bit bashfully. Bree frowned.

"How?" she asked.

"My Mommy bedazzled my stinky bits," Fury explained. "They can never stink again."

Bree stared at her in mid-undress.

"Go away," she grumbled. And so Fury did, reluctantly. Eventually Bree finished, and they found another room, this one like a walk-in-closet. Tons of glittering clothes hung there, along with shelves of underwear and stockings and all sorts of accessories.

Fury's eyes lit up and she rushed to these, pouring over the uniforms.

"Look at all these!" she exclaimed, picking up a glittering swimsuit. One that had been fashioned of surprisingly little fabric. "Ooo!"

"Just choose something," Bree grumbled, looking through the clothes herself. Apparently she wasn't much for fashion, because she clearly wasn't enjoying herself. Unlike Fury, who studied each uniform with fascination. For while she had an impressive array of clothes at home, she'd never seen – or worn – clothes like *these*.

"Ohmygod I just wanna wear them *all*," she gushed, pulling out a super-skimpy pink uniform.

"Idiot," Bree grumbled, picky a relatively plain purple outfit, a one-piece with a plunging neckline. She started undressing, and Fury turned around to give her some privacy, continuing to look through the marvelous clothes. At length she found something *super* spectacular: a rainbow-colored one-piece jumpsuit of sorts, with rather intriguing cut-outs. She got undressed, putting it on. It was, she found, a perfect fit. And what's more, it was, stylistically speaking, a perfect fit for her personality.

"Ta-da!" she exclaimed, turning around to show Bree. Bree eyed her with grudging approval.

"That actually looks good on you," she conceded.

"I know, right?"

"But you *do* know it's a little see-through, right?" Bree pressed. Fury frowned, realizing that it was. She shrugged.

"That's okay," she replied. "I like it anyway."

"Everyone's gonna like it," Bree warned.

"I know, right?"

"That's not a good thing," Bree stated exasperatedly. "But don't take it off," she added hastily. "We need to make the buyer think we're all-in." She paused. "And then strike before *they're* all-in."

"Huh?"

"Accessories," Bree prompted. Fury smiled, happy to accessorize. A few rainbow bracelets and anklets later, and her outfit was complete. "Alright," Bree stated. "We need a plan."

"I thought you already had one," Fury stated.

"My plan was to get here, then figure out who the buyer was," Bree replied. "When we do, you do your thing."

"My thing?"

"The whole 'glowing eyes and meat cleavers' thing."

"Oh." Fury frowned. "But I don't know how."

"Better figure it out," Bree shot back. "Or we're screwed." She paused. "Like, literally."

Just then, they heard a knocking on the door at the other end of the hall.

"Coming!" Bree called out. "Get ready," she warned, striding toward the door. Fury followed behind, feeling anything *but* ready. And also feeling that this had been a horrible mistake. But momentum once again pulled her toward Bree, and their shared destiny. For there was no turning back now.

Bree opened the door, and they went upstairs, far too quickly for Fury's liking. They emerged into the bar, finding Percy waiting for them. As well as the various patrons at the bar. All eyes turned to them...and then widened. And then stared.

The assembled men made noises then. Noises that poorly socialized men made when those of the opposite sex wore revealing outfits. Unsexy noises. *Creepy* noises. Utterances that guaranteed that said men would never get what they so obviously desired, akin to trying to catch fish by using one's stool as bait. Indeed, it was likely that such men would then blame the fish for not biting in lieu of blaming their choice of lure.

"Oh *my*," Percy murmured, getting two eyefuls. "I daresay your buyer is going to be *quite* pleased."

"Great," Bree grumbled, clearly uncomfortable with the assembled men's attention. "Where is he?"

"He?" Percy replied.

The door to The Moist Cookie burst open then, and the scrawny gentleman Herbert returned. Followed by an elderly woman, tall and slender, with short, wavy silver hair. A very distinguished-looking lady, dressed in a very distinguished-looking black dress. Her silver eyes noticed Fury and Bree, and she eyed them for a long moment, standing just beyond the doorway.

"I ordered one," she stated in a crisp, no-nonsense voice.

"They came as a pair," Percy replied, a bit apologetically.

"Hmm," the woman murmured. "Which one is the original?"

"Me," Bree answered. But the woman's eyes dismissed her, focusing on Fury.

"You've been upstaged," she stated, to Bree's obvious irritation. "What is your name, girl?" she asked.

"Fury," Fury replied. Honestly.

"A hothead, then?" the woman inquired.

"Um…not really," Fury admitted.

"Definitely not," Bree agreed. "Unless you fuck with her," she added.

"I won't be the one fucking with her," the woman stated. "I trust you'll behave?" she asked, clearly not trusting her to do so at all.

"I'm a good girl," Fury answered. Which was pretty darn true.

"Good," the woman replied. "My name is Gertrude Silverette," she introduced. "But you can call me 'Madame Silver.'"

"Yes Madame Silver," Bree replied.

"Yes Madame Silver," Fury copied.

"Have you any experience in your future profession?" Madame Silver inquired. Bree glanced at Fury, who shook her head.

"My only work experience is at a magic shop," Fury admitted.

"I see," Madame Silver replied. "Well I daresay you'll be making magic of a kind for my customers."

"Aren't we a little young?" Bree asked, brazenly. Madame Silver eyed her.

"Your paperwork will say you're dead," she replied. Fury blinked.

"What paperwork?"

"The official, very *legal* paperwork I'll draft for you," Madame Silver answered. "Dead girls have no rights," she added. "Keep that in mind."

Fury stared at her, then stole Bree a sidelong glance.

"Come," Madame Silver prompted, leading the way toward the door to downstairs. Fury glanced at Bree, who gestured for her to follow, and the three went downstairs to the hallway they'd been in before. Madame Silver led them to the first bedroom. "This is your office," she declared, gesturing at the bed. "I expect you to keep it tidy."

"Okay…" Bree replied. And then paused, giving Madame Silver a funny look.

"What?" the woman asked.

"It's just…I wasn't expecting you to be a woman," Bree admitted.

"Yeah, we thought you'd be like, a creepy old guy or something," Fury piped in.

"In my experience, men aren't cut out for this sort of work," Madame Silver replied. "It's like having an alcoholic run a bar."

"Why do you do it?" Bree asked. "Selling underage girls," she added, as if the woman needed clarification.

"I give an income stream – and thus a future – to girls society leaves behind."

"Oh, so you're doing us a *favor* now," Bree grumbled.

"I am," Madame Silver replied evenly. "Economies are based on goods and services, and you are merely entering into an apprenticeship for the oldest service industry in human society."

"So this isn't wrong at all," Bree concluded, crossing her arms over her chest. While looking remarkably unimpressed.

"It's as right or wrong as you think it is," Madame Silver replied. "Bartenders serve liquid poison to people, knowing full-well it's destroying their lives and marriages. Blacksmiths forge swords knowing they'll be used to maim and kill. Prostitutes have relations with married men, knowing they're helping break the sacred bonds of trust between husband and wife. All," she added with an arch of a silver eyebrow, "…for a little coin."

"Great, so that makes it okay," Bree shot back.

"Being mouthy won't work in your favor," Madame Silver warned. "I have no patience for difficult girls."

"Oh yeah?" Bree asked. "And what happens to 'difficult girls?'" Madame Silver eyed her coolly.

"They quickly learn the error of their ways," she replied. Her lips curled into a smirk. "The…*hard* way," she added.

"What's the hard way?" Fury pressed, too curious *not* to ask.

"Letting one of my…rougher customers teach you a lesson," Madame Silver answered.

"Like a mean teacher at school?" Fury asked. Innocently.

"You're sick," Bree snapped at Madame Silver. Which wasn't true at all, because the woman – despite her age – looked quite healthy to Fury.

"Your uncles insisted you were on board with this," Madame Silver replied, crossing her arms over her chest.

"Yeah, well we're not," Bree shot back. "We can't let you take advantage of us…or any girls like us."

"Take advantage?" Madame Silver inquired with an arch of her eyebrow. "I pay my girls the highest rate in Tabula."

125

"They're underage," Bree shot back.

"They're precocious," Madame Silver countered.

"They're precious," Bree argued. "And they're not mature enough to make decisions like this on their own."

"That's a rather mature thing for an underage girl to say," Madame Silver pointed out. Bree grimaced.

"You're a sleazy hag trying to pretend you're doing these girls a favor," she snapped. Madame Silver's eyes went cold.

"It looks like you're going to have to learn some manners, girl," she replied icily. "The *hard* way."

"Not gonna happen," Bree declared. "Fury, do your thing!"

Fury blinked, then pointed to herself.

"Me?"

"Yes you!" Bree snapped. "Do the glowing-eyes thing!"

"Um...you mean attack her?" Fury pressed.

"Yes!"

"But...she hasn't hurt us," Fury pointed out.

"Percy!" Madame Silver called out, clearly not concerned in the least. Mostly because Bree and Fury were both dressed in miniscule clothing that, being a bit see-through, made it clear they held no weapons of any kind.

"She's a madame buying underage girls into prostitution!" Bree snapped at Fury. "Take her out before she hurts more girls like us!"

Fury just stood there, eyeing Madame Silver. She raised a hand as if to slap the woman, then lowered it.

"I can't," she stated. Bree stared at her, then pulled at her own hair, then swore to herself.

"Fine!" she snapped. "I'll do it!"

And then lunged at Madame Silver, shoving her onto her back on the bed.

"Get her!" Bree yelled, leaping atop the woman and punching her right in the goddamn face. Over and over again. Blood spurted from Madame Silver's nose, coating Bree's fists and flying all over the place, splattering Fury in the face.

"Pthhbpth!" Fury spat as some got in her mouth. "Yeccch," she complained, wiping her lips with the back of her hand. She felt a tingling on her skin there, and glanced down at the back of her hand...

...and saw the red circle tattooed upon it start to glow with an eerie crimson light.

"What...?" she blurted out...and then saw the blood smeared on said circle suck into it, vanishing from sight. "Oh," she murmured, feeling a strange warmth spread up her hand and forearm, then to the rest of her body. Warmth that grew hot, and then burned...*oh* so pleasantly.

"Ohhh," she moaned, a vision of the stone dragon coming to her, eyes glowing with a blood-red light. "Ohh *yeah.*"

Surrender to me, Proeliator.

And given that at least in this case, surrendering promised to be *extremely* pleasant for her, that's precisely what Fury did. And the moment she did so, hollow dragon-fang shafts shot out of her palms, blood forming and crystalizing into crimson meat cleaver blades.

She realized that Bree had stopped punching Madame Silver, and had in fact backed away quite a bit, eyes wide with terror. All while Madame Silver lay on the bed, staring up at Fury with a bloodied, shocked-looking face.

"What in the bloody hell...!" the woman blurted out. Fury's lips curled into a grin.

"Mama's *thirsty*," she purred.

And then she had a drink.

Chapter 20

While the journey to Old Langsroth had taken days for Pravus and Templeton to complete on horseback, their journey via fire dragon took mere hours to complete. Such that they found themselves landing on the now-dry, flat land of the Great Flat. After dismounting, the fire dragon curled up and got comfy, leaving the two men to their adventure. Ahead, the great wall of Old Langsroth stood, just as it had six years ago, the only way through it into the city a closed portcullis. Just before the wall were the ruins of a settlement, no longer submerged in water.

"Look at all those bones," Templeton stated, eyeing said ruins with wonder. For there were heaps of bones littering the ground, most clustered near the wall. Human bones, naturally.

"Bodies finally allowed to rest in peace," Pravus replied.

"A great gift, that," Templeton mused.

"Death?" Pravus inquired.

"The peace that comes with it," Templeton clarified. "A final letting go of all roles, and the responsibilities that come with them."

"Hmm," Pravus murmured, rubbing his chin. For he couldn't very well deny his cousin's logic. Death was, however, the letting go of all joys as well, so on balance, it was a bit of a wash. Neither bad nor good, or rather, the *end* of bad and good...and all other dichotomies. Something he wasn't prepared to do, as the good still outweighed the bad, at least for him. But one day, the balance was bound to shift, as it had for his poor father. For, with the potions of youth having lost their effect over the centuries, old King Pravus the Seventh had succumbed to a particularly deplorable dementia, transforming into a vile, hurtful codger that frankly, everyone had been relieved to bury. Pravus could only hope he had the presence of mind to end his life before becoming so great a burden, instead of hanging on with a grip so strong it strangled his loved ones.

"Shall we?" Templeton inquired, arching an eyebrow whilst gesturing at the wall ahead. Pravus smiled.

"We shall!" he replied, and set forth at once toward Old Langsroth. It didn't take long at all to arrive at the familiar portcullis, which Templeton asked to lift. For the man hadn't been able to lift it before, and clearly looked forward to the prospect of a second attempt.

"Hrrngghh!" Templeton groaned as he gripped the bottom of the portcullis, lifting with perfect deadlift form. His veins bulged deliciously as he struggled, the portcullis screeching in protest.

"Go into the pain, Templeton!" Pravus cried from right behind his cousin, in the spirit of support. All while committing the scene to memory, to support an altogether different future activity.

Templeton did just that, and to Pravus's delight, this time the man managed to lift it all the way to chest-height. After which he shifted his grip one hand at a time, then transitioned into a military press. He managed to bring the weight a few inches upward…and then his arms and legs began to shake.

"I have you, cousin!" Pravus cried, stepping in and pressing up with him, but only with the slightest of force. Thus Templeton's impossible task was rendered possible, and he struggled against the still-enormous resistance to complete it.

"Ha!" Templeton cried, not in triumph over another, but over himself. They passed through the portcullis, and Templeton stacked stones to prop it open, after which Pravus let it down gently. "Thank you cousin," Templeton added, wiping sweat from his brow.

"Thank you for the opportunity to help," Pravus replied. Still, Templeton's thanks inspired the kind of elation that only gratitude could bring, and why, he found himself practically beaming with joy. For the first time in quite a while, in fact. For the problems in his life had gotten so heavy that they'd proven impossible to lift. Now that he had temporarily cast that burden aside, he could enjoy a challenge of a more manageable size.

"Ready for adventure?" Templeton inquired, gesturing down the tunnel.

"To Old Langsroth!" Pravus cried with gusto. And with that, the two men strode through the tunnel in the wall, ready to enter the once-doomed city, and to meet whatever resistance its dangers offered. For while said resistance might prove too much for one of them to bear, together it was a weight that might just be hefted!

Chapter 21

Fury stood triumphantly over Madame Silver, who lay sprawled out on the thoroughly mangled mattress of the basement room's bed. Twin streams of blood flowed from the older lady, flying through the air to suck into the hollow handles of Fury's meat cleavers. A rather large amount of blood, which Madame Silver had generously donated. Involuntarily, but still. It wasn't long before the woman didn't have anything more to give, and was very, *very* dead. And what's more, had gone to pieces quite literally in the end.

"Thank you for your donation," Fury purred.

A man burst through the doorway into the room, and Fury whirled around, seeing Percy standing there.

"I heard shout…" he began, the words dying in his throat. "Oh," he blurted out, staring at the horrid, bloodless scene of Madame Silver's body-parts strewn across the bed. "Shit."

"Hi," Fury greeted.

"Um," he replied, taking a step back.

"Aww, don't go," Fury protested. While chucking one cleaver at his shoulder. It slammed into his flesh, throwing him back into the wall…and pinned him there.

Percy *shrieked*.

"Fill me *up* big boy," she prompted, sauntering up to him. He stopped in mid-shriek, looking awfully confused. She swung her other meat cleaver at his neck, which turned out to be more efficient than she would've preferred. Still, the rapid jets of blood that magically flowed from his carotids and jugulars made up for this fact, filling her cleavers to the very brim.

At length, when the man's blood had left him for good, he hung there against the wall, still pinned by her other cleaver. She yanked it out, letting him fall to the floor with a satisfying *whump*.

With no one else to murder, Fury felt her fury fading. She instantly missed it, desperately trying to hold on to the heady rush. But instead, her meat cleaver blades re-liquified, sucking back into her bone-handles, and those handles began plunging back into the glowing circles in her palms. They pulsed as they did so, releasing their blood into her veins. A far greater volume than the first time it'd happened to her, she soon discovered.

A warm, pulsing feeling rushed up her arms and spread across her body, followed by a pleasure beyond anything she'd ever experienced. Ecstasy beyond description, far stronger than it'd been the first time, experienced by every last inch of her.

"Ohhhh*ngggghhhh*," she moaned, her eyes rolling into the back of her head. Her legs wobbled, and she fell onto her hands and knees on the floor, trembling uncontrollably.

"Fury!" Bree gasped. "Are you okay?"

"Nghhh!" Fury gasped, flash-sweating. Nearly a minute passed, and the feeling finally faded, which was both a relief and a goddamn shame. She collected herself, then rose unsteadily to her feet, feeling lightheaded, but incredibly good. Like, *incredibly* good, as if she'd had a great meal, a great sleep, and everything was just…great. "Wow," she breathed.

"Damn," Bree murmured, staring at the bodies of Percy and Madame Silver. "Well that worked."

Fury blinked, then took in the scene before her. One of unimaginable horror and brutality, though not a speck of blood remained. She put a hand to her mouth, feeling incredibly *un*-good. And then turned away from the sight, bending over to puke her brains out.

"Okay," Bree soothed when she was done, patting her back. "Let's go."

She led Fury out of the room, closing the door behind them, then went down the hall where they'd left their clothes. Bree took off her outfit, putting her normal clothes back on, while Fury just put her clothes over her outfit numbly. Then Bree led her up the stairs to the bar, and they straight-up walked right out of it. The big bouncer eyed them as they did so.

"Where's Percy?" he asked.

"With Madame Silver," Bree answered. The bouncer's eyes twinkled.

"*Oh*," he replied.

"Better leave them be," Bree warned. "They said they were gonna be a while."

And with that, they left The Moist Cookie behind. And with the violence they'd wrought within its walls, it would never be the same. For as fate would have it, the Moist Cookie ended up being quite a bit bloodier after they came.

* * *

Committing a double-homicide, it turned out, had a strange effect on Fury's psyche. On the one hand, it didn't seem real, and a part of her firmly believed that it hadn't actually happened at all. A second part of her blamed the whole thing on being possessed by an evil, demonic dragon-thing, which nicely avoided any and all culpability for having committed murder. But a third part of her was absolutely convinced that *she* was responsible for what she'd done, and what's more, that she very much deserved to be punished for it.

"I'm turning myself in," she insisted for the third time, as they neared the city exit.

"You're really not," Bree replied, gripping her by the upper arm and walking beside her.

"I have to," Fury insisted, setting her jaw firmly. She eyed the guards guarding the exit, determined to confess to her crimes. For despite her being of three minds about her crimes, the guilty mind was by far the most influential. For guilt was one's conscience pointing out that you'd done something against the nature of your true self, and there was no escaping it. There was no end to the creative ways in which people attempted to flee their consciences, engaging in vices and distractions of every kind, or convoluted rationalizations invented by one's logical mind. But in the end, such attempts were always – *always* – in vain. For the conscience was the wisest and surest part of oneself, and the only way to silence it was to act according to its prescriptions.

"You do, you'll get us *both* arrested," Bree hissed, gripping Fury's arm a bit harder. "Shut up and walk."

"But…"

"Aren't you supposed to save the world?" Bree interrupted. "How're you gonna do that from prison?"

Fury paused, finding that she didn't have an answer.

"That's right," Bree stated triumphantly, clearly sensing her success. And also the fact that, while they'd been talking, they'd passed out of the arched exit. Bree forced Fury down the wide path leading down Tabula's mesa, and Fury gave up on her quest to confess, her shoulders slumping in surrender. They reached the bottom of the path, nearing the guards there. They turned to look at Fury, and she felt a pang of terror.

They know!

"Leaving so soon?" one of them asked.

"Um!" Fury began. Bree elbowed her, smiling sweetly at the guard.

"We stocked up on supplies," she replied.

"Well have fun," the guard told them. "And be careful," he warned. "The world isn't a safe place for girls like you two."

"We'll be careful, thanks!" Bree replied cheerfully. Which was quite out of character for her. Still, the act was sufficient to let them pass without incident, and they soon left Tabula far behind. Going southwest, Fury noted glumly. For now that she wasn't so afraid of getting caught, she'd turned to beating herself up.

"I can't believe I did that," she muttered, tears welling up in her eyes.

"You did good," Bree replied.

"Good?" Fury blurted out incredulously. "I *killed* people!"

"Just like we planned," Bree pointed out.

"I didn't plan on killing them!"

"Um, you came with me and I told you I wanted you to do the glowing-eyes thing," Bree reminded her.

"Yeah, but I didn't think I'd *kill* them," Fury insisted.

"How else were we going to stop them?" Bree asked. "By talking to them?"

"Well…yeah."

"Pfft," Bree scoffed, shooting her a glare. "No way that would've worked. And even if you tried reporting them to the authorities," she added before Fury could take this tack, "…chances are the authorities are some of their best customers."

"No," Fury protested.

"Yes," Bree retorted. Convincingly. "And even if the authorities eventually *did* do something, it'd be like, *years* from now, and chances are Percy and Madame Silver would've just skipped town and gone somewhere else to do the same thing."

"You don't know that," Fury argued.

"I do," Bree shot back. "People don't change, Fury."

Fury blinked.

"What do you mean?" she asked.

"People don't change," Bree repeated.

"Yeah-huh," Fury shot back. Which was terrible reasoning, but all she could come up with at the moment. And to be fair, it was *most* people's reasoning for their beliefs. Few ever really thought very hard about what they believed, because to do so was to threaten those beliefs with alternative points of view. Thus, the majority of people played it safe, choosing what seemed right – which meant following the crowd – and then never giving it a second thought. "They can too," Fury added. Because it seemed true.

"Maybe they can, but they don't," Bree stated. "The majority of them, anyway. People are what they are, and that's that. It's a good thing sometimes," she added. Fury furrowed her brow.

"How?"

"Well, you just killed two people, and you're still you," Bree pointed out. Fury grimaced.

"Ugh, you *had* to remind me."

"See?" Bree pressed. "You're still the same girl I met yesterday."

"Am I?"

"Yep," Bree confirmed. "That glowy-eyed chick isn't who you are now...because now you wouldn't hurt a fly."

"I mean unless it was an accident," Fury conceded. For she'd stepped on a few flies in her life, to her chagrin at the time. Still, the possibility that Bree's argument might be right made her give a little smile.

"There she is," Bree replied, smiling back. "You feel bad now, but one day you'll realize you saved a whole lot of girls from being manipulated and used by those predators."

"I mean *maybe*," Fury mumbled, lowering her gaze.

"Hey, I don't know what the whole 'bloodthirsty psycho bitch' thing you do is all about," Bree stated, putting a hand on Fury's upper back. "But I'm damn sure it's magic...and that it's what Imperius sent you to get."

Fury nodded, having to concede that once again, Bree was right. For it'd been none other than Imperius that'd charged her with finding the fabled land of Ferra Linn...and she'd found it, and the stone dragon therein. Whatever being the Proeliator of that dragon meant, well, it had to be part of her quest. So it really wasn't her fault she'd gotten mixed up in all of this, considering she never would've done so if it hadn't been for Imperius.

And such was the power of having someone else to blame – or at least, not being *entirely* to blame for her acts – that Fury found herself feeling quite a bit better.

"Thanks Bree," she stated, grabbing Bree's hand and giving it a squeeze.

"You're welcome," Bree replied, reluctantly accepting this.

The two continued walking, hand-in-hand, making their way southwest toward the legendary city of Belfast. And while Fury's heart was still heavy after the heinous acts she'd committed, the fact that Bree still liked her gave her hope. That one day, she'd be able to forgive herself, and thus *feel* like herself once more.

Chapter 22

By the time the sun set over the horizon, Fury and Bree had left Tabula far behind. They decided to make camp at a fortuitous clearing in the woods far southwest of Tabula, gathering dry sticks for a campfire. Something that Fury didn't know how to light, but Bree did, using two sticks and a fair amount of friction. That done, they sat side-by side near the warm, flickering flames. Fury found herself thinking back to the events of the day. Particularly how she'd dismembered Madame Silver and Percy. And *enjoyed* it, at least in the moment.

"You okay?" Bree asked, clearly sensing Fury's glum mood.

"No," Fury answered. Bree put a hand on her shoulder.

"You did the right thing," she insisted, for the umpteenth time that day.

"It doesn't *feel* right," Fury replied.

Bree paused, lowering her head in thought. Then she turned to Fury.

"How many bad people have you met in your life?" she asked. "Before meeting me, I mean."

Fury paused.

"Well, none, actually," she confessed.

"Right," Bree replied. "So you never learned that bad people existed."

"Mommy and Daddy told me," Fury argued. "They had to fight all sorts of bad people, actually."

"Yeah, but you never *met* anyone bad," Bree retorted. "So you never knew what they were like."

"They're not *bad*," Fury countered. "They're people like you and me, just...confused. Or misunderstood."

Bree paused again.

"You know that feeling you have now?" she asked. "Feeling guilty because you thought you did something wrong?"

"I *did* do something wrong."

"Well some people don't get that feeling," Bree continued, ignoring her. "Some people are born without a conscience, Fury. It isn't their fault," she added hastily. "But when they do something that would make us feel bad if we did it...well, they don't get that feeling. They *can't*. And that means they do whatever they want without the...without the *good* that's in the rest of us telling them it's wrong. And when other people tell them it's wrong, they don't understand, because feeling guilty is foreign to them."

"I don't know," Fury mumbled.

"Well I do," Bree retorted. "My older uncle was one of them."

"But both your uncles were going to sell you," Fury pointed out.

"Yeah, but Uncle...the younger one just went along with it," Bree countered. "A lot of people without a conscience are dumb, just like a lot of regular people are. But some are really smart...and charming. They learn how to fake being like everyone else. They manipulate people like my younger uncle. And...me," she added, lowering her gaze to her lap.

Fury paused.

"Do you think Madame Silver was like your uncle?" she asked.

"I do," Bree replied. "Nothing we could've said would've stopped her. The only way to stop people like that is to convince them it's in their best interest to do good, or imprison them. Or kill them."

Fury considered this. She'd never imagined that such people could exist, people who didn't know right from wrong. Or rather, didn't *feel* right from wrong. For it was the feeling that was far more important. A person's conscience was perhaps the most powerful part of their psyche, a tireless advocate for doing right by others. It was like another person, really. A best friend that quietly guided you to consider others when acting. A friend whose main way of communicating was guilt.

Without that feeling, what would Fury have done throughout her life? Without guilt, why, she would be capable of doing anything she wanted...without any emotional consequences whatsoever.

"But if they're born that way, do they really deserve to die?" Fury asked. It seemed horrible that someone should be born so broken. It wasn't their fault, after all.

"If they're going to keep hurting others, they need to be stopped," Bree answered. "And we have to stop them any way we can."

"By doing the wrong thing?" Fury pressed.

"Killing people isn't always wrong," Bree replied.

"It *feels* wrong," Fury shot back. "And if it feels wrong, that means my conscience thinks it is."

Bree grimaced, but held her ground.

"Did your...alter ego think it was wrong?" she inquired. This time, it was Fury's turn to grimace. She lowered her gaze. The answer was obvious, of course. She hadn't thought it was wrong at all. In fact, not only had she thought it was right, but it'd *felt* right.

No, it'd felt *incredible*.

"Well, she's bad," Fury reasoned.

"And you're good," Bree pointed out, clearly sensing an angle. "So she really isn't you, is she?"

Fury frowned. It was true, she realized. The homicidal blood-sucking murderous bitch within her wasn't like her at all. It was as if there was another person inside of her, who sometimes came out to play. By chopping people into pieces and sucking their blood into her veins, but still.

"I guess you're right," she decided.

"So if she isn't you, then you're not to blame," Bree concluded, smiling triumphantly. Fury hesitated, then smiled back.

"Yeah," she agreed, feeling suddenly much better. "Yeah!" she repeated, with feeling. And in feeling that it was true, she found herself...well, herself again. For knowing everything was okay wasn't terribly convincing, but *feeling* it was utterly so. In feeling that she hadn't done anything wrong, she could finally let her guilt go. "Thanks Bree," she stated, wrapping an arm around the girl's shoulders and giving her a squeeze. Bree stiffened, pulling away, which made Fury frown. "What's wrong?" she asked.

"Nothing," Bree grumbled. "It's just...I don't like to be touched too much."

Fury blinked.

"What? Why not?" she asked.

"I just don't," Bree replied with a shrug.

"Huh," Fury mumbled, taking a moment to process this. "Well, I do," she stated.

"Yeah, I kinda figured that out," Bree grumbled. "Thank you, by the way," she added. "For coming to Tabula with me."

"Well you're my friend," Fury declared. "And friends do stuff for each other, because they care."

Bree paused, eyeing her. To the point where Fury frowned.

"What?" she asked.

"Nothing," Bree replied automatically. "I mean, it's just...I haven't had many people tell me they were my friend."

"Why not?" Fury asked. Bree shrugged, lowering her gaze to the fire.

"I guess I'm hard to get along with," she admitted. "I rub people the wrong way."

"Well you rub me the right way," Fury stated resolutely. Bree lifted her gaze to arch an eyebrow at her. "And I think you're easy, not hard."

"To get along with," Bree added on to this statement.

"Right," Fury confirmed with a big ol' smile. "So like, wanna be my bestie?"

"What?"

"My best-est girlfriend in the whole wide world," Fury translated. "My Mommy's bestie is a zombie wizard," she explained. "You can be mine!"

"Your mom's...what?" Bree blurted out.

"Do you wanna be my bestie or not?" Fury stated, putting her hands on her hips. Bree paused, then shrugged.

"Sure I guess," she replied. "Why not?"

"Yay!" Fury exclaimed, twisting around to give Bree a hug. Bree jerked away. "Oh," Fury mumbled, taken aback. "Um, can I hug you?"

"No," Bree replied. "Not much of a hugger."

"But...hugs are the *best*," Fury pressed, unable to stop herself from this protest. "Try it," she pleaded.

Bree paused, then did so, reluctantly.

"See?" Fury asked. "Isn't this nice?"

"I guess," Bree grumbled.

"You *like* it," Fury insisted. Because saying it made it so. But Bree refused to succumb to this infallible logic, continuing to be all tense. "Relax," Fury soothed, petting Bree's back.

"All right, enough," Bree snapped, extracting herself from Fury's love. Fury pouted.

"Aww."

"Look, if we're going to be besties, we gotta lay some ground rules," Bree declared, standing up and crossing her arms over her chest.

"Rules?" Fury asked. For the idea seemed silly. Besties just *were*, knowing each other so well that it all worked out. Without any effort at all, because relationships were supposed to be...well, effortless. Like Mommy and Daddy's marriage, which didn't require any work for them, and probably never had.

"If I want a hug, I'll hug you," Bree stated.

"But if *I* want a hug, I can't hug you?" Fury asked. Which seemed awfully one-sided. Bree grimaced.

"You can ask," Bree compromised. Fury considered this for two microseconds.

"That's fucking stupid," she replied. And then gasped, covering her mouth with her hand. "Shit! I mean, sorry!"

Bree just stared at her, clearly taken aback.

"What I meant to say was that having to ask for love and affection isn't good," Fury explained. "We should want to do it, and do it."

"I *should* want to do it?" Bree inquired, raising her eyebrows.

"Well yeah," Fury replied, as if it were obvious. Because it was. "Everyone wants love and snuggles."

"Sometimes," Bree compromised.

"*All* the time," Fury corrected.

"Maybe you do," Bree stated. "But I don't."

"But that doesn't make any sense!" Fury protested, even stomping her foot.

"Did you want love and snuggles from Percy?" Bree inquired. Fury made a face.

"Ew, no."

"Exactly," Bree concluded, triumphantly.

"But he's a guy and we're girls."

"And?" Bree pressed.

"Girls don't wanna...you know," Fury said. And waggled her eyebrows like Daddy did to Mommy.

"Don't wanna what?"

"You know, sex each other," Fury added, when Bree just stared at her. Which the girl continued to do. "What?" Fury asked.

"You think girls don't want to...sex each other?"

"Well yeah," Fury replied. "Duh." For Bree had been quite specific when describing sex earlier, and it'd involved pee-pees.

140

Bree rubbed her face with her hands, then sighed.

"God, you're so *sheltered*," she complained. "It's like you grew up in a goddamn cave." She went to Fury's pack, taking out the sleeping bag and unrolling it on the ground a ways away from the fire. Fury frowned, putting her hands on her hips.

"Wait, girls boink each other too?" she asked. Bree gave her a look.

"Yes Fury," she replied. "Girls…boink each other."

"But you said…"

"Girls boink boys, girls boink girls, and boys boink boys," Bree declared exasperatedly, throwing up her hands. "We boink what we wanna boink, and that's that."

Furry blinked, lowering her hands to her sides.

"So like, how does it work?" she asked. But Bree ignored her, climbing into the sleeping bag.

"Goodnight Fury," she stated wearily.

"How does it work?" Fury pressed.

"Ask your parents," Bree grumbled. "They're the ones who should've told you. Like, five years ago."

Fury grimaced, her shoulders slumping. She got into the sleeping bag with Bree, this time as the big spoon, but hardly enjoyed it as much as the first time. For while Bree's outside was "hubba hubba *wowee*," her personality was anything but. Fury sighed.

"I guess I won't touch you, unless I ask you first and you agree," she decided.

"Great," Bree muttered. "Works for me." Which was the only person it really worked for. For Fury found herself frustrated by the fact that she couldn't really be spontaneously herself with Bree, because everything she liked, Bree seemed to get irritated by. But being besties meant putting in the work to *make* things work, and so that's what Fury would do.

"G'night bestie," she murmured.

"Night."

And with that, they went to sleep.

* * *

The next morning, Fury woke to find Bree already out of the sleeping bag, eating some rations from Fury's pack.

"Good morning, day!" Fury greeted, for it was as sunny as her disposition. Bree gave her a look.

"Really?"

"Who's a grumpy grump-kins," Fury cooed, giving her a pouty face. "This is your face," she added, pointing to her own. Bree rolled her eyes, turning around to pointedly ignore her. Fury got out of the sleeping bag, stretching, then reaching for her pack for the ol' choosing of the day's outfit. She rummaged around, then found a cute little orange shirt and pants. She took off her clothes, then realized she still had the rather scandalous outfit she'd gotten from The Moist Cookie underneath. Which was really awfully cute, if also awfully revealing. She took it off, stuffing it in the pack, then putting on her new outfit. Thusly dressed, she addressed her bestie. "How are you feeling?" she asked.

"I don't need you checking in on my feelings," Bree grumbled, still chewing on her breakfast. A piece of jerk chicken, which was appropriate, 'cause Bree was being a bit of a jerk herself. Fury decided to leave her alone, having dealt with this situation before. Both Daddy and Chaos were grumpy-kins when they were hungry, after all.

Fury focused on finding a bit of breakfast for herself instead, eating jerk without resorting to being one. When she was done, she eyed Bree, a bit apprehensively. But in lieu of asking her if she was ready to go, Fury decided to just assume it was so, slinging her pack onto her back and striding southwest. To her relief, Bree followed behind her. Wordlessly, which was probably for the best. Sticks and stones could break your bones, but words could break you emotionally.

Onward they went, Bree trudging while Fury stepped and skipped intermittently. And while Bree's sour mood and presence pressured Fury to suppress her usual happy vocalizations, Fury decided to be herself and vocalize anyway. She wasn't about to give up her ways just to please Bree, and certainly wouldn't expect Bree to do that either. For if everyone had to suppress who they were just to be around anyone else, why, everyone would die in a suppression-induced depression!

In this frame of mind, Fury enjoyed the land of Grissam, one that looked a bit different than that of the kingdom of Pravus. The rocks and soil had a reddish hue, and the grass was sparser, the trees not quite as lush. But on balance, the clash of blue sky on reddish land was beautiful, and thus satisfied her aesthetic appetite.

142

After many hours, they reached the tree line of a forest, one with towering evergreens that…well, towered over them. The forest floor was a bed of their dead needles, the scent of pine quite pleasing.

"Isn't this just *wonderful?*" Fury exclaimed as they continued into the forest.

"It's a bunch of trees," Bree replied.

And this was an exchange that revealed a surprising fact to Fury, one she'd never considered before. That one's relationship to reality could be far different than another's. For while a tree was just a tree, it was also a towering creature that'd once been a tiny seed, with massive roots plunging deep into the earth. Strong enough to hold up branches weighing hundreds if not thousands of pounds, sometimes straight sideways. It was a being clad in layers of tough bark-armor that could survive fires or lightning strikes, and that was itself a miniature world for all sorts of living things. It provided shade for plants that liked shade, its branches and leaves buffering wildlife from the wind. And when rain fell upon it, it directed water in a steady drizzle to the land below, giving the soil time to absorb it.

In short, a tree was a miracle, with mysteries yet to be revealed. But it was also just a tree…if a person wanted it to be. To see it that way was to ignore most of its properties, or to take it for granted. It was to reduce the tree to a word instead of seeing it for what it was.

And that was the difference between a girl like Fury and a girl like Bree…that the latter reduced reality. To reduce was to make something smaller than it was, and there was perhaps no better tool for accomplishing this purpose than words.

Reality was magical, but in being reduced, it was merely mechanical.

"You got quiet," Bree noted, eyeing Fury.

"Thinking deep thoughts," Fury replied.

"Yeah right," Bree muttered, almost too quietly to hear. Fury ignored her, continuing to enjoy the forest for what it was.

After another few hours, they came upon a campfire that – though they had no way of knowing it – Chaos had…ah, come upon not so long ago. Soon after *that*, they spotted the end of the forest, beyond which was more rocky grassland. The ground sloped upward gently as they continued, leading up a rather large hill. Fury's legs burned rather pleasantly as they trekked, and she picked up the pace just to enjoy the challenge it brought. Bree, in contrast, slowed down considerably, looking miserable. As usual.

"Almost there!" Fury exclaimed.

"Yay," Bree replied, unconvincingly.

It wasn't long before they did reach the top of the hill, Fury doing so long before Bree. The summit gave Fury a marvelous view, one that took her breath away. For the hill ended abruptly in a near-vertical drop to a great bit valley far, far below…and a few miles further, this valley dropped again into a massive canyon the likes of which she'd never seen. A canyon that had to be at least a mile wide, and thousands of feet deep. And one that seemed to break the earth in two, for the canyon went to the left and right for as far as Fury's eyes could see.

"Wo*wee*," she breathed, taking it all in.

Bree caught up with her, a bit out of breath, and stood at her side, looking below.

"There it is," she stated, pointing ahead. For there was a narrow rocky pass that went across the canyon, held up by three huge pillars of reddish rock. Or rather, the near and far sections of the passage were narrow. It flared out into a big flat circle above the middle of the canyon, one that rather ambitious people had built a walled-off city upon.

"Is that…?" Fury asked.

"Belfast," Bree confirmed. "See that?" she added, pointing across the canyon, to a large, misty-looking forest at the other end.

"The forest?"

"The *Dark* Forest," Bree corrected. Fury's eyes widened, her breath catching in her throat. For if that was the Dark Forest, then she'd nearly arrived at her destination…and her great adventure had nearly come to its end.

A fact that kinda bummed her out, for it hadn't been all that long of an adventure.

"Well shoot," she swore, stomping with one foot. Bree frowned.

"What?"

"It's just that…well, I was hoping it'd take more time," Fury explained. Bree looked at her as if she'd said something stupid.

"Why?"

"Adventures should take a while," Fury stated. "I was hoping it would be, like, *epic*."

144

"I just want to get it over with," Bree countered. It was Fury's turn to give Bree a look.

"Why?"

"So I get can back to my life," Bree explained. Fury furrowed her brow.

"But...this *is* your life," she protested, gesturing at the scenery before them. Which was objectively awesome, by the way. "Adventuring is the most living we'll ever do."

"We didn't adventure, we traveled," Bree retorted.

Fury gave her a funny look, for she realized that Bree just didn't understand. Or rather, that she didn't see it Fury's way.

"What?" Bree snipped.

"Nothing," Fury replied, turning to take in the sight of Belfast. A gosh-darned city built over a gosh-darned canyon, the last defense against a great zombie horde! One that'd risen quite unexpectedly from a dark, misty forest, one from which no man – or woman – had returned since the Dark Rising. "Goll-*y*," she breathed, feeling a chill run through her. Not of terror, but of awe.

"Let's go," Bree grumbled, turning left and continuing along the edge of the cliff. Fury tore her gaze from Belfast, following behind her grumpy friend. And in this way, they made their way closer to the end of Fury's quest.

Chapter 23

The aftermath of the siege on Belfast was the most depressing day of Chaos's life.

After spending that night beating back the last of the undead, the sun rose, heralding the end of the zombie assault. Belfastian soldiers set out with the grim task of throwing the bodies of their brethren into the canyon. Other than burning the bodies, it was the best way to ensure that their comrades were not added to the undead army. Looking down from the edge of the land bridge over the canyon, Chaos watched as the bodies fell into the abyss far below.

Most horrible of all was the knowledge that these bodies would eventually turn into undead, and rise every night at the bottom of the canyon. Just wandering about aimlessly, tens of thousands of men, doomed to go on and on. Many of the undead the Belfastian soldiers been forced to fight had been former friends. Looking into the eyes of the soldiers that night had been haunting, the damage done to their souls even more devastating than any wound could've been.

Chaos heard more than a few soldiers wondering if they'd be able to withstand another night like that. A thought he and Destiny shared.

Later that next morning, Destiny set out to heal the wounded, conserving Vita's magic for those who needed it the most. Chaos helped to repair the southern portcullis and the wall, using his Omen-63's magic to absorb all the debris and deposit it in convenient piles for the city's construction workers. A small army of soldiers set about to repair the barricades and the pendulum, like resetting a horrifying amusement park. Others dressed the wounds of the soldiers less seriously wounded, and comforted those who'd lost loved ones. It was monumentally depressing, a scene of unimaginable suffering. Both in body and in mind.

Chaos bore witness to it, absorbing that tragedy. And after years of looking forward to joining Destiny in war, it'd only taken a single day of battle to never want to see war again.

At noontime, Destiny returned to her home below the bell tower, and Chaos joined her for lunch. None of them said much as they ate what amounted to unseasoned gruel. When they were done, they both sat back, and Destiny eyed him critically. Or was maybe just looking at him…he couldn't be sure.

"What?" he inquired.

"You did good last night," she stated. And while Chaos would've normally taken this opportunity to make a glib quip, he didn't. Instead, he lowered his gaze to the tabletop.

"Doesn't feel good," he admitted.

"It isn't supposed to," she replied. "War is hell," she added. "A night like last night can torture you for a lifetime."

He lifted his gaze to hers.

"How do you do this?" he asked. "Day after day, for years?"

"Because if I don't, I'll have to live with my guilt for the rest of my life." She leaned over the table, grabbing his hand in her own. "Dying is the end of hell, not the beginning of it. And there's no greater hell than a life filled with regrets."

Chaos nodded silently, and she squeezed his hand.

"Life is as wonderful as it is terrible," she told him. "It's easy to forget the good when it's bad."

"Yeah, well I wish you could heal wounds to the mind instead of just the body," he mumbled. She arched an eyebrow.

Who says I can't?"

"Huh?"

Destiny stood from the table, pulling him bodily toward the bed. And it wasn't long before she showed him quite definitively that there was still good in the world…and that it was most definitely worth fighting for.

* * *

It was a bit past noon by the time Fury and Bree strode across the narrow land bridge crossing over the canyon, reaching the wall surrounding the city of Belfast at last. The entrance was a large portcullis, guarded by men in chainmail armor, identical in color to the rock of the canyon, and the wall behind them. Fury walked right up to the men, smiling and waving cheerfully.

147

"Hello!" she greeted, stopping a few yards away.

The guards eyed her and Bree with looks Fury couldn't quite read, then glanced at each other. And then eyed mostly Fury this time.

"Afternoon," one of the men greeted, with just exactly the gruff kind of tone she'd imagined a brave soldier would speak in. The kind of tone a man who'd seen war might use. A guy who'd *seen* some shit. "Who're you?"

"I'm Fury Little and this is Bree," Fury answered. "We came here to…" she glanced at Bree. "…to come here," she finished. Lamely.

"She was sent by Imperius Fanning to enter the Dark Forest and save the world," Bree corrected. The soldiers frowned, eyeing each other again, before eyeing Fury once again.

"You a wizard then?" one of the men asked.

"Um…yes," Fury replied. "I think," she added, with was honest, but also wishy-washy. It was honest to express doubt about one's own opinions, but the world at large largely saw this as weakness. For the masses, it was better to be sure and wrong than unsure and right, and to never change one's position on things. Largely because the masses were a bit simple, and thus easily managed by those who knew how simple minds worked.

"You think?" the man inquired.

"She's humble," Bree interjected. "I've seen her use magic twice myself."

"What's your power?" the guard asked.

"To turn into a killing machine," Bree answered before Fury could. "Believe me, you don't want to be there when she does it."

The guard eyed Bree, then Fury, clearly not believing either of them.

"Ooo wait," Fury blurted out. "Isn't Destiny here? She could vouch for me!"

He blinked.

"She is," the guard replied. Guardedly. "You know her?"

"Well *duh*," Fury stated. But the way she said it, it wasn't an insult. "She's dating my brother Chaos."

The man's eyes widened, and he glanced at his fellow guards, who smiled, nudging each other.

"We heard Chaos…*came* yesterday," the guard stated. The other guards sniggered. "He's with Destiny now."

"Wait, he's *here?*" Fury gasped. "Gasp!" For while she'd known that Chaos had left home to be with Destiny, she'd forgotten that Destiny had been in Belfast.

"That's right," the guard confirmed.

"Yay!" Fury exclaimed, turning and giving Bree an impromptu hug. Bree stiffened, clearly not comfortable with said affection, and gently but firmly pushed Fury away. "Ooo, let's go see them!" she added, hopping up and down excitedly.

"We'll have to confirm…" one of the other guards began, then stopped when all the other guards turned murderous glares on him.

"Hold on a sec ladies," the guard who was clearly in charge stated. He called out to the soldiers inside the wall, and they opened the portcullis post-haste. "Welcome to Belfast," he added, gesturing for them to go inside. "Please stay as long as you like."

"Thanks!" Fury replied, beaming a smile at him. Which made his cheeks flush, which was kinda adorbs, even if he was kinda not. Still, he smiled bashfully, and such was the power of smiles that it helped unattractive people a tad. Well, depending on how many teeth one had.

In any case, Fury curtsied, and then stepped through the gate and into the city, Bree following behind her. And the guards inside the gate all waved and said hello and smiled, and were just so gosh-darn *nice*, like all guys were. Except for Earl, the man in the village of Erp who'd been a bit rude during the battle over his bulge.

"Wow," Fury breathed as she took in the sights of Belfast. The city wasn't nearly as interesting aesthetically as Tabula, nor as well-kept as Southwick, but Fury could appreciate it for what it was: a city designed purely for defense, every tan stone building heavily fortified, every window barred, and with soldiers and weapons and such just…*everywhere*. It was a city that had survived six years of nightly sieges…and that success was in large part due to its design.

Functional could be beautiful, Fury knew. And by golly, Belfast was proof of that.

The soldiers of Belfast were all-too happy to be of help to Fury and Bree, directing them toward where they could find Destiny: in the tallest building of the city, which was a great big belltower in the center of the city. They went inside the building, taking the stairs all the way up to the apartment just below the big ol' bell. Fury reached the door, getting ready to knock…

…and then heard muting shouting from beyond it.

She frowned, pressing her ear against the door, and heard distressed-sounding cries from beyond.

"They're in trouble!" she cried, and turned the knob, shoving the door open and rushing inside.

And that, dear reader, was when Fury was suddenly subjected to a rather startling lesson on the facts of life. Taught to her by Destiny, which was fine, and her brother, which was not. For it became instantly clear that the two were not, in fact, under attack.

"Oh," Fury blurted out, putting a hand to her mouth. Whilst unable to tear her eyes away in time.

"Rrrrghhh!" Chaos groaned, in the very throes of involuntary ecstasy. "Ngghh...not *again!*"

And then, at least for Chaos, things came to a rather disappointing end.

Chapter 24

"Fury?!" Chaos blurted out, covering himself with Destiny's bedsheets. Destiny, on the other hand, didn't bother covering up, nor did she seem bothered, unlike Fury's brother. "What're you doing here?!"

"Um, hi?" Fury replied, blinking rapidly. "Um," she continued, then didn't know quite what else to say. "Whatcha doing?" was all she could come up with.

"Having sex," Destiny answered, to Chaos's obvious chagrin. His cheeks flushed furiously. "Hi Fury," she added, giving a little wave.

"Ohhhh," Fury replied, finally putting Bree's previous description and reality together. "I get it now!" she exclaimed, turning to smile at Bree. Who was standing behind her, doing her very best not to make eye contact. Or have her eyes make contact with any other part of Chaos and Destiny.

"Who's your friend?" Destiny asked.

"Um, this is Bree," Fury replied. "My bestie."

"Eh," Bree mumbled.

"Why'd you barge in here?" Chaos complained. "Knock next time."

"I heard shouting," Fury explained. "I thought you were being attacked or something."

"Just...uh...wrestling," Chaos stated, blushing again. Fury's eyes widened.

"Ohhh," she murmured. "Wait, *that's* what Daddy and Mommy do?" she gasped, putting it all together now. For they wrestled at least twice a day, with similar vocalizations, now that she thought about it.

"...yeah," Chaos replied. "Can you like, leave for a second while we get dressed?" he asked.

"Oh, sure!" Fury replied. And then promptly went outside with Bree. She closed the door, waiting for a bit, until the door opened and Destiny gestured for them to come back in. Chaos was seated at a small table, making minimal eye contact.

"Have a seat," Destiny offered, pulling up a few chairs. They all sat at the table, with only Destiny appearing unfazed by recent events. "Why the visit?" she asked Fury.

To make a long story short, Fury caught everyone up on the events that'd led to this moment, with Bree interjecting to add details from time to time. When the tale was told, Destiny leaned back in her chair, eyeing Fury with an expression Fury couldn't read.

"What?" she asked. "You're *super* pretty, by the way," she added before Destiny could reply. Because she totally was. Like, even prettier than a year ago.

"Thanks," Destiny replied. "You're not a wizard," she added. Fury blinked at this sudden change in topic.

"Huh?"

"She totally is," Bree countered, folding her arms over her chest. "I saw her magic myself."

"Not her magic," Destiny retorted. "She's like me."

Fury blinked.

"Huh?" she repeated. And while her mother had a tendency to say it innocently, for the purposes of avoiding culpability, Fury did it honestly.

"You're a...vassal," Destiny explained. "And a vessel for the power of your god."

"My...what?"

"Your god," Destiny repeated. "Mine is the goddess Vita, and yours must be this Ferra Lin."

"Okay, now *I'm* confused," Chaos interjected. "You're saying my sister's a paladin?"

"A paladin is a holy warrior," Destiny stated. "Ferra Lin called you his Proeliator. That's more of a...combatant."

"You're saying that dragon-statue was Ferra Lin?" Fury asked incredulously.

"That's right," Destiny confirmed. "And that underground temple was his land."

"The fabled land of Ferra Lin," Fury breathed, her eyes widening. "Ohmygod you're *right!*"

"But what's he the god of?" Chaos asked, clearly disturbed by the fact that his sister had become the bloodthirsty er, combatant of a dragon-god...thing.

"Well, I'm not sure," Destiny admitted. "Fury, you said that the dragon had three heads, with the river of blood going into one of them, coming out of another, and the third that spoke to you?"

"That's right," Fury confirmed.

"So Ferra Lin sustains a river of blood, which starts and ends with him," Destiny deduced, rubbing her chin. "And when you maim people, their blood goes into the handles of your weapons…and then into you."

"Right," Fury replied, impressed with Destiny's ability to bring it all together. "I'm impressed with your ability to bring it all together," she told the paladin, never one to hold back a compliment.

"Thanks," Destiny stated.

"So wait, what happens to you when you take all that blood inside of you?" Chaos asked. "Like, what are the effects?"

Fury paused.

"Um, well, it ah…" she began. And then stopped. "Huh?"

"I think Chaos is wondering what effect absorbing blood is having on you," Destiny clarified.

"Well, it um, feels…good," Fury answered. Destiny arched an eyebrow.

"Good?"

"She like, looks like she's having a *real* good time when it happens," Bree translated, giving Destiny a significant look. "Like when Chaos finished…ah, wrestling."

"I see," Destiny replied. "But how it *feels* doesn't give us much information on what it is *doing*. We need to figure that out if we're going to use your Proeliatorship to help defeat the evil in the Dark Wood."

"How do we do that?" Fury asked.

"First I'll ask Vita," Destiny answered. "But chances are she either won't know, or will want us to figure it out for ourselves. If that's the case, we'll need to run some experiments before tonight."

"Experiments?" Chaos asked.

"Let me consult with Vita," Destiny stated. "We'll go from there."

* * *

After consulting with Vita, Destiny informed everyone that the goddess had declined to provide an answer, as expected. Thus Destiny decided to run an experiment...which apparently involved leaving the belltower, and traveling across the city to the prison. The prison looked like any other building in Belfast, in that its windows were barred and such, but inside, Fury found a long hallway with cells on either side...almost all of which were filled with zombies.

"Graarrghh," they graarrghed in zombie unison as Destiny led them down said hallway, Fury, Chaos, and Bree following close behind.

"Aww," Fury cooed. "Reminds me of Zora. *Gosh* I miss her."

"Me too," Chaos confessed. While giving Destiny an apologetic look. For Destiny had made it clear that she didn't approve of the Little family harboring a zombie. So it was both fortunate and unfortunate that Zora had vanished from their home in Southwick six years ago, along with Epic, Zora's son.

"We'll pick this one," Destiny stated, stopping before a cell with a rather well-preserved looking zombie. Which was a lie, because *she* was the one who did the picking, not them. She inclined her head at a nearby guard. "Unlock the door," she ordered. And to Fury's surprise, the guard did. Fury swung the door open, gesturing for Fury to step inside. "Go on," she prompted.

"Go on and what?" Fury asked, staying right where she was.

"Kill that thing."

Fury glanced at the zombie – very un-fresh compared to Zora, who'd been perfectly preserved, if a bit drooly. This one was a man, quite nude, with saggy skin and a single yellow-brown snaggle-tooth.

"Ew," she said, making a face.

"It has blood in it," Destiny said.

"Like the Fallen Blood?" Chaos asked.

"That's right," Destiny confirmed. Chaos frowned.

"Won't that do something bad to Fury if she absorbs it into herself?"

"According to Vita, no," Destiny answered. "But even if it does, Vita's magic can dispel its effects." She gestured for Fury to go in again. All while the zombie just stood there, looking rather dazed.

"Why isn't it attacking?" Fury asked, staying right where she was.

"It's daytime," Destiny explained. "Most undead are lethargic when exposed to the sun." Which, Fury noted, was beaming in from a small, barred window at the rear of the cell.

"Not Zora," Fury pointed out.

"So I've been told," Destiny stated, glancing at Chaos. "She must have been an exception. Now quit stalling and fight it," she ordered, shoving Fury into the cell. And right into the zombie, grossly enough. While she managed to keep her balance, the zombie toppled over, landing on its back with a *thump*.

"Ugh," Fury complained, wiping invisible zombie-stain from her front.

"Go on, hit it," Destiny prompted, even pantomiming a swing of the ol' fist.

"You can do it," Chaos told her. Supportively.

"Fuck it up," Bree added. Sadistically.

Fury eyed the zombie, which just sort of laid there.

"I kinda feel bad for it," she admitted. "Poor zombie," she added. One with particularly poor dental care.

"Chaos, use your Omen-63," Destiny prompted. "Make it bleed."

"Yes ma'am," Chaos replied with a cheesy but adorable salute. And promptly took his shovel from his back, striding right into the cell and gently pushing Fury aside. He took a surprisingly violent swing of his shovel, the edge of it striking the zombie in the right upper arm...and taking it clean off, in a spray of blood. Or rather, not a spray, but a kind of gentle gurgle-vomiting of blood, for zombies' hearts did not beat.

"Urrghh," Fury blurted out, holding back some gurgling vomit of her own.

"All right," Bree stated. "Now you'll see it." And then waited. And *waited*.

"Nothing's happening," Fury pointed out, her hand still covering her mouth.

"I think you have to get it on you," Bree stated. "Those circles on your hands always start glowing when you do, and then you transform."

Fury eyed the maroon, gloppy blood oozing from the zombie's shoulder. And promptly didn't get it on her. Then, rather non-consensually, Chaos dipped a finger in the blood, then turned said finger on her.

"Ew!" she protested, putting up a hand to stop him…and he promptly slid his bloody finger across her palm.

The red circle on said palm began glowing bright red…and the blood sucked into it, making Fury feel some kinda way.

"Oh," she murmured, giving a little shudder. Goosebumps rose on her arms.

"Holy shit," Chaos blurted out, staring at her for some reason. "Her eyes!"

"Her hair," Destiny added.

"Mamma wants *more*," Fury purred, giving a lil' shiver.

And then her cleavers came out.

What happened then is best hinted at, for to describe it in exhaustive detail would turn too many stomachs. Suffice it to say that when Fury was done, the zombie's snaggle-tooth was the only way to identify it. When the last of its blood had sucked into the shafts of Fury's cleavers, said cleavers sank back into her palms. She moaned as the blood pumped into her veins, her eyes rolling back into her head.

"Oh," Chaos mumbled, averting his eyes and grimacing.

"Wow," Destiny murmured, doing the opposite.

"See?" Bree stated rather smugly, her hands on her hips. "Told you she goes crazy."

And with that, the experiment was a success.

* * *

Destiny decided to have everyone re-convene back at her apartment, and they all sat 'round her little table for a debriefing. Fury felt a bit embarrassed about having gleefully hacked a zombie into pieces and sucked out all its blood, particularly given how everyone had seen her reaction at the end.

"So blood activates your transformation into Ferra Lin's Proeliator," Destiny stated. "And your cleavers collect the blood you draw."

"And then that blood goes into you," Chaos added, grimacing at the memory.

"Question is, what does it do?" Destiny wondered, leaning back in her chair.

"What do you mean?" Fury asked.

"Vassals of gods have different ways of accessing their god's power," Destiny explained. "I do it through prayer. Yours has something to do with blood."

"Well, maybe her transformation *is* her power," Bree argued.

"Perhaps," Destiny replied. "But there might be more. Blood enters you, and you crave it...which means Ferra Lin craves it, and wants you to collect it."

"But why?" Fury asked, disturbed at the thought.

"I don't know," Destiny admitted. She leaned forward then, eyeing Fury. "Can you still feel the blood in you?"

Fury frowned, focusing inward. Then she shook her head.

"Not really."

"When I pray to Vita, I focus on the feeling of her warmth and love," Destiny stated. "Of her golden light bathing me. Her love is how I connect to her, and how she connects with me. As Ferra Lin's Proeliator, you should be able to connect with him."

"But how?" Fury asked.

"Close your eyes," Destiny instructed. "Try to focus on how the blood felt surging through your body...and try to visualize Ferra Lin."

Fury did so, shutting her eyes and scrunching her face, because face-scrunching was an essential part of concentrating. As well as a general stiffening of the body, to show that you were trying real hard.

"Relax," Destiny said. Fury cracked an eye open.

"But you said to focus," she pointed out.

"Focusing means narrowing your attention to one thing," Destiny countered. "And that means letting go of everything else."

"Okay," Fury replied, reasonably sure Destiny was wrong. But she closed her eye, giving it a shot, because there was nothing to lose in giving it a try. She forced herself to relax...or rather, relaxed herself by not forcing...and instead imagined herself standing in a great big underground chamber, facing the middle head of Ferra Lin. Those glowing red eyes seemed to stare into her soul, the sound of a river of blood rushing in and out of the dragon's other two heads.

And as she stared into those glowing eyes, she felt a rushing of blood within her, flowing into her heart and out of it in precisely the same way.

Something within her stirred...and when she opened her eyes, she saw that Destiny's apartment had disappeared. She found herself standing before the great stone dragon, in the chamber he resided in.

You learn quickly, my Proeliator, a deep voice boomed in her head.

"My name is Fury," Fury stated, not vocally, but with telepathy. For if she was going to be a god's vassal or vessel or whatever, it seemed only fair to be on a first-name basis. "What's yours?"

I am Ferra Lin, the dragon replied in her head.

"So like, what are you the god of?" Fury asked.

That will become apparent in due time.

She rolled her eyes.

"Just *tell* me already."

The blood you take flows within you, but at the same time, within me, he explained. *This is your Lifeblood.*

Fury frowned.

"Wait, how can it flow inside me and you at the same time?"

We are united, Ferra Lin explained. *I exist within you, as you exist within me.*

"Uh...okay," Fury replied. Though it didn't seem okay at all. "Did we connect when you penetrated me?"

Indeed, Ferra Lin replied. *The blood of your enemies is theirs...until it passes through you and is transformed. Bring it out of you to harness our true power.*

And with that, the image faded, and Fury found herself once again seated at Destiny's table. She blinked, realizing that everyone was staring at her.

"What?" she asked.

"You've been staring off into space for like, three minutes," Bree stated. "Didn't even blink." Which explained Fury's irritated eyes. She blinked, then rubbed them.

"What happened?" Destiny asked.

"Well, that dragon was definitely Ferra Lin," Fury answered. "And he said the blood I absorb is my true power."

"How so?" Chaos asked. Fury shrugged.

"Didn't get that far."

"Ah."

"But he did tell me to bring the blood back out of me, and that this was how I could use it somehow," she added. "I think," she added to this addition, less definitively, but more accurately.

"Bring it out of you, huh?" Bree stated. "How do you do that?"

"She already does it when she summons her cleavers," Chaos pointed out. "Blood comes out of their handles and forms the blades, then hardens." Which was true.

"Yeah, but I don't have to think about it," Fury countered. "It just happens."

"Maybe you can do other things with blood," Fury reasoned. "It's worth doing more experiments. Without having to hack apart zombies in the prison," she added when Fury's face fell.

"What're you thinking D?" Chaos inquired. Which was Destiny's nickname, apparently.

"Your hand-portals suck blood in, and this activates your...furious mode," Destiny explained. "Maybe you can activate that mode by trying to take blood *out* of them."

"Furious Fury," Chaos quipped.

"Shush," Destiny chided. "Give it a try, Fury."

"Now?" Fury asked. For it really didn't seem like the proper venue for transforming into a psycho homicidal bitch.

"Now," Destiny confirmed.

Fury sighed, then focused on doing just that. Which meant she nearly made another scrunched-up frowny-face, until she recalled Destiny's advice. So she relaxed instead, focusing on the circles on the backs of her hands. She felt the faint pulsing of her blood in her fingertips, and imagined that blood shooting out of her hand-circles.

But nothing happened.

"Well shoot," she complained.

"If something doesn't work, that doesn't mean give up," Destiny told her. "It means try something else."

"Oh," Fury replied. "Okay."

She closed her eyes, focusing inside once again. And instead of having an agenda, she merely paid attention to what was going on. And there was quite a bit of that, she realized rather quickly. Not only her thoughts, which came in a never-ending stream and mostly came to nothing, but all the stuff her body was doing. Like beating her heart and hearing stuff, and salivating and swallowing said saliva, and breathing and well, all sorts of things. Most of which she had absolutely no control over, and furthermore, didn't even realize was happening unless she attended to them.

It turned out that being alive was, by and large, automatic. A doing that did itself. Strange that she trusted her body implicitly to carry out this complex symphony of countless little activities, and

159

that it all worked so well. And yet, at the same time, that so many people worried incessantly about matters beyond their control, when their very existence proved that control was inferior to trust. And trust was surrendering to that which one could not control, which meant that anxiety was a lack of trust. In oneself to be able to handle whatever might happen, or in the universe that so often seemed against you.

Yet here she was, breathing air that was available in abundance, on a planet that held her firm to its bosom. Birthed from a mother that fate had provided, warmed by the sun, having been created and sustained by all of creation.

Surrender.

She did so, letting her mind go where it pleased. And it pleased her mind to picture the river of blood flowing in, then out of Ferra Lin. At the same time, she felt her heart *lub-dub* in her chest, and the corresponding pulse of blood in her fingers.

I exist within you, as you exist within me.

Three heads. One taking in, the other letting out, the third a sentient being.

In, out, mind.

When blood touched the red circles on her hands, it sucked in automatically. There was no need to think about it, to will it to happen. It was automatic, like her breathing. So…

"Wake up!" she heard Bree snap.

Fury jerked her head up from the table, blinking rapidly. She realized that everyone was looking at her…and that she'd drooled on the table.

"Oh," she blurted out. "I fell asleep?" Which was a dumb question, because she already knew the answer. She could've saved face by adding that it was a rhetorical question, had she cared about not seeming dumb.

"Great experiment," Bree groused. "Super effective."

"You must be tired," Destiny told Fury, ignoring Bree's negativity. Which seemed the best way of dealing with it, actually. "Your body is telling you to sleep…so sleep."

"But…" Fury began.

"We have a long night ahead of us," Destiny warned. "Most of us sleep during the day so we can be alert at night."

"What about Vita's Boundless Vigor?" Chaos asked.

"I need to conserve Vita's healing magic for emergencies," Destiny replied. "And if tonight is anything like last night, we'll

160

have more than enough of those to deal with." She turned to Fury and Bree. "I'll have the guards bring up cots for you two, and we'll all get some sleep."

"We're going to need it," Chaos warned, his expression grim. "Believe me."

Chapter 25

The ancient city of Old Langsroth was mostly like Pravus had remembered it from six years ago. At least, mostly like it'd been after they'd defeated the Fallen Sky. For when he and Templeton passed through the wall and into the city, they found a glorious blue sky high above, the sun shining its light on a city unlike any other. It was a radially arranged city, with one-story buildings at the periphery, and two, then three, then four-story buildings as one approached the city center. All the way up to the nine-story-tall Temple of Langsroth at the center, a circular, domed building some two hundred feet in diameter…and where he and Templeton had faced off against Fallen, the Vessel for the Fallen Sky.

Six years in the sun had dried up most of the mold and moss and such from Old Langsroth's fine white stone buildings, and from the innumerable sky bridges that served as roads connecting the buildings on each of the city's eight stories. Excluding the ninth, of course, seeing as how it only consisted of one building.

But it was not this splendid scene that drew Pravus's eye. No, it was not what was above, but what was below that aroused his curiosity. For the water level, having once been near his knees, had dropped considerably. Such that he could easily see the broad stone floor extending a good sixty feet ahead, and to the left and right along the wall. There was a fifty-foot-wide chasm beyond it, and then a white stone platform supporting the buildings beyond. He could even see the bridge leading from this platform into the city, no longer submerged in water as it'd been.

But the water level had dropped even further, such that he caught a glimpse of what was below this sky-bridge.

Pravus strode toward the edge of the chasm ahead, stepping over the bleached bones of a great many skeletons. And when he reached the edge, he found himself gazing down at something most unexpected: a city *beneath* the city, as deep as Old Langsroth was tall. For the buildings and sky-bridges continued downward, radially configured as they were above, with the deepest buildings near the center of the city, and the shallowest at the periphery.

"Oh my," Templeton breathed after catching up with Pravus, gazing down at this scene with awe. "A marvel!"

"To think that ancient peoples could build such a thing!" Pravus exclaimed.

"It boggles the mind," Templeton replied.

"Look at the carvings and embellishments," Pravus prompted. "They clearly had their priorities right."

"Indeed," Templeton agreed. "A city built as a celebration of beauty, and not purely functional."

"Or built purely for efficiency," Pravus added. "For the concentration of money." His expression darkened. "I fear we are the last country in the world that hasn't bowed to that inane obsession."

"I celebrate it," Templeton countered gently. "For it gives us the opportunity to offer our way of life as an antidote to Borrin's cultural poison."

Pravus nodded, and felt a sudden stirring in his soul as he gazed up the ancient city.

"I will build something like this," he vowed, surprised at his sudden certainty. "Not like its structure, but like its heart. A magical place that will stir the hearts of men, so that merely to gaze at it will teach them that there's more to life than production and consumption!"

Templeton said not a thing, the dear man, merely gazing at Pravus with his kind blue eyes. And while most people were immediately seized with the urge to temper their peers' enthusiasm, and point to the impracticality of unusual aspirations, Templeton did no such thing. A fact that Pravus was grateful for.

It was a strange compulsion, to need to temper the enthusiasm of others. For enthusiasm was the fuel upon which great things were done…and done joyfully rather than as a grim duty. It was telling that the toys and rooms of children were colorful, whilst those of adults had been drained to a depressing, dull hint of the palette they'd once enjoyed. As if growing up meant abandoning the very things that made life worth living.

"I'll build it in the sky," Pravus decided. "So that it stands, visible to all, as the very height of human living!"

"I can't wait to see it," Templeton declared, beaming a gorgeous smile. And oh! It made Pravus simply *yearn* to kiss him.

He tempered this enthusiasm, for he knew that his cousin would not approve. But enthusiasm so abruptly buried was painful indeed…and was becoming more so with each passing year.

"I'll need to bring a sample of stone back to our engineers, so that we might build a city that lasts like this one," Pravus stated.

"After we're done with our quest," Templeton agreed.

"Speaking of which," Pravus said, gazing down. The water level had dropped about two-thirds of the way down, the deepest three stories of the city still submerged in crystal-clear waters. "It appears our path to the catacombs beneath the city is no longer so inaccessible." He paused. "Or at least *less* inaccessible," he added.

"Fancy a stroll through an ancient city?" Templeton inquired.

"With my best friend at my side?" Pravus replied. "Indubitably!"

Chapter 26

When Fury's eyes fluttered open, and she sat up from her cot in Destiny's apartment, the sun was nearly setting. Destiny was already up and getting dressed, and Chaos was clad in suit of black leather armor with dark red stripes on upper arms, and was in the process of slinging his Omen-63 over his back. Bree was sitting up in the cot beside Fury, rubbing her eyes grumpily.

"I got you some armor, Fury," Destiny stated, gesturing to folded-up clothes resting on the table.

"Ooo!" Fury exclaimed, leaping out of bed with her usual verve and rushing to check them out. "Check *these* out!" She unfolded a red leather jacket, which looked super cute. And then red leather pants that were like, a *perfect* match. And even little red leather gloves and red leather boots. "Yay!" she exclaimed, rushing up to Destiny and giving her a big hug. "Thanks D!"

"Got you armor too," Destiny told Bree, who was still rubbing her eyes. Bree lowered her hands, glaring at the world at large. "Not that I want you in combat," Destiny added. "We'll need all the help we can get in the medical suite with the wounded."

"Do I look like a medic?" Bree grumbled.

"You'll learn on the job," Destiny replied, not at all offended by Bree's foul mood. "Get up. Get dressed." Bree gave her a nasty look. "Or sit there and die," Destiny offered as an alternative. One that Bree decidedly decided against. "Girls gotta get dressed," Destiny told Chaos. "Get out."

And so Chaos did.

Bree and Fury got dressed, and Fury found herself wishing Destiny had a mirror. For she was pretty sure that she looked *awfully* cute in her armor.

"Wish I had a mirror," she stated with her hands on her hips, never one to hold a thought back.

"You look hot," Destiny assured her.

"Annoyingly hot," Bree added. Annoyedly.

"On second thought, better not wear those gloves," Destiny advised Fury. "Don't want to cover up your palm portals."

"Aww," Fury pouted. She peeled them off, but stuck them in her pockets for future use.

"'Palm portals' sounds lame," Bree complained. Fury frowned, realizing she was right.

"How about dragon portals?" she proposed. Bree made a face. "Dragon circles? Serpent circles? Um…" she frowned, rubbing her chin. "Blood gates?"

"How about Vena Draco?" Bree suggested. "Dragon veins," she translated, before Fury had to ask. Fury considered this, finding it fitting. Because her circles brought blood into the circulation of a dragon god. And also her, because apparently her and Ferra Lin were one.

"I'll call 'em Vena for short," she decided.

"Great," Bree replied. "Can we go now? I'd like to not die."

"Let's go," Destiny prompted.

She led them downstairs, exiting the belltower and continuing down the street toward the southern wall, where Fury saw a portcullis guarding the exit, much like the one she and Bree had entered from the north the day before. Beyond this portcullis, she could see a land bridge continuing southward over the canyon, to a dark forest over a mile beyond. *The* Dark Forest, she presumed. But there was a gap in the land bridge, right beyond the portcullis. One a good fifteen feet long. A series of long wooden planks bridged the gap, forming a…well, a bridge over it. Beyond, Fury could see soldiers climbing ladders up to tall stone towers spaced at regular intervals on the land bridge at either edge, lighting big round braziers atop them.

"So wait," Fury stated, putting her hands on her hips. "Can't we just pull those planks and the zombies won't be able to cross?" For zombies were, as Zora had taught her, very bad jumpers. In fact, she couldn't remember ever seeing Zora jump.

"It'll stop the regular zombies," Destiny replied. "But not the Zhimeras."

"Ohhh," Fury stated.

"Zhimeras?" Bree asked.

Destiny explained what Zhimeras were, after which Bree looked rather pale.

"Oh," she mumbled.

"Go to the medical clinic at the northeast corner of the city," Destiny told Bree. "The nurses there will train you."

"Okay," Bree replied instantly, clearly eager to be as far away from the fighting as possible. She turned to leave, and Fury waved.

"Bye bestie!" she called out.

"Yep," Bree said, without so much as turning her head. Or slowing, much less stopping.

"I'm not sure she sees your relationship the way you do," Destiny stated. Fury turned to the paladin with a frown.

"Huh?"

"Besties aren't besties because you say so," Destiny explained. "Words often lie. Actions rarely do."

Fury's frown deepened, but on reflection, she couldn't deny that Bree seemed far less enthused about being besties than Fury. A troubling thought, one that was thankfully interrupted by soldiers returning from lighting the braziers. The last of them pulled the planks away from the gap in the land bridge, dragging them into the city. With that, the portcullis closed.

"What now?" Fury asked.

"Now we go up to the ramparts," Destiny answered. She led them up some stairs on the inside of the wall, leading up to the top. Then she went rightward. "The wall over the portcullis is still fresh," she warned. "We need to let it settle tonight."

"Hopefully they don't smash through again," Chaos grumbled. "That wall was a hell of a lot of work."

"Wait, they smashed through the wall?" Fury asked. For zombies were strong, but not *that* strong.

"There was a zombie giant, like Rocky," Chaos explained. Fury's eyes widened.

"Oh."

"Right," Chaos replied grimly. "If they have another one, we're in deep..." he began, but was interrupted by a deep, unexpected *DONG!*

Fury turned, seeing the giant bell atop the bell tower tolling. *DONG! DONG!*

"It begins," Destiny declared, looking out over the land bridge to the Dark Forest beyond. Fury squinted, spotting pale shapes illuminated by the braziers at the far end of the land bridge. A truly massive army of zombies...numbering easily in the thousands.

"Oh shit," she blurted out. And then covered her naughty, dirty little mouth with one hand. "Sorry!"

"Don't be," Destiny replied. "It won't be the last time you swear tonight."

"The slow zombies won't have a chance at crossing that gap," Chaos noted. "But the fast zombies might."

"And the Zhimeras," Destiny piped in.

"If they have another dwarf giant, we're in deep trouble," Chaos warned. "My magic beat the last one, but it's not exactly reliable."

The pale-bodied masses were a quarter mile away from the first barricade, moving slowly toward it. Everyone watched as the enemy continued forward, an army extending all the way back to the Dark Forest.

"Ohmygosh the *size* of it!" she exclaimed, putting a hand to her mouth. For it was easily the largest number of people she'd ever seen in one place.

"That's what Destiny said when she first saw it," Chaos quipped. Destiny rolled her eyes.

"Alright, silence from now on unless you have a warning or an idea," Destiny stated, her gaze on the approaching army of undead. Which was impressively large and intimidating.

We got this, Fury told herself, setting her jaw firmly and putting her hands on her hips. A posture that screamed "I'm not scared" even though to be honest, she was scared enough to scream.

The slow march of the zombie hordes brought their front line to the first of the barricades, about halfway across the land bridge. They impaled themselves rather stupidly on the sharpened ends of the wooden stakes jutting out of the barricade, causing a big traffic jam behind it. Zombies fell, and the zombies behind them trampled the fallen, then fell themselves, and were trampled in turn. Again and again, in a cycle of mindless obedience to their master. It was not unlike Daddy's description of the workplace at Evermore Trading Company, where employees trampled each other just to get ahead. All because their masters told them to, for the promise of a great big goody at the end.

But the only true end was death. In this case, un-*un* death, which would be brought to these zombies by the hands of Chaos, Destiny, and Fury.

"Yeah!" Fury exclaimed, her fear replaced by faith. That they could *totally* do this.

"Shh!" Destiny scolded, shooting her a glare.

"Oops," Fury blurted out, putting a hand to her mouth. And promptly scowled, telling herself to shut up already. But shutting up was hard for her to do, for while sadness was quiet, joy tended to be loud.

The zombie army eventually piled up so high in front of the first barricade that the zombies behind them were able to walk right up and fall over it, landing rather hilariously on the other side. Hilarious, that was, except for the fact that it brought them closer to murdering everyone in Belfast.

"First barricade breached!" Destiny yelled.

"Why aren't they using the fast zombies first this time?" Chaos wondered.

"They may be saving them for last," Destiny replied. Chaos eyed the fifteen-foot gap in the land bridge, right before the southern gate, then grimaced. Though why, Fury didn't know. The zombie hordes breached the second, third, and fourth barricades in the same way, then went over the fifth...where some Belfastian soldiers with long metal poles awaited them. The soldiers used said poles to sweep the zombies off the sides of the land bridge, making them fall – again, hilariously, at least to Fury – to the bottom of the canyon far, far below. It was everything she could do not to laugh, honestly.

But given the sheer size of the enemy army, the soldiers were quickly overrun, and escaped via ropes hung down from the sixth barricade, which of course the zombies couldn't climb. They piled up in front of the barricade, then spilled over it, and the process repeated itself for the remaining barricades. In less than an hour, all ten were breached, and zombies flowed over the last barricade, rushing toward the southern gate.

And then went right to the edge of the gap in the land bridge, and promptly ran off it in a steady stream.

"Zombie waterfall!" Fury exclaimed, hopping up and down, unable to hold herself back. Destiny smirked, and Chaos chuckled. Because really, it was pretty funny. In her defense, had they been creatures with souls, or with feelings of any kind, she would've found the scene absolutely horrifying. But then she thought of Zora being among them, and quickly became troubled.

Zora's different, she told herself. But then again, how could she be so sure? For who knew the inner experience of a zombie, or even another human, or animal for that matter? Borrin was notorious for making the a priori assumption that nothing other

169

than humans were conscious. An assumption that conveniently allowed them to "ethically" abuse and commodify other living things. Fury didn't have time to ponder this for long, however. Not because of any particular event, but because of a rather short attention span.

"Ooo, look at that!" she exclaimed, pointing off into the distance, at the other end of the land bridge. For a very large number of very fast-moving zombies was rushing forward, shoving through their slower brethren.

"There they are," Destiny stated. "And there's a Zhimera."

Fury frowned, making a squinty-face, and saw what looked like a zombie human centipede following behind the fast zombies. One whose eyes glowed red in the darkness of night, unlike the other zombies. Two more of the Zhimeras followed behind the first, crawling over the over zombies.

"Three this time," Chaos noted grimly. "And no pendulum."

"Three of us too," Destiny countered.

"True," Chaos had to concede.

They watched as the slow zombies continuing pouring over the edge of the gap in the land bridge, like lemmings following each other to their dooms.

At length the first of the three Zhimeras made it to the edge. But instead of falling off, they leapt off instead…and bridged the gap with ease, landing to cling onto the portcullis of the southern gate.

"Get ready," Destiny warned. Fury looked down at the horrible creature…right as it started climbing up the wall toward them!

At that moment, faced with imminent danger, Fury found herself struck with an overwhelming urge. To flee.

But before she could, Destiny lowered her head in prayer…and a shockwave of golden light shot outward from her in all directions, including the direction of the Zhimera. It struck the vile creature, flinging it from the wall…and it tumbled toward the canyon far, far below.

"Oh thank…" Fury began, but the Zhimera reached out with one multisegmented limb, managing to grab on to the portcullis blocking the southern gate. It hung there, baleful red eyes glaring up at them, with sphincter-spasming effect. "…shit," she concluded, terror gripping her as tightly as her sphincter was currently gripping itself. Thereby guaranteeing that shit was the one thing she wouldn't emit.

170

But to her immediate relief, the soldiers behind the portcullis immediately started bashing the Zhimera's zombie hand with their warhammers, and the Zhimera's grip failed it. It gave out one last spine-chilling shriek as it plummeted over a thousand feet to the canyon floor below, vanishing into its utter darkness.

"Yeah!" Fury exclaimed. But then the second centipede-like Zhimera leapt across the gap, clinging to the wall and climbing up. It skittered to the left away from them, out of range of Destiny's previous shockwave, then made its way up, vaulting over to land atop the rampart. The soldiers to Fury's left rushed to battle with exceptional bravery, wielding hammers and swords and axes with grim resolve.

And were promptly torn to shreds by the vile creature.

"Go go!" Destiny barked. But instead of running away, she ran toward the Zhimera, wielding her silver and gold mace. Chaos rushed forward at her side, Omen-63 in hand. All while Fury stood there, frozen in place, staring as the Belfastian soldiers were literally torn limb from limb. Chaos swung his magic shovel, flinging stored-up rock out of it at the Zhimera's head. The rock struck it between the eyes, and it flinched backward...just as Destiny leapt over the bodies of two fallen soldiers, smashing her mace atop its skull.

The creature's skull caved in, and its long body spasmed, and Chaos reached the thing, cutting off its head with a single Omen-63 swing.

"Throw it off!" Destiny barked, picking up the disembodied head and flinging it over the edge of the rampart. Then she helped Chaos and the surviving soldiers drag its body over the edge as well...

...just as the third Zhimera finished climbing the wall to Fury's right, rushing across the rampart toward her!

Fury shrieked.

The two soldiers between her and the Zhimera rushed to fight it, and the creature grabbed both of them, throwing them off the rampart and into the canyon. Then the Zhimera lunged at Fury, swiping at her face with one pale hand. It raked its fingers across her cheek, tearing at her flesh and snapping her head to the side. She fell against the chest-high inner wall of the rampart, feeling dazed.

Before she could recover, the Zhimera grabbed her by the neck, lifting her up...and threw her over the edge into the city.

171

* * *

Destiny finished dragging the Zhimera Chaos had beheaded off the rampart, then heard screams to her right. She turned, spotting a third Zhimera climbing atop the rampart a good thirty feet away, then charge toward the few soldiers between it and Fury.

"Zhimera, go!" she shouted, leaping over the bodies of her fellow soldiers, then sprinting toward Fury. Chaos followed behind her, as did a few soldiers.

But the Zhimera threw the soldiers protecting Fury off the rampart, then lunged at Fury herself, clawing at her face. Fury lurched to the right, slamming her right flank against the inner rampart wall...and then the Zhimera grabbed her by the neck.

"No!" Destiny cried. But it was too late. The Zhimera tossed Fury off the inner wall of the rampart...and Fury fell a full sixty feet to the street below.

Destiny grit her teeth, looking away right before Fury struck the cobblestones.

"Shit," Chaos swore. "Save her!"

"On it," Destiny replied, rushing down the stairs toward the street level. She found Fury lying on her back on the street, a halo of blood forming around her head. Destiny ran up to her, kneeling, and focused inward, sending Vita a silent prayer. Vita's warm filled her, and her hands glowed with golden light. Lay on Hands would surely save the girl, as long as she was still alive. But it would mean no more magic until tomorrow...and that meant if she saved Fury, she might be dooming the entire city.

Destiny paused, eyeing Fury, then looking up at the soldiers in the streets. She heard Chaos's footsteps approaching rapidly, and he skid to a stop behind her.

"What are you waiting for?" he demanded. "Save her!"

Still Destiny hesitated, gritting her teeth.

"Destiny!" Chaos pressed, grabbing her wrist and pulling her still-glowing hand toward Fury. Destiny let the prayer go, the golden light fading. "What are you doing?!" Chaos blurted out incredulously.

"Give me your shovel," she ordered.

"But..."

Destiny ignored him, grabbing the head of his shovel and sliding her palm across its razor-sharp edge. Blood welled up from

172

the wound, and she reached down, grabbing Fury's hand with her wounded one. The red circle on Fury's palm began to glow…and Destiny's blood started sucking into it.

Come on…

She heard frantic shouting from somewhere to the east, and ignored it, gripping Fury's hand tightly.

Come on!

Then Fury's hair started to turn blood-red, from the roots all the way down to the tips.

The girl's eyes fluttered open, glowing with a crimson light, and her own blood began streaming up through the air to enter her other hand.

"Fury!" Chaos gasped.

Fury's eyes rolled into the back of her head, her lower back arching. Chaos grabbed her shoulder, shaking it.

"No," he blurted out. "No no no!"

"Nghhh!" she moaned. In a way that made it quite clear that she was not, in fact, dying like he'd feared. Chaos blinked, and Fury finished moaning, her eyes refocusing. She looked at Destiny, then at Chaos, then sat up without any trouble at all. And without any evident injuries, Destiny noted.

"You okay?" she asked Fury.

"I'll be better," Fury replied, her cleavers rising from her palms as she got to her feet, "…as soon as I kill some shitty-shit *sheeit.*"

At that very moment, Destiny heard more shouting from the east. Frantic shouting, followed by soldiers streaming down the stairs from the ramparts toward her, gesticulating wildly while screaming her name.

"The hell?"

"It made it out of the canyon!" one soldier shouted as he approached, skidding to a stop breathlessly before her. His eyes were wide with terror, his face slick with sweat. "They're climbing up the eastern wall!"

"What's coming?" she asked.

"Everything," he replied.

Chapter 27

King Pravus found his foray into the streets of old Langsroth quite different than it'd been six years ago, not in the least because he wasn't being attacked by hordes of bloodthirsty undead. The sun shining down on the ancient city gave a marvelous view of its beauty, and of the ingenious nature of its design. And, without the need to hurry through the previously flooded streets, Pravus found that he and Templeton could spend time appreciating Old Langsroth a fair bit more than before.

"What marvelous bas-reliefs!" he exclaimed as they strode toward the center of the city, still on the ground floor. Many of the massive white stone columns supporting the streets on the level above them had reliefs carved into them, and were of remarkable quality, made with uncommon skill.

"And statues," Templeton noted, eyeing a statue of a rather elegant looking woman dressed in a flowing robe, in a sort of town square ahead. "I notice they favored octagonal plinths."

"I noticed the same," Pravus replied. For the tall pedestals supporting each statue were indeed octagonal.

"I do enjoy the elegant colonnades supporting the level above," Templeton stated, gazing upward to admire a row of columns.

"The entablatures are remarkable," Pravus pointed out. For they very surely were. And if you don't know what those are, dear reader, don't feel ashamed; I had to look it up too.

In this way, the two men enjoyed their journey through Old Langsroth's ground level, which was large enough to constitute a full city from their kingdom on its own. But with eight floors above and below this one, Old Langsroth was, in terms of sheer usable square footage, larger than any city in the Kingdom of Pravus, if not the world.

"Odd that we haven't seen any stairs leading down," Templeton mused. Which was true.

"Plenty going up," Pravus noted. And while not being able to find what he was looking for was usually a tried-and-true recipe for regal irritability, now he wasn't miffed in the slightest. For being with Templeton, exploring an ancient city they'd saved, was also what he'd been looking for, in that it was time well spent with the man he loved, doing what interested them both.

It was at precisely the end of this thought that Pravus spotted a small, domed building ahead, one with an arched, open entrance that led to a spiral staircase beyond. One that went down, naturally.

"Ah," Templeton stated, smiling at the sight. "Our way down is revealed."

Upon reaching said staircase, they followed it downward, spiraling clockwise. Being an open staircase with an elegant white stone rail – likely to prevent drunks and children from suffering the unfortunate fate of a fatal fall – Pravus and Templeton were treated to quite the spectacular view. For as above, so below…and thus the levels of Old Langsroth beneath the ground level were equally architecturally interesting. In fact, Pravus found he could see through the various gaps in the sky-bridge-streets below, to the water level near the sixth understory of the city. A formidable distance, and one that caused a bit of vertigo to behold.

Reaching the bottom of the stairwell, they found themselves on a wide, white stone street on the first sub-level. One with more buildings on either side of the street, most appearing to be long-abandoned shops.

"It seems the commercial district was near the ground level," Templeton observed. "I suspect the lower levels will be primarily residential."

"Possibly," Pravus replied. "Although it is equally possible the Great Flat was once the location of a large town exterior to the city, and that most commoners lived there."

"If such a town were composed of wood structures, it would have long since rotted away," Templeton agreed. "Thus the appearance of a barren land."

"In any case, all mysteries will be penetrated," Pravus declared.

And penetrate they did, plunging ever deeper into the bowels of Old Langsroth. A journey that involved walking the maze-like streets of each level, searching for the next spiraling stairwell leading to the next-lowest level. Abandoned as the city was, they found themselves utterly unmolested during their trek, which was rather disappointing, to Pravus at least. For he would've fancied a fight or two, a bit of resistance to spice up their adventure. But as it turned out, his hopes were in vain, for there was simply no evil left in Old Langsroth to battle with.

At length, they made it all the way to the sixth sub-level of the city. The water line was a few inches above the street, such that they found themselves splashing with each step. And with the shadows thrown by the levels above, the going was a bit harder, on account of it being nearly as dark as night in some areas. Still, it was hardly dangerous, and as such, this particular adventure seemed far from adventurous. A conclusion that Pravus found impossible to keep to himself, try as he might.

"You seem subdued," Templeton noted. "Is something bothering you?" Pravus paused, then nodded.

"Something is," he confessed. "I admit I was expecting...more of this mission."

"I as well," Templeton revealed.

"Really?"

"Indeed," Templeton confirmed. "A bit more resistance, if you will."

"A struggle," Pravus concurred.

"Adversity to overcome," Templeton added.

"But thus far we've encountered none," Pravus noted with dismay. Templeton gazed off at the long-abandoned city.

"Perhaps there is a lesson in this," the man mused. "That important deeds might require little effort, other than to put in the time to achieve them."

"Hmm," Pravus murmured, rubbing his chin.

"I daresay a toilet-scrubber's job is vital to the health and comfort of a lord, though the job requires little effort and even less glory."

"Quite so," Pravus had to agree.

"Heroism comes in many forms," Templeton declared.

"All in service to the good," Pravus mused. "I suspect you're right."

They walked a bit longer.

"Still, it *would* be nice to have a challenge," Pravus stated.

"I suspect we already have," Templeton replied. "For the past six years."

Pravus frowned, realizing that, once again, his cousin was correct. And furthermore that this meant their current mission was a reprieve from struggle. Which was technically a vacation, really. Something to enjoy rather than lament.

With this revelation, Pravus felt his perspective shift…and he found himself smiling in lieu of a frown. For a vacation with his favorite cousin – indeed, his favorite person – was something to cherish.

Unfortunately, he didn't get to cherish it for long. For as soon as his perspective had shifted, his gaze shifted to what lay directly ahead on the street. It was a town square of sorts, with a large circular pool in the center, filled to the brim with water. And in the center of the pool was a boulder.

A submerged stone.

"Damn," Pravus swore, eyeing this with a grimace. He stopped in his tracks, staring at the stone.

"What is it?" Templeton inquired. Pravus sighed.

"Time to go it alone," he replied.

Chapter 28

Fury followed Destiny and Chaos as they mounted the rampart steps again, reaching the top of the wall. The soldier who'd warned Destiny led them to the eastern wall of the city, and gestured for Destiny to look down. She did so, as did Chaos and Fury, and when they did, Destiny blurted out something *extremely* inappropriate. In fact, it was by far the worst single stream of words Fury had ever heard the girl utter.

And when she saw what had inspired said words, she spouted an inappropriate word of her own.

"Fuck," she swore.

"Whelp, we're dead," Chaos declared. Fury ignored him, eyeing Destiny.

"What's the plan?" she asked. Destiny grimaced, her eyes on what was down below.

"Die," Destiny replied. "Horribly."

Which was, Fury knew, the most likely end to this night. For there, far below, she could see the dark, yawning maw of the canyon, from which rose up one of the three gigantic stone pillars that supported the land bridge and Belfast itself. There, crawling up the side of the pillar over a hundred feet down, was something pale and gigantic. A zombie dwarf giant, it appeared. One that looked a bit like Rocky, but without the rocky exterior.

And hanging from its back was a long chain of zombies holding on to each other's ankles. A chain that extended all the way down into the darkness.

"They're forming an undead ladder," Destiny realized, her face turning pale. "Every zombie we've ever thrown into the canyon is going to come back up."

"Fuck," Chaos swore. Fury put her hands on her hips.

"Fucking isn't a plan," she retorted. Obliviously. "And neither is dying horribly. If we can stop that giant from climbing up, they'll all fall back down," she reasoned.

"And then climb back up again," Destiny retorted. "As soon as the giant heals. Which he will."

"So we need to destroy him," Fury stated.

"Which means burning him or decapitating him and burning the head," Destiny replied.

"But won't another zombie be able to graft its head onto his body, and become a giant Zhimera?"

"Yep," Destiny replied.

"So we burn the body and the head," Fury replied. "Easy-peasy."

"Easier said than done," Destiny argued.

"Well it's better than rolling over and dying," Fury reasoned. Which was rather sound reasoning, if she said so herself.

"Do we have any cannonballs or something that we can drop on it?" Chaos asked.

"We have hot oil," one of the soldiers nearby said.

"Takes too long for bodies to burn, especially really big ones," Destiny argued. "We'd just end up fighting a flaming giant."

"Oh," the guard mumbled, lowering his gaze and feeling stupid.

Fury looked down at the upcoming giant, who was only fifty feet or so now from the bottom of the city wall. Its glowing red eyes seemed to bore into hers. Which were also red and glowing, or so she'd been told. It occurred to her then that she had no idea what she looked like in Proeliator mode; she'd have to find a mirror at some point to have a look.

But the giant's glowing eyes gave her another idea.

"Wait," she blurted out. "Aren't the giant's eyes glowing because they've got lots of Fallen Blood in them?"

"That's right," Destiny replied.

"So instead of burning it, what if we *bleed* it?" she proposed. Which was a really, *really* good idea. "That's a really, *really* good idea," she added, because despite being a blood-lusting Proeliator, she was still Fury Little. Destiny frowned, considering this.

"You mean what if you absorb the giant's blood?" she asked.

"Yeah."

"It would work," the paladin conceded. "But there's no telling what effect that much Fallen Blood would have on you."

"Back in Old Langsroth, it would make you bleed easier, and if you lost half your blood, you'd turn into a zombie," Chaos explained.

"Got any better ideas?" Fury inquired. Everyone paused, then shook their heads. "Then let's *do* it," she exclaimed, lifting her cleavers to showcase them. "Wish me luck, bye!"

And with that, she leapt right off the frickin' rampart.

"Holy...!" Chaos blurted out, lunging to try to catch her. But Fury fell like a stone toward the giant and his hangers-on. The gut-wrenching lurch of free-fall took her, her heart pounding in her ears. And while before she would have interpreted said sensations as utter terror, as a Proeliator, she felt them as a thrill.

"Wooo!" she cried, wind tearing at her face as she fell, faster and faster with every passing second. The wall of Belfast gave way to the rock of the pillar as she plummeted, the giant's big, ugly face getting rapidly closer. She twisted around 180 degrees, so she was facing the pillar now...

...and then plunged her cleavers downward when she reached the giant, chopping into his big-ass frickin'...well, ass. For her blades struck his monstrous, pale right butt-cheek, sinking into his flesh...and then tore down his right hamstring, stopping behind his knee. The sudden stop nearly tore the cleavers from Fury's hands, and she gripped them as tightly as she could, hanging from the giant's leg.

The giant roared, kicking said leg again and again, trying to shake Fury free. She held on for dear life, her cleavers thankfully lodged quite firmly into the back of his knee joint. Looking down, she saw the thousand-ish foot drop to the canyon far below. A distance she'd surely fall for, if she didn't do something...and quick.

She looked up, and realized that blood was flowing from the wounds she'd created, dripping down her cleavers. A smirk curled her lips.

"Ooo, come to *mama*," she purred.

And by virtue of her magic, the blood did just that, streaming into the bottoms of her cleaver handles. The giant roared, kicking again, but still she hung on. The kick, however, dislodged the chain of zombies hanging on to its big ankle, sending them tumbling into the dark void below.

"One down, one to go," Fury mused, smirking at the sight. The giant, clearly sensing its mistake, decided to plant its feet in fortuitous footholds in the rock pillar, then reach down with his right hand to grab her.

Fury yanked her left cleaver out of the thing's flesh, then swung away from the approaching hand, sinking her cleaver into the inside of his lower thigh. Then she kicked off, twisting around 180 degrees, and buried her cleavers into the giant's other knee...and just out of reach of his grasp.

More blood flowed from his growing number of wounds, all streaming through the air magically to enter her cleaver handles.

The giant shifted his grip on the pillar, using his left hand to try to grab her. So she just swung back to the right leg, because she was small, and thus a whole lot faster. At length the giant tired of this game, and decided to do the one thing that no woman could abide: he ignored her.

Up the pillar he went, using his big, powerful hands to smash handholds into the rock with every step upward. The base of Belfast's defensive wall was only ten feet up or so...which meant that whatever Fury was going to do, she needed to do it quickly. But without a clever plan in mind, she resorted to doing what she loved best.

She started hacking the living *shit* out of the giant's legs.

The giant roared as she chopped into its flesh again and again, slashing and hacking and whacking with what soon became unfettered glee. To the point where, with a rapidly growing number of blood-streams flowing into her handles, she forgot all about the people of Belfast. And even Destiny, and her own brother.

All that mattered was her lust for blood, and she sated it with furious intensity.

The giant howled, trying to kick her off again. It even slammed its legs against the pillar, but any attempt to dislodge her was in vain. For with one cleaver wedged deep in the back of its knee joint, its own bones were holding it in place.

So the giant did the only thing it could, continuing to climb. It reached the bottom of the wall, smashing handholds up it until it was very nearly at the top, where Destiny and Chaos and a whole lot of Belfast's soldiers were standing on the rampart.

But even as it did so, dozens of streams of blood flowed into Fury's cleavers, every wound serving as another fountain of the stuff. And as its Fallen Blood was drained, the speed at which the giant climbed slowed considerably. And, Fury noticed, the rate at which its wounds were healing was also slowing.

181

It continued to climb, only a dozen feet from the top now, but it was clearly struggling.

"It's weakening!" Fury called out to Destiny and Chaos.

"Hold your fire!" Destiny ordered, apparently talking to the archers flanking her. "Flanking positions!"

The soldiers, Chaos, and Destiny moved to either side of where the giant was climbing toward, giving it ample space. The giant roared, slowing even more, but managing to get one big hand over the rampart wall. It paused, then grunted, hauling itself up until it was resting its belly over the rampart, Fury still dangling behind its knee.

"Get up here Fury!" Destiny urged. And Fury was happy to oblige. She used her cleavers to hack her way up the back of the giant's leg, reaching his butt...and his back, which was arched over the rampart. Streams of blood continued to flow to her, for apparently any wound her cleavers made bled into their handles. At length, she made it to the horizontal portion of the giant's back.

"Ha!" Fury exclaimed. And then promptly rushed up to the back of the giant's neck, and began hacking away at it.

The giant *roared*, reaching back to swipe at her, and this time it managed a lucky hit. Fury flew to the side, landing on the rampart next to Destiny, who helped her to her feet.

"Cut off its head," Destiny ordered her men. A few with axes rushed to complete this task.

"Uh uh," Fury replied, leaping onto the thing's back again. "This big bad boy is *mine*."

She ran to his neck again, then started hacking away again. And again, he tried to swipe her off. But this time she was ready, dodging easily, then continuing to hack and whack. And by golly she didn't stop whacking until the deed was done, and the giant head fell in a spurt of blood. Blood that came to her, of course, filling her bloodthirsting cleavers. The giant's head fell a good sixty feet to the city street, denting the cobblestones a bit there.

"There," Fury exclaimed, beaming a smile at Destiny. "Day saved. You're welcome," she added, like a little bitch.

"The day isn't saved until we see the sun rise," Destiny replied. "Should've cut off his leg first," she added. Fury frowned.

"Huh?" she asked. Destiny's gaze went to the giant's posterior, where to Fury's surprise, a bunch of zombies were climbing. The chain of zombies that'd held on to its left leg, to be precise. Other zombies were using said chain as a rope to climb up from the canyon to the top of the city wall. "Oh," Fury mumbled.

"Archers! Fire at the base of the chain!" Destiny ordered.

A few archers lit fuses on their arrows, then shot them at the giant's left ankle. A moment later, the arrows exploded…and the zombie chain was no more, falling to the canyon floor.

"Burn the body where it lies," Destiny commanded. A soldier from the southern part of the rampart ran toward them, flagging Destiny down. "What is it?" she asked.

"A centipede Zhimera is using its body as a bridge across the gap, and the fast zombies are crossing it and climbing up the wall."

"What?" Chaos blurted out. "How can they climb up it?"

"The mortar is still wet in the section we rebuilt today," the soldier replied. "They're using the spaces between stones as handholds and footholds."

"Shit," Chaos swore. Destiny immediately started striding toward the southern wall, Fury in tow. Chaos leapt over the giant's body to follow them.

"Take out the Zhimera with exploding arrows," Destiny ordered as she went. "We'll take care of the zombies that crossed over it." Then she glanced back at Fury. "Good work with that giant," she congratulated. "If we get to see the sun rise, you'll be the one we thank."

Chapter 29

After a composed and heartwarming goodbye, King Pravus left the sunshine of his life behind, separating from sweet, dearest Templeton to stride past the submerged stone to whatever came next. Which happened to be a dead-end street, leading to a single, domed building. One that was made of black stone, in contrast to the rest of the city's stark white. A single, large stone door served as the gateway into said building. Pravus strode up to it, stopping before it. Studying the door, he found elaborate pictorials engraved in its surface. Most of which depicted skeletons, morbidly enough. Which, considering that the doors must have been constructed before the cursing of Old Langsroth, meant that this building had something to do with housing the dead.

"A catacomb," Pravus deduced, putting his hands on his hips. Which by definition was an underground cemetery. As such, he was right where he needed to be. It didn't escape him that six years ago, this catacomb had been submerged beneath about a hundred feet of water. And that, as such, it would have been particularly difficult for him to get to, even after destroying the Fallen Sky. Which meant that perhaps he and Templeton had not, in fact, been destined to reach the catacombs at that time. Imperius Fanning's magic worked in mysterious ways, after all. Perhaps everything was going precisely according to its mysterious plan.

He focused, trying to make out what the door's pictorials were displaying. For while art often was merely decorative, in more culturally advanced societies, it was a communication medium far more profound than that of mere words strung together. Indeed, one could reliably determine the maturity of a culture by the profundity of its art. The least mature cultures devalued art by making it purely functional, like the Republic of Borrin.

In any case, it appeared that this door told a story of Old Langsroth's concept of the dead crossing over into the great beyond. For corpses were depicted being carried to this very door, which served as a gate to their final resting place. Once within the catacombs, their souls appeared to depart, pulled to a sort of tunnel in the sky. One with a great star or light or something at the other end.

"All right Pravus," he told himself, cracking his knuckles in proper manly fashion. "Time for a solo adventure." With that, he grabbed the stone handle of the stone door, pulling it open. To his surprise, it came open with ease, once again displaying the fine craftsmanship of the ancient Langsrothians. Beyond, he saw a stairwell leading downward as far as his lantern's light would let him see. To his further surprise, there was no water inside said stairwell, despite it going below the water line.

Pravus paused, then stepped through the doorway, following the stairs downward. He took his time, making sure to study his surroundings, not wanting to be surprised by anyone with ill intent. Foolish men rushed headlong into danger, whilst wise men tread cautiously. A mere six years ago, he'd made the mistake of being incautious in Old Langsroth, and had nearly paid for it with his very soul. If he was a wise man, he owed it largely to his failures, for the wisdom of others had been too often ignored.

Ever-downward the stairs went, bringing him deeper below the surface of Old Langsroth's lake. Until at last Pravus made it to the bottom: a narrow corridor of pure black stone, with an arched ceiling. He strode forward, for it was the only way to go; it wasn't long before the corridor opened up into a small cylindrical room, one hosting another stairwell, this time a spiral one going down.

"Thank goodness it wasn't leg day yesterday," Pravus quipped, feeling a bit antsy with the silence. And the fact that he was alone, which was a rare thing for a monarch. He found himself wishing Templeton were here, almost reflexively.

When was the last time you were alone?

He hadn't even thought to ask such a question, so busy had he been with his duties. Being king had taken up so much of his time over the last six years that it'd taken up all of...well, of *him*.

"Focus," he chided himself, for now was not the time for gathering wool. He descended via the spiral staircase, which soon opened up into a four-way intersection of hallways. And on each wall of each hallway, he saw stone coffins without lids on them, within which skeletons laid. Coffins packed so tight that a sheet of paper couldn't have been shoved between them.

"Oh my," he breathed, slowing, then stopped on the open spiral stairwell, having a look around. This place must have been

185

the burial grounds for the citizens of Old Langsroth, or at least the aristocracy and richer members of the mercantile class. The serfs, of course, would have been buried outside the city, for within a city, square footage was limited. With only his lantern, he couldn't see very far, but it was clear from the echoes his ejaculation had generated that each hallway went a very long distance.

Pravus studied this somber scene a bit longer, then continued to descend. The stairwell allowed him to exit onto this floor, but he continued down through to the next lowest floor instead. An identical scene greeted him, with legions of the dead resting within their stony coffins. He paused to eye them, knowing that each had been alive once. A living man or woman, filled with hopes and dreams, with fears and resentments. Each skull had held a brain, a universe of its own, with memories unique to itself.

And it occurred to him, descending into the depths where only the dead rested, that one day, he too would be reduced to this. No matter how hard he'd developed his muscles, they were doomed to be eaten away. Every memory he had would be gone, as if his whole life had never been lived. Until he was reduced to a skeleton, an inert object instead of a man.

That's what I am, he realized, staring at the nearest skeleton, then feeling his own cheekbones. *They were like me, and I'll be like them.*

Pravus found the idea chilling, and once again, he found himself yearning for Templeton's cheer. But in its absence, he could only suffer his morbid thoughts, while descending further into the darkness of the catacombs. Which, it being his destiny to do so, he did. But the sight of the dead forced him to wonder just what he wanted to do with what remained of his life, before he too was reduced to remains. The prospect of his life being nothing more than a continuation of what already was…well, he found it rather horrifying.

Who am I when I'm not a cousin or a king?

The question troubled him, and it troubled him further that he couldn't answer it. But there was one thing he knew was missing in his life, a hole he'd spent decades hoping to fill. With his cousin Templeton, of course. But it was a fool's dream, and with each passing year, he felt the hole in his life more keenly, and the yearning to fill it only grew.

"You *are* a fool," he muttered to himself as he descended, making it to yet another story of the catacombs, identical to the other two. This time, he kept moving, determined to act instead of indulging himself with depressing thoughts. Down he went, until he reached the bottom of the stairwell...and the small, cylindrical chamber it ended within.

Ahead, a closed, black stone door barred his way. Pravus grabbed the handle, pulling it open...

...and saw a long tunnel beyond, with a man standing in his way.

Pravus's breath caught in his throat.

For the man barring his way was even taller than Pravus, though slender. He was clad in all-black leather armor, his face unnaturally pale in Pravus's lantern light. He was bald, and clean-shaven, and roughly middle-aged. In fact, he would've been rather handsome if it hadn't been for the fact that his eyes were glowing with a ghostly silver-blue light.

A light that froze Pravus where he stood...and filled his heart with sudden terror.

"What...urrghh!" he blurted out, cut off as the man grabbed him by the throat with one pale hand. Cold fingers curled around his neck with inhuman strength.

Pravus gripped the man's hand, prying the fingers free. Or at least he tried to. For though his grip strength was second-to-none – on account of countless deadlifts, naturally – the stranger's grasp proved impossible to break.

"Guurghh!" Pravus gasped, kicking at the stranger's groin. But the blow had no effect, despite perfect aim. Pravus focused, prying at the man's fingers with all his might, and felt them start to come free...

...and then the stranger head-butted him, and the world went black instantly.

Chapter 30

After the harrowing battle with the zombie giant – and a long, drawn-out battle with the zombie hordes afterward – Chaos, Destiny, Fury, and the soldiers of Belfast did indeed manage to see the sun rise.

It was a victory, for sure, but to Fury's surprise, no one celebrated too much. She realized that *every* day had to be like this…each sunrise a gift, but also a curse. Because each soldier in the city was doomed to suffer through another night of terror, a night which very well could be their last.

But it wasn't long before word got out that Fury had been visited by the great Imperius Fanning himself, Arch Wizard of the Order of Mundus. And that it had been ordained that she would be the one to defeat the great evil in the Dark Forest, thereby saving all the land.

With this realization, the mood of the previously hopeless city changed. For – after a very long nap – Fury joined Chaos and Destiny, traveling down to street-level. There, they found men's faces lighting up at the mere sight of them, their lips breaking out into big smiles. Those close by rushed up to the three, to shake their hands or just say a kind word, while those farther away hollered and cheered. And not in the usual cat-calling way that Fury had become slightly accustomed to, if not comfortable with. Rather, they saw her and Destiny as the strong, brave, selfless women that they were. And they saw Chaos as well. Assumedly.

Destiny slung an arm around Fury's shoulders as they walked down the street, basking in the cheer all around them.

"You did good," she congratulated.

Fury eyed the growing crowd of cheering soldiers, glancing at Destiny. She hardly felt like she'd done good. It'd *felt* good, at least at the time. But now that she wasn't in Proeliator mode, it felt like she'd been very bad. For she'd thoroughly enjoyed hacking things to pieces and sucking out their blood. The only good had been in the result; it seemed grossly inappropriate that an evil process

188

could do good. For as she'd been taught since childhood, the ends didn't justify the means.

"I don't know," she mumbled, feeling undeserving of the accolades thrown her way.

"Feeling guilty?" Destiny guessed. Fury nodded. "You'll learn," Destiny assured her.

"Learn what?"

"For one, that despite what people have taught you, sometimes violence *is* the answer," Destiny replied.

"Mommy tells me that like, *all* the time," Fury admitted.

"...and that killing things can be an act of love," Destiny continued. Fury frowned.

"It can?"

"Sure," Destiny confirmed. "The zombies you took out are tortured beings. To end their un-lives is a kindness. And in doing so, you protected the people of Belfast. People that were terrified that we wouldn't last the night."

"I've never had to worry about that," Chaos joked. The two girls ignored him.

"The point is, you've been held back this whole time," Destiny stated. "You never got to experience negative emotions...like anger, rage, jealousy, sadness..."

"I've been sad," Fury argued.

"You've felt sad momentarily," Destiny corrected. "But when have you felt sad for days? Or weeks, or months on end?"

"Ew, never," Fury replied, making a face. She paused. "That can happen?"

"It happens all the time," Destiny replied. "To people who don't have a magical tooth-necklace around their necks their whole lives."

Fury frowned, reaching for said necklace, which wasn't there, on account of her losing it back in the fabled land of Ferra Lin.

"What do you mean?" Chaos asked, butting in.

"I've been thinking about it the whole morning," Destiny admitted. "Why Fury is the way she is...and why Ferra Lin chose her. I remember your father telling me about how he made your magic necklace, and how you never threw a tantrum after you started wearing it."

"Huh," Fury replied. "Wonder why?"

"I did too," Destiny stated. "Until I figured it out this morning. Everything your dad makes absorbs and releases something. That

189

tooth absorbed your negative emotions your whole life, so you never got to feel them."

Fury blinked.

"Wait, what?"

"Your necklace prevented you from feeling negative emotions, so you never felt bad," Destiny explained. "Your dad knew it, but wanted to protect you from ever feeling bad, so he let you keep wearing it."

"Oh," Fury mumbled. "Aww," she added, breaking out into a smile and clutching at her bosom. "That's so sweet!"

"It's also stupid," Destiny retorted. "Because in trying to protect you from feeling bad, he stopped you from knowing how to *deal* with negative feelings. So every negative emotion you have feels unacceptable to you, and you try to avoid them."

Fury considered this, feeling stunned.

"Wow, that makes total sense," Chaos stated, shaking his head in wonder.

"It does," Destiny agreed.

"Dad did the same thing to Fury that he did to me," Chaos realized. "He made me so safe and secure it almost killed me. My spirit, anyway." Which to be fair, were pretty much the same thing.

"And kept Fury safe not just from others, but her own emotions," Destiny said. "The terrible things we do trying to do good," she mused.

That, Fury realized, was terribly true. There was no doubt in her mind that Daddy – and Mommy – had wished her the best. But in trying to protect their children from the very hardships that'd made them fully realized and functional – and happy – adults, they'd hamstrung their children, so to speak. Perhaps it was better to allow one's children to experience hardship, in a dose proper to their ability to manage it. Thus the role of a parent was more appropriately to portion out difficulty than it was to abolish it. Like hardening an indoor plant by exposing it to the elements for longer and longer periods each day, it ensured that said plant would be able to endure a life outside the safety of the home, and perhaps even thrive, even in the face of adversity.

"Well they didn't *mean* to," Fury decided.

"Of course not," Destiny agreed. Fury paused, a horrible thought coming to her.

"Wait, does this mean that who I was this whole time…wasn't really me?" she asked, putting a hand to her mouth in horror.

"Not at all," Destiny answered. "You haven't worn it in a while, and yet..." she added, gesturing at Fury. Who was dressed in a *super* cute pink-on-pink ensemble. "It just wasn't *all* of you."

"Oh," Fury replied, quite relieved.

"Whoever you've been since Ferra Lin is who you are," Destiny assured her.

"And that's not much different than the sister I grew up with," Chaos added with a smile.

"Aww, thanks big brudder!" Fury exclaimed, leaping at him and giving him a big ol' hug. Chaos chuckled, hugging her back.

"Yep, same old Fury," Destiny quipped. Fury pulled away from Chaos, putting her hands on her hips.

"So you're saying I have to learn how to deal with my bad feelings?"

"Feelings aren't bad or good," Destiny corrected. "They just are. *Actions* are bad or good, insofar as the effect they have on others."

"But good feelings feel good," Fury argued.

"Not everything that feels good *is* good," Destiny countered. "Like satisfying your addictions, for example."

"Ah," Fury replied. "Right."

"Anyway, you don't have to learn to deal with your negative emotions," Destiny stated. "Just accept them. Learn how to deal with your actions."

"Got it," Fury stated confidently. "I think," she added, ruining the aforementioned adverb. "So what's next?"

"Well, Imperius said your destiny was to go into the Dark Forest and save the world, right?" Destiny stated.

"Right," Fury confirmed.

"Then that's what's next," Destiny decided. "And we're coming with you."

"Really?" Fury blurted out, her eyes widening. "Yay!" she exclaimed, giving Destiny a hug this time. And then Chaos, because he was technically part of the "we" implied by Destiny.

"Didn't Vita tell you not to go into the Dark Forest?" Chaos asked Destiny.

"Not to go *alone*," Destiny corrected. "Fury is the key, like you were for Old Langsroth."

"Huh," Chaos murmured. "Guess Dad was right."

"About what?" Fury inquired.

191

"Littles do a lot," he recited with a smile. Fury smiled right back.

"We sure the fuck do!" she agreed. And then put a hand to her mouth. "Shit, sorry!"

Everyone chuckled at that, and even Fury had to join them.

"Okay, let's go!" she prompted, turning toward the portcullis and marching away.

"Hold up," Chaos stated. "First of all, the southern exit is that way," he informed her, pointing in the opposite direction. "And if we're going into the Dark Forest, we need to be prepared. With provisions, weapons, armor, lighting sources, and so forth."

Destiny smiled at him, punching him in the shoulder. Pseudo-gently.

"Look at you," she stated proudly. "All grown up."

"I had help," Chaos stated, throwing her a wink.

"A lot of it," Destiny agreed. Chaos rolled his eyes.

"Ass," he grumbled.

"A lot of that too," Destiny stated with a smirk.

"Well that's true," Chaos replied, brightening up a bit.

"Let's go prepare!" Fury stated fervently.

So that's just what they did.

* * *

Destiny was kind enough to let Chaos shine in his role as Fury's instructor in the ways of preparing for an adventure, bringing Fury through each of the items they would need – and some they might need – for a potentially prolonged quest in a dangerous land. Fury proved an excellent student, having inherited her mother's memory. And not only that, but by virtue of her enthusiasm for the task, which lent itself not only to *wanting* to learn, but in forming far better memories by virtue of not wanting to get said learning over with already.

This was of course the common failure of most schooling, in that it turned most lessons into grim chores. Chores that teachers scolded students for not being interested in, despite that lack of interest being, in reality, the failure of the teacher or the curriculum, not the student. For excellent teachers have the gift of understanding what makes their students tick, and provide the environment for one's natural curiosity to take charge. For it is curiosity itself that is a fuel for learning, a fact known and repeated by great men and women every generation since antiquity. But sadly, largely unbeknownst to administrative types in charge of designing educational systems. Who, in classic management style, fail badly, then blame the teachers for their failures.

In any case, Fury paid attention to each step of the preparatory process with glee, committing each step and the underlying reasoning to memory. Not in the least because it was information she would most definitely use.

When they were done, their packs packed and their armor on, they made their way to the southern portcullis, which was in the process of being repaired once again.

"We're heading out to the Dark Forest," Destiny told the guards there. "We should be back before sunset."

The soldiers glanced at each other, swallowing visibly. For each of them knew what would happen if the three *didn't* return.

"Let's go," Destiny prompted Chaos and Fury. And with that, they strode through the open portcullis. Fury waved at the guards as they passed.

"Bye bye!" she told them. To which two blushed, one smiled idiotically, while the other just stared. Creepily. But before they could really leave, none other than Bree ran up to the gate. "Oh, hey!" Fury greeted.

"Hey," Bree replied. She hesitated. "Thanks for saving us," she offered.

"No problem," Fury replied. "We're going to the Dark Forest. Wanna come?"

Bree stared at her for a long moment.

"No," she answered at last.

"Oh," Fury mumbled. They faced each other a bit awkwardly, until Bree stirred.

"So, I'm not going to hang out with you anymore," she stated. Fury blinked.

"Huh?"

"It's just...you're great, but you're...a lot," Bree explained, grimacing at Destiny and Chaos. "You're just too...um...*cheery* for me."

"Oh," Fury mumbled, utterly confused now. For it seemed odd that happiness would be something off-putting. "So uh, whatcha gonna do then?" she asked.

"I'm going to hang out here," Bree answered. To the nearby guards' clear delight. For as one of the only girls there – and by far the most attractive – she was a sight for sore eyes.

"Okay then," Fury stated. "Bye," she added with an awkward wave.

"Yeah," Bree replied. And promptly walked away. Fury watched her go, feeling totally blindsided. Destiny put a hand on her shoulder.

"Believe me, it's better this way," the paladin told her. "She was a bitch." Fury smiled reluctantly at that.

"A little bit," she had to agree.

"Come on," Destiny prompted, continuing forward along the land bridge. Fury followed her and Destiny across the long wooden planks covering the gap in the land bridge near the gate, then continued across the long rocky pass over the canyon, stepping around the barricades men there were busily re-building. Chaos glanced back at the gap in the land bridge, then eyed Destiny.

"You know, Belfast probably should've just destroyed part of the land bridge to stop the zombies a long time ago," he stated. Destiny gave him a look.

"Tried that," she replied.

"What happened?" he asked.

"Wait and see," she answered. Chaos frowned, but decided to do just that instead of pressing the issue. Meanwhile, Fury recovered quickly from being dumped by her pseudo-bestie, beaming a big ol' smile as she walked and feeling positively giddy.

"I can't believe I'm actually here, going on an adventure with you two!" Fury exclaimed. "Gosh, I wonder if this is what Mommy and Daddy felt like, going on an adventure together."

"From what I remember, it did feel like this," Chaos said. "But to be fair, I was like, four at the time."

"It's like we're honoring them," Fury said, smiling at the thought. "Like we're the next generation of Littles, saving the world like our parents did!"

"Trying to, anyway," Chaos corrected.

"That's all we can do," Destiny stated.

"That's right," Fury agreed. "We'll try so darn hard that...we'll...like, really, *really* try!" she finished rather lamely.

They continued onward, making their way toward the opposite end of the canyon, eventually passing the halfway point. Ahead,

Fury saw a portion of the land bridge that looked rather odd; it was as if a huge gouge had been made in the stone, and zombie bodies had been packed into it.

"That's what happened when we tried to make a gap," Destiny informed them. "Every night, zombie bodies would fill it and be crushed by the weight of their peers. During the day, they're dormant, and we had to get rid of all the bodies before we could start digging again. Eventually it took so long to get rid of the bodies that we gave up."

"Oh," Chaos mumbled. "Didn't think about that."

"The land bridge is over a hundred feet thick in places," Destiny informed him. "Your magic was the only thing that could destroy it."

They crossed the zombie-filled gouge, which was so densely packed that it provided surprisingly stable footing. Continuing their journey, their eyes on what stood beyond: a great forest of tall, dark pine trees, a dense mist floating in the air between the trees. Mist that went from the forest floor all the way up to a good twenty feet high.

"We're gonna have a hard time making our way through that mist," Chaos noted. "I'm worried about us getting lost."

"We brought compasses," Destiny pointed out. "But you're right."

"We'll need a source of light," Chaos stated. Fury gave him a little smile.

"You rhymed," she noted.

"I'm a wizard," Chaos replied with a wink. "It's what we do."

Fury nodded, but lowered her gaze a bit.

"What's wrong?" Chaos asked.

"It's just...I guess I'm not," she told him. "A wizard, I mean."

"Maybe not, but you're still pretty awesome."

"I don't know," she mumbled.

"Hey, who saved our butts back there last night?" he asked her, raising an eyebrow. She smiled reluctantly.

"I guess I did," she conceded.

"Hey, Destiny's not a wizard," Chaos continued, "...but her relationship with Vita gives her magic that's incredibly useful. How many lives have you saved with it?" he asked Destiny, who shrugged.

"Never counted," she replied.

"A lot," Chaos answered for her. "Don't need to be a wizard to be magical," he stated. "Or to be important."

"Aww," Fury cooed. "You're the best big brudder I've ever had!"

Chaos and Destiny just looked at her.

"That I could ever imagine having!" Fury corrected.

They reached the end of the pass – and the canyon – continuing onward toward the Dark Forest ahead. To a place that so many brave people had entered, determined to bring the undead threat to an end. Not a single soul had ever returned from the mists of the Dark Forest, and Fury darn well knew it.

And as she stepped into the swirling mist of that cursed land, plunged into surprisingly dark darkness, she couldn't help but wonder if she would ever see the sun again.

Chapter 31

King Pravus opened his eyes. Which meant that, to his surprise, he wasn't dead.

He found himself sitting propped up against a cold stone wall, his nose throbbing and goopy with blood. He'd somehow been transported to a large chamber, clearly still within the catacombs. It was circular, with a domed ceiling twelve feet high, and wrought of the same black stone as the rest of the catacombs. In the center of said room stood a circular dais, upon which a single coffin lay. A coffin that had a lid, unlike the others he'd seen…a lid that'd been slid slightly ajar.

Standing to one side of the head of the coffin was the stranger in black leather armor who'd accosted Pravus, his eyes glowing with that ungodly silver-blue light. And at the head of the coffin stood a second person. A man wearing a black suit, with a black shirt and black tie that matched his short, spiky black hair. He had skin as pale as the other man, but his eyes did not glow with that creepy blue light. And a bit oddly, he appeared to be wearing dark gray lipstick.

Pravus grunted, then rose to his feet, glaring at the two men. He reached for his purple-pink greatsword…and found to his surprise that it was still sheathed at his hip. He unsheathed it, holding it before him.

"Who are you?" he demanded.

The man in the suit lifted his gaze from the coffin, eyeing Pravus with unnatural calm. For it would have been natural to be concerned that Pravus was awake and so impressively armed. The blue-glowing-eyed man strode toward Pravus, but the man in the suit held up a hand.

"Please Tylo," he murmured, his voice surprisingly quiet and gentle. "Be kind to our guest."

Tylo stopped, staring at Pravus with those unnerving glowing eyes.

"Your first mistake was letting me live," Pravus declared, glaring at Tylo. "Your second was leaving me armed."

"My only mistake was allowing you to be harmed," the man in the suit replied, again in that quiet voice. "I apologize."

Pravus blinked.

"Pardon?" he asked.

"You are King Pravus," the stranger stated. Pravus frowned.

"I am," he confirmed. "How did you know that?"

"Suffice it to say that I do," the man replied. Pravus lowered his sword a bit. But only a bit.

"And what is your name?" he inquired.

The man paused, then gave a little smirk.

"It's a long story," he answered.

"I didn't ask how you were named," Pravus countered. "Or why. I merely asked what it was."

"You can call me...Ka-La-Meh-La," the stranger replied. Pravus frowned.

"Pardon?"

"Ka-La-Meh-La," the stranger repeated.

"Is that four names or are they hyphenated?" Pravus inquired.

"Hyphenated."

"I see," Pravus replied. "Never heard of you."

"By design," Ka-La-Meh-La stated. "I have no desire to be known by your kind."

Pravus's eyebrows rose at that.

"My kind?" he inquired.

"The unkind," Ka-La-Meh-La explained. "Those who put themselves above others."

Pravus paused, for he'd been about to argue that he was not, in fact, unkind. But as king, he did put himself above his subjects. In a kind way. Mostly.

"What are you doing here?" he demanded.

"Visiting someone I held dear," Ka-La-Meh-La answered, lowering his gaze to the coffin. He reached inside, retrieving a skull, and gazed at it with an expression Pravus couldn't read. Mostly because it was a no-expression kind of expression.

Pravus paused, then sheathed his sword reluctantly. He eyed the skull in Ka-La-Meh-La's hands.

"I doubt very much that you held the owner of that skull dear," he stated. "Old Langsroth fell to the Fallen Sky millennia ago."

Ka-La-Meh-La didn't reply at first, staring at the skull in his hands. Then he stirred, lifting his gaze to Pravus's.

"You helped end the Fallen Sky," he stated.

"I did," Pravus replied.

"Did Imperius send you here?" Ka-La-Meh-La inquired, changing the subject rather suddenly.

"He did," Pravus admitted. "So that I might find the means to defeat the greatest villain of my generation, or some such."

Ka-La-Meh-La stared at him for a long, uncomfortable moment.

"Anyone can be a villain if someone names them so," he replied at last. "A true villain puts themselves above others, though."

Pravus frowned.

"Are you implying that I'm a villain because I'm king?" he inquired.

"If so, only a minor one," Ka-La-Meh-La replied. "You've a heart that yearns to do good, even if good isn't always what you've done." He gazed at the skull in his hands then. "The owner of this skull, however, was a villain beyond compare...and is the very villain that is the cause of your despair."

Pravus crossed his arms over his chest.

"And that is?" he pressed.

"Zarzibar," Ka-La-Meh-La revealed. "Necromancer of Old Langsroth, creator of the Fallen Sky. Mastermind of the Dark Rising, and the lich who enslaves those that die." His lips drew into a thin line, his dark eyes hardening. "A man who cares nothing for others, and yearns only to serve himself."

"I see," Pravus stated. "So it's true that the man behind the Fallen Sky and the Dark Rising are one and the same?"

"Yes."

"Very well," Pravus replied. "I came here to find the means to defeat Zarzibar. Can you help me?"

"I can," Ka-La-Meh-La answered. "And I will."

"Then I shall forgive your man Tylo for his aggression against me," Pravus declared magnanimously. Tylo just stared at him with those eerie glowing eyes, his expression as flat as the floor.

"Forgiveness is divine," Ka-La-Meh-La murmured, lowering his gaze to the skull. "We are men yearning to be the gods we are."

"So...regarding the means of defeating Zarzibar," Pravus prompted, not particularly in the mood for philosophizing.

"This requires context," Ka-La-Meh-La stated. "Which I can provide."

Pravus sighed.

"Fine," he grumbled, gesturing for Ka-La-Meh-La to continue, whilst preparing himself for a prolonged monologue.

"Zarzibar was rejected from Old Langsroth millennia ago," Ka-La-Meh-La began. "For the crime of necromancy, which was his gift, he was jailed. His sister had attempted to cover up Zarzibar's crimes, and for that, she was jailed as well. By the time Zarzibar managed to escape, he found his sister dead in her cell."

"I see," Pravus replied, his interest piqued. For like so many housewives in his kingdom, he was quite the fan of murder mysteries, as you may recall.

"He escaped, then vowed to return to gain his revenge," Ka-La-Meh-La continued. "Thirty years later, he made good on his promise, creating the Fallen Sky and dooming Old Langsroth's citizens to eternal enslavement."

"Seems a bit disproportional," Pravus stated.

"It was," Ka-La-Meh-La agreed. "Because the real reason for Zarzibar's anger was not his sister's death, but rejection. And the purpose of the Fallen Sky was not revenge, but power."

"Power?"

"Zarzibar was getting older," Ka-La-Meh-La explained. "He desired immortality as a lich. But to do so required creating a Soul Crystal...a crystal fashioned of enormous soul-power that could serve as his soul's eternal home."

"So you're saying that the Fallen Sky was created to take the people of Old Langsroth's souls from them...to make a crystal?" Pravus asked.

"Zarzibar concentrated the Fallen Blood into a crimson Soul Crystal," Ka-La-Meh-La confirmed. "Then came down here to this very room. He killed his body, releasing his soul with his blood...and that blood completed the Soul Crystal, binding his soul to it."

"Vile," Pravus spat. "To cause the deaths of so many for personal gain!"

"Something kings are fond of doing," Ka-La-Meh-La replied coolly. "With wars against their enemies."

"I have started no wars during my rule," Pravus shot back with pride, puffing out his chest.

"Yet," Ka-La-Meh-La countered.

"In any case…" Pravus grumbled, gesturing for him to continue.

"As a lich, Zarzibar gained standard lich powers," Ka-La-Meh-La stated, "…such as killing anything he touched. But his original magic was to bind one's soul to their blood…and after dooming old Langsroth, he went to what is now called the Dark Forest, with a plan to create an army of undead there to guard his Soul Crystal."

"As he's doing now?" Pravus guessed.

"Yes," Ka-La-Meh-La confirmed. "The Evermore Trading Company raided the Dark Forest nearly a century ago, stealing Zarzibar's crystal and enslaving him as a specter."

"So now he's been freed, and he's back at it again in the Dark Forest," Pravus concluded. "So how do I defeat him?"

"Zarzibar's enslavement taught him that he needed to grow his power," Ka-La-Meh-La replied, which wasn't an answer to Pravus's question at all. Still, it was clear the man's monologue was incomplete, and as such, that Pravus would have to suffer it a bit longer. "He vowed to never be enslaved again. So he's using his ability to remove souls with people's blood to fill a cistern with soul-power."

"To do what, exactly…?"

"To create a new Soul Crystal," Ka-La-Meh-La answered. "One made of the souls of millions upon millions of his victims, so that he can become a lich too powerful to destroy."

Pravus considered this.

"So he's created a second Fallen Sky?" he guessed.

"No," Ka-La-Meh-La told him. "The Fallen Sky was too centralized. Now each zombie carries a tiny bit of soul-blood within them, which animates them. The more soul-blood they carry, the more powerful they are. The most powerful have red glowing eyes, and often graft other zombie parts to themselves."

"The Zhimeras," Pravus realized.

"A fitting name for them," Ka-La-Meh-La replied. "Each zombie serves as its own Fallen Sky, for every drop of soul-blood has the power to do what the Fallen Sky did."

"Thus making it nearly impossible to stop, unless we kill all the zombies," Pravus realized, a chill running down his spine.

"And remove all the blood from them," Ka-La-Meh-La added grimly. "Every soldier that falls fighting the undead is turned into an undead slave as well, and thus Zarzibar's pool of soul-blood grows. For each new zombie is bled into the cistern, and blood-sucking zombies gorge on the blood of the living, then regurgitate it to fill that cistern even more."

"How can we possibly defeat him?" Pravus wondered, a chill running down his spine.

"Stop the fighting...or drain the cistern," Ka-La-Meh-La answered. "Or destroy Zarzibar's existing crystal before he can make a new one."

"His existing crystal?" Pravus asked.

"A diamond hand," Ka-La-Meh-La revealed. "One created by one of the most powerful wizards alive."

Chapter 32

The omnipresent mist within the Dark Forest was so thick that it wasn't long before it soaked through Fury's clothes, making her feel all moist and gross. It also blocked most of the sunlight, such that, despite it still being barely noon, she felt like it was night-time. She could only see five or so yards ahead of her nose, which was enough to dodge trees and low branches as she walked. And the ground, subject to constant moisture, was mossy in some places, puddly in others, and downright mucky in most. Such that everyone's boots made squelching farty sounds as they walked.

Fury giggled, and Chaos chuckle-snorted, while Destiny just kept on keeping on. For while the Little family appreciated inappropriate humor, others apparently did not. Which was awfully strange to Fury, for she'd made the assumption for most of her life that most people were mostly like her. But different people were, well, vastly different. And as such, what was uproariously funny for one could be immature drivel to another...and both views were correct.

In any case, Destiny ignored both of them, probably, while leading them further into the aptly named Dark Forest.

"Do you sense anything?" Chaos asked Destiny in a hushed voice. For as a paladin, she could sense the presence of the undead, unless there was magic preventing it.

"No," she answered.

"Huh," Chaos murmured. "Maybe they're hiding because it's daytime."

"Maybe," Destiny replied noncommittally.

Fury peered ahead through the mist, trying to make out what lay ahead of them, but the mist was so thick that it was impossible to see much. She had to trust that Destiny would be able to sense what they couldn't see. Luckily, trust was something that came easily to Fury, but apparently quite a bit less so for Chaos.

"What if there's magic like in Old Langsroth, when you couldn't sense that Zhimera that ambushed us until it was too late?" he asked.

"Then we fight," Destiny answered. Which was a badass line.

"Badass line D," Fury congratulated, beaming a smile at the paladin. Destiny smirked.

"But seriously," Chaos pressed.

"You're anxious," Destiny told him. He frowned.

"Not *anxious*," he countered, which was a lie. "Just trying to have a plan here."

"I trust that whatever happens, I'll be able to deal with it," Destiny stated. "I had a plan over a decade ago, and I executed it."

"What plan?" Chaos asked.

"Train. Prepare. Until I was the type of person who was trained and prepared for anything."

"Damn D," Fury mused. "You're like, *full* of badass lines."

"So you've already planned for this, and you don't need a plan anymore," Chaos translated.

"Right," Destiny replied. "And so have you," she added, putting a hand on his shoulder. "You just don't trust yourself enough yet…and you shouldn't."

"Um…" Chaos began.

"You'll trust yourself when you prove to yourself that you can do things," Destiny told him. "Over and over again. You have to earn that trust. And that means risking failure."

"Which would mean death in this case," Chaos argued.

"You chose to save the world," Destiny reminded him. "And so did we. If we fail, we die."

"You seem oddly comfortable with that," Chaos noted, clearly not at all comfortable himself. Destiny shrugged.

"Death is a part of life," she replied. "It'll happen to us all one day. I accept that, and so I don't fear it. Which means I'm not afraid to live fully."

"Huh," Chaos murmured.

He fell silent then, and they trekked through the woods in said silence, save for the aforementioned mud-sucking fart sounds. Which still made Fury giggle. And then snort.

Minutes passed, and then a good half-hour, without any evil enemies leaping out to molest them. Which was odd, because Fury had been told that no one had ever come out of the forest alive, at least since the Dark Rising. She was about to ask Destiny why they hadn't been attacked when Destiny stopped suddenly, putting her finger to her lips. She stayed in place, staring off into the mist, then pointed ahead and to the left.

"Enemies ahead," she whispered. "Half-mile away or so. Silence from now on."

Chaos and Fury nodded. Silently.

Chaos took his Omen-63 from his back, and Destiny held her mace at the ready. Fury, for her part, focused inward, on the *other* within her. For Ferra Lin was inextricably linked to her, she now knew, and in a way, he *was* her…and vice versa. As a Magus, he was bloodlust incarnate, unable to stay in this plane of existence as a manifested entity for long. But as his Proeliator, Fury was his connection to the material world, in the same way as Destiny was Vita's vassal.

Fury focused on his presence, on those unholy glowing dragon eyes…and on the sight of the rightmost dragon head, from which the never-ending stream of blood flowed outward. And to her surprise, she felt a warmth in her palms, and looked down to see her Vena glowing bright red. She willed the hollow fangs of Ferra Lin out from them, the handles of her cleavers, and in moments, she too was armed.

And while before she was a bit nervous, now nervousness was a foreign concept to her. For Ferra Lin was bloodlust manifested, and a warrior in the throes of fury feared nothing. In fact, she couldn't *wait* for something to leap out and try to attack them. For Ferra Lin was all about fucking evil up.

Unfortunately, as fate would have it, evil would be the one doing the fucking. And when it came, it did so not from the front, but from behind.

* * *

By the time Chaos heard the *whump* behind him, it was too late. For a Zhimera had leapt from the branches of a tree behind him, landing less than a yard away. He spun around, readying his Omen-63 for a vicious swing…

…just as the Zhimera flung him headlong into the trunk of a tree.

Chaos's head struck the wide trunk in a glancing blow, one that twisted his head sharply. He heard a loud *crack*…and then the world went black.

Pain exploded in his temple, spreading across his skull and shooting down his neck. He cried out…or at least he tried to, but no sound came out. The back of his head struck something soft, and then he felt himself come to a stop.

His vision slowly cleared…and he saw the ghostly shadows of countless tree branches high above him, obscured by ever-swirling mist.

There was shouting, and then a blood-curdling *shriek*.

Get up!

Chaos willed himself to rise…but nothing happened. He tried again, but his body would not obey. His head began to swim, and it took him a moment to realize why.

He wasn't breathing.

Chaos tried to take a breath in, but nothing happened. He tried again, but still, no breath came. It was only then that he realized that he couldn't feel the usual burning in his lungs, the telltale sign that they were hungry for air.

In fact, he couldn't feel *anything* except for his face.

Terror gripped him.

Help!

He willed his lungs to pull air in, even as black spots appeared in his vision. He tried to call out for help, but it was as if his body below his neck no longer existed. A shrill scream pierced the air, followed by muffled swearing.

Destiny!

Panic gripped him, and if he could've used his body, he would've thrashed his limbs violently. But all he could do was wait until he suffocated to death.

Then he spotted something moving in the tree branches some twenty feet above; a pale, bloated zombie with a huge gut standing on a large branch right above him. A type of zombie he'd never seen before. As Chaos watched, the creature leapt from the tree branch, falling toward him…and landed with a *whump* beside him, less than a yard away.

Help!

The black spots in Chaos's vision grew, until he could barely see at all. Until the last thing he saw was the zombie getting down on all fours over him, its horrid mouth opening to bite the side of his neck.

206

Chapter 33

Destiny should have felt the Zhimera's presence long before it attacked Chaos, but she didn't.

The warning came too late, as a kind of pressure on her mind, coming from behind. She whirled around, seeing the huge, many-limbed body of a Zhimera landing on the forest floor behind Chaos. Her reflexes kicked in immediately, and she swung her mace at the grotesque creature's head.

But fast as she was, she was still too late.

To his credit, Chaos was already swinging his Omen-63 at the creature as well, but the Zhimera grabbed him by the shoulders, throwing him violently to the side. He flew through the air with shocking speed…smacking head-first into a tree trunk some forty feet away.

Destiny heard a loud *crack*. One that made horror grip her.

Chaos!

Her mace struck the Zhimera's jaw in a glancing blow, shattering it and dislocating it. But the Zhimera ignored the injury, kicking her in the chest. Vita's Crystal Skin absorbed most of the blow, but while she wasn't hurt, the kick sent her flying backward. She landed in the dirt, and got to her feet quickly, sending out a silent prayer…and felt Vita respond. Not with words, but with the warmth of her love.

A dome of golden light exploded outward from Destiny in all directions, striking the Zhimera and sending it flying backward a full fifty feet.

Thank you, she told her goddess silently. And then she got to work.

"Got it!" Fury cried, charging after the fallen zombie, who was scrambling to its many feet. Destiny grimaced, knowing that the thing might be too powerful for the girl. But she couldn't help fight the thing, not with how hard Chaos had struck that tree. She turned to look for him, and saw him lying on his back on the forest floor by the tree he'd struck, looking upward. But something was terribly wrong.

His body was facing the opposite direction.

Shit!

Destiny sprinted toward her love…just as something dropped from the trees above, landing beside him and lowering its gaping, fanged mouth to his neck.

A Bloodsucker…a type of zombie that fed on its victims' blood.

Destiny cursed, charging at the thing as quickly as she could. It bit down on Chaos's neck, blood spurting from the wound, its throat contracting rhythmically as it sucked.

She reached the vile beast, swinging her mace at its flank. It connected with a *crunch*, the thing's ribs caving in under the sheer power of her blow.

The Bloodsucker detached from Chaos's neck, tumbling to the side…and Destiny followed up with an overhead chop that caved in the thing's skull.

She swung again, bashing its face in, then knelt over Chaos. He was just lying there, eyes wide open, his bloodied neck twisted at that grotesque angle. Blood pumped from two puncture wounds on the left side of his neck, forming a pool on the forest floor.

It took her a moment to realize he wasn't breathing.

Shit!

She placed a hand over his puncture wounds, applying pressure to stem the flow of blood. And while her first instinct was to pray to Vita, to use Lay on Hands to heal Chaos instantly, she knew that doing so would prevent her from using magic for the rest of the day. Which meant that, even if they aborted the mission and tried to flee back to Belfast, if they were attacked again along the way, she'd be all but useless to Chaos and Fury.

Don't fear, think, she told herself. *He needs to breathe.*

And if he couldn't do it, she would do it for him.

She leaned over, placing her lips over his, and breathed into his mouth as hard as she could. But with his body lying chest-down on the ground, she couldn't tell if it was working. She grabbed his shoulder, rolling him slowly so that he was lying on his back…while keeping his head facing upward as well. Doing so had almost certainly caused more damage to his spinal cord, but it couldn't be helped.

She placed a hand on his chest, giving him another breath, and to her relief, she felt his chest rise. Slightly, but hopefully it was enough. She felt his heart beating against her palm, thank Vita.

"I've got you," she told him. And to her relief, her voice was calm, though she was anything but. But she knew he was terrified, and she had to seem calm, for his sake. She gave him another breath, knowing that if she kept him alive for long enough, Vita's Trickling Regeneration would heal him.

Come on, love…

She heard a shrill scream from behind, and twisted around, seeing Fury still battling the Zhimera…and a second Zhimera, this one charging toward *her*.

"Shit," she swore, giving Chaos another breath. "Sorry love," she added. "I'll be back."

Then she got to her feet, gripping her mace tightly, just as the Zhimera closed the distance between them. It had a single head, but three torsos stuck end-to-end like the segments of an insect, each with a pair of arms. It lunged at her…and she swung her mace at it in a horizontal arc, aiming for its left temple. It blocked the blow with two left forearms, which fractured with the impact. But it slammed its shoulders into her chest, sending her flying onto her back on the forest floor.

Her breath exploded from her lungs, her mace flying from her hand.

Destiny cursed, rolling onto her belly and scrambling toward her weapon on all fours. She reached out for it…

…just as the Zhimera grabbed her ankle, yanking her backward.

"Little help here!" she shouted, kicking at the thing's hand. But its grip was like iron, and it didn't react to pain the way a living person would. It dragged her across the forest floor a few yards, then flung her right at the tree Chaos had been thrown into. She struck it with her lower back with a *whump*, falling onto her side on the ground beside Chaos.

The pain was excruciating.

Destiny gasped for air, struggling to get to her feet. But her legs were like rubber, and she fell onto her butt. The Zhimera let out a shriek, then charged at her with terrifying speed.

She called out to Vita, starting a silent prayer…but Vita wasn't the one to answer it. For without warning, the creature's head toppled off of its shoulders, its body falling chest-first to the ground. It slid up to Destiny, stopping a foot away…and lay still.

Destiny lifted her gaze from the Zhimera's decapitated body, seeing Fury standing behind it, her eyes glowing with crimson fire. She smirked at Destiny.

"Miss me?" she quipped.

Destiny extended a hand, and Fury helped pull her to her feet. She went to Chaos's side…and saw that his face was pale, his lips blue. She rushed to give him a breath, then another, and saw his skin pink up a bit.

"Need a room?" Fury asked, arching an eyebrow. "I mean I get it, 'cause when Mama's got an itch, Mama *scratches* it."

"He broke his neck," Destiny retorted. "I need to breathe for him until my magic heals him.

"Oh. Makes sense," Fury replied. There was a blood-curdling shriek behind them, and then a third Zhimera lunged out of the mist at Fury, yanking her backward into the swirling fog…and out of sight.

* * *

Fury felt herself being pulled into the mist away from Chaos and Destiny, by a horrid zombie, no less. It was something out of her greatest nightmares, at least before she'd entered the fabled land of Ferra Lin.

But now *she* was the nightmare. And that meant her attacker was about to get royally fucked.

She chopped at the arm that'd grabbed her, feeling a satisfying *thunk* as it split flesh and met bone. And then severed said bone, because her cleavers were frickin' sharp as hell. She aimed her next blow right between the glowing red eyes glaring at her from within the swirling mist…and chopped the Zhimera's stupid little zombie head in half.

"Ha!" she cried as the Zhimera fell to the forest floor, its many limbs spasming. She cackled then, because traumatic brain injuries were funny when it happened to someone else. After she'd enjoyed the spasming for a bit, she chopped the thing's head off. And then kicked said head a fair distance away.

Then she strode back to Destiny, who was busy giving Chaos intermittent breaths. Chaos's hands twitched, and then his legs did too. He took a deep, gasping breath in, then starting trembling all over.

"Oh god," he blurted out. "Thank god!"

"Thank me," Fury replied with a smirk. "And Destiny, I guess."

"Stay down," Destiny told Chaos as he tried to get up. "Your vertebrae may not be totally healed yet." He obeyed, giving her a lopsided grin.

"Might need another breath," he quipped. Destiny smirked, then leaned in, kissing him rather passionately. And while Fury would've normally found such a display super cute, now it seemed like a waste of time.

"Quit with the foreplay," she stated. "Just *do* it already."

Chaos blinked, and Destiny turned to give Fury a strange look. Which meant that there definitely wouldn't be a show, to Fury's disappointment. She turned away from the spoilsports, spotting the Bloodsucker zombie still lying by the tree, its head a bit less caved in than she'd left it. Which meant it was healing, and would reanimate soon. Rather quickly on account of its magical blood…which she could *feel* inside of it, just begging to come out.

"Chop!" Fury exclaimed gleefully, leaping into the air quite unnecessarily, then executing an overhead chop. One that severed the zombie's head…and let the blood come out. Lots of it, to her delight. It flowed up to her cleaver handles, sucking up inside.

When she'd sucked the zombie dry, she let the cleavers back into her Vena…and enjoyed quite a few pumps of blood into her circulation.

"Mmm," she murmured, breaking out into a smile. "Nnghhh *yeah*," she exclaimed with a shudder.

"Ugh," Chaos muttered, risking breaking his neck again to avert his gaze. "*So* wrong."

"You can get up now," Destiny stated. Chaos did so, gingerly at first. He stood all the way up, then smiled, giving Destiny another kiss.

"Thanks babe," he told her.

"Anytime," Destiny replied. "Let's go," she added. "Since I can't rely on my ability to sense undead, we need to be more cautious."

"I can sense their blood," Fury stated, feeling her bloodlust fade away. Until she was just plain ol' Fury again. "The ones that have a lot of it, anyway."

"Gee thanks sis, would've helped earlier," Chaos grumbled.

"Sorry brudder," Fury apologized with a pouty-face. "I didn't realize it until now."

"Can you sense blood when you're not in Proeliator-mode?" Destiny asked. Fury frowned, focusing on the paladin. But she felt nothing at all, except for love and admiration, of course.

"No," she answered.

"Could you sense my blood when you *were* in Proeliator-mode?" Destiny pressed.

"Um...I don't think so."

"Maybe you can only sense the blood of those Ferra Lin wants you to kill," Destiny stated.

"Like, evil things?" Fury asked.

"Right," Destiny replied. "Try to feel it while we walk," she prompted. "If you sense something, let me know."

"Okay!" Fury replied instantly, eager to be of help.

"But otherwise, shut up," Destiny added.

"Okay," Fury mouthed.

They continued forward through the misty forest, traveling slower this time. Fury found herself admiring the creepy aesthetic of the forest, with its dark, twisted trees shrouded in swirling mist, and had to remind herself to focus on the feeling of blood instead of the Dark Forest's dark beauty. For while she preferred rainbows and butterflies and blue skies and cheer, she could also appreciate the darker aspects of life. Because even the ugly things were still beautiful to her, in that they were beautifully ugly. Like turkeys.

In this way, they trekked through the Dark Wood, thankfully not accosted by any more Zhimeras. And less thankfully, by any Bloodsuckers, whom Fury would've rather enjoyed draining. In fact, they met with no zombies at all, continuing through the forest unmolested. And while not being molested was nice, it was also strange. For in the very heart of evil, molestation was typically a given.

At length, Destiny slowed, her eyes narrowing. She stopped, holding up a hand for the others to do the same. Then she rotated to the left a bit.

"Zombies ahead," she warned, pointing in the direction she was facing. She immediately strode toward it, which was proof positive that she was a hero, for cowards would've run the other way. Chaos followed, and Fury followed behind them, her skin slick with moisture. Whether sweat or misty deposition, she couldn't be sure, but probably both. For while Destiny and Chaos were like, *totally* brave, Fury was only partially so. Unless she was in Proeliator-mode, that was. But even then, she wasn't so much brave as fearless…and it occurred to her then that bravery wasn't an absence of fear, but the act of overcoming it.

Which meant that, in being scared and sweaty, but following Chaos and Destiny anyway, perhaps Fury was braver than she'd given herself credit for.

Huh, she thought, suddenly wondering if Mom and Dad had been afraid, back when they'd gone on their various adventures. But she didn't have time to wonder for long. For soon the mist began to clear ahead of them…or rather, they moved beyond the mist to a clearing within the forest. There was a huge hill of dark brown dirt in the middle of this clearing, with tons of human-sized holes dug into it. It looked for all the world like a squat termite mound she'd seen in books back home, or one of those mushrooms with all the holes in their caps. Either way, it was kinda gross-looking. And it smelled of decay.

"Ew," she blurted out, pinching her nose. For the hill's holes were clearly extra moist, their walls coated with objectionable fluids.

"Shh," Destiny scolded. She stopped to study the hole-filled hill, then waved them forward, walking toward the terrible thing. Fury followed…and promptly slipped and fell into a fluid-coated hole in the ground.

"Eeek!" Fury squeaked, landing a good seven feet down. On her feet, thank goodness. But it was an oddly soft landing, and she felt something writhing beneath her. She looked down…and saw hands. Lots and lots of pale, grabby hands…and glowing red eyes.

She'd fallen right on top of them.

"Graarrghh!" zombie voices called out, grabbing her ankles and pulling her further down.

"Eeek!" Fury repeated. "Help!"

Something fell over her shoulder from above; it was a rope, she realized. She grabbed it, and was promptly hauled out of the hole. But two zombies held onto her ankles, pulling themselves up along with her…and more zombies held onto *their* ankles, and so on, in a long zombie chain.

"Um!" Fury warned. Nonspecifically.

Destiny and Chaos dragged her out, and Chaos promptly used his Omen-63's peerless edge to sever the arms of the zombies holding on to her. This caused the zombie chain to fall back into the hole, which was nice. But the disembodied zombie hands still gripping her ankles were decidedly not. She yanked them off, making a face as she did so, and threw them in the pit.

"Watch your footing," Destiny chided.

"Sorry," Fury replied.

"Be careful and you won't be," Destiny shot back. Which was a pretty darn good line.

"That was a pretty darn good..." Fury began, but Destiny shooshed her. Fury's mouth snapped shut, and she nodded in silent understanding. Then Destiny led them forward, around the pits in the ground, toward the pitted hill ahead. But when they'd nearly reached the bottom of the hill, Fury heard sounds coming from behind. *Moist* sounds.

She turned...and saw zombies crawling out of the pits in the ground. Like, *tons* of them...along with at least half a dozen red-eyed Zhimeras.

"Forward!" Destiny snapped, rushing toward a large hole in the base of the hill. The largest hole, Fury realized; they entered it, their boots squishing on the overly moist floor. Fury glanced back...and saw hundreds of zombies rushing after them, including over a dozen Zhimeras now.

"Crap!" Chaos blurted out.

"Don't look back!" Destiny snapped. The hole they'd entered sloped upward for a bit, then suddenly dipped down, utter darkness ahead. Destiny prayed for a light, and one appeared, illuminating the way. They rushed further downward and forward, then turned left as the tunnel curved that way. The sounds of graarrghing came from behind, along with the ear-piercing screeches of the Zhimeras. The much *faster* Zhimeras, who charged down the tunnel after them, gaining on them steadily.

"Faster!" Destiny ordered, rushing ever downward and to the left. For the tunnel spiraled into the earth, deeper and deeper, until they had to be over a hundred feet below the surface. The tunnel straightened, its downward slope leveling out.

Then it ended. In a dead end, unfortunately. Which, given the army of zombies chasing them, was an awfully appropriate name for it.

"Fuck," Destiny swore, skidding to a stop. She turned around, gripping her mace tightly before her. "Guess we fight and die."

"Not today," Chaos declared bad-assedly, stepping in front of her.

"Yeah, problem is, we don't have a choice," Destiny shot back. Chaos smirked, switching his grip on his shovel and waggling his eyebrows unsexily.

"When there's a problem, the answer is the Omen-63," he recited. Which was literally the shovel's tag line.

He held the shovel out ahead of him, then rotated it so its scoop was facing down. A whole lot of stone and dirt poured out of it, forming a rapidly growing pile ahead of them.

"Yeah!" Fury exclaimed, pumping a fist. "Way to go, Chaos!"

The sounds of zombies approaching grew louder, along with a cacophony of hisses and graarrghs.

"Incoming!" Destiny warned.

Then Fury spotted a few pairs of glowing red eyes piercing the darkness beyond the growing pile of earth, getting rapidly closer.

"We're not gonna make it," Chaos warned, continuing to pour. "I need more time!"

"On it!" Fury replied immediately. And then made a running leap over his pile, landing beyond it. Two of the closest Zhimeras charged at her, closing the distance between them with frightening speed.

Frightening, that was, until Fury went, as her mother Valtora would have surely said, all Proeliator-mode and *sheeit*.

A thrill went through her as her Vena glowed red, cleavers forming in her hands. She did leap and a downward chop at the two Zhimeras, embedding both of her cleavers in their foreheads. Then she yanked the blades free, leaping straight up and kicking them both in their chests, sending them stumbling backward into the Zhimeras behind them.

Fury rotated in midair, landing on all fours, then rushed over the rapidly growing pile Chaos was heaping, rejoining him and Destiny. The pile was nearly halfway up to the ceiling now…but the Zhimeras without cleaved foreheads recovered, rushing toward them far too quickly.

"Or I could've just done this," Destiny grumbled, closing her eyes in prayer. A golden dome of light exploded outward, sending the Zhimeras flying backward through the tunnel with extraordinarily satisfying violence.

"Spoilsport," Fury grumbled, feeling her fury fading. Her cleavers sank back into her hands, barely any blood pumping into her veins for her trouble. Chaos finished blocking off the tunnel, then set his Omen-63 against the tunnel wall, wiping the sweat from his brow.

"Well that worked," he declared, clearly rather self-satisfied.

"Good job Chaos!" Fury exclaimed, giving him a hug.

"Thanks sis."

They all stood there in the rather small length of tunnel they'd blocked off.

"So like…what now?" Fury asked.

"The Zhimeras dig through to us or we run out of air and die," Destiny replied.

"No, seriously," Fury pressed.

"Yes, seriously," Destiny retorted.

"Well, what if we make a new tunnel?" Chaos asked, picking up his Omen-63. "We could dig our way to the surface."

"And?" Destiny inquired. Chaos blinked.

"And…not die?" he answered.

"We haven't completed our mission," Destiny reminded him.

"We're outnumbered," Chaos shot back.

"I've been outnumbered every day for the last six years," Destiny argued, crossing her arms over her chest. "Hasn't stopped me yet."

"*Damn* D," Fury exclaimed. "Bad*ass*."

"It kinda was," Chaos had to admit. "So what's your plan?"

Destiny stood there for a moment, staring off into space. Then she stirred.

"I can sense something powerful below us," she stated. "This way," she added, pointing down and to the left of the dead end.

"What is it?" Chaos asked.

"Not sure," Destiny replied. "But it's more powerful than anything I've ever sensed."

"More powerful than that asshole from Old Langsroth?" Chaos pressed.

"Yep," Destiny answered. To Chaos's clear dismay.

"Great," he grumbled. "So glad I visited."

"Dig us down there," Destiny ordered.

"Are you really sure we should do that?" Chaos asked.

"Do it *before* we run out of air," Destiny replied. Which answered his question without answering it. Chaos got reluctantly to work, digging in the direction she'd ordered him to.

"This is a bad idea," he complained. While still digging.

"So is going back up," Destiny argued. "There's an army of undead waiting for us."

"And a super-powerful evil bad guy down there," Chaos shot back. "Who totally wants to murder us to death."

"If we kill the source of the Dark Rising, we save Belfast and the world," Destiny stated. "If there's something worth dying for today, it's that."

Chapter 34

After his impromptu meeting with Ka-La-Meh-La in the catacombs of Old Langsroth, King Pravus left the man – and his rather rude sidekick Tylo – to ascend the spiral stairwell to join up with Templeton again. He reached the last set of stairs going up to the catacomb's exit, and saw Templeton there waiting for him.

"My liege!" Templeton gasped, regarding Pravus's bloodied nose with dismay. "Are you badly hurt?"

"No," Pravus replied. "But I'm afraid we must fly back to Belfast at once. I'll explain along the way," he promised.

"Of course, sire," Templeton replied immediately, without questioning Pravus. For Templeton trusted him implicitly, a fact that warmed Pravus's heart. For his part, there was no man Pravus trusted more than sweet Templeton...a man whose heart was as pure as the cheer he brought to the world. Pravus smiled, then frowned, noticing a white stone in Templeton's hands.

"What's this?" he inquired.

"A sample of stone to take back to Cumulus," Templeton explained. "For your future city in the sky."

Pravus blinked back sudden moisture in his eyes, struck with the urge to kiss the man.

"Thank you Templeton," was all he could manage. "Come!"

They set off at once, ascending the six understories of Old Langsroth, until they reached the ground floor at last. To the tunnel through the wall they went, emerging onto the Great Flat. To Pravus's surprise, the fire dragon was still there, having apparently waited for them.

"To Belfast at once!" Pravus cried. And then made the long climb up the rope ladder to the top of the dragon's back. Templeton followed behind, mounting the beast behind Pravus. "To Belfast at once!" Pravus cried a second time, and this time, the dragon complied. Up and away they went, leaving Old Langsroth behind.

"What did you learn, cousin?" Templeton shouted over the shriek of the wind. Pravus relayed the specifics of his meeting with Ka-La-Meh-La, which took considerably longer than it should have, on account of said wind. By the story's end, Pravus spotted a great chasm ahead...and bridging it, the city of Belfast. A city he'd visited a few times in the last six years, to provide morale support...and troops and loads of supplies, of course.

"Bring us to the northern wall!" Pravus commanded the dragon. The dragon did so, not out of fealty, but out of friendship. At length they reached Belfast, and the dragon deposited them before said northern wall. Much to the consternation of many of the troops guarding said wall. For not all knew of Pravus's predilection for fiery dragon steeds.

Having landed, Pravus nearly leapt off his steed. But then he remembered that he was without his magical monarch's uniform, and that as a result, said fall would have killed him. So instead he unfurled the rope ladder down the dragon's side, climbing down in a more mundane way. That done, he strode up to the Belfastian guards at the northern gate.

"I am King Pravus the Eighth," he declared valiantly. "I require an audience with your leader!"

"Um...she's gone," one of the guards replied, glancing at his fellows. Pravus arched a perfectly plucked eyebrow.

"Gone?"

"Destiny went to the Dark Forest," the man explained. "With Chaos and Fury."

"Fury?" Pravus inquired.

"Fury Little," the guard replied. "Chaos's sister."

"I see," Pravus stated. "When did they leave?"

"This morning," the guard answered. "Sire," he added, clearly realizing he hadn't been using Pravus's proper honorifics.

"We must go to them at once, Templeton!" Pravus exclaimed. "The fate of the world hangs in the balance!"

"Then go we shall, sire!" Templeton replied with gusto. "Shall we take the dragon?"

Pravus considered this, then shook his head.

"No," he answered. "We go on foot, to maintain the element of surprise." He regarded the guard. "Open the gate at once!" he commanded. And, being king – and having a sizeable proportion of soldiers within the city under his rule – his command was immediately carried out. "Come, Templeton!" he prompted.

And with that, they entered the city of Belfast, determined to help the newest generation of Chosen Ones save the day.

Chapter 35

With each shovel-full of dirt Chaos's Omen-63 absorbed, the tunnel leading forward and downward toward whatever evil awaited Chaos, Destiny, and Fury grew. But as the tunnel's volume increased, the amount of air remained the same...and as such, it was forced to grow quite thin. Thin enough that Fury soon found it rather hard to breathe. As evidenced by the fact that she was breathing hard.

"Hurry up," Destiny urged Chaos.

"Going...as...fast as I...can!" Chaos gasped, his face dripping with sweat.

"You can...do it!" Fury gasp-exclaimed, even clapping for him. "Ooof, lightheaded," she added, swaying a bit.

"Almost there," Destiny reassured...just as Chaos's shovel struck air. "Stop," she hissed, putting a finger to her lips. Chaos did so, but as it turned out, the air rushing into the relative vacuum of the tunnel had other ideas. For it made a loud whooshing sound, blowing dirt in their faces. Fury turned away from the earthen assault, closing her eyes, and waited for the wind to subside. Which it did in short order.

Then they all stood there, taking deep, gulping breaths, while Chaos rested for a bit. Luckily, he recovered quickly, on account of Vita's Boundless Vigor.

"Okay," Destiny whispered. "Now we need to..."

And then the tunnel collapsed beneath them, and Fury entered into free-fall.

She didn't even have time to scream.

Mostly because she only fell about six feet, into a tunnel below. A tunnel that was a good nine feet tall, but with the few feet of dirt that'd collapsed below her, it'd narrowed a bit. Luckily this dirt cushioned her fall.

"Pthhh!" Fury spat, for dirt had gotten into her mouth.

"Mmf," Chaos groaned, sitting up, then standing.

"Shh," Destiny warned, rising to her feet as well. Fury looked around; the tunnel sloped downward ahead of them, and upward behind them. Its size – nine feet tall and twice as wide – made it clear it was a major tunnel, unlike the one they'd first come into the hill through. Destiny pointed down the tunnel, then gripped her mace. Chaos took the hint and carried his Omen-63 appropriately, while Fury focused on Ferra Lin within her, her Vena glowing with crimson light. Her cleavers appeared in her hands, and trepidation turned to eager anticipation.

"Let's *do* this," she purred like a sexy little badass. 'Cause that's exactly what she was.

"Shh!" Destiny shooshed.

They continued down the tunnel, Destiny lighting the way magically, and eventually said tunnel's slope leveled out. Ahead, Fury saw it open up into a much larger chamber…and something within called to her.

Blood.

With every step she took toward the chamber ahead, the sheer *presence* of the blood compelled the following step. And the next.

"Slow down," Destiny hissed.

But Fury couldn't.

The blood-presence was unlike any she'd ever felt. So powerful that it would not be denied. She *had* to go to it. She had to consume it. To bring it into the great circulating river of blood that passed through Ferra Lin…and the circulating river of blood within her.

Seek the blood, my Proeliator, the dragon-god commanded in her mind. *Bring it to us.*

Fury's pace quickened, for she was compelled to obey.

* * *

Chaos watched as Fury broke ranks with them, striding down the tunnel toward the chamber ahead.

"She's acting weird," Destiny warned. "We need to stop her."

Chaos rushed to catch up with his little sister, Destiny matching pace beside him. They reached her, and Destiny grabbed her arm, pulling her back.

"Wait!" Destiny hissed. But Fury turned a glowing red glare on her, yanking her arm free with surprising strength…and promptly ran right into the chamber.

"Fury!" Chaos scold-whispered, rushing after her...

...and then he entered the chamber beyond, and skid to a stop, his eyes widening. For he found himself standing in a huge, circular subterranean cavern a hundred feet in diameter, the domed ceiling easily thirty feet high. And in the center of said chamber was a large circular pool.

A pool not of water, but of blood.

The blood glowed bright red, as bright as Fury's eyes. And when Fury saw it, her eyes widened in surprise.

She skid to a stop before it, her mouth agape. And then she made a sound. It was the kind of sound that, suffice it to say, Chaos had worked hard to evoke from Destiny, but had never wanted to hear from his sweet little sister.

"Holy *fuuuuuck*," Fury moaned, staring at it for a bit longer. And then she charged toward the edge of the pool, clearly determined to jump in. Which she very surely would have, if Destiny hadn't leapt to intervene.

Destiny tackled Fury to the ground, holding on to her tight. Fury cursed, struggling to break free.

"Let me *go!*" she yelled. But Destiny did no such thing. "I said..."

"Graarrrgh!"

They both froze, then turned to look to the right of the pool. Chaos followed their gaze, and to his surprise, he saw a zombie standing nearby. A slouched-over, drooling, pale, and rather pathetic-looking zombie, but also drop-dead gorgeous. And awfully familiar.

"Zora?!" he blurted out.

"Gasp!" Fury...gasped, her eyes immediately stopping their crimson glow. "Let *go* of me already!" she ordered Destiny, scrambling to her feet. "Zowa!" she cried, rushing up to the zombie and giving her a big ol' hug.

"Graarrgh!" Zora graarrghed happily. Maybe.

Fury let Zora go, and it was Chaos's turn to hug her. Then he frowned, looking at Zora's left hand. To his surprise, Zora's diamond hand was gone...it'd been cut off at the wrist, apparently.

"How'd *you* get here, Zowa?" Fury asked, putting her hands on her hips. Zora just stood there, looking...stumped.

"So this is the zombie who lived with you?" Destiny asked, fingering her mace.

"Yes," Chaos answered. "Don't kill her," he added, necessarily.

"Sorry babe, but I'm a paladin," Destiny replied. "I'll let you say your goodbyes," she offered.

"Destiny..." Chaos began. And was promptly interrupted, not by Zora, but by a man. Or rather, a spirit that rose up from the middle of the blood-pool. His body was skeletal and translucent and glowed white, in the manner of ghosts. But his eyes burned with a ghastly red fire. One far brighter than that of even a Zhimera, or Fury's.

WELCOME, its voice boomed in Chaos's head. Everyone else's eyes widened, making it clear that they heard it too. Or sensed it, or whatever.

"You must be Zarzibar," Destiny declared.

"He is," Chaos confirmed, having met the lich before. Mom had prompted Zora to occasionally let the guy out to meet the kids. Which was, in retrospect, questionable parenting.

YOU'VE COME TO DEFEAT ME, Zarzibar stated, clearly aware of what was up.

"Not necessarily," Chaos replied. "We just want to stop you from hurting the people of Belfast."

I OFFER THEM IMMORTALITY, Zarzibar argued.

"You offer them enslavement," Destiny retorted.

ETERNITY HAS ITS PRICE.

"They didn't choose to become zombies," Destiny shot back. "You didn't 'offer' anything...you took it."

THE STRONG TAKE FROM THE WEAK, Zarzibar pointed out. Which was historically accurate, but unfortunate. And also a classic example of villain logic. For Chaos knew from his time with Destiny that the vast majority of life's interrelations were cooperative rather than competitive. It was the propaganda of ultra-competitive systems that they were simply mimicking nature's design. Naturalists, of course, knew better, having studied nature in a more holistic way, and thus they knew that the natural order was not merely predator-prey.

"Which is why we'll take your un-life from you," Destiny replied coolly.

"Badass, D!" Fury cheered, pumping a fist in the air.

"Aww come on Zar," Chaos interjected. "We don't want to fight. You're a part of our family."

"Yeah!" Fury agreed, playing both sides. Not because she was an opportunist or disloyal, but because she generally wanted everyone to be happy.

"Yeah, no," Destiny retorted.

YOUR FAMILY WAS ENTERTAINING FOR A TIME, Zarzibar admitted.

"Darn straight," Fury agreed.

BUT THAT TIME HAS PASSED, Zarzibar continued.

"Come on Zar," Chaos insisted, but the lich cut him off.

YOU HAVE OUTLIVED YOUR USEFULNESS TO ME, Zarzibar declared. *NOW YOU ARE A LIABILITY.*

"Definitely a wizard," Fury observed. "Wish I could rhyme like that."

"We're more than our use for each other," Chaos argued. "You spent almost twenty years with my mom and dad. Doesn't that mean anything?"

Zarzibar paused.

NO, he replied. Fury blinked.

"Really?" she asked. "You don't care about us at all?"

NO, Zarzibar repeated. *I WILL ADD YOU TO MY ARMY OF UNDEAD,* Zarzibar proclaimed. *AND YOUR BLOOD AND SOULS WILL JOIN MY CISTERN.*

Chaos frowned, glancing questioningly at Destiny.

"Cistern. Noun. An underground reservoir," Fury recited, having spent loads of quality time on the couch with Mommy, reading the dictionary.

"He means the pool of blood," Destiny explained, gesturing at said pool.

"I don't want to fight you," Chaos warned.

THAT WILL MAKE THIS EASIER, Zarzibar replied.

"There's nothing easy about any of this," Chaos retorted. "But if you won't stop using people, then it's time to kick your undead ass."

"Past time," Destiny agreed. "Ready guys?"

"Ready," Chaos replied.

"Ready," Fury replied in unison. Then she paused. "Wait," she blurted out. The focused, and her Vena began to glow, her cleavers appearing in her hands. "Ready," she repeated. Zarzibar gave a ghostly smirk.

I SINCERELY DOUBT THAT, he replied.

And with that, he attacked!

Chapter 36

Zarzibar zoomed across the cistern of glowing blood, heading right toward Fury. She faced the lich fearlessly, readying her cleavers for epic swings. As he drew near, she dodged to the side at the last second, swinging her cleaver at his ghostly face.

It passed right through. Harmlessly.

Zarzibar shot past her, then flew toward her back, and Fury spun around, dodging and swinging again. This time, he swiped at her left arm with his hand, and it passed through her left forearm. Harmfully.

Fury gasped at a sudden, horrible pain in said arm, the cleaver instantly falling from her grasp. She clutched her forearm, biting back a scream...and looked down at it, her eyes widening in disbelief. Her forearm was pale gray where Zarzibar had touched her, the tissue clearly dead.

"What the..." she began.

"Fuck!" Chaos screamed as Zarzibar zoomed into his legs, collapsing on the ground even as the lich flew through him. Then Zarzibar charged at Destiny, who dodged out of the way...mostly. The lich managed to strike her right shoulder, and her mace fell from her grasp, her whole arm instantly dead.

And with that, the battle was done.

Zarzibar flew back over to the center of the cistern of glowing blood, giving them a ghostly smirk.

YOU THOUGHT YOU COULD DEFEAT ME? he bellowed, his voice booming in Fury's head. *I AM THOUSANDS OF YEARS OLD. YOU ARE CHILDREN.*

"Fuuunnnghhh," Chaos groaned, rolling on the ground in pain.

"By...Vita's...light!" Destiny cried, closing her eyes in prayer. Golden light filled her body, and a glowing golden dome shot outward in all directions, slamming into Zarzibar. Who rippled. A little bit.

FOOLISH GIRL, the lich sneered. *YOUR POWER IS MINISCULE.*

"Whelp, we're fucked," Destiny declared.

"Nnghhh…no we're not," Chaos retorted. Which seemed needlessly argumentative, as well as factually incorrect. For none of their weapons could touch Zarzibar, while his touch could destroy them.

YOU REALLY ARE THOUGH, Zarzibar argued, echoing this sentiment.

"Oh yeah?" Chaos asked. "Time for a surprise, asshole!"

Which as you are well aware, dear reader, is Chaos's magic.

Zarzibar zoomed at him, but was instantly blown backward. He fell into the cistern, vanishing under the surface of the blood.

Fury blinked, staring at where he'd been.

"So…did we win?" she asked, daring to hope.

"I wouldn't bet on it," Destiny answered, reaching down for her mace with her left hand. No sooner did she finish saying it when something burst out of the middle of the cistern in a spray of blood. Something sparkly. Something *gorgeous*.

A diamond hand.

"Gasp!" Fury gasped. "That's Zora's hand!"

"Graaarrrgh," Zora replied.

The diamond hand levitated over the pool…then shot right at Destiny, its fingers curling into a glittering fist!

Destiny swung her mace instead of dodging, smashing it into the diamond hand. But rather than shatter, it just flew backward a bit, then stopped in midair.

"The hell is Zora's hand fighting us for?" Chaos asked, trying to get to his feet. But his dead legs made the feat impossible. Destiny frowned, peering at it.

"Zarzibar's inside of it," she stated. "I can feel him."

"Inside?" Fury asked. "Why?"

"Chaos's magic must have trapped him inside," Destiny reasoned. "That must be his Soul Crystal…what his spirit is bound to. Except Chaos's magic changed the rules, and bound him to it physically, so he can't get out."

Fury blinked.

"How the hell did you figure that out so quick?" she demanded.

"Vita told me," Destiny replied. Which was awfully convenient.

The diamond hand – or Zarzibar, rather – flew at Destiny again, and Destiny took another swing with her mace. But this time, Zarzibar dodged the swing at the last second, and then slapped her across her face. Hard enough to knock her off her feet.

227

She landed on the dirt floor, looking dazed...and Zarzibar grabbed her mace, lifting it up over her head in preparation for a fatal blow.

Fury sprang into action, flinging her cleaver at the diamond hand. Her aim was perfect...and the cleaver caught Zarzibar by surprise with a loud clang.

Zarzibar jerked to the side, but held on to the mace, righting himself in midair and trying for another blow. Fury went to fling her other cleaver, then realized her other arm was still dead.

Shit!

Zarzibar chopped the mace down on Destiny's head...but Destiny rolled to the side just in time, the mace missing her by mere inches. A dome of golden light expanded outward from her, and this time it blasted Zarzibar backward. For apparently, being trapped in his Soul Crystal, he was more susceptible to her magic.

Fury reached down to pick up her remaining cleaver, which she'd dropped after Zarzibar'd killed her forearm. And then blinked, because she was grabbing it with *both* hands.

She looked down, seeing that her dead forearm was somehow fine again.

What the...

"Little help here!" Destiny shouted, even as Zarzibar flew at her with mace in hand. She scrambled to her feet, and released another blast of golden light, knocking Zarzibar back again. And Zora, who fell onto her butt on the dirt, looking dazed. But then again, that was how she always looked.

Fury broke out into a sprint, charging toward Zarzibar, and swung her cleaver in a vicious horizontal arc, smashing it into the diamond hand. Zarzibar dropped Destiny's mace, flying to the side...and right into Chaos's chest.

"Oomph!" Chaos grunted, falling onto his back. Fury dropped her cleaver, putting her hands to her mouth.

"Oops!" she blurted out.

Zarzibar made a fist, rising up and then slamming down on Chaos's chest. Again...and again. Until Destiny's third golden-domed blast flung the lich-hand away.

"Running out of magic," Destiny warned, picking up her mace.

"Ow," Chaos gasped, rolling into his side and clutching his battered breastbone.

Zarzibar's hand zoomed back toward Destiny, who swung her mace at him. He dodged once, then again, clearly getting more used to being a hand. Fury retrieved her cleaver, rushing at the lich while winding up for an overhead chop.

But Zarzibar flew right at her with surprising speed, punching her right in the frickin' face.

Pain exploded in Fury's nose, her vision going instantly black. She stumbled, then fell onto her back, the air blasting from her lungs. Her vision began to clear…just in time to see Zarzibar levitating above her, her cleaver in his grasp.

He swung it down at her head in a vicious chop…and she didn't even have time to scream.

* * *

Chaos watched in horror as Zarzibar knocked Fury down, then picked up her blood cleaver, lifting it over her head.

"No!" he screamed…just as the lich slammed the cleaver down on Fury's forehead.

A blast of golden light struck the lich a split-second too late, flinging him away. The diamond hand slammed into the surface of the cistern's blood-lake, vanishing from sight.

"Fury!" Chaos cried, rolling onto his belly and military-crawling toward his sister. But as he approached, his eyes widened, his blood running cold.

The cleaver was embedded deep within Fury's forehead, blood and brain matter oozing out of the wound.

"No!" he blurted out, reaching her at last. He stared at her sweet face, then horrid wound, bile welling up in the back of his throat. Tears blurred his vision, and he shook his head. "No no no."

Destiny reached their side then, kneeling before Fury. Her jawline rippled when she saw the wound.

"Save her," Chaos pleaded. "Use Lay on Hands."

"If I do, that's it," Destiny warned. "No more magic for the fight."

"Do it!" Chaos urged. Then he swallowed. "Please," he pleaded, tears streaming down his cheeks. Destiny hesitated, then nodded.

"Okay," she agreed.

And then something rose from the surface of the blood-pool in the distance. A glittering diamond hand. But this time, it was attached to churning, rippling blood in the shape of a man. A blood body with two glowing red eyes.

TIME FOR THE REST OF YOU TO DIE, he proclaimed.

He levitated over the cistern toward them, and Chaos grit his teeth, focusing on the lich…and then the universe at large. He sensed its intrinsic order, and willed it to *shift*.

The ceiling above the cistern cracked, then crumbled, hunks of earth falling down from it. But just as quickly, blood tendrils shot out of the cistern, reaching the ceiling and forming a flowing web that held the ceiling up. Zarzibar glared at Chaos with those horrid eyes.

FOOLISH BOY, he stated. *I'VE ENJOYED OUR LITTLE BATTLE.*

Chaos swore, focusing on creating another surprise. At the same time, he saw Destiny lower her head in prayer, golden light spreading out to her hands. She lowered them toward Fury's head…

…but Zarzibar sent a blood-tendril at them, wrapping it around Fury's ankle and yanking her away.

"No!" Chaos cried, his concentration breaking. He tried to get up, and found that this time, he could. His legs were healing, slowly but surely thanks to Vita's Trickling Regeneration. He limped toward Fury, at the edge of the cistern now. But Zarzibar yanked her away again, using the blood-tendrils to fling her right into the cistern. She sank below the surface, vanishing from sight.

YOU'RE NEXT, the lich vowed, pointing his diamond finger at Chaos. Tendrils of blood shot up from the cistern, wrapping around Destiny and Chaos's bodies and pinning them in place. Chaos struggled in vain, then glared at the lich.

"How could you do this to us?" he asked. "You were part of our family!"

Zarzibar lowered his diamond hand.

YOU WERE A MEANS TO AN END, he countered. *YOUR IDIOT FATHER SAVED ME FROM EVERMORE, AND I SPARED HIS LIFE IN RETURN. BUT I OWE YOU NOTHING.*

"But you lived with us for decades!" Chaos protested. "Don't we matter to you at all?"

YOU DESTROYED MY FALLEN SKY, Zarzibar retorted. *AND CAME HERE TO DESTROY ME.*

Chaos paused. For that was undeniably true.

"Only because you keep attacking Belfast," he argued. "Stop doing that and we'll leave you alone."

I NEED MORE SOULS, Zarzibar declared. *I WON'T STOP UNTIL I HAVE WHAT I NEED.*

"For what?" Destiny piped in. "What are you using these souls for?"

TO CREATE A SOUL CRYSTAL TO HOUSE MY SPIRIT IN, the lich proclaimed. *ONE THAT WILL GRANT ME ENOUGH POWER TO NEVER BE ENSLAVED AGAIN.*

"But…you didn't have to worry about being enslaved," Chaos pointed out. "We saved you."

YOUR FATHER SAVED ME, Zarzibar retorted. *HE WAS A FOOL, BUT I REWARDED HIM BY SPARING HIM…AND YOUR MOTHER.* He gestured at Zora. *AND I RESSURECTED HER FOR YOUR FATHER, AS A GIFT TO HIM.*

"Oh, so now you're the *good* guy," Destiny grumbled.

I AM NEITHER AS GOOD AS YOU WANT ME TO BE NOR AS BAD AS YOU BELIEVE I AM, Zarzibar replied.

"Right," Chaos replied. "Says the guy who murders Belfast's people every night."

AS YOU DESTROY MINE, Zarzibar retorted.

"It's not the same," Chaos insisted. "Your people aren't *your* people…they're soldiers who would never have wanted to join you."

I GIVE THEM IMMORTALITY IN RETURN FOR SERVICE, he argued.

"It's not a gift if they don't want it," Destiny shot back. "It's a curse."

YOU MORTALS LACK PERSPECTIVE, Zarzibar stated. *BUT SOON YOU WILL SEE…AFTER YOU JOIN ME.*

"I'll never join you!" Chaos spat. "You killed my sister!"

SHE WILL JOIN ME AS WELL, Zarzibar vowed. *AND YOU WILL ALL BE TOGETHER AGAIN. BUT ENOUGH TALK,* he declared. *IT'S TIME…FOR YOUR SOULS TO BE MINE!*

Then Zarzibar strode from the edge of the cistern toward Chaos, diamond hand curled into a fist. Chaos focused, trying to create another surprise. But he found himself exhausted by his previous two attempts, his power temporarily drained. Trapping an ultra-powerful lich inside of its Soul Crystal had taken most of his magical reserves.

231

Destiny struggled against the blood-tendrils trapping her in place, and Chaos did the same. But it was futile; all they could do was watch as Zarzibar strolled slowly up to Chaos, then stopped before him. The lich's evil eyes bore into his, and Chaos grit his teeth, glaring back at the man.

"Traitor!" he spat.

Zarzibar grabbed him by the throat, wrapping his cold, hard fingers around Chaos's windpipe.

Then he squeezed…and Chaos heard a horrifying *crunch* as his windpipe caved in.

The pain was beyond description.

He tried to cry out, but only a gurgle issued from his lips. Blood poured down his airway, filling his lungs, and he coughed violently, blood spraying from his mouth. He tried to breathe in, but there was no air.

He was drowning from the inside, in his own blood.

Terror seized him then, and he thrashed wildly against the tendrils that bound him, even as Zarzibar pulled his diamond hand away. More blood spewed from Chaos's mouth, along with a frothy red foam.

"Chaos!" Destiny cried. But he barely heard her. He continued to thrash, his lungs burning, his vision blackening.

It was then that he knew he was going to die.

The realization brought a strange sense of calm, which came with surprising suddenness. Chaos ceased his struggle, knowing that it was pointless. What would be would be. This was the end.

These were the final moments of his life, short as it'd been.

He turned toward Destiny then, barely able to see her face through the dark veil falling over his vision. Still, he smiled at her, mouthing three simple words.

I love you.

Then, having said everything he'd wanted to say, Chaos rested, letting the tendrils of blood hold him up and support him instead of trap him. And in that moment, he realized that *he'd* been the one that'd determined which it was, merely by his frame of mind.

There was never anything to fear, because the worst isn't so bad.

And with that, Chaos closed his eyes, and let himself die.

Chapter 37

The second the cleaver struck Fury between the eyes, darkness claimed her.

She floated within it for what seemed like an eternity, without thought or feeling. Without anything but pure awareness. There was no pain, no fear. For pain and fear were creations of her body, and in this state, she *had* no body.

So she floated in oblivion. For days or weeks or years, there was no way to tell. It was timeless here, though she somehow knew that the entirety of time existed here, all at once. How she knew this, she couldn't say. And she didn't care. It was pure knowledge, without source. It merely *was*, as she was.

Then she felt something. A soft, gentle *push* from behind.

Fury had the sudden sensation of moving forward, while still feeling that she was floating. She had no body, though she did feel that she had *something*. A form, nebulous and spread out, but moving ever-forward through the darkness. She felt herself changing shape, curving to the right...and then to the right again.

Then, somehow, she saw without eyes, beholding a dragon's gaping maw.

She flowed right into it, and there was darkness once more.

Rise, Proeliator.

Fury felt herself rising then, and at the same time, her spread-out shape drew itself inward in a more definite form. There was a burst of red light...and then she could see. She opened her eyes, looking down at herself.

She was standing on a stone pedestal, rising from a pool of blood there. And she *was* blood, her chest and belly a rippling mass of it. The centers of her hands glowed with a bright red light.

Return to me.

Her body solidified, blood turning to flesh before her eyes. Until she was standing on the cool stone pedestal, utterly nude...but whole.

She lifted her gaze, seeing a statue standing across a narrow underground hallway opposite her. A statue of a man with long hair, wearing real scale armor, a longsword in his right hand. His eyes glowed with a crimson light, as did circles on the palms and backs of his hands.

Fury paused, then stepped down from the stone pedestal, looking around. She was, she realized, back in the underground hallway the blood-river had taken her to near the beginning of her quest, in the fabled land of Ferra Lin.

She stood in the hallway, trying to remember how she'd gotten here. Then it came to her: the fight with Zarzibar. How Chaos had lost his legs. Destiny's dead arm.

And Zarzibar wielding her cleaver in his glittering diamond hand, sending it crashing into her skull.

Fury felt her forehead, rubbing it gingerly, and half-expected a large dent to be present there. But her skin was smooth and unmarred. She was, she found upon looking down at herself again, fully intact.

But Chaos and Destiny…

Her blood ran cold, her heart leaping into her throat.

"They're in trouble!" she blurted out. "I have to help them!"

She ran down the hallway, which ended in a left turn. She took the turn, nearly running into the wall in the process, going down another hallway with stairs leading up to another statue-lined hallway. This opened up into the familiar bridge across the bloody river, which she crossed quickly, entering into another tunnel beyond. Down another set of stairs she went, coming to the end of the tunnel…and the large, hexagonal chamber beyond.

The chamber of Ferra Lin.

She skid to a stop in the middle of said chamber, facing the three-headed stone dragon there.

"Help!" she cried. Then she paused. "Hi," she added, giving a little wave. For it was only polite. "Help!" she repeated. "Chaos and Destiny are in trouble!"

Be at ease, my Proeliator, the dragon's voice boomed in her head.

"But…"

When you are here, time does not pass in your realm, he reassured. Fury blinked, then relaxed.

"Oh," she replied. "But like, they're still in trouble," she countered. "I have to help them."

We will, Ferra Lin replied.

"How?" she asked. "If I'm here, that means they're a million miles away!" Or at least, it certainly felt that way.

Here is not a place, the dragon countered. *This is another dimension. In your realm, you are where you were.*

"Oh," Fury stated. "So...how do I get back?"

Through me, he answered.

She considered this, then frowned, crossing her arms over her chest.

"How did I get here?" she demanded. "And how am I not dead?" A pause. "Wait, *am* I dead?"

You are in-between, he replied. Fury blinked.

"Huh?"

Your hands bring blood into our river, the dragon explained. *When you die, the blood you've collected flows to me...and carries you with it.*

"So you're saying...all that blood I absorbed brought me here?"

Yes, Ferra Lin confirmed. *But in returning here, it is no longer within you. If you die again before filling the river of blood within you, you die permanently.*

Fury processed this.

"Got it," she replied. "So how do I get back?"

As you did before.

"And that means...?"

She heard a rushing sound to the right, and saw the reverse-waterfall of blood flowing upward there. The bloody elevator she'd taken before, to get back to Rocky. She strode toward it, then paused, turning to face the dragon.

"So what *are* you anyway?" she asked. "And what are you doing with me?"

I am Ferra Lin, Magus of Blood, he replied. *Your role is to bring me the blood of those who sin.*

"Sin? Like, breaking rules and stuff?" Fury asked.

Sin is a parasite, taking from others with no regard for them, Ferra Lin clarified. *I chose you to excise these parasites from your realm.*

"But why?" she pressed. "Why do you want all this blood?"

Suffice it to say that I do, he replied. She put her hands on her hips.

"But why me?" she asked.

Your purity, he answered. She frowned.

"What does virginity have to do with it?"

Your purity of heart, he clarified. *I trust that you will only seek out those who sin, and shed the blood within.*

"Huh," she murmured. Then she shrugged. "Makes sense. Can I go now?"

You may.

She went to step toward the blood-elevator again, then paused, looking down at her naked body.

"Um..."

Clothe yourself in blood, Proeliator.

"Right," she muttered.

Then she stepped into the upside-down blood waterfall, and felt herself immediately shoved upward by the raging geyser of blood. Faster and faster she went, blood roaring in her ears...

...and then she shot up into a lake of warm fluid, her ascent slowing, then stopping.

Crimson light surrounded her, the taste of blood filling her mouth. It *pulled* at her soul, this blood. She yearned for it.

Feed, my Proeliator, the voice of her god boomed in her mind.

She looked down, seeing brightly glowing red circles amidst the glowing blood...and then the feeding began.

Blood coursed through her Vena, spreading down her forearms and upper arms to her chest, then radiating throughout her body in an explosion of utter pleasure. She gasped, arching her back and throwing her head backward, feeling as if her body was expanding, ready to explode. But still the blood came, a veritable river of it, pouring into her.

All reason left her then. There was no thought. There was only the blood, and it promised her everything she could ever want.

Ecstasy wracked her, and she thrashed in the water, unable to stand it any longer. It was too much, this pleasure. Too great for any one person to bear. She felt as if she would explode, as if she would be annihilated by it.

But still the blood came, and she with it.

Then, far beyond what she'd thought was her limit, the torrent of blood ended. And with that, she found herself lying naked on her back on the bottom of a large, circular hole in the ground, easily thirty feet deep. High above, she saw a rocky ceiling, with tendrils of glowing blood forming a web across it. She was in the cistern, she realized. But all of its blood was gone. Or not gone, but in *her*.

Rise, Proeliator, her god commanded. And so Fury did. The movement was far too easy, as if she was far too strong for her puny body. She looked down at her naked flesh, and willed blood to flow from her Vena, forming a suit of blood armor around her. Belly-baring, of course, and sleeveless, which was super cute. And with boots and tight pants that were *super* flattering.

Then twin fangs shot out of her Vena, and her cleavers formed their blades. She gripped them with a loose, easy grip, then gazed up at the edge of the cistern, thirty feet up. A bright red spotlight shone wherever she looked, and it took her a moment to realize it was because of her glowing eyes.

IT'S TIME, she heard Zarzibar's voice boom in her head, *...FOR YOUR SOULS TO BE MINE!*

"Nope," she replied.

And then she jumped.

* * *

Destiny watched in helpless horror as Chaos thrashed in Zarzibar's deadly grip, his throat crushed by that awful diamond hand. He coughed up bloody foam, his eyes wide, thrashing his head from side to side...and when Zarzibar let go of Chaos's throat, Destiny saw that it was utterly crushed.

"Chaos!" she cried, struggling in vain against Zarzibar's crimson tendrils.

Then Chaos stopped thrashing, and turned his head toward her, giving her a warm, bloody smile.

I love you, he mouthed.

And Destiny's heart was crushed.

She cried out, even as Chaos's eyes drifted closed, and he fell limp in his blood-tendril prison.

No!

Destiny closed her eyes, willing Vita's power to flow into her. Not asking this time, but demanding.

Save him!

But the goddess's power refused to be compelled. For as Destiny knew all too well, grace could only be given, not taken.

Please, she pleaded, tears streaming down her cheeks. *Let me save him.*

But plead as she might, Vita remained silent.

Zarzibar turned to Destiny then, striding up to her. He gazed down at her with his horrid glowing eyes, and in that moment, he was evil incarnate.

YOUR GODDESS IS WEAK, Zarzibar sneered, lifting his diamond hand to her neck. He wrapped his fingers around her throat then. I HAVE SURPASSED HER, he continued, AND SOON I WILL SURPASS ALL OF THE MAGI.

Destiny swallowed past a lump in her throat, blinking tears from her eyes.

"And then what?" she asked.

But she never got an answer.

For something appeared behind Zarzibar, flying up out of the depths of the cistern. A figure dressed in blood-red, belly-baring armor, wielding twin crimson cleavers. A girl, young and beautiful, with long, flowing red hair. And with eyes burning with the most intense, blood-red fire that Destiny had ever seen.

Fury, Proeliator of Ferra Lin, dragon god of blood.

Destiny watched as Fury reached the apex of her leap, arcing toward Zarzibar, her cleavers held high over her head. Zarzibar noticed the direction of Destiny's gaze, and turned to face what was coming...

...just in time for Fury's cleavers to chop through his blood-arms, severing them from his frickin' body. Fury followed up with a horizontal swing, decapitating him.

But his arms and his head merely flowed back into his body, re-forming almost instantly. Then tendrils of blood shot out from Zarzibar, wrapping around Fury and binding her in place.

FOOL, he stated. WITH MY POWER, YOU CANNOT DEFEAT ME.

"What power?" Fury inquired.

THE FALLEN BLOOD, he answered.

"Oops, sorry, I drank it all," she replied. Then she smirked. "Now your power is mine."

And with that, her Vena glowed impossibly bright, and the tendrils of blood flowed into them...as did Zarzibar's blood body, until all that was left was his diamond hand. It fell to the ground before Fury with a clatter, palm-up. But it quickly flipped around, flying upward toward Fury's throat.

"Nope," Fury said, her cleavers starting to glow with that same bright light. She slashed at Zarzibar's hand with one of them...

...and it shattered into a thousand glittering little pieces.

A burst of blue energy shot out from the impact, flying outward in all directions, with a soul-chilling scream that echoed through the chamber. It faded away, and Destiny felt Zarzibar's evil presence go with it. Until only she and Fury remained.

"Chaos!" she blurted out, even as the tendrils binding her dropped away, sucking into Fury's hands. She rushed to Chaos's side, sending a heartfelt request to Vita. But this time, she didn't have to ask, for Vita was already in the process of giving.

Grace, it appeared, came when it was ready, and not a moment sooner.

Golden light flowed from Destiny's heart to her hands, and she laid them on her lover. It bathed Chaos, spreading not only to his neck, but to his entire body. His windpipe filled out, his eyes fluttering open...and to her utter joy, he took a deep, shuddering breath in.

"Chaos!" Destiny cried, embracing him just as tightly as she could.

He grunted, then hugged her back, and they just stood there, holding each other. And in that moment, Destiny never wanted to let him go.

"I love you too," she murmured, kissing him full on the lips. The kind of kiss that meant something. No...the kind of kiss that showed him he meant *everything* to her.

At length, they separated, and Destiny pulled back, gazing at her love.

"Well that's a relief," Chaos replied with a little smile. "Would've been kinda awkward if you didn't."

Destiny rolled her eyes, but couldn't help but chuckle, and she heard laughter from behind. She turned, seeing Fury standing there, her eyes no longer glowing, and her hair no longer red. Fury beamed a smile at them, opening her arms wide.

"I love you guys too!" she exclaimed. "Group hug!"

Chapter 38

Having destroyed Zora's crystal hand – the home of Zarzibar's soul – the lich, whose life had spanned millennia, was put to rest at last. Destiny and Chaos helped Fury climb out of the now-empty Cistern, after which Fury dusted off her awesome new blood-armor.

"Isn't this blood armor awesome?" she asked, gazing at her getup rather proudly.

"Sure is," Chaos replied with a smile. He leaned in, giving her a hug. "Good job sis," he told her. "You're something else, you know that?"

"Isn't everything?" Fury replied. She turned to Destiny, who looked a bit fucked up. "You look fucked *up*," Fury stated, but not in a mean sort of way. Some seeming insults were just descriptive.

"I am," Destiny replied with a grimace, clutching at her broken shoulder. Her golden shirt was a bit shredded, which hinted at shredded skin beneath. "But I'm only one nap away from being fine."

"Man, that was close," Chaos stated, rubbing the back of his head. "I thought you were dead," he told Fury.

"She *was* dead," Destiny answered. Fury blinked.

"I was?"

"According to Vita, you were," Destiny confirmed. "But somehow you came back."

"I think the blood I collect has the power to resurrect me," Fury explained.

"Which means if you didn't have enough left, you would've died permanently," Destiny reasoned. Which, while reasonable, wasn't particularly comforting, for obvious reasons.

"Well I've got *tons* of blood now," Fury stated. Which was literally true. Like, *tons* of tons. In fact, she felt positively *buzzing* with the stuff. And to be honest, it felt...well, incredible. "I feel like I'm like, fucking powerful as hell," she added. And for once, didn't recoil from having sworn.

"You swear more when you absorb more blood," Chaos noted.

"I noticed it too," Destiny stated.

"Huh," Fury replied. "And it doesn't bother me as much."

"Maybe your furious self gets stronger the more blood you're holding," Destiny proposed. "In any case, we should really get out of here before an army of undead corners us."

"We killed Zarzibar," Chaos argued. "All of the zombies should die, like they did in Old Langsroth."

"Afraid not," Destiny countered. "Each zombie was like their own little Fallen Sky, remember? Killing Zarzibar won't change that."

"Oh," Chaos mumbled. "Crap." He grimaced. "How the hell are we supposed to fight our way out of here?" he asked. "You don't have any magic."

"I don't, but *she* does," Destiny stated, gesturing at Fury. Which was true, in a way.

"Yeah," Fury replied, putting her hands on her hips and adopting what she assumed was a badass look. "I'm like, filled to *bursting* with blood. I can totally get us out of here!"

"Graarrrghh," a voice called out from a few yards away. Everyone turned, spotting none other than Zora shambling toward them, all dead-eyed and drooling and such. But on balance, she was awfully beautiful, having been Mommy's body in the distant past. And what's more, having been perfectly preserved, without a single trace of decay.

"Zora!" Fury exclaimed, rushing up to the zombie and giving her a hug. Then she held the zombie at arms' length. "Come on, we're taking you home!"

"Yeah, I don't think so," Destiny grumbled, holding up her mace.

"Now hold on," Chaos blurted out.

"Sorry guys, but she's a zombie and I'm a paladin," Destiny replied. She limped up to Zora, who was still staring at Fury with an awfully dull expression.

"Don't!" Chaos shouted, reaching for Destiny. But Destiny stopped suddenly, her eyes narrowing.

"Wait a second," she stated, frowning a bit. Then her eyes widened. "She has a soul!"

"Well of course...she does?" Fury asked.

"She does," Destiny confirmed, studying Zora intently. "But zombies aren't supposed to have one."

"Told you she was different," Chaos piped in. For as you may recall, dear reader, he'd done just that a good six years ago. After their adventure in Old Langsroth, when they'd returned to Borrin to meet his parents. Which in retrospect had been rushing the relationship a bit, but still.

"You were right," Destiny replied. "I was wrong." Which was a rare thing for many women to confess to their partners. But for Destiny, it wasn't because she was averse to admitting fault, but because she was usually right. "Guess I don't need to destroy her after all."

"Really?" Fury asked, daring to hope.

"Really," Destiny confirmed.

"All right!" Chaos exclaimed. He leaned in to embrace Zora, even giving her a kiss on the cheek.

"Grrarrrgh!" Zora graarrghed rather violently, happy to see Chaos and Fury. Probably.

"Aww!" Fury cooed. "C'mere Zowah!" And with that, she gave Zora another big ol' hug. During which Zora drooled on her shoulder a bit. "Ew," Fury blurted out, extracting herself.

"All right then," Chaos stated. "Since you're the only one not injured, you'll have to lead the way," he told Fury.

"On it!" she exclaimed, saluting sharply.

She did just that, leading Chaos and Destiny and Zora out of the large underground chamber of the Cistern, making her way up the shallow slope of the wide tunnel beyond.

"You should probably go Proeliator mode," Chaos prompted.

"Right," Fury stated. "Pro-mode it is!" she exclaimed, making up a cute nickname for her bloodthirsty alter-ego on the spot. In a considerably shorter period of time than it usually took her to summon her inner mass-murderer, her meat cleavers sprouted from her palms, her eyes glowing red and her hair turning red as well. "Let's *go*," she purred, charging up the slope.

"Slow down," Chaos complained. "Destiny's injured."

"And we have Zora," Destiny pointed out, gesturing at the zombie. Who was managing the slope slightly better than she managed stairs. Which was to say, not well.

"Right," Fury grumbled, tapping her foot impatiently as they caught up. Eventually they did, and Fury tried to settle into a slower pace. One that in her current condition, felt slug-like.

In this way, they eventually reached the part of the tunnel that'd collapsed, and Chaos used his Omen-63 to make a ramp back up to it. They helped poor Zora up the slope, then continued until they reached the earthen blockade Chaos had made.

"Well crap," Fury blurted out.

"When there's a problem, the answer is the Omen-63," Chaos recited. "Wanna try it out?"

"Fuck yeah," Fury replied, grabbing the shovel's shaft. And soon she found that the shovel's tagline was in fact quite accurate, uncommon as that was. For the Omen-63 cut through that blockade like her cleaver had cut through zombie necks, making quick work of excavating all that earth. It wasn't long before the tunnel ahead was visible again, and the hole was wide enough for them to go through.

And also wide enough for them to see a horde of zombies rushing down the tunnel toward them!

"Ooo," Fury exclaimed, handing the shovel back to Chaos and retrieving her cleavers. "Mama needs a *drink*."

But before she could engage, the zombies were cleaved in two rather messily by a truly massive purple-pink blade. One that Fury soon found was held by an equally massive man. A man clad in purple-pink platemail armor that was just *gorgeous*. Like, it really had to be seen to be believed.

Behind this man was another man, one muscular and toned, wielding a slender blade more akin to a fencing coil. A man that Fury found quite startlingly handsome. So much so that she blushed, lowering her gaze…and felt some kind of way. A "hubba hubba *wowee*" kind of way, much as she'd felt when she'd first met Bree. Which was rather startling, in that it seemed that she was precisely half as picky with said feeling as she'd expected to be.

"Have at you!" the bigger man exclaimed, cleaving the last of the zombies between them with remarkable strength. Then he frowned, looking straight at Fury and her family and friend. "Hold now," he stated. "Is that Chaos Little I see?"

"And Destiny," the smaller man stated.

"King Pravus!" Chaos exclaimed.

"Indeed," the large man confirmed, striking a truly epic pose. Fury found herself quite impressed.

"You're King Pravus?" she asked.

"I am," King Pravus proclaimed, eyeing her. Specifically, her red hair, which made him grimace. "And who are you?" he inquired.

243

"Her eyes are glowing red," Templeton noted, seeming a bit confused as to how to approach this.

"Oh," Fury replied. She sucked her cleaver handles back into her Vena, then returned to her usual self. "I'm Fury," she greeted, giving a cute little wave. "Fury Little."

"Chauncy's daughter," Templeton told King Pravus.

"Ah yes," Pravus replied. "Templeton and I came as quickly as we could, to warn you of a dire evil that lurks within this land."

"You mean Zarzibar?" Fury asked. Pravus frowned, clearly taken aback.

"Yes."

"Already killed him," Destiny notified. Pravus blinked.

"Really?"

"Yep," Chaos confirmed. "Fury smashed his Soul Crystal."

"He's like, *dead* dead," Fury stated. Then she paused. "Like, *un*-undead."

Pravus stared at them all for a bit, looking rather disappointed.

"Oh," was all he could manage. "I see," he added, managing just a bit more.

"Bravo," Templeton offered, beaming them a smile. And quite strangely, Fury found that he no longer seemed nearly as interesting. Handsome yes, but not in a *wowee* kind of way. Which was odd, really. She paused, then focused on entering Pro-mode again…and instantly the *wowee* feeling returned.

Huh, she thought, reverting back to herself. Again, the feeling faded.

"Bravo indeed," Pravus agreed. "You two are a credit to the Little name, I suppose. And your efforts are also appreciated," he added, inclining his head at Destiny.

"The Little name is getting so good I'm starting to want to have it," Destiny quipped, giving Chaos a look. Chaos blinked, looking enormously taken aback.

"What?" he blurted out.

"Relax," Destiny chided, glancing down. For while some people wore their emotions on their sleeves, Chaos displayed them a bit further south. Fury caught Pravus looking rather appreciatively.

"My how you've grown, Chaos," the king murmured.

"Happens so quickly with children, doesn't it," Templeton mused. Obliviously.

"In any case, thank you all for helping us defeat Zarzibar and save the land and such," Pravus stated.

"I'd say it's our turn to help," Templeton added. "Shall we escort you up?"

"Please do," Destiny replied.

"Graarrghh," Zora added.

And so they did. Suffice it to say, with the help of two of the strongest and most resilient men in the land, that our heroes soon found themselves free of the underground lair that'd nearly imprisoned them. And soon after that, they left the dark, misty Dark Forest behind, returning to the city of Belfast.

Chapter 39

It hardly needed to be said that, upon their only daughter's inaugural flight from the nest, so to speak, that poor Chauncy Little felt horrible indeed. For his sweet, loving daughter, who'd shown him perhaps the purest form of love a man could be bequeathed, had been torn from him by fate to go on a journey that practically guaranteed to change her for the worse, if not kill her.

Thus Chauncy found himself at home, feeling terribly terrible, and what's more, inconsolable. This despite his loving wife's rather spectacular attempts to keep him otherwise occupied. Mostly through the act of occupying *her*.

But after many days of said distractions, Chauncy found his appetite for occupation nearly sated.

Nearly.

"Get it, Chauncy-poo!" Valtora exclaimed, whilst engaged in an activity guaranteed to give it to him instead.

"I'm…a…gonna!" Tip exclaimed, in rhythmic increments.

"Rrghhh!" Chauncy groaned, near to completing the task Valtora had given him. Which was when, quite vexingly, there came a knock upon his door.

"Fuck," Valtora swore.

"Keep going!" Tip urged.

"The door!" Chauncy blurted out, extracting himself from this situation. He leapt out of bed, opening the door and bounding downstairs.

"You're nude!" Valtora reminded him.

"Crap!" Chauncy sort-of-swore, rushing back upstairs. Or rather, beginning the attempt. One that was aborted by the sight of none other than ZoMonsterz perched at the top, gazing down at Chauncy with loving purple-pink eyes. Eyes that used to fill his heart with warm, gushy feelings…and now filled it with sphincter-spasming terror.

He *shrieked*.

"Chauncy?" Valtora called out. He saw her poke her head out of the bedroom, looking down at him. Then she noticed ZoMonsterz. "Oh hey poopy-dooz," she greeted, giving the hellcat a loving behind-the-ear scratch.

There was a second knocking on the door.

"Crap!" Chauncy blurted out, still nude. Tip said nothing at all, as he was no longer up. Luckily, Valtora threw down Chauncy's purple robe, and he donned it quickly, then opened the door...

...and saw none other than Chaos and Destiny standing on the porch. And behind them, Fury!

"Oh!" Chauncy gasped.

"Big Daddy Nyum-Nyums!" Fury exclaimed, leaping at him and giving him a big hug. The kind of firm embrace that made it absolutely crystal clear that she really *had* missed him. Not the obligatory kind of hug that most ended up being, but an act straight from the heart, truly and deeply felt. And as such, it evoked the same feeling in him.

"Oh thank goodness you're okay!" Chauncy cried. And then cried.

"Aww," Fury cooed, rubbing his back tenderly. Which only made his crying worse. He sobbed, releasing the pent-up tension of days and days of worry. For now there was nothing at all to worry about. Fury was safe and sound. As was Chaos, and Destiny, whom he'd worried considerably less about. At length, Fury pulled away, to Chauncy's dismay. Then Chaos took his turn, giving his dad a hug, as did Destiny.

"What are you guys doing home so soon?" Chauncy asked. For he'd expected Chaos to be in Belfast with Destiny for quite a while, if not indefinitely.

"Well, seeing as how Fury saved the world, we really didn't have much else to do," Chaos quipped. Chauncy's eyes widened, and he turned to Fury.

"You did it?" he asked, trying not to sound too surprised. And failing.

"*We* did it," Fury corrected, throwing an arm around Destiny and Chaos. Just then, Valtora came downstairs.

"Who is it?" she demanded. And then spotted Fury. "Fury-kins!" she gasped, shoving past Chauncy and leaping into Fury's arms. And almost throwing them both off the porch stairs. "Ohmygod I *missed* you!"

"Mommy!" Fury cried. And then starting crying, because girls treated mommies and daddies differently.

"Gimmee *hugs*," Valtora commanded, squeezing Fury tightly.

"Hi Mom," Chaos greeted.

"Hey Valtora," Destiny piped in. Valtora extracted herself from Fury, giving each a big hug. Then she eyed Destiny approvingly.

"*God* you look good," she stated.

"Thanks," Destiny replied.

"Like, hot as *fuck*," Valtora continued. "Ever thought about getting bedazzled?"

"Not really," Destiny admitted.

"Not that you need it," Valtora stated, "...but you should *totally* try it."

"I'm not opposed," Destiny replied.

"Neither am I," Chaos stated. Destiny gave him a look.

"Why am I not surprised?"

"I mean I'm happy with you as you are," he clarified. "But I'm just saying if that's what you wanted, you could do it."

"So you're saying I need your permission?" Destiny asked, raising an eyebrow.

"No, that's not what..."

"Typical man," Valtora interjected, putting her hands on her hips and shaking her head at him.

"And here I thought you were different," Destiny groused.

"I didn't...that's not..." Chaos stammered. Both women glared at him.

"Relax," Chauncy told him. "They're just messing with you."

"Aww," Valtora said, pouting. Then she turned to Destiny. "But seriously though, hit me *up* and shit."

"Alright," Destiny agreed.

"Ooo! Then you can have big ol' teddy bears like me and Mommy!" Fury exclaimed, hopping up and down. Destiny blinked.

"Teddy bears?" she asked, glancing at Chaos, who blushed furiously.

"She means titties," Valtora explained. "When she was six, she thought we were saying 'teddies,' and then..."

"Anyway," Chauncy interjected, eager to change the subject.

"Graaarrrghh!" a feminine voice graarrghed from behind. Chaos and Destiny stepped to the side, and none other than Zora shambled up the stairs toward them!

"Zora!" Chauncy blurted out. And then Zora tripped on the steps, landing flat on her face on the porch. "Ooo," Chauncy said, wincing. For Zora had really hit the porch quite hard. He and Destiny helped the zombie up.

"Zora, you're alive!" Valtora cried, giving the zombie a hug. "I mean undead!" she corrected. Then she noticed Zora's missing left hand. "What the hell?" she blurted out. "Rooter!"

A moment later, the gneiss little golem waddled adorably out onto the porch.

"Unheal Zora already," Valtora ordered. For while healing healed the living, un-healing healed the undead.

"Better step back," Chaos warned, for un-healing meant harming those with a pulse. Everyone did so, and within moments, Zora's hand had grown back. But unlike before, it was merely a fleshy hand, not a diamond one.

"Well crap," Valtora muttered. "Chauncy, switch bodies with me."

Chauncy blinked.

"Like...now?" he asked. For it was usually something they did in private.

"Just *do* it already," Valtora urged. And despite Chauncy's better judgement, he did just that, putting his left hand on her shoulder, then focusing seeing himself in her. There was a sudden shift, and then he was in her body, and she was in his. "Okay," Valtora stated, turning to Zora and putting her left hand on the zombie's shoulder.

"Wait!" Chauncy blurted out. "You don't know what'll..."

But it was too late...for there was a sudden change in Valtora's posture. Or rather, Chauncy's body's posture. For it went from Valtora's sass to something else entirely: a kind of breezy, confident, and mildly dangerous pose.

"Graarrghh," Zora's body graarrghed. Which confirmed Chauncy's greatest fears: for now Valtora was trapped in Zora's body, a dumb zombie...and Zora was in Chauncy's body. Which meant that Chauncy's body was now inhabited by a dumb zombie mind, one that would be too dumb to switch bodies back.

"Crap," Chauncy blurted out. Zora – in Chauncy's body – turned to gaze at him.

"Well well *well*," she stated, eyeing him up and down. "It's been a long time since we talked, darling."

Chauncy blinked.

"Huh?" he mumbled.

"Oh come *on* dear," Zora-in-Chauncy stated, stepping forward in sashaying kind of way, and putting a hand on his cheek. "You know who I am."

"Grarrrgh," Valtora graarrghed, in Zora's body. Just looking as dull and dumb as could be. Her eyes unfocused further, if that was possible, and she slouched a bit more…and suddenly, her left hand turned into a diamond one, as it'd been before.

"Oh," Chauncy blurted out. "Wow."

"I missed our conversations," Zora-in-Chauncy's-body stated, turning Chauncy's head to face her.

"Um…hey Zella," he stated, swallowing in a suddenly dry throat. "So…you ah, you were aware of who you…were all this time?"

"Of course," Zella replied. For that's who she truly was.

"We weren't sure what your experience was like," Chauncy stated. "As a um, zombie."

"You never switched bodies with me," Zella pointed out.

"We didn't know what would happen," Chauncy argued. "If your mind was still…zombified, and you got in my body, we might never change bodies back."

"You change bodies back naturally in a few hours, remember?" Zella shot back. "Like in the earth-hut Harry made for me so many years ago."

"Ah," Chauncy mumbled. "Right."

"Unless the original body dies," Zella continued. Which was also right.

"Are you…uh, mad?" Chauncy asked. A bit lamely.

"Mad? Hardly," Zella replied. "The Order of Mundus would've executed me or put me in jail for eternity. Honestly, sixteen years in a zombie body was a gift."

"Oh," Chauncy mumbled. "Well that's good."

"And I got to enjoy being with you," Zella continued, sliding a hand down his cheek to his neck. Which, her being in his body, was touch he didn't really appreciate. But, little bitch that he was, he just took it. "My husband, just like I wanted."

"Um, yes," Chauncy replied. "We are married," he added, which was obvious. But to be fair, the woman he'd married was a brain-dead bombshell, and now that she'd gained a considerable amount of intelligence, he was having second thoughts. Not that he minded the idea of being married to a slightly psychopathic bitch, him having married Valtora as well. Still, Zella was dangerously psychopathic, while Valtora was entertainingly so. "So um, what now?"

"Hi Zella!" Fury interjected, waving to Chauncy's body.

"Hello daughter," Zella replied, turning to embrace the girl. "And hello son," she added, hugging Chaos.

"Good to finally talk with you," Chaos admitted.

"Glad I didn't choose to destroy you," Destiny offered. Zella smirked.

"And I'm glad I wasn't successful in destroying you all," she replied. "Apologies for strangling you and threatening to kill you," she told Chaos.

"Honestly, I don't even remember it," Chaos replied.

"You were a newborn."

"Well that explains it," Chaos stated, glancing at Chauncy a bit nervously.

"Well isn't this delightful?" Zella mused, eyeing everyone. "I could get used to being smart again."

"Um," Chauncy began. For while Zella being smart was something he could get used to – maybe – Valtora being trapped as a zombie was decidedly not.

"Graarrgh!" Valtora graarrghed, shambling up to Zella and giving her a hug.

"I love you too Valtora," Zella replied, giving her a hug and a kiss. On the lips, and rather vigorously, which was awkward, at least in front of the kids. She turned to Chaos and Fury then. "Thank you for coming to save me from Zarzibar," she stated.

Chaos glanced at Fury, and they both gave her a weak smile.

"...yeah," Chaos replied.

"Like, mission totally accomplished!" Fury exclaimed. Chauncy frowned.

"So uh...what happened to you?" he asked. "You and Epic just disappeared one day."

"I'm afraid I don't really know," she confessed. "While I'm a zombie, I'm not very smart."

"Oh," Chauncy replied.

"I mostly live in the now when I'm Zora," Zella explained. "It's actually quite refreshing to do."

"So you don't remember what happened to you and Epic?" Fury pressed.

251

"I know that Zarzibar talked with Epic quite a bit," Zella answered. "And that we left Borrin to go to the Dark Forest. Then Epic left, and you and Chaos and Destiny came to save me."

"So Epic's still alive?" Fury asked, clutching her hands to her bosom hopefully.

"He is," Zella confirmed.

"Where is he?" Chaos asked.

"I'm not sure," Zella admitted. "But in my defense, I was brain-dead at the time."

"We have to find him!" Fury exclaimed.

"That might not be a good idea," Zella warned.

"Why not?" Fury pressed incredulously. Zella paused.

"I'm not sure," she admitted. "But trust me when I say my gut tells you not to."

Everyone glanced at each other, not at all knowing if they *could* trust Zella. As a braindead zombie, she was quite trustworthy. But as an intelligent woman who thought for herself, she was dangerous and unpredictable. Which was why the very best students and employees were like zombies, incidentally. Indeed, the main purpose of Borrin's educational system was to transform children into complacent completers of repetitive tasks, workers who would be unlikely to question or fight back against their masters.

"So...what now?" Chauncy asked. "With you I mean."

"Relax Chauncy dearest," Zella purred. Which sounded weird coming from Chauncy's voice-box. "You'll get Valtora back. It's actually rather pleasant to be a bit brain-dead," she mused. "A break from the trauma of endless cycling thoughts."

"It is?" Chauncy pressed.

"Quite," Zora confirmed. "To merely exist, without the weight of responsibilities, without worries of any kind. I found that most of my suffering before being a zombie was a result of self-inflicted wounds, setting expectations for the future, then having them dashed."

"So as a zombie, you had no expectations," Destiny piped in. "And therefore you didn't suffer."

"Exactly," Zella agreed. "I could focus on what was happening in the moment, without anxiety about the future or reliving pain from the past. It made me realize what was *really* important to me."

"Like...?" Chauncy inquired. She smiled, putting a hand on his shoulder.

"My husband," she replied. "And my wife."

"Graaarrgh?" Valtora asked. Maybe.

"Well that's how I see it," Zella stated. "After all, considering what we've done together, and with Chauncy, I'd say we're all married to each other."

"Hurrghh," Chaos retched, covering his mouth with his hand just in time. Destiny made a face, and Fury just kept smiling, sweet, adorable, clueless little girl that she was.

"I don't mind being Zora," Zella continued. "But it'd be nice to switch off with Valtora from time-to-time. I do miss being in my own body."

"Graarrgh," Valtora agreed. Brain-dead-ed-ly.

Zella put her hand on Chauncy's shoulder, and with that, Chauncy felt another shift. Suddenly he was in his own body again...and Zella was in *her* original body, all tatted up and ultra-gorgeous.

"Oh *yes*," Zella purred, gazing down at herself. Then she eyed Chauncy with a predatory look. One that made him take a step back involuntarily. "This is going to be *fun*."

"Um..." he began.

"So anyway," Chaos interjected, doing his very best not to glance at the rise Zella had gotten out of Chauncy, "...I was going to say we all came home to stay a while, but I think I'll go back to Belfast."

"Guess it'll stay a long-distance relationship," Destiny quipped, "...because I'm not going back."

"Yeah, about that," Chaos stated. "I was planning on waiting until Harry and Nettie were around to give the news, but..." he trailed off, looking profoundly uncomfortable.

"What news?" Chauncy asked. Zella draped an arm around his waist, pressing her side against his.

"And I'm up," Tip exclaimed.

"Did it just...talk?" Destiny asked, eyeing Tip's tent whilst clearly wishing she wasn't.

"What news?" Chauncy repeated hurriedly, clasping his hands over the devilishly demonic mod for his rod.

"Yeah, what news?" a voice called out from midway down the stairs. Chauncy turned, seeing Nettie limping her way down to them. She'd slept in, having stayed up rather late the night before.

"Yeah, what news?" a warbly voice called out from the top of the stairs. For it was none other than Harry, coming down after her.

"Nettie! Harry!" Fury gasped, rushing to give both of them an embrace.

"Good to see you, kid," Nettie stated, smiling at Fury.

"She thought you wouldn't make it," Harry notified Fury.

"Huh?" Fury asked. Harry slid a finger across his throat.

"She placed a bet on it," he revealed. Nettie elbowed him, then yelped, rubbing said elbow.

"Shut up Harry!" she snapped. "I told ya it was a damn joke!"

"Good one!" Fury exclaimed, even though it really wasn't. Certainly not from Chauncy's parental point of view. Nettie turned her glare on Chaos.

"All right, spit it out," she ordered. Chaos hesitated.

"Um...on second thought, I'll do it some other time," he decided.

"Bull," Nettie retorted. "We're all family. Come on now, whatever it is, just get it off yer chest already."

"If ya want to," Harry added, earning another elbow from Nettie. Chaos hesitated some more, shifting his weight from one foot to the other, then sighing.

"Alright," he decided. "So...well, the thing is, when I was a kid, I dreamed of a day I'd be like my dad, and go off on a great adventure. I waited and waited for Imperius Fanning to come to my door and give me my destiny."

He turned to Destiny then, smiling at her and grabbing her hand.

"And now that I have you," he continued, "...I know that we're destined for something more."

With that, Chaos lowered himself to one knee, gazing up at his Destiny.

"Gasp!" Fury gasped.

"Grargh!" Valtora graarrghed, in gasp-like fashion.

"Will you marry me, Destiny?" Chaos asked, clasping Destiny's hand in both of his.

"Graarrgh," Valtora graargh-whispered in Chauncy's ear.

"Yes, I know he rhymed," Chauncy whispered back, unable to help but smile. For, brain-dead or not, she was still Valtora.

"Eh," Destiny answered.

Chaos blinked.

"What?"

"Not sure if I want that much chaos in my life," Destiny stated. Chaos stared at her, then suddenly looked so crestfallen that it broke Chauncy's heart. But to everyone's relief, Destiny broke out into a grin.

"Kidding," she said, leaning down and giving him a kiss on the lips. "Yeah I'll marry you."

"Graarrrrgh!" Valtora exclaimed. Chauncy jerked his head away, for her lips were still near his ear.

"Eeeeee!" Fury squee-d.

"Yeah!" Chaos exclaimed, leaping to his feet and picking Destiny up by the waist. They kissed again, this time in a way that frankly, Chauncy was uncomfortable witnessing. Still, he found himself smiling from ear-to-ear.

"Guess our Little family is getting bigger," he stated.

"Come on everyone," Nettie declared, turning to go back inside. "Let's celebrate!"

Chapter 40

After helping to defeat Zarzibar in the Dark Forest, King Pravus the Eighth employed the fire dragon's services, having it burn every last zombie at the bottom of the canyon. That done, he traveled back to the capitol city of Cumulus with sweet, dearest Templeton, feeling rather refreshed after their little vacation. But when he returned to his castle to resume his duties, Pravus found himself feeling rather removed from the day-to-day activities he'd been compelled by the circumstances of his birth to carry out. Not in the sense that he removed himself from having to do them; rather, he did them with practiced efficiency, but without any attachment to what he was doing. It was merely a series of tasks, unworthy of emotional investment. So it was that he found himself in his oversized office, seated in his well-worn chair, finishing his day neither irritated nor pleased, but merely feeling…well, finished.

He signed the last of the legal documents on his desk, then leaned back in his chair with a sigh. All of the work he'd done that day seemed suddenly pointless, filled with putting ink on pieces of paper and little more. Then again, even his most recent foray into Old Langsroth had proven utterly pointless, as he hadn't found anything useful within the catacombs. The greatest evil in the land had been defeated by Fury's hand, with no help from him. Other than the services of his dragon, who'd taken care of the residual zombie army.

It didn't make any sense, really. Why had Imperius sent him to the catacombs? The Arch Wizard was no fool, of course, and his magical gut was never wrong. Still, Pravus couldn't for the life of him understand how his most recent adventure had made a lick of difference.

He couldn't help but feel that, in the grand scheme of things, he'd been utterly useless.

It was in this frame of mind that Pravus lifted his gaze to find Desmond still standing by the office door, waiting as usual to assist. Or more likely, waiting for time to pass in his usual dour way, so he could do it all over again the following day. Pravus was struck with the urge to make some snippy comment to the old man, but even this seemed…wrong. Instead, he studied Desmond intently, realizing he'd never really gotten to know the man.

"You know Desmond, I don't feel that I really know you," Pravus confessed, feeling in a particularly honest mood.

"What is there to know?" Desmond droned in his usual monotone.

"Well that's just the thing," Pravus replied. "What *is* there to know about you?"

Desmond paused.

"The vast reality of my internal world," he answered at last. "And the universe from my point of view."

"My point exactly," Pravus stated.

"Was it though, sire?"

"I mean that I know so little of your internal world," Pravus clarified, giving the man an irritated look. But he didn't feel that irritated, which was unusual. And a bit irritating.

"You can't know it," Desmond replied. Pravus frowned.

"I can't?"

"Only I can," Desmond explained. Pravus eyed the man, then crossed his arms over his chest.

"But you *can* explain your thoughts," he pointed out, feeling a tiny thrill at the prospect of an argument. Arguments were battles, after all, a pitting of wit against wit. And an argument with Desmond promised to be challenging indeed, for he was no nitwit.

"Words are the wrong tool for the task," Desmond countered.

"They communicate what you're thinking," Pravus shot back.

"What I'm thinking is a stream of words," Desmond replied. "Streams of words are the least part of my experience."

"Thoughts are the least part of *most* people's experience, unfortunately," Pravus quipped. For as he knew all-too-well from dealing with the problems of the general public, the general public was generally thoughtless, otherwise they would've solved their problems themselves. A fact that gave the aristocracy something to do; why, if people didn't require the aid of authority to solve their problems, kings and kingdoms wouldn't exist.

"Indeed," Desmond agreed.

"I daresay you're more thoughtful than most," Pravus pointed out.

"And yet thoughts are a fraction of the experience."

"You mean *your* experience," Pravus corrected.

"I *am* the experience," the old man shot back. Pravus frowned.

"You mean you're *having* an experience," he retorted.

"I am the experience of having an experience," Desmond countered.

"We're going in circles," Pravus stated a bit peevishly. But he was eager to trap Desmond with Desmond's own logic.

"That is the precisely the experience," Desmond replied instantly.

"Explain."

"There is the experience of being, and the experience of being a being experiencing being," Desmond stated. Pravus paused to parse this.

"So you're saying that the feeling that you're a person having an experience is just the experience," he translated.

"Yes sire."

"And thoughts are a small part of it," Pravus continued.

"The least part, sire."

"So thoughts are unimportant?" Pravus pressed.

"Importance is not a matter of proportion," Desmond countered. "My eardrums are no less important for being small."

"So you mean your thoughts are a tiny fraction of your experience."

"And vocalizing them can only show you a fraction of what there is to know about me," Desmond concluded.

"You being the sum total of that experience," Pravus stated.

"Correct, sire."

"Hmm," Pravus murmured, uncrossing his arms and rubbing his broad, classically masculine chin. "So I can't know you."

"Only my appearance and my words," Desmond replied.

"And your actions," Pravus argued. Desmond paused.

"And those," he agreed.

Pravus considered this, and found himself troubled.

"Well that's depressing," he stated.

"It is, sire," Desmond agreed. Depressedly.

"If we can never truly know each other – without *being* each other – then what are we to do?" Pravus wondered. "Remain strangers forever?"

"I regret so, my liege."

Pravus stared at Desmond for a long moment, then felt a sudden pang of sadness. That they were doomed to remain strangers – that *everyone* was doomed to remain strangers to each other, never truly understanding what each other's lives were like. He supposed that was what made it so easy for people to treat each other poorly, that they could remain blissfully unaware of the trauma they caused one another. In their ignorance, they needn't ever suffer the suffering they sowed. It was their own experience that mattered, simply because it was the only one they could ever fully know.

"Go away Desmond," he muttered, waving the old man away. "As usual, you've depressed me."

"Terribly sorry, sire."

"You most certainly are," Pravus grumbled. The old man bowed, then tottered away with slumped-over shoulders and a rounded back. Signs of neglected external rotators and a poor posterior chain, he knew. But in the end, it was not the specifics of the musculoskeletal system, but the neglect that was the key. For while Desmond's mind had clearly not been neglected, his spirit had. And as such, his mind and body suffered…and the experience that Desmond surely was suffered as well.

Perhaps this, Pravus thought, was what spirit really was. A word to describe experience from one perspective. Not merely the body or one's thoughts, that constant stream of words flowing from who-knows where. But the sum total of experience, which no other spirit could fully know.

The thought prompted him to recall his most recent adventure, plunging into the catacombs of Old Langsroth by himself. One of the few times he'd felt truly alone, and in doing so, had been forced to connect with himself. Perhaps this was the value of spirits being individual experiences, that – thusly isolated – they had to go it alone for a time, and thus connect with parts of their natures. And if that were the case, they perhaps after death, spirits might ascend as he had, to rejoin with others to share what they'd learned. Not in the sort of judgmental way popularized by the masses, but in the spirit of discovery, of revelation. And in this way, of learning more about the greater self.

Pravus stirred, turning to look at the countless books resting on his office's bookshelves. Each written by a different hand, words from a different experience. All a kind of sharing, for few wrote a book for only themselves to read.

"I should read more," he realized, staring at those tomes. His attitude toward books had been forged by schooling, to see reading as a compulsory activity. And as he'd often mused, anything compulsory was contemptible to the human spirit. But from this new perspective, reading was discovery. If not of the whole of another's being, then at least a sliver of it.

If we can never truly know each other, then what are we to do?

He thought of Templeton then, his sweet, dearest cousin. The man who'd held his heart captive since the moment he'd been able to feel the magnetic pull of attraction to another. How many years had Pravus pined over the man, desperate to have what he could never possess? And how many years had he denied himself the prospect of meeting someone attainable, for fear of giving up on the dream of being with Templeton?

"You're a fool," he realized, a chill running down his spine. "Why, you're just like Desmond." For in denying himself what his heart wanted – by indulging in hopeless fantasy – he'd been forever the author of his own suffering.

Which meant that he'd suffered because he'd wanted his fantasies more than he'd wanted to not suffer.

"You're a damn fool," Pravus muttered, shaking his head. "You already have Templeton in your life. Allow someone else love you the way he doesn't."

Imperius's words came to him then:

You may bring your cousin with you, until you see the submerged stone. But at the entrance to the catacombs, you must part with him and go it alone.

Pravus felt a sudden surge of emotion, and swallowed it back down.

You must part with him.

Not as a friend or as family, of course, but as the lover of his dreams.

"Alright," Pravus muttered, heaving a heavy sigh. "Alright."

And so it was that, despite his day's work having been complete, it was a good long while before Pravus stood from his chair, leaving his office at last. He did so knowing that Desmond was right, as usual. He never could know another as he knew himself. But perhaps that wasn't the point. For if he'd learned anything from his dear cousin Templeton, it was that warmth and cheer – and above all else, kindness – was perhaps the most potent of all magic. Sure, fireballs and staves of wind and destiny-delivering guts were powerful, and useful in countless ways. And those with such powers were called Chosen, and set off every generation or so to save the day.

But if every spirit was an isolated experience, never able to truly know each other's point of view, then by being kind to each other, each could make the other experiences a little bit better...and in the end, perhaps that was the very best a spirit could do.

Chapter 41

Having set off on her destined path toward to vanquish the great evil lurking in the Dark Forest, Fury Little felt a little bit different than the girl she'd been. Not a whole lot, but enough for Mommy and Daddy to notice. And Harry and Nettie, to boot. But despite her fears, Fury's Proeliatorship to the great god Ferra Lin hadn't hardened her heart or blackened her soul. For at her core, she was essentially the same.

There was a lesson in this, she thought as she cleaned the dishes after a nice celebratory dinner with the fam. She gazed out of the kitchen window, seeing the stars twinkling in the night sky. Chaos and Destiny had gone to bed rather early, and Mommy and Zella had gone to bed with Daddy. Or rather, zombie Mommy, for Zella was still in Mommy's body. Or rather, Zella's body, which Mommy had stolen years ago. In any case, Nettie and Harry were the only ones still up, and the above were the reasons why. Harry was outside, doing something or other, while Nettie was helping clean up.

"You alright girlie?" Nettie asked her, whilst wiping the table.

"Mmhmm," Fury replied. Then she frowned, trying to recall what she'd just been thinking.

"Whatcha thinkin'?" Nettie asked, interrupting said recollection a second time.

"I can't remember," Fury replied. Nettie gave her a look, then continued wiping. At which point Fury recalled what she'd pondering. That there was a lesson in having stayed the same core person despite having grown so much…and perhaps it was that a quest's purpose was not to grow out of something, but to grow *into* the person you'd always been. To peel away the layers of conditioning that peers and authority had placed upon you, to make you less like yourself and more like everyone else.

In Fury's case, it'd been a lifetime of being denied negative emotions by virtue of the magical fanged necklace her father had placed upon her. A necklace that he'd had her wear her whole life, partially to protect her from unhappiness, but also – almost assuredly – because it'd made her far more pleasant to parent.

"You remember yet?" Nettie asked.

"Hmm?"

"What you were thinkin'," Nettie clarified.

"Just that the magic necklace Daddy gave me stopped me from feeling bad, but that it made me miss part of what it means to be alive," Fury replied. "And that I was worried that I might not be who I thought I was all my life, but it turns out I am who I always was, just with more depth."

Nettie blinked, then stopped what she was doing, staring at Fury with a funny look on her face.

"I guess I had to learn how to accept the negative side of me, and that it didn't define me," Fury continued. "And that it's good to feel bad sometimes."

Nettie just continued to stare.

"I mean, if I love someone, and I lose them, it should hurt," Fury explained. "Like when Epic and Zora left." She paused, lowering her gaze, and felt a sudden sadness come over her, one that surprised her. For sadness of anything more than a minor amount was foreign to her. She realized then that her magical fang necklace must've prevented her from feeling this emotion too. When Zora and Epic had disappeared six years ago, she hadn't been too upset. A little sad, but any time she'd think of them, she'd soon forget. The necklace had prevented her from being crushed by her younger brother's disappearance…and only now was the full weight of her loss apparent.

"Aww, c'mere kid," Nettie prompted, limping up to her and giving her a hug. Fury hugged her right back, feeling some of the sadness go away. Such was the power of embraces that they lifted psychic weights, making the greatest of burdens easier to bear. For a hug was connection, and to be connected was to share. The good *and* the bad.

They separated, and Fury wiped a tear from her cheek.

"I guess feeling bad isn't bad," she stated. "Unless I think it is. It's just my heart telling me the truth, and if I avoid it, I'll be living a comfortable lie."

"In the short-term maybe," Nettie stated. "But lies always hurt more in the end."

"Yeah," Fury agreed. Nettie paused, then grimaced.

"Speaking of comfortable lies," she stated. "I suppose I owe you an apology."

Fury frowned.

"For what?"

"Well, I think I…underestimated you all these years," Nettie admitted.

"Huh?"

"I guess I assumed I knew who you were, so I never tried very hard to figure it out," Nettie explained. "Y'know, what was going on in that pretty little noggin of yours."

"Aww," Fury replied. "It's okay."

"Like hell it is," Nettie scoffed. Then she smiled. "But it will be. Gonna hafta have lots more conversations with ya."

"Oh yay!" Fury exclaimed. "I'd love that!"

"I know," Nettie replied. "There's more to you than I gave you credit for, kid." She shook her head ruefully. "Strange that happy people seem like fools, while bitter people seem smart."

"Really?" Fury asked. For she'd certainly never seen it that way. Bitterness was a bad relationship with the world, which included oneself. And staying in a bad relationship didn't seem smart at all, at least to her.

"You might be smarter than I thought," Nettie stated, putting a hand on Fury's cheek. "But yer love is what I love most about ya."

Fury smiled, blinking back more tears, and gave Nettie another hug.

"I love you Nettie," she murmured.

"Love you too Fury," Nettie replied. They held each other for a long while, until Nettie pulled back. "All right kid," she stated. "I'm headed off ta bed. You see that lousy husband of mine, tell him to get his ass up to bed too."

"I will," Fury promised at once.

With that, Nettie hobbled into the foyer, then went upstairs, leaving Fury all alone in the kitchen. She finished drying the final dish in the sink, then turned to gaze at her small kitchen. With everyone in bed, the house was pleasantly silent, the patter of gentle rain drumming on the roof the only sound. She smiled, feeling right at home. Not just because she *was* at home, but because she knew that this was where she belonged. Adventures were fun and exciting when they came, but in the end, her heart was with her family. A growing family, with Destiny destined to join it. Luckily, Fury's heart was plenty big enough to love a Little family of any size.

She lowered her gaze, thinking suddenly of Epic...the one member of her family who'd left and never returned.

Don't try to find him.

Zella's warning stung, because they implied that Epic didn't *want* to come back. How that could be, Fury couldn't possibly understand, for she loved him dearly and would give so much to have him home again.

She sighed, feeling awfully depressed...but at the same time, she knew that the depth of her sadness was precisely the depth of her love for him. And so, as terrible as she felt, she knew it meant she'd loved him terribly as well.

I'll find you, she told herself, straightening her shoulders and fixing the kitchen with a steely-eyed, slightly squinty glare. The kind of look a badass hero gave, which made sense, because that's precisely what she was. When she had to be, anyway.

For as she'd noted before, she'd remained the Fury she'd always known, for without her suppressive necklace, she was still her happy self, but with a fair amount of once-suppressed rage that liked to come out and play once and a while, by way of murderous rampage. A great power indeed, though it was not technically hers to own, but to rent. For the power was, in the end, the magic of Ferra Lin, and Fury had no claim to it other than through her connection to him.

But while Fury wasn't technically a wizard, she made up for it by being herself. For as Nettie had told her, her love was the best part of her. Love, as it turned out, was even more powerful than the magic of Ferra Lin. For while it wasn't technically magic that could open the silver doors of the Gate, it had an even greater power: to open the hearts of those whose lives she touched.

So it is, dear reader, that we find ourselves at the end of this particular tale, a journey into the Dark Forest, but also the darker parts of Fury's soul. And as Chauncy had once thought of his visits with Harry and Nettie, this was time with the Little family that may have seemed a bit too short.

But rest assured, while Fury's tale is complete, there are many more stories yet to tell. Not the least of which is the story of what happened to the last remaining member of the Little family who has yet to be addressed: one Epic Little, the most mysterious member of Chauncy's magical family.

Now, dear reader, while Fury's story was rather short and sweet, Epic Little's tale will prove to be anything but. In fact, it is a tale that you may find the most epic of them all...and one told with a truly epic amount of epically inappropriate magic.

Epilogue

The catacombs in the depths of Old Langsroth were pitch-black, the air cool and moist. For the vast network of subterranean hallways and chambers were still submerged in some forty feet of water. While the stone had been sealed against flooding, the humidity within the catacombs was oppressive, making the floor and walls slick. Within the deepest chamber of the catacombs, the pitch-blackness was pierced by two eyes glowing with a marvelous silver-blue light.

The light of a soul having returned to the body it'd occupied in life.

The man who called himself Ka-La-Meh-La sat cross-legged in the center of this chamber, next to his blue-eyed companion Tylo. He cradled the skull he'd taken from the coffin in the center of the chamber, gazing down at the empty sockets from which its eyes had once gazed, transforming the light of the sun into brilliant color. A familiar bitterness rose up within him, and he found himself clutching the skull so hard his fingertips turned white. He forced himself to relax. To accept rather than resist what'd been done to him.

Find the lesson, he told himself. A well-worn mantra in his mind. Everything had its lesson, and the more painful that lesson, the more important it was, and the better it was learned. Pain was communication. A message that what he'd done had been a mistake. The greater the pain, the bigger the mistake.

The lesson was to never make this mistake again.

He found himself feeling suddenly antsy, and stood, grimacing at the stiffness in his legs and back. He hooked his fingers into the skull's eye sockets, lifting it to carry it at his side. Then, without a word, he turned and strode toward the chamber's exit, his footfalls reverberating off the bare stone of the tunnel beyond. His constant companion followed dutifully behind him, the light from his glowing eyes illuminating the way. Faithful as always, unlike the owner of the skull Ka-La-Meh-La held. Those he brought back

267

always were. Not in the forced way that Zarzibar's zombies were, by slavish addiction to blood. Not by making them incomplete, and therefore yearn to be what they'd been in life. But by giving them everything, in an act of kindness. By understanding who they *really* were.

The journey out of the catacombs took nearly an hour, for Ka-La-Meh-La refused to hurry. There was no point to it. No need for ceaseless rushing from destination to destination. Nothing mattered more than anything else...and no one mattered more than anyone else.

When at last Ka-La-Meh-La emerged from the darkness of the catacombs, ascending the spiral staircase to the sixth understory of Old Langsroth, he found the stars peeking out between the maze of layered sky bridges and buildings. They cast the white stone of the city in the faintest glow, though most of the sixth understory was cast in shadow. He wondered what sort of lights the ancients who'd lived in this city had used thousands of years ago, before it'd been cursed by the Fallen Sky.

Never again, he thought, feeling another pang of bitterness. He glanced down at the skull in his left hand, then tore his gaze away, focusing on what he was doing. Putting one foot in front of another, making his way out of the city. To whatever happened next.

He continued to ascend, until he reached the ground floor of the city at last, his companion following behind him. Not in the typical shambling, mindless way that most of Zarzibar's abominations did, but with agency. Slavery was abhorrent to Ka-La-Meh-La. He had never once ordered his companion to do anything. His power lay not in compulsion, but in connection. A connection purer than that of most humans, as Zarzibar's betrayal had proven. As most of the humans in Ka-La-Meh-La's life had proven...at least until they crossed over.

It changed people, crossing over. Made them realize what they *really* were. And what a great gift to have that understanding while he was still fully alive.

He crossed over the bridge to the platform leading to the city exit, continuing onward through the fifty-foot-long tunnel passing through the wall surrounding Old Langsroth. He spotted the portcullis ahead, closed as it'd been when he'd first come here.

Ka-La-Meh-La stopped before the closed portcullis, stepping to one side to let his companion reach it. The man walked right up to it, squatting and grabbing the bottom of it...and lifted it up over his head in one smooth motion. Ka-La-Meh-La inclined his head, stepping through the open doorway into the Great Flat beyond. His companion twisted so that he was facing the tunnel, then stepped backward. There was a muffled *pop* as the companion's left shoulder jerked downward out of its socket, muscles snapping under the great weight. The portcullis slammed shut with a loud *clang*.

The companion did not grimace, though his shoulder was grotesquely deformed, and terribly painful. The man was no longer under the illusion that his body was *him*. It was merely a vessel, the thing which bound him to this world. His shoulder would heal, of course. His soul would see to it.

Ka-La-Meh-La stood there, staring outward at the Great Flat...and at the wide expanse of sky above. The heavens were devoid of clouds, stars glittering like jewels in the flawless sky. They told the truth of the world, that it was one of many. For to the stars, his world was a tiny speck, unseen in the darkness of the void. For it cast no light of its own. To the heavens, it was invisible. It might as well not even exist.

Perhaps it shouldn't, he thought, lowering his gaze to the skull in his hand. Without a material plane, souls would never have to leave their home.

He felt a sudden *shift*, and a *pulling* sensation in his mind. A presence within his awareness which had not been there a moment ago. His eyes widened, and he felt a chill run down his spine.

He crossed over!

Ka-La-Meh-La stood there, staring at the skull, feeling numb. He'd expected nothing less, of course. Imperius Fanning's magic had made it all but guaranteed that Zarzibar would be defeated. Zarzibar's desperate attempt to grow his power such that he could avoid this fate had been in vain. Just as Ka-La-Meh-La had warned him it would be.

And Zarzibar had used him. Brainwashed him into serving his cause. All so that Ka-La-Meh-La would use his magic to bring him back when the inevitable came to pass.

He turned to face the wall of Old Langsroth, black stone contrasting with the pure white stone of the interior. Zarzibar's quest for power hadn't been for any cause other than his own preservation. He'd used the people of Old Langsroth to gain

269

immortality, and then tried to use Ka-La-Meh-La to cheat death once again. And like a fool, Ka-La-Meh-La had believed in him.

Never again.

It was clear now that there was only one living being that he could trust. Only one person he could believe in. There was no one still living that he could know the heart of…other than himself.

If he brought Zarzibar back, of course, then he would know the man's heart. For in bringing souls back from their resting place, Ka-La-Meh-La connected with them in a way that living things never could.

He stood there, staring at the wall, then let his fingers go lax. Zarzibar's skull slipped from his hand, landing on the packed dirt of the Great Flat, joining the countless other skulls there. Then he took a gray handkerchief from the breast pocket of his suit, wiping away the ash he'd applied to his lips earlier.

It's finally over.

Ka-La-Meh-La turned away from Old Langsroth then, making the first step of his journey toward whatever happened next. And while he didn't know yet what that was, he took comfort in knowing that it would not be a quest for power. It would not be for personal gain. What he did next would be for the countless souls trapped in their limited bodies, living their small lives clueless as to what they truly were.

He would show them what they were, the only way he knew how. Because for humanity, death was the greatest lesson of all.

The following is an excerpt from
HUNTER OF LEGENDS
Book 1 in the Fate of Legends series

PROLOGUE

Taylor stood in a small cavern a hundred feet below the surface, looking up at the uneven, rocky ceiling above. There was a dark, narrow vertical shaft there, with a rope dangling through it, just long enough to reach the cavern floor. He pointed his flashlight up the shaft, seeing his wife Neesha rappelling down the shaft toward him. He aimed the flashlight just below her, so she could see where she was going.

"You okay?" he asked as she continued downward. At a faster pace than he had, he noted with dismay. She smirked at him.

"Better than you were," she replied. Five foot one, with chocolate-colored skin and big, beautiful eyes, she was a sight to behold. He'd been damn lucky to find her…and even luckier that she'd said "yes" so many years ago.

"Show-off," he grumbled. Neesha reached the bottom, disconnecting her harness from the rope. She brushed past him, checking him with her shoulder as she did so. He stumbled to the side, catching her smirking as she strode forward through the small cavern beyond. Lanterns had already been set up in the cavern by her grad student, Mark. Taylor spotted a small tunnel ahead, extending beyond the cavern.

"Try to keep up," Neesha quipped, striding toward the tunnel. Taylor hesitated.

"Hey, let's take a picture," he proposed. She stopped, turning to give him a look.

"Really?"

"For Hunter," Taylor explained. Neesha sighed.

"Fine," she grumbled.

She pulled out her phone, leaning in next to Taylor and snapping a picture. Then she put her phone in her back pocket, striding toward the tunnel again. Taylor followed behind, admiring his wife's well-shaped buttocks as she walked. An amateur powerlifter, her posterior was damn-near perfect…and she knew it.

"I know you're staring at my ass," Neesha said, not even bothering to turn around.

"Can you blame me?"

"Not really," she conceded. "Come on baby, try to focus on your work."

"Right now," he replied, "…I'm focusing on what I'll be doing *after* work."

"Dirty boy," she murmured. But the way she said it, he could tell she was smiling.

They continued down the tunnel, using their flashlights to illuminate the way ahead. After a few minutes, the tunnel opened up into another small cavern. Lanterns lit the cavern as before, and two men were standing by the far wall, talking to each other. They stopped in mid-conversation, turning to face Taylor and Neesha.

"Oh, hey professors," one of the men greeted. It was Mark; tall and lanky, he was the best archaeology grad student Neesha had ever had. The shorter, beefier man beside Mark was Corey, a linguistics grad student.

"Whatcha got?" Neesha asked, stopping before the two men. Taylor studied the wall before them. It was mostly composed of rough granite. But embedded in the far-left side of the wall was a thick black stripe of what looked like metal extending from the floor to the ceiling, its surface perfectly smooth save for small symbols carved into it. The stripe was about a foot thick, and curved away from them as it went upward, vanishing into the wall.

"I'm not sure," Mark admitted. "We've been excavating this thing all morning. Or trying to, anyway."

"Do you recognize the symbols?" Taylor asked. Corey shook his head.

"They're not like anything I've ever seen," he confessed. "I took some pictures," he added. "I'll have to do a database search once we get back to the surface."

"Interesting," Neesha murmured. She reached out with one gloved hand, touching the black metal. It was obvious that the two students had spent a great deal of effort digging a few yards to the right of it, a large gouge in the wall present there, with rubble moved to one side of it. "Keep digging."

"Yes professor," Mark replied. He grabbed a pickaxe resting against the wall, and Neesha and Taylor backed away. Mark got to work, swinging the pickaxe at the wall, without much effect. After a few swings, Neesha stopped him.

"Let me do it," she stated, grabbing the pickaxe from him. Mark stepped back, and Neesha planted her feet, then swung the pickaxe in one smooth motion, slamming it into the wall. The rock crumbled with the force of the blow, and Neesha swung again, striking the wall a second time. A hole appeared in the wall, about the size of a fist. Inky blackness lay beyond.

"Damn," Corey breathed, staring at Neesha in admiration. Taylor grinned.

"Yeah," he replied. "My wife's a badass."

Neesha lowered the pickaxe, peering through the hole, using her flashlight to illuminate what lay beyond.

"What do you see?" Taylor asked.

"There's another chamber beyond," she answered. "I can't get a good look at it yet. We need to widen this hole." She handed the pickaxe to Mark. "Come on buttercup, put some muscle into it."

"What muscle?" Corey quipped. Mark rolled his eyes, but got to work, widening the hole swing by swing. After a few minutes, the hole was large enough to fit a leg through. Taylor took over, taking a few swings himself. No stranger to lifting weights, he was in almost as good shape as his wife. He made quick work of the wall, broadening the hole. When he tired, Neesha took over, making them all look bad, as usual.

"Not bad for being eleven weeks pregnant, eh?" Taylor quipped. He swiped Neesha's phone from her back pocket, snapping a few pictures. Mark and Corey didn't respond, no doubt feeling utterly emasculated.

When Neesha dropped the pickaxe at last, the hole was large enough for a person to squeeze through. Taylor peered into it, seeing nothing but blackness beyond.

"I can't see much," he said.

"I'll go first," Neesha offered. Being the shortest of them, it was the most logical choice. Taylor nodded, and Neesha stepped through the hole, vanishing into the darkness. Moments later, her head poked through. "Mark, hand me a couple of lanterns."

"Yes professor," Mark replied, retrieving a few and handing them to her. She vanished from sight again.

"Holy shit," they heard Neesha blurt out.

"Hon, you okay?" Taylor asked. A few seconds later, Neesha's head poked back through the hole. She gestured for them to follow.

"Come on," she urged. "You've *got* to see this!"

Taylor gestured for Mark to go in first, followed by Corey. Then he followed them, barely squeezing through the narrow opening. He straightened up, then froze, his eyes widening. There, illuminated by the lanterns, was a tunnel running left to right. A *huge* tunnel. The ceiling was over twenty feet high, the walls curving inward in a perfect upside-down U-shape. To the right, the tunnel ended abruptly in an irregular rock wall. To the left...

"Holy shit," he blurted out.

There, not five feet from where he stood, was a huge arch of the same black metal they'd seen earlier, matching the curvature of the ceiling perfectly. Small symbols were carved into the arch along its entire length. And while the tunnel ended at the arch, it was not with a stone wall like he would've expected. Rather, there was a perfectly smooth wall of utter blackness.

"I know, right?" Neesha stated.

"What the hell *is* that?" Corey asked. Neesha shook her head.

"I have no idea," she admitted.

"Do you recognize any of these symbols?" Mark asked Corey. Corey walked up to the arch, peering at the symbols carved into the jet-black metal. Then he shook his head.

"Afraid not."

"Look at the walls," Neesha said, gesturing at the curved rock walls around them. Mark's eyebrows furrowed.

"What about them?"

"They're perfectly smooth," Taylor answered for Neesha, walking up to one of the walls and running a gloved hand across it. The granite was as polished and smooth as a countertop. As was the ceiling...but not the floor.

"This is so weird," Mark murmured, running his own hand over the wall. "What is this doing a hundred feet below the surface?"

Taylor glanced at Neesha. She was staring at the black wall bordered by the metal arch, pointing her flashlight right at it.

"Guys," she called out. "Check this out."

"What?" Taylor asked, walking up to her side.

"It's not reflecting any light," Neesha explained, scanning the wall with her flashlight. She was right; no matter where she shined her light on that utter blackness, no light was reflected.

"A wall that doesn't reflect any light?" Taylor asked. "That doesn't make any sense." He'd heard of materials that could absorb any light that shined on them, but they were incredibly high-tech, made of carbon nanotubes ten thousand times smaller than a human hair. Certainly not something that would be found in a cave.

"Interesting," Neesha murmured.

"How old do you think this thing is?" Mark asked her.

"I have no idea," she admitted. She pointed her flashlight at the arch bordering the darkness, peering at the symbols. "The first step is to figure out these symbols." She grabbed her smartphone from Taylor, walking up to the arch and taking some pictures.

"That arch is metal," Mark observed. "But I don't know what kind. Whatever it is, it's really strong."

"What makes you say that?" Taylor asked. Mark gave a sheepish grin.

"I...may have hit it by accident a few times when I was trying to make that hole earlier," he admitted. "Before you guys came." He shook his head. "The pickaxe bounced right off. Didn't even make a scratch on it."

"Really?" Taylor pressed. "A full swing?" Mark nodded.

"I hit it pretty damn hard," he confirmed. "Not a scratch."

"Yeah, well we've both seen you try to swing a pickaxe," Neesha teased. Mark blushed. "Alright, so it's made of metal," she stated, snapping a few more pictures. "Building it would've involved smelting and molding. South Americans had that capability maybe two and a half thousand years ago."

"You mean the Mocha," Mark deduced.

"Right. But they were in Peru," she said. "Smelting wasn't used in North America in pre-Columbian times."

"So you're saying this is at most what, five hundred years old?" Corey asked. "That doesn't make sense...these symbols aren't like anything I've ever seen."

"And neither is this wall," Taylor added, eyeing the wall's utter blackness. Neesha finished taking pictures of the arch, and turned to focus on the wall. She stared at it for a long, silent moment. "What are you thinking, hon?" he asked.

"That we have a lot of work to do," she answered. "We need to excavate this whole thing. We're going to need more people to do that."

"We could call in the MCX-CMAC," Taylor offered. That was the U.S. Army Corps of Engineers' Mandatory Center of Expertise for the Curation and Management of Archaeological Collections. Neesha glared at him.

"Day one and you're ready to bring the damn government in," she grumbled. "No thanks."

"Just a thought," Taylor stated. "They have better toys than we do."

"Think of something else," Neesha shot back.

Corey grabbed one of the lanterns by the hole they'd made in the granite wall, bringing it up to the inky black wall. Again, no light reflected off of its surface. He put one gloved hand on the wall, sliding it side to side.

"It's so smooth," he murmured. "And cold."

"We *are* in a cave," Neesha reminded him. "It's like fifty degrees in here."

"Yeah, but it's colder than the arch," Corey countered.

"Probably just a better conductor of heat, like metal," Taylor ventured. "So it feels colder." Corey hesitated, then took off his glove, placing his bare hand on the black wall.

It passed right through.

"What the..." he exclaimed. His hand had vanished *into* the wall, up to his wrist. Beyond his wrist, there was only blackness...as if he'd dipped his hand into a pool of black liquid. But no ripples appeared on the wall's surface.

"Woah," Taylor blurted out. "How in the hell...?"

"It went right through," Corey stated in disbelief, staring at his exposed wrist. "Like it wasn't even there!"

"But you just put your hand on it earlier," Mark protested. "It was solid."

"Well it isn't now," Corey countered.

"You were wearing your glove the first time," Neesha recalled.

"You're right," Corey replied. He dipped his arm further in, until it was up to the elbow. "Weird," he stated. "It feels cold at my elbow, but I can't feel anything past that." He concentrated for a moment. "I can't feel my hand," he added. "It's like it isn't even there."

"Really?" Mark asked.

"Yeah," Corey replied. "In fact, I..." He frowned then.

"What?" Mark pressed. Corey grimaced.

"My arm's stuck," he answered. "I'm trying to pull it out, but it won't come."

"What do you mean it won't come?" Neesha demanded, taking one more picture, then lowering her phone.

"I'm pulling on it," Corey explained. He jerked his whole shoulder back, but still his arm remained elbow-deep in the inky blackness. Neesha set her phone down on the ground, then walked up behind him, grabbing his shoulders and pulling backward.

He didn't budge.

"Hold on," she told him.

She grabbed Corey around his flanks, planting her feet wide and pulling backward. Her arm muscles tensed, the veins at her temples bulging with the effort. But still, his elbow remained stuck. She let go, beads of sweat glittering on her forehead.

"Well shit," she swore. She glanced at Taylor. "Want to lend me a hand?"

"Uh guys," Corey interjected. "My arm…"

They turned to look at Corey's arm, and saw that his elbow was no longer visible. He was up to his mid-bicep in the wall now.

"Damn," Neesha swore. "Don't put your arm any further in."

"I didn't," Corey retorted.

"Are you sure?"

"Pretty damn sure," he insisted. He tugged again at his arm, then stopped, staring at it for a moment. His face paled. "Aw, shit!"

"What?"

"It's being pulled in!" Corey exclaimed. Taylor stared at the student's arm, realizing that he was right. As Taylor watched, Corey's arm sank slowly but steadily into the wall.

"You're not leaning into it?" Neesha pressed.

"No, I'm not fucking leaning into it," Corey retorted, his voice rising in panic. "Pull me out!"

"Grab his waist on the left," Neesha ordered, nodding at Taylor. "I'll get the right. Mark, you pull his shoulders from behind."

"Got it," Taylor said. He wrapped his arms around Corey's waist, as did Neesha. He planted his feet, then pulled backward, as did Mark. They strained, but it was no use…Corey didn't budge. In fact, he'd been pulled in even further; he was up to his shoulder now.

"Come on guys!" Corey shouted. "Get me out!"

"Grab his legs," Neesha ordered. "Pull him by his legs!"

Taylor grabbed Corey's left leg, and Neesha tore off her gloves, grabbing his right leg. They lifted Corey's legs off of the ground, leaning backward and pulling as hard as they could.

Nothing.

"Damn it!" Neesha swore.

"Guys!" Corey yelled. His shoulder passed through the wall, his upper chest sinking slowly into the blackness. His face was only inches away from the inky surface now. He twisted his head away from it. "Guys!"

"Pull damn it!" Neesha shouted. She heaved backward, and Taylor followed suit, straining as hard as he could. Sweat trickled down his forehead, stinging his eyes, his biceps burning. But it was no use.

Corey screamed as the right side of his face touched the blackness, sinking into it.

Then his eyes rolled in the back of his head, and his left arm and leg began to jerk uncontrollably. Taylor's grip on Corey's leg slipped, and he stumbled backward, falling onto his butt on the stone floor.

"Come on!" Neesha urged, yanking on Corey's leg again. "Mark, help me!" Mark rushed up to Corey's still-spasming leg, trying to grab it. But he was kicked in the chest, and fell backward as well. Neesha swore, grabbing both of Corey's legs and leaning backward, the muscles of her arms going taut.

The rest of Corey's head was sucked into the blackness, and then *both* legs started jerking, yanking Neesha forward. She stumbled, letting go of Corey's legs and falling onto her belly on the ground.

"Neesha!" Taylor exclaimed, rushing to her side. "You okay?" She was pregnant after all, and had fallen right on her belly. But she waved him away.

"Grab him!" she ordered, struggling to get on her hands and knees. Taylor grabbed one of Corey's legs, realizing that the poor guy's head and neck had passed all the way into the blackness. And that he was being drawn in faster now, the darkness greedily consuming him.

"Shit," Taylor swore, pulling backward as hard as he could. But it was no use...Corey's upper body vanished through the wall, his waist passing through rapidly, and then his upper legs. When Corey's knees passed through, Taylor let go, backing away from the wall quickly.

Corey's legs and feet vanished into the wall, the blackness swallowing him whole.

"Well shit," Neesha swore. Taylor stared at the spot where Corey had been, unable to believe his eyes.

"What the hell just happened?" he asked.

"Babe," Neesha said.

"I can't believe he just..."

"Babe!" Neesha repeated, louder this time. Taylor looked down at her. She was still on her hands and knees near the wall, staring at her left hand.

The tip of her index finger was touching the wall.

Taylor rushed to her side, dropping to his knees. His blood went cold.

"Can you pull it out?" he asked. Neesha ignored the question.

"Get out your knife," she ordered. Taylor stared at her blankly. She glared at him. "Your knife!" He hesitated, then reached for his belt, for the hunting knife there. He unsheathed it. Neesha twisted to the side, exposing her stuck finger.

"What do you…"

"Cut it off," Neesha ordered.

"What?"

"Cut my finger off," she clarified, her voice icy calm. He just stared at her. She grabbed the knife from his hand, then pressed the blade against her index finger, just beyond the last knuckle.

"Babe!"

"Shut up," she commanded. Her jaw rippled, and she slid the blade across her finger, blood welling up immediately, the skin parting easily. Yellow fat was exposed beneath, blood pouring out of the wound. She bit back a scream as she sawed into her own flesh, the sound of metal grating on bone echoed through the large tunnel.

And then her finger began to suck into the wall.

"Babe!" Taylor repeated. But Neesha ignored him, biting back another scream, sawing faster. Blood began spurting out in regular intervals, spraying the blade and Neesha's other hand. Mark backed away, his face turning deathly pale, and promptly vomited.

"God *damn* it!" Neesha shouted.

"What?"

"I hit the goddamn wall with my goddamn knife!" she exclaimed. She was right; the tip of the knife had plunged into the wall. She pulled on it frantically, but it didn't budge.

"Move your finger against the blade," Taylor offered. Neesha glared at him.

"I *can't* move my finger!"

"Can you move the blade at all?" he pressed.

"No," she answered. She leaned back, jerking her left arm from the wall. Her partially-severed finger continued to spurt blood, but it held. "Oh come on!"

Then the finger was sucked further into the blackness, the wounded part vanishing beyond it.

"Mark, do you have a knife?" Taylor asked. Mark fumbled through his equipment, then shook his head. Taylor swore, turning back to Neesha. Her finger was now entirely engulfed by the blackness…and as he watched, her hand joined it. "Baby, grab my hand," he ordered, reaching out to her. She swatted his hand away.

"Get back," she told him. Taylor stared at her uncomprehendingly.

"What?"

"Get away from the wall," she clarified. "You can't get trapped too."

"Babe, we have to…"

"You're not getting me out," she interrupted, her tone icy calm. "You need to be there for our son."

"We can still…"

"I love you hon," she said, reaching out and touching his cheek. She gave him a sad smile. "I'll always love you."

"Baby, no!" Taylor insisted, grabbing her hand and pulling it back, trying to pull her free. It was no use...the blackness consumed her, pulling her in past the wrist now. Her forearm vanished, then her elbow.

"Let go babe," Neesha requested, her tone gentler. Her shoulder passed through, her head only inches from the wall now.

"No," Taylor shot back, his vision blurring as tears welled up in his eyes. "No baby, no."

"Take care of our son," she pleaded. "He can't lose both of us."

"Baby, please..."

"Kiss me," she demanded. He hesitated, then leaned in, pressing his lips against hers. He felt the soft crush of her lips, smelled the sweetness of her breath, of her skin. That intoxicating scent that meant everything was going to be okay...that he was home.

She pushed him away, staring into his eyes.

"Goodbye love," she murmured, smiling at him again, tears dripping down her cheeks.

And then the back of her head passed into the darkness.

"*No!*" Taylor shouted.

Her face stiffened, her eyes rolling into the back of her head. Her arm spasmed, then her legs, convulsing rhythmically. Her face passed through the blackness, then her right shoulder, her arm sucking inward rapidly. Her hand reached out for him, her fingers spreading wide.

And then she was gone.

CHAPTER 1

Hunter sighed, drumming his fingers on his desk. He watched as a young woman got up from her chair, walking up to Mr. Stanson's desk to pass in her test. It was Tiffany, easily the hottest girl in school. She had the kind of body that kept a guy up at night...in more ways than one. Tall, slender, with a cute butt and long, luscious golden hair, she was like a magnet for the eyes...and his eyes tracked her as she walked back to her desk to sit down.

God damn, he thought.

He glanced at the clock on the wall; it'd been over twenty minutes since he'd finished the exam, being the first to do so, as usual. He'd always been pretty good at tests, even if he didn't know the material that well. A gift he'd gotten from his father...one of the few.

Hunter fidgeted in his chair. There were still another ten minutes left before class ended. His mind wandered, and he found himself gazing at Tiffany again. Not only was she easy on the eyes, she was also one of the nicest people he'd ever met.

Man, he mused. *What I wouldn't give to be with her.*

Fat chance of that ever happening, of course. He'd pined after Tiffany for years now, always from afar, never quite having the guts to ask her out on the rare occasions that she'd been single. And she certainly wasn't single now; she was dating a dumb jock in class called Tyler. But hey, a guy could dream...and he planned on doing just that later on tonight. Among other things.

More students got up to pass in their exams, and eventually the bell rang, signaling the end of class. A tall, muscular guy in the back row hurried up to Mr. Stanson's desk to drop off his test, and Hunter found with no small amount of satisfaction that it was Tyler, Tiffany's boyfriend. The colossal prick was usually the last to finish. God only knew how he managed to stay on the football team with his lousy grades.

"Alright," Mr. Stanson declared. "Class dismissed."

Everyone bolted from their chairs, and Hunter got up as well, joining the rush toward the exit. But Mr. Stanson caught his eye, gesturing for him to come up to the front desk. Hunter hesitated, waiting for the last of the students to leave, then walked up to his teacher's desk.

"What's up?" he asked. Mr. Stanson, a short, middle-aged man with reading glasses, handed Hunter some papers. Hunter took them, realizing that it was his test.

"I graded yours already," Mr. Stanson declared, leaning back in his chair and eyeing Hunter disapprovingly. "Almost as quickly as you took it."

"Thanks," Hunter mumbled. He glanced at the score, written in bold red marker on the top of the page. 82%...not bad.

"You made some pretty stupid errors," Mr. Stanson told him. "If you'd taken your time, you might have gotten a better score."

"Not bad for not studying," Hunter countered. Mr. Stanson sighed, leaning forward and propping his elbows on his desk.

"You know Hunter," he began, "...every year I get someone like you. Smart, but lazy. I used to think it was because they weren't stimulated enough...that things were just too easy for them." He took a sip from a glass of water on his desk. "You wanna know what I think now?"

Hunter just stared at him.

"I think you," Mr. Stanson stated, jabbing a finger at Hunter, "...are afraid."

"Of what, getting an A?"

"Of what you might be able to accomplish if you actually tried," Mr. Stanson corrected.

Hunter glanced down at his test, then back at Mr. Stanson. He felt a familiar bitterness rise up within him.

"My parents tried," he replied at last. "It didn't work out so well for them."

Mr. Stanson sighed, leaning back in his chair.

"You can't use that as an excuse forever, you know," he retorted. "You've had it rough, I get it. But sooner or later you're going to have to take a chance, Hunter. You're a good kid, and you have a lot of potential...don't waste it."

"It's not an excuse," Hunter countered.

"Yeah, well next time, don't hand in your test until time's up," Mr. Stanson ordered. "Now go on, get out of here."

Hunter was all-too-happy to oblige, walking out of the classroom and into the hallway. He trudged toward his locker at the far end, spotting his friend Sam there. Short, with black curly hair and glasses, he was a total geek...and one of the awesomest, most loyal people Hunter had ever met.

"What did Mr. Stanson want?" Sam asked, opening his own locker – which happened to be next to Hunter's – and dropping his books into it.

"Just busting my balls," Hunter answered. "He was mad I got a B."

"What a douche," Sam muttered.

"Nah," Hunter replied. "He's pretty cool, actually." And it was true; as much of a hard-ass as Mr. Stanson was, he was the only teacher who actually seemed to give a damn about his students. He was also the only teacher who knew the truth about Hunter's dad...and his mom.

"You want to hang out later?" Sam asked.

"Sure," Hunter agreed, dropping his pre-calc textbook into his own locker.

"Hey Hunter," he heard a voice say. He looked up, seeing Tyler – Tiffany's boyfriend – walking up to him.

Great, he thought. *This again.*

"Finished early again, huh?" Tyler asked.

"Uh huh."

"Heard that was a problem for you," Tyler quipped, smirking at him. "Caught you staring at my girlfriend again," he added. "Need to change your underwear?"

Hunter ignored him. He felt more eyes staring at him, and knew that Tyler's buddies had swooped in to enjoy the show. As usual.

"Get lost Tyler," Sam interjected. But Tyler ignored him.

"Aww, it's okay man," he continued, patting Hunter on the shoulder. "You'll get laid someday. Somewhere out there, I'm sure there's a guy that's *perfect* for you." Tyler's friends laughed at that, and Hunter rolled his eyes.

"You volunteering sweetheart?" he asked, not even bothering to look up. He shut his locker, spinning the lock.

"Oh damn," one of Tyler's friends blurted out. "Tyler, I think he wants you!" Tyler laughed.

"Yeah, you know what," he said, "…I think I *did* catch him trying to sneak a peek at my dick in the bathroom." He sneered at Hunter. "You a faggot, *boy*?"

Hunter froze.

"I asked you a question," Tyler pressed. Hunter turned to face him.

"You sure had a hard time finishing that test," Hunter replied coolly. "Maybe you should switch to the special needs class."

Tyler stared at Hunter for a long moment, then stepped in closer. He was a good eight inches taller than Hunter, and a whole lot bigger.

"You calling me a retard?" he shot back. "Careful boy," he added, "…or I'll hit you so hard I'll make *you* a retard."

"Right," Hunter muttered, turning back to his locker. "Is that what you did to Tiffany?" he asked. "That explains why she's going out with you."

Tyler stepped in even closer, glaring down at him.

"What did you say, boy?"

Hunter ignored him, zipping up his backpack and closing his locker door. Tyler shoved him backward, and Hunter slammed into Sam, knocking his friend over. Sam fell to the floor, his glasses flying off his face. Hunter managed to keep his balance, and looked down, seeing Sam's glasses on the floor.

They were broken.

Hunter helped Sam up, handing him his glasses, then turned to see Tyler stepping toward them again.

"I asked you what you said," Tyler growled. Hunter clenched his fists, feeling anger rising within him.

"Need me to talk slower so you can understand?"

Tyler went to shove Hunter again, but this time Hunter pushed back, and they both moved back a step. Tyler's face turned red.

"You little black piece of shit," he spat. Hunter smirked.

"Dumb *and* racist," he shot back. "You're nothing but white trash, Tyler." Tyler shoved him again, pushing him back a few steps.

"At least my white trash dad didn't knock up some dirty nigger *ho*," he spat.

The rage was instant.

Hunter burst forward, swinging his fist at Tyler's face as hard as he could, his knuckles slamming into the jock's nose with a loud *crack*. Tyler dropped like a stone, landing on his back on the floor. Blood spurted from his nose, gushing over his face and onto the floor.

He was out. Cold.

"Jesus!" one of Tyler's friends blurted out.

"Anyone else wanna talk shit about my mom?" Hunter asked, stepping toward one of Tyler's friends. Then he felt arms grab him from behind, pulling him away. He resisted, trying to break free.

"Stop it!" he heard a man shout. "Stop *now!*"

It was Mr. Stanson, he realized. Holding him from behind.

Well shit.

* * *

Hunter slumped into the passenger seat of his dad's car, putting his seat belt on. He felt Dad's eyes on him, and avoided making eye contact, staring straight ahead. Dad sighed, starting the engine and pulling out of the high school parking lot. They drove in silence for a while, and Hunter turned to stare out of his side window glumly.

"What happened?" Dad asked at last.

"Some kid dressed up as a punching bag," he answered. "It wasn't my fault," he added. "The costume was so realistic. How was I supposed to know?"

Dad just glared at him.

"Some douchebag started pushing me and Sam around," he admitted. When Dad didn't say anything, Hunter turned away from the window to look at him. "He broke Sam's glasses."

"You broke his nose, Hunter," Dad countered.

"He started it," Hunter insisted. "I tried to talk my way out of it, but he kept going after me."

"Okay," Dad replied. "But now you're suspended."

Hunter said nothing, lowering his gaze. He *was* suspended...for a week. He was damn lucky he hadn't been expelled. With only a year left, that wasn't a mistake he could afford to make. Even his suspension might cost him dearly. With his dad's salary, he *had* to get a good scholarship if he wanted to have any chance of going to college with Sam and the rest of his friends.

"Sorry Dad," he muttered.

"I am too," Dad replied. "That was really stupid, Hunter."

"I know."

"You can't just hit people when they piss you off," he continued. "You have to learn how to control your temper."

"I *know*," Hunter repeated. He'd heard the lecture a thousand times.

"If you *knew* it," Dad pressed, "...you'd *do* it."

Hunter sighed, staring out of his side window, at the houses whizzing by. They were close to home now, only a half-mile away. He swallowed past a lump in his throat.

"He made fun of Mom."

Dad slowed, then stopped at a red light. His jawline rippled, and he accelerated rapidly when the light turned green, his tires squealing a bit.

"He called her a..."

"I don't want to know," Dad interjected. "I *really* don't want to know."

"He used the N-word," Hunter continued. Dad grimaced.

"I understand why you got upset," he conceded. "But it isn't an excuse to hit someone." He turned down a side street. "You could've gone to a teacher, you know. Then you wouldn't have gotten suspended."

"Yeah, well," Hunter muttered, still gazing out of his window. They were passing a few greenhouses now. "Mom would've hit him."

Dad slowed down, then turned into their driveway, parking the car in the garage. He pulled his keys from the ignition, getting out of the car without saying anything. Hunter sighed, opening his own door and getting out. They both went into the house, taking off their shoes and walking into the kitchen.

"She would've," Hunter insisted. Dad turned to glare at him.

"I know she would've," he replied. "That doesn't make it right."

"Yeah, but..." Hunter began, but Dad put up a hand.

"Stop," he ordered. Hunter obeyed, glaring at his father silently. "You screwed up," he stated. "And now this suspension is going on your permanent record. Think about that," he added. "You wanted to go to college with your friends? Too bad. You wanted to get into a good college at all? Good luck." He turned away from Hunter, his jawline rippling. "I need to cool down for a bit," he stated. "We'll finish this conversation later." He walked to one of the kitchen cupboards, retrieving a tall glass. "Go to your room."

Hunter complied, walking out of the kitchen and into the foyer, then taking the stairs up to the second floor. He went into his room, closing the door behind him and throwing himself onto his belly on the bed. He buried his head in his pillow, taking a deep breath in, then letting it out.

Great.

Dad was right, of course…and Hunter knew it. Tyler deserved what he got, there was no doubt about it. But it sure hadn't been worth getting suspended over. He'd screwed himself over…again. And without a scholarship, he wouldn't be able to afford to go to college with Sam and the rest of his friends. All the plans he'd been making for the last year had just been destroyed. His future was gone. His life as he knew it was over.

Just great.

He felt a heavy paw on his back, and rolled onto his side, seeing a black cat standing there. It meowed, rubbing the side of its head against his shoulder, purring loudly.

"Hey Charlie," he mumbled, petting the cat absently. He'd named her after his mom's old black cat. She purred louder, and he scratched around Charlie's ears, earning a truly blissful look. He sighed, rolling onto his back and letting her walk onto his belly and sit down, positioning herself perfectly for maximum petting.

Turning his head to the side, he spotted a framed photo on his nightstand. It was a picture of him and his mom when he'd been nine. The last picture they'd taken together, before she'd died. Dad was white Mom had been black, but Hunter mostly took after his mother, being just slightly less brown. It wasn't exactly an advantage. White kids at school shunned him for being black – while pretending not to – and black people shunned him for not being black enough…and didn't bother pretending otherwise. Points for honesty, he supposed.

Hunter stared at the picture, trying to remember what she'd been like, his mom. She'd died about eight years ago, and each year he had a harder time recalling memories of her. He'd have already forgotten her voice if it hadn't been for the videos Dad had saved of her.

Like everything else in his life, she was slipping away. And there wasn't a thing he could do about it.

He felt his eyes growing moist, and wiped them dry with his sleeve. He turned back to Charlie, running a hand over her back. Her butt rose in the air as he reached her tail, and she continued to purr, her eyes nearly shut.

"You're the only one here who isn't broken, Charlie," Hunter told her.

He turned back to the picture of his mom, staring at it. Mom had died on a work site, according to his father. Her and Dad had been rappelling down a tunnel when her equipment had failed, and she'd plummeted to her death. After that, Dad had quit being a professor at the university, going to work as a consultant for the Army Corps of Engineers.

Hunter felt suddenly antsy, and turned onto his side, causing Charlie to hop off his belly and onto the floor. He got out of bed, walking out of his room and into the hallway. The pull cord to the attic was right outside of his bedroom door; he pulled it slowly, so as not to alert his dad, watching as the folded wooden stairway descended. He unfolded the stairs, then climbed up to the attic, flipping the light switch on the wall as he went up. Charlie joined him, following close behind. The attic smelled musty, and was oppressively hot; he ignored this, stepping onto the plywood floor. He turned toward the far end of the attic, spotting a few boxes there.

Mom's stuff.

He walked up to one of the boxes, kneeling before it and opening it. There was a stack of old photos inside, ones he'd long since memorized. A few of her favorite books. A bottle of Egyptian musk, her favorite perfume. He paused, grabbing this and opening it. Taking a whiff, he closed his eyes, feeling an immediate sense of peace.

It smelled like *her.*

He held the feeling for as long as he could, but it slipped away as quickly as it'd come, and he sighed, capping the perfume and setting it down. Charlie rubbed against his leg, and he smiled at her.

"*You'd* never leave me," he said, scratching under her chin. Then he turned back to the box. There were a pair of workout gloves, still reeking of sweat and dust. Her favorite jacket – pink, a color she'd hated, strangely enough. A notebook. An old smartphone.

He paused, staring at the phone, then picking it up. It was practically ancient, at least nine years old. Blowing the dust off the screen, he turned it around in his hands. He'd never really paid the phone much mind. He tried pressing the power button, but of course it didn't turn on. And he didn't recognize the port for the phone charger. He sighed, and was about to put the phone back in the box when an idea struck him.

There was a box of old cords in the spare bedroom.

Hunter stood, going back down the attic stairs. He waited for Charlie to come down, then folded the stairs back up, pushing the trapdoor to the attic shut. Walking into the spare bedroom, he found a few boxes stacked to one side in the closet. He rummaged through them, eventually finding the box of cords.

He checked each cord methodically, trying to plug each of them into the phone's charging port one-by-one. After a few minutes, he found one that matched.

Bingo.

He plugged the cord into the wall, then stared at the phone. Nothing happened.

Come on…

He waited a few seconds, but the screen remained blank. He shouldn't have been surprised. The phone was so old that the battery must have died. He was about to unplug it when the screen suddenly turned on.

Yes!

He smiled, watching as the phone booted up. Rows of icons appeared on the screen. He scrolled through them, then found what he assumed was the icon for camera photos. Tapping it made row after row of thumbnails appear. He scrolled through them, then clicked on a random one. It was a picture of Mom and Dad in their old office at the university, along with a tall, lanky younger man Hunter didn't recognize. He swiped the screen, seeing the next picture…a dirt path leading up a hill, with a sign on the side of the path.

Welcome to Smuggler's Cave, it read.

Hunter swiped again, seeing another picture of the path, this time showing it lead to the mouth of a cave ahead. Dad was ahead, his muscles bulging out of his t-shirt. Those were back in his bodybuilding days, before Mom had died. He sure as hell didn't look like that anymore. The only thing bulging out of his shirt now was his belly.

Hunter swiped again. Now they were inside the cave. A few more pictures of Dad walking, which meant Mom must've taken them. Then a picture of Dad standing in a cramped cavern, pointing his flashlight down a large hole in the ground. It was a long vertical shaft, descending as far as the eye could see. A rope had been tied to a large rocky outcropping near the hole, and was dangling down the shaft.

Hunter hesitated then, realizing that he was almost certainly looking at the pictures Mom and Dad had taken right before her death. She'd fallen down a shaft, after all. It had to be *this* shaft. His finger hovered over the screen, and he felt a twinge of fear in his gut.

He took a deep breath in, then swiped again…and frowned.

For they'd clearly reached the bottom of the tunnel…both of them. They were smiling into the camera, Mom having taken a rare selfie with Dad.

What the hell?

The next picture was of Mom swinging a pickaxe at a rock wall. A tall, lanky guy and a shorter man were off to one side, and to their left was a thick band of black metal that extended halfway to the ceiling. Strange symbols were carved into the metal.

The next picture showed Mom standing beside a hole in the rock wall with a rather satisfied smile on her face. He found himself smiling back, and swiped again.

He frowned, trying to understand what he was looking at.

There was a large tunnel, that he could tell. It looked to be made of pure rock. Ahead, there was a huge black metal arch, shaped like an upside-down "U." It looked to be a continuation of the black metal he'd seen earlier. The arch surrounded a perfectly flat wall of utter blackness. To one side, he saw his dad and the two other men standing by the arch; Dad was pointing to one of the symbols there.

He swiped again.

More pictures of the symbols, close-ups now. He swiped through them quickly, until he found a photo of the arch again. This time, the shorter man had his hand on the black wall, and his dad and the tall guy were watching him. Hunter swiped again, then blinked.

288

The next picture showed the shorter guy touching the wall again. But this time his hand was going *through* the wall. Or rather, it had disappeared *into* the blackness.

That's weird.

The next picture showed the man again, but this time his arm had vanished into the wall all the way up to the elbow. Hunter's eyebrows furrowed, and he stared at the man's face.

He looked terrified.

Hunter hesitated, then swiped again. But that was the end of it...there were no more pictures. He stared at the final picture, at the man with his arm in the wall. It looked like he was trying to pull his arm back...and obviously not succeeding. Dad and the taller guy looked alarmed.

Hunter stared at the picture for a long moment, then shut the phone off. He left it where it was, letting it charge. Then he went back to his own room, sitting down at his desk and booting up his laptop. Charlie hopped on his desk, trying to sit on his keyboard, as usual. He put her on his lap instead, then waited for his computer to boot up.

Welcome to Smuggler's Cave.

He did a quick search for the cave, and found a web page about it within seconds, along with a street address. It was about an hour's drive from here. He got the directions, printing them out. The whirring of the printer spooked Charlie, who hopped off his lap and bolted out of the room. He grabbed the printout when it was done, folding it and stuffing it in his pocket. Then he went back into the spare room, waiting for the phone to charge for a bit longer, then unplugging it and walking out of the room to go downstairs.

There Dad was, in his usual spot on the couch, watching TV with a tall glass of brown liquid in his hand. Whiskey, as usual. It was already half-empty.

"Dad," he called out. Dad turned to face Hunter. His eyes were glassy.

"What?" he slurred. Then he frowned. "You're supposed to be in your room."

"And you're not supposed to drink anymore," Hunter shot back, reaching for Dad's glass. Dad pulled it away just in time, cradling it to his chest. "Come on Dad," he insisted. "Give it to me."

"What do you want?" Dad demanded, refusing to give it up. Hunter grit his teeth, then gave up, crossing his arms over his chest.

"What happened to Mom?" he demanded. Dad's brow furrowed.

"What?"

"What happened to Mom?" Hunter repeated. He held up Mom's phone. Dad stared at it.

"What are you..."

"You know exactly what I'm talking about," Hunter interjected. He turned on the phone, the last picture appearing on the screen, and tossed the phone at his father. It bounced off Dad's chest, landing in his lap.

Dad flinched, then set his glass down on the coffee table carefully – far away from Hunter – and picked up the phone.

His face paled.

"You told me Mom died falling down that tunnel," Hunter accused, pointing at the phone. Dad stared at the picture, his Adam's apple bobbing up and down. Then he glanced back up at Hunter.

"Hunter…"

"How did she die?" he demanded. "Tell me the truth."

"She fell after we were climbing back up…"

"Don't lie to me Dad," Hunter interjected. "She's my mom. You *owe* me the truth."

Dad stared at Hunter mutely, then glanced back down at the phone. At the photo of the man's arm in the wall. At the panic in the man's face. Then he sighed, his shoulders slumping.

"Alright," he muttered. "She…she didn't fall down the tunnel."

"Then what happened?"

Dad shook his head mutely, staring at the TV. *Through* the TV.

"I don't know," he admitted at last. "She…it happened so fast."

"What happened?"

"That damn wall," Dad answered. "It took her."

Hunter stared at him uncomprehendingly.

"What do you mean?"

"It sucked her in," Dad explained. "Just like it sucked Corey in."

"Corey?"

"The guy with his arm in the wall," Dad clarified. "He touched the wall, and his arm went right through. He tried to pull it out, but he couldn't. Then it pulled him in, and he never came back."

Hunter processed this for a moment, hardly believing what he was hearing.

"And Mom?" he pressed. Dad sighed, lowering his gaze to his lap.

"She got caught in the wall trying to save Corey," he replied. He raised a finger. "One damn finger was all it took."

"Wait," Hunter stated. "She got caught in the wall too?" Dad nodded, swallowing visibly. He reached for his drink then, taking a big gulp, then setting it back down.

"One finger," he muttered. He took another gulp. "One *goddamn* finger."

"Why didn't you pull her out?" Hunter pressed. Dad turned to glare at him.

"You think I didn't try?" he shot back. "I couldn't save her. It was too late. There was nothing I could do." His eyes turned moist, tears dripped down his cheeks. "I watched her die."

"How do you know?" Hunter asked. Dad frowned, glancing up at him.

"How do I know what?"

"That she's dead?" Hunter pressed. "You don't even know what happened to her."

Dad didn't answer.

"She could still be alive!" Hunter exclaimed, his heart racing. He walked forward, grabbing the phone and pointing at it. "We could go here and…"

"No," Dad interrupted, his tone cold. "We can't."

"But…"

"The government's all over that place now," Dad interrupted. "The Army Corps of Engineers took over after I called them." He shook his head in disgust. "I asked them to help me find Neesha, and instead they took over and blocked me from ever going there again…even after I started working for them."

"But she's *there*," Hunter insisted. Dad raised his eyebrows.

"Where?" he asked. "In the wall?" He shook his head. "She's gone, Hunter."

"Well, why didn't you go after her then?" Hunter pressed. "You just watched her get sucked in, then *left*?"

"I didn't just *watch* her get sucked in!" Dad shouted. Hunter flinched, staring at his dad, who glared at him furiously. "You act so high-and-mighty, thinking you know what you're talking about. But you don't know *shit* Hunter."

Hunter stared at his father silently for a long moment, resisting the urge to snap at the man. He crossed his arms over his chest.

"You should've gone after her," he insisted. Dad just stared at him mutely, his jawline rippling. "*I* would've gone after her."

"You think I didn't want to?" Dad retorted, his voice cracking. He stood up from the couch, swaying slightly. "Is that what you think?"

Hunter said nothing, glaring at his father.

"I was *going* to go after her," Dad insisted. "But she told me not to." He took a deep, shaky breath in, letting it out, then pointed one finger at Hunter. "The only reason I didn't go after her was because of *you*," he spat.

Hunter felt his blood go cold.

Dad lowered his finger, grabbing his glass and taking another gulp. He stared at Hunter for a long moment, his mouth quivering. More tears spilled down his cheeks.

"She was the love of my life," he said, his voice cracking again. "But I stayed for you."

Hunter stared at Dad, then at the mostly-empty glass in the man's hand. He thought back to every after-school game Dad had missed, every party Hunter hadn't been able to go to because he had to stay home and make sure Dad didn't fall and kill himself. Or drive and kill someone else.

"I wish you hadn't," Hunter muttered at last. "You could've been a hero," he added. "But now you're just a lousy drunk."

Dad's eyes widened, and he shot up from the couch, lunging at Hunter and whipping the glass at Hunter's head. Hunter dodged at the last minute, and the glass hurtled through the air, smashing into a framed photo on the wall behind him. It shattered, sending the photo crashing to the floor, glass spilling outward in all directions. Hunter backpedaled, half-expecting Dad to come after him and beat him. But instead, the man froze in place, his eyes on the ruined photo on the floor.

It was a blown-up photo from Mom and Dad's wedding.

Dad stared at it, his face turning deathly pale. He stumbled backward, landing on the couch and sitting there, his eyes unblinking. Then he looked up at Hunter.

"You're right," he muttered at last. "I *should* have left you behind."

CHAPTER 2

Hunter slammed the door to the garage behind him, staring at the two cars parked there. One was a new SUV – his dad's car – and the other was a beat-up sedan. He stood there for a long moment, clenching and unclenching his fists. His father had stormed off upstairs a few minutes ago, going to his bedroom and locking the door. Which was fine with Hunter; the bastard could stay there the whole weekend for all he cared.

Lousy drunk.

He wiped moisture from his eyes, taking a deep breath in, then letting it out, staring at the cars. He reached into his pants pocket, fingering the keys there. He was supposed to be grounded because of the suspension, but it wasn't like Dad was about to stop him from going out. He was probably drinking himself into oblivion now anyway, like he did every day. He'd gone upstairs, which meant there was a chance he might fall down the stairs again later tonight. Which would mean another visit to the hospital.

Hunter grit his teeth.

I'm done babysitting him.

He reached into his other pocket, feeling the paper he'd printed out earlier there. He took it out, unfolding it and staring at it. Directions to Smuggler's Cave.

To Mom.

He stared at it, then at the two cars.

I can make it there in an hour, he reasoned. *Dad would never know.*

He walked toward the beat-up sedan, unlocking the door and getting inside. He turned it on, then swore. The gas tank was almost empty, and he didn't have any money on him. He could go back inside the house and steal some money from his dad's wallet after the guy passed out, but that might take a while, and Dad had locked his door anyway.

But his keys are on the kitchen island.

Hunter went back into the house, finding the keys there and grabbing them. Then he hesitated. If he was going to try to get to Mom, he'd need rappelling equipment. Luckily Mom had taught him how to use it when he was a kid. Dad's old equipment was probably in the basement. He grabbed his backpack, then went downstairs, finding a bunch of dusty old boxes in the corner labeled "work." He searched through them, and after a few minutes found what he was looking for. Harness, clips, rope...everything he needed, except gloves. He stuffed these in his backpack, bringing it back upstairs and into the garage. He threw the backpack into the front passenger seat, then got in, turning the keys in the ignition. The engine roared to life; to his relief, there was a full tank of gas.

He hesitated then, staring at the steering wheel, feeling doubt trickle in. If he was going to do this…if he was going to go after Mom, then it might very well be a one-way trip. Hell, there was a possibility that Mom had even died getting sucked into that thing, whatever it was. If so, and he tried to go after her, then he'd be next. But it wasn't as if he had much to live for here. A drunkard for a dad, no mom, no girlfriend. A future in shambles. Even a chance of getting his mom back was worth the risk.

He took a deep breath in, then let it out, gripping the steering wheel with both hands.

All right, he told himself. *Let's do this.*

Hunter hesitated then, opening the car door and stepping out. He went back into the house, making a clucking sound. He'd hardly needed to; Charlie was already trotting up to him. He picked her up, cradling her against his chest, feeling her warmth, and the steady vibration as she purred. He felt a burst of affection for her, for the one thing in his life he could love without being punished for it.

"Bye Charlie," he whispered.

He set her down then, walking back into the garage and getting into the car. Then he looked around the cabin. He might need some cash for the tolls, after all. He found a couple of dollars in the center console, then popped the glove compartment, reaching inside. He froze.

There was a gun inside.

He grabbed it, pulling it out. A silver revolver. It felt heavy, and very real. He turned it over in his hands, vaguely recalling going to the range with his mother so many years ago. He hadn't shot a gun since she'd died. He popped the cylinder, spinning it around. There was a single bullet inside.

He stared at it, feeling a chill run through him.

Jesus Dad.

Glancing back at the glove compartment, he saw another few bills laying there. He grabbed them, then shut the compartment, looking for the safety on the gun. He couldn't find one, of course. Revolvers didn't have safeties. But it did have a hammer…he vaguely remembered that he had to cock the hammer first before he could fire. He hesitated, then stuffed the revolver in his backpack.

Opening the garage door, he pulled out of the garage and down the driveway. Then he accelerated forward down the street, following the signs for the highway.

* * *

The sun was hovering over the hills in the distance by the time Hunter pulled up in front of a tall chain-link fence blocking the dirt road. He glanced at the directions he'd printed out, then at his phone. Both said

294

he'd come to the right place...Smuggler's Cave. Past the fence, the road continued forward toward a large hill perhaps a quarter mile away. Deep tire-marks ran through the dirt road ahead, as if heavy construction equipment had rolled over it. But that must've been a long time ago; grass had partially overtaken the road, along with a few gangly shrubs.

Hunter got out of the car, slinging his backpack over his shoulder and walking up to the fence. A sign on one side of the fence said: "DO NOT ENTER" in big red letters, and the chain-link double-doors blocking the path ahead had been chained and padlocked shut. But the padlock was rusty, the fence in disrepair, much like the road.

Interesting.

He tested the padlock, pulling on it vigorously, but it held. Looking upward, he spotted razor-wire at the top of the fence. He sure as hell wasn't going to be able to climb over. He walked back to the car, popping the trunk. Dad occasionally still went to dig sites. He always kept random equipment in boxes in his car just in case he needed it. Hunter searched through one of the boxes, finding exactly what he'd been hoping to find: a pair of heavy-duty bolt cutters. He grabbed them, walking back to the fence. He looked around, suddenly nervous that someone might spot him. After all, if his dad was right, the place had been taken over by the government. If they caught him now, he probably wouldn't get another chance at finding Mom.

But there was no one around...the place was deserted.

Hunter used the bolt cutters on the padlock. With a little effort, the padlock snapped, and Hunter pulled it from the chain looping around the fence doors. Unwrapping the chain, he opened one of the doors, stepping through to the path beyond. He decided to leave the door open. If someone caught him here before he could get to that thing that took Mom, he needed to make sure his escape route was clear. And if he wasn't caught, it hardly mattered if someone discovered the open door afterward. If he managed to find Mom and bring her back, he'd deal with the consequences of his trespassing later.

Alright then.

He continued forward down the path, following it as it wound gently to the right. The path rose upward at a slight angle ahead, just as it had in the pictures he'd seen on Mom's old phone. In the distance, he saw a sign by the side of the road. As he drew closer, he saw its familiar greeting: "Welcome to Smuggler's Cave."

He slowed his pace, staring at the sign, feeling a chill come over him. This was where *she'd* been. Walking on this very path, seeing this very sign. He imagined her snapping a picture, Dad a few steps ahead. Probably laughing at one of Dad's silly jokes. Back when Dad used to tell jokes.

He sighed, trudging past the sign, continuing forward and upward.

The path narrowed a bit, squat rocky walls rising some five to six feet high on either side. A strong breeze blew up the path, pushing him from behind. He switched his backpack to his other shoulder, his back starting to ache from the weight of it. After a few minutes, he saw the path end abruptly, blocked by a tall rock wall. And there, in the middle of the wall, was the opening to a small cave…just like Mom's photo.

He glanced back, seeing the path winding down the hill. Far in the distance, he could see his dad's car beyond the fence.

Hunter continued up the path, reaching the entrance to the cave. A few feet into it, the path was plunged into utter darkness. He retrieved his phone, turning on its flashlight and checking its battery. It was at 42%. Running out of juice while rappelling into the bowels of the earth wouldn't just be inconvenient…it'd be deadly. And he needed enough battery life for the trip back, assuming he ever got back. He'd have to be quick.

He aimed the light into the cave, then strode inside.

There was a narrow tunnel beyond, the ceiling just high enough that he didn't have to stoop. The light from his phone was barely bright enough to guide his way, sending inky black shadows like long fingers across the irregular walls on either side. He strode forward, glancing from side to side as he went. The photos from Mom's phone had shown a hole in the wall…the one that had led to the long shaft traveling downward.

The cave wound through the earth, twisting left, then right, angling slightly downward. He followed it, moving quickly. He glanced at his phone…40% battery left. It was draining pretty quickly. He switched it to power-saving mode, turning off wi-fi and putting it into airplane mode.

Onward he went, the tunnel widening a little ahead. He tread carefully, not wanting to roll an ankle on rocks littering the cave floor. While the temperature outside must have been in the 70's, the air here was much cooler, and he shivered, suddenly wishing he'd brought a jacket.

Minutes passed.

Suddenly the tunnel ended, a rock wall blocking his way. Hunter stared at it, then shined his light on the walls on either side. There was no hole in the wall like he'd seen in his mother's photos…just a dead end.

The hell?

He turned back the way he'd come, shining the light down the length of the tunnel. Shadows stretched across the walls on either side. He moved forward, the shadows shifting as he went. He angled the light side-to-side as he walked, and after a few minutes, he saw what he'd missed the way in: a waist-high hole in the wall to the left. The shadows thrown by his light must have hidden it earlier. He squatted in front of it, shining his light through. Beyond, there was a small cavern, with a hole in the ground. A rope hung from a hook embedded in the ceiling, extending downward through the hole.

Bingo.

He crawled through the hole, his backpack scraping against the top of it. Squeezing through, he stopped before the vertical shaft. Slipping his backpack off and setting it to the side, he took the rappelling equipment out, putting it on. That done, he clipped his harness to the rope, picking up his phone and glancing at the screen.

36% left.

He grimaced, aiming the light down the shaft. It plunged downward as far as he could see, vanishing into the shadows. He retrieved his backpack, then grabbed the rope with one hand, lowering himself into the hole, bracing his feet against the walls of the shaft. He hesitated then, staring downward, realizing just how long it'd been since he'd done something like this. He took a deep breath in, then let it out.

Here goes...

Downward he went, slowly at first, then more quickly as his muscle-memory kicked in. It wasn't long before he saw the bottom of the shaft below. He dropped toward it, his feet striking the rocky floor a few moments later. Unclipping his harness from the rope, he shined his light forward. He was in a cavern, exactly the same as he'd seen on his mother's phone. At the far end of the cavern was a tunnel; it was bigger than he remembered from the pictures; tall enough for him to walk through without stooping, and wide enough to fit two people side-by-side.

Hunter strode forward into the tunnel, glancing at his phone again. 32% battery left...he'd managed to make it using only a quarter of the phone's charge. It'd take longer to climb back up the shaft, but he could probably get away with not using the light while doing so. So far, so good.

Suddenly, he heard voices in the distance.

He froze, quickly turning off his light. He stood there in the tunnel, pressing himself against the wall and straining his ears. He heard the voices again, echoing through the tunnel. They were coming from ahead, unintelligible but clearly male.

Shit.

Hunter hesitated, then turned on his light again, aiming it downward so it wouldn't travel as far. If there were people ahead, he didn't want them to know he was coming. If he got caught, he'd have to pretend he was just some stupid kid spelunking. He'd have to get past them somehow, and make a run for the archway his mother had vanished through. But what if he *couldn't* get past them?

He stood there in the darkness, hearing the voices again in the distance, and had the sudden urge to turn back. Then he pictured his mother the last time he'd seen her. Her big brown eyes, high cheekbones. Long curly hair tied back into a ponytail. Her laugh.

She'd been the strongest woman he'd ever known, the glue that had held their family together. She would have done anything for him, and for his father. And his father had abandoned her.

If Hunter didn't do this, he'd be no better than his dad.

He took off his backpack, setting it on the ground, then unzipping the main compartment. Reaching in, he felt cold metal under his fingertips. He grabbed it, pulling it out.

It was Dad's revolver.

He stared at it, then glanced down the tunnel. If the people ahead were armed, it was game over. But if they weren't, and they gave him trouble, the revolver would give him the upper hand. But there'd be no coming back from that…his future here would be over.

If he was really going to do this, he had to commit.

Hunter glanced at the revolver one more time, then stuffed it in his pants, hiding it under his shirt.

Here goes…

He slid his backpack on again, then moved forward through the tunnel. The voices got progressively louder as he continued down the tunnel, which soon led to a small chamber ahead. It was well-lit with electric lanterns set on the rocky floor, and a large hole carved into the far wall leading to another room beyond. Hunter turned off the light on his cell phone, shoving it in his pocket and ducking low. He was still far enough away from the light to be invisible in the darkness…he hoped.

Suddenly a man ducked through the hole into the chamber, carrying a few boxes stacked on top of each other. He was middle-aged and overweight, and wore a red jacket with the words "Bridge Corporation" on the back of it.

"Come on Gus," the man urged. "We're almost done."

A younger man ducked through the hole, also carrying a few boxes. They lowered these onto a large pallet on the floor of the chamber.

"Yeah yeah Harvey," the younger man grumbled. "What is this shit anyway?"

"Bunch of leftover equipment from the Corps," Harvey answered, stretching his back. "Company wants this crap outta here."

"Why the Bridge Corporation would want this place is beyond me," Gus muttered. "We're a goddamn tech company!"

"Who cares?" Harvey shot back. "Two more boxes to go," he added, gesturing at Gus. "Go get 'em."

"Your back hurting old man?" Gus teased. But he did as he was told, vanishing through the archway and returning moments later. He set these on the pallet with the rest. "This is stupid," he stated, gesturing at the pallet. "Why don't we just throw this shit into that black wall?"

"Won't work," Harvey replied. "Unless one of us touches it first. They say it's activated by living things touching it. You volunteering?"

"Uh…no."

"That's what I thought," Harvey replied with a smirk.

"That wall creeps me out," Gus confessed. "I heard the people who found this place got sucked into it. Never came back."

"That's what I heard too."

"You think it's real?" Gus asked.

298

"You can test it if you like."

"Yeah right," Gus muttered. "Age before beauty old man."

"Let's just get the hell outta here," Harvey grumbled. "I gotta get up early tomorrow to drive to the Cape."

"Weekend with the wife?"

"Yeah," Harvey confirmed. He picked up one of the lanterns, as did Gus, and the two men started walking toward the tunnel.

Toward Hunter.

Hunter cursed under his breath, backtracking as quickly as he could, until he reached the chamber he'd climbed down into earlier. He glanced at the rope dangling down from the vertical shaft above.

I could climb it, he thought.

He glanced back, seeing the light from the men's lanterns in the tunnel growing brighter as they approached. There was no time to climb the rope...they'd almost certainly see him, and then the jig would be up. He walked to the wall just beside the tunnel, pressing his back against it...and reaching down to touch the revolver stuffed into his pants.

He heard footsteps behind him, getting louder.

Maybe they won't see me, he thought. *Maybe...*

And then Harvey and Gus stepped into the cavern, stopping a few feet from the dangling rope.

Hunter froze, staring at their backs...and then bolted down the tunnel!

"What the..." he heard Harvey say from behind. "Hey!"

Hunter sprinted down the tunnel as fast as he could, soon plunging into total darkness. He cursed, grabbing his phone and fumbling to turn on its flashlight. His right shoulder scraped against the tunnel wall, and he stumbled, nearly dropping his phone.

"Hey you!" a voice from behind shouted, footsteps clambering after him. "Stop!"

Hunter ran as fast as he could, keeping one hand on the wall to his right so he wouldn't slam into it again. He spotted light ahead – the chamber with the pallet and a few remaining lanterns.

"I said stop!" Harvey shouted. The footsteps were getting closer, Hunter realized. He resisted the urge to turn around and look, focusing on the chamber ahead. Moments later, he burst into it, leaping over the pallet and ducking into the hole in the wall beyond.

And found himself in a huge underground room.

He skidded to a stop, looking around quickly. The room was long, with a tall arched ceiling high above his head. To his right was a flat stone wall in the distance, illuminated by a few more of the electric lanterns. To his left...

His blood went cold.

For there, a few yards away from him, was an inky black wall bordered by a dark metal archway, runes inscribed into the archway's surface. It was just as he'd seen in the pictures from Mom's phone…except that a few feet in front of the wall stood a long wooden fence, a sign with huge red block letters in the center of it.

DO NOT PASS, it read. *DO NOT TOUCH WALL.*

He hesitated, glancing back, seeing Harvey and Gus sprinting down the tunnel and into the smaller chamber. They ran around the pallet, ducking through the hole after him.

Hunter ran to the left toward the fence, vaulting over it, then stopping. He was only a few feet away from the black wall now; he turned, seeing Harvey and Gus skidding to a stop, turning to stare at him.

"Hey kid!" Harvey yelled. "Get the hell away from there!"

"Don't touch the wall!" Gus added.

Hunter glanced at the wall, then at the two men, his heart pounding in his chest. He was struck with the sudden realization that this was it. That if he did this, there was no going back.

And that these could very well be the last moments of his life.

"Come on kid," Harvey insisted, stepping toward Hunter slowly. "Come back over the fence."

"I can't," Hunter retorted.

"Why not?"

"My mom went through," he explained. "I have to get her back."

Harvey glanced at Gus, then turned back to Hunter. He grimaced, shaking his head.

"Aw shit kid, I'm really sorry," he said. "Really, I am. But you gotta understand, no one comes back. Once they go in…" He trailed off, shrugging helplessly.

"I have to try," Hunter insisted.

"What's your name?" Harvey asked. Hunter hesitated; if he told them, they'd know his identity. Which meant that they'd at least be able to tell Dad what'd happened to him.

He owed Dad that much.

"Hunter," he admitted.

"Okay Hunter," Harvey replied. "I understand you miss your mom, but I can guarantee you she wouldn't want you going through that wall."

Hunter said nothing, knowing damn well that Harvey was right. Mom hadn't wanted Dad to go through either.

"Come with us," Harvey pleaded, taking another step toward him. "We'll help you get home. You won't get in trouble, I promise."

Hunter glanced at the wall again, then lowered his gaze to the floor. His resolve wavered, and he was struck with the sudden realization that he could be making a terrible mistake. That he might be throwing his life away for nothing…and leaving his dad – and Charlie – alone, with no one to care for them.

"Come on Hunter," Harvey urged. "You mom's not coming back."

Hunter looked up at the man, swallowing past a lump in his throat. He imagined himself stepping over the fence, joining these two men. Going back to the surface, then back home. Living the rest of his life taking care of Dad, until the guy died of liver failure, or a fall that Hunter wasn't there to prevent. A life without Mom.

He took a deep breath in, then let it out, squaring his shoulders.

"Then I'm going to her," he replied.

And plunged his left hand into the wall.

Hunter felt his left hand go instantly numb as it vanished into the darkness, feeling as if it had been instantly and painlessly severed. He pulled back reflexively, but the wall resisted, his arm not moving an inch. Panic seized him.

Oh shit.

He yanked his left arm again, and again it didn't budge. He tried clenching his left fist, but felt nothing. It was as if his hand was gone. Maybe it *was* gone. Maybe the wall had dissolved it, and the rest of him was next.

Oh shit oh shit!

He glanced back at Harvey and Gus. Both were staring at him, their eyes – and mouths – wide open.

Something *pulled* on him.

Hunter turned back to face the wall, realizing that he was moving forward. Slowly but surely, the wall was sucking his arm into it. He saw the bump at the end of his wrist pass through, felt it vanish from his awareness just as his hand had.

What have I done?

He jerked his arm back a third time, but it was pointless. His forearm gradually disappeared into that utter darkness. The wall was consuming him more quickly now, pulling him into its unholy maw.

"Help!" he cried, turning back to the two men. "Help me!"

They just stared at him.

"Damn it!" he swore, yanking at his arm again and again. He felt his elbow pass through, vanishing from existence, and then his left bicep. He nearly lost his balance, stepping back with his left foot…and feeling it go numb as it passed through the wall.

No!

The wall tugged at him relentlessly, sucking his arm and leg into it. He was nearly shoulder-deep into the darkness now, his head mere inches from the deadly void.

"Help me!" he pleaded, glancing back at Harvey and Gus. The older one shook his head.

"Sorry kid," he apologized. "No one can help you now."

Hunter cursed, pulling his head as far away from the wall as possible. He felt his left shoulder become non-existent, then his left calf. He continued to struggle, but it was futile.

He was going to die.

Hunter felt the left side of his chest go numb, and his left thigh. He stopped struggling, feeling the darkness consuming him, pulling him into its nothingness. In another few seconds, his head would be pulled in. He turned to face that horrible void, that utter nothingness, and felt terror grip him. He grit his teeth, pulling the revolver from his pants and pressing the barrel against his own temple.

I'm coming Mom.

Then he threw himself into the darkness.

To read more, get Hunter of Legends, the 1st book in the Fate of Legends series!

Available in print, ebook, and audiobook formats.

About the Author

Clayton Taylor Wood is the author of the Runic series, the Fate of Legends series, the Magic of Havenwood series, the Magic of Magic series, and the Masks of Eternity series. He's been a computer programmer, graphics designer, martial-arts instructor, and now works in the medical field. He has a wife and three wonderful children.

Writing was always Clayton's passion, but it wasn't until the birth of his first son that he found the inspiration necessary to finish his first book. Five years later, he published Runic Awakening, the first entry in the Runic Series.

Connect with me on my website and/or join my newsletter:

https://www.claytontaylorwood.com